30126 00255584 2

KALEIDOSCOPE

Books by Arthur Koestler

Novels

The Gladiators*
Darkness at Noon*
Arrival and Departure*
Thieves in the Night*
The Age of Longing*
The Call-Girls*

Autobiography

Dialogue with Death*
Scum of the Earth*
Arrow in the Blue*
The Invisible Writing*
The God that Failed (*with others*)

Essays

The Yogi and the Commissar*
Insight and Outlook
Promise and Fulfilment
The Trail of the Dinosaur*
Reflections on Hanging*
The Sleepwalkers*
The Lotus and the Robot*
The Act of Creation*
The Ghost in the Machine*
Drinkers of Infinity
The Case of the Midwife Toad
The Roots of Coincidence
The Challenge of Chance
(*with Sir Alister Hardy and Robert Harvie*)
The Heel of Achilles
Suicide of a Nation? (*ed.*)
Beyond Reductionism: The Alpbach Symposium
(*ed. with J. R. Smythies*)
The Thirteenth Tribe
Life After Death
(*with Arnold Toynbee and others*)
Janus – A Summing Up
Bricks to Babel: Selected Writings

Theatre

Twilight Bar

* Available in the Danube Edition

ARTHUR KOESTLER

Kaleidoscope

Essays from Drinkers of Infinity, *and* The Heel of Achilles *and later pieces and stories*

THE DANUBE EDITION

HUTCHINSON
London Melbourne Sydney Auckland Johannesburg

To Pat Kavanagh
with love and gratitude

Hutchinson & Co. (Publishers) Ltd

An imprint of the Hutchinson Publishing Group

17–21 Conway Street, London W1P 5HL

Hutchinson Group (Australia) Pty Ltd
30–32 Cremorne Street, Richmond South, Victoria 3121
PO Box 151, Broadway, New South Wales 2007

Hutchinson Group (NZ) Ltd
32–34 View Road, PO Box 40–086, Glenfield, Auckland 10

Hutchinson Group (SA) Pty Ltd
PO Box 337, Bergvlei 2012, South Africa

This selection first published 1981

Set in Linoterm Bembo
by Book Economy Services, Cuckfield, Sussex

Printed in Great Britain by The Anchor Press Ltd,
and bound by Wm Brendon & Son,
both of Tiptree, Essex

British Library Cataloguing in Publication Data
Koestler, Arthur
Kaleidoscope. – Danube ed.
I. Title
082 PR6021.04

ISBN 0 09 145950 8

CONTENTS

AUTHOR'S NOTE

Parts One and Two of this volume in the uniform Danube Edition contain selections from *Drinkers of Infinity – Essays 1955–1967* and *The Heel of Achilles – Essays 1968–1973*. But unlike the earlier collections of essays reissued in Danube (*The Yogi and the Commissar* and *The Trail of the Dinosaur*) the present volume also includes new material not contained in the original editions. Thus Part Three consists of "Some Later Essays", written after *The Heel of Achilles,* and Part Four, "Tales of the Absurd", consists of short stories.

Two of these short stories also appear in the original edition of *The Call-Girls* (1973), but were omitted from the Danube Edition (1979) of that novel, and are resurrected here. The reasons for this bit of jugglery are explained in the postscript to the Danube Edition; I mention it merely in case some readers of the original edition of the novel should have a feeling of *déjà vu*.

Similar feelings might be aroused by three items in the present collection which also appear in *Bricks to Babel – Selected Writings with Author's Comments* (1980). The latter is an omnibus volume, containing selections from some thirty books published over the last fifty years – including those three items from *Drinkers of Infinity* and *The Heel of Achilles*. It would perhaps have been more satisfactory if the present volume had appeared *before* that overall selection, but for technical reasons this was not possible.

Some of the essays in Parts One to Three consist of writings and lectures addressed to such varied audiences as the Nobel

Foundation, the British Academy, the Brain Research Institute of the University of California and various scientific or literary congresses – but also to the broader readership of *The Times, The Observer,* etc. The items in the collection thus differ in style and weight, ranging from academic papers to excursions into journalism, including book reviews. Yet in spite of this diversity, most of these essays and stories were intended as variations on certain themes: the creativity and pathology of the human mind – which are by and large also the leitmotifs of the books I wrote in the period covered by this collection (*The Act of Creation, The Sleepwalkers, The Ghost in the Machine, The Roots of Coincidence,* etc.). Some of these books are fairly long and go into technical details; in the essays, on the other hand, I have endeavoured to pick a single thread out of the complex pattern to make it more easily discernible. A glance at the list of contents may give the impression of a kaleidoscope; yet I hope that a closer look through the tube will reveal the basic elements which enter into the changing images and lend them some unity in diversity.

London, February 1981 A.K.

PART ONE

DRINKERS OF INFINITY
ESSAYS 1955–1967

THE GREATEST SCANDAL IN CHRISTENDOM*

"Alas," the old man of seventy-three wrote to his admirer, Diodati, "your friend and servant Galileo has been for the last month hopelessly blind; so that this heaven, this earth, this universe, which I, by marvellous discoveries and clear demonstrations, have enlarged a hundred thousand times beyond the belief of the wise men of bygone ages, henceforward for me is shrunk into such small space as is filled by my own bodily sensations. . . ."

All the main ingredients are there, contained in a few lines: the grandeur, the boastfulness, the self-pity, the elegance of style.

The letter is dated from Galileo's villa, Il Giojello, at Arcetri where he spent the last years of his life. It stands on a hill among olive groves overlooking Florence, but its name, the jewel, sounds today sadly ironical. The garden, where he received Milton and a stream of other celebrities, is covered with weeds; the sixteenth-century house, with its old beams and high ceilings, is occupied by tenants and contains no trace of the past. On the outside of the massive stone wall which separates the garden from the one and only street of the village of Arcetri, there is a sort of niche containing an old marble *pissoir* without a door or screen; close to it is a decayed memorial plaque with a bust of Galileo sternly watching the urinators. Whether this is intended as a deliberate insult – a kind of *Clochemerle* in reverse – I was unable to discover; but it certainly testifies to a lack of

* First published in *The Observer* on the 400th anniversary of Galileo's birth, February 1964.

reverence of the powers that be towards the memory of the man who, in the words of his one-time admirer, Pope Urban VIII, had "given rise to the greatest scandal throughout Christendom". Its shadow still lingers over the desolate house.

The scandal is one of the historic causes which made post-Renaissance Europe a divided house of faith and reason. Legend has turned Galileo into a martyr of the freedom of thought, Urban into its benighted oppressor, and the conflict into a kind of Greek tragedy ennobled by the stamp of historical inevitability. In fact it was a clash of temperaments wantonly provoked and aggravated by unlucky coincidences.

To elucidate what really happened, a word must be said about the background – the grand topography of the universe, as Galileo's contemporaries saw it.

For the last two thousand years, according to the orthodox doctrine, the solid earth had been regarded as the centre of the world round which the sun, the planets and the stars revolved in their orbits; it was based on the legacy of Aristotle and had been elaborated in detail by Ptolemy, an Alexandrian astronomer of the second century AD. As against this there existed another grand scheme of even more ancient origin. The Pythagorean school, which had flourished between the fifth and third centuries BC, had taught that the earth rotated on its own axis; and at least one Pythagorean, Aristarchus of Samos, held that in addition to its daily rotation, the earth also travelled through space in its annual revolutions round the sun; the five known planets did the same, so that the sun, and not the earth, was the centre and hub of the universe.

The geocentric system of Aristotle and Ptolemy had prevailed, but the rival heliocentric system of the Pythagoreans was never quite forgotten. It was preserved in the writings of the Latin compilers; it was finally revived and elaborated in detail by Canon Koppernigk or Copernick, called Copernicus, a somewhat crotchety cleric in the godforsaken province of Varmia on the Baltic Sea.

Copernicus had died in 1543, twenty-one years before Galileo was born; his book, *On the Revolutions of the Heavenly Spheres*, which outlined the heliocentric system, was published in the last year of his life. For more than half a century it aroused very little interest. It was addressed, as the title page said, "to mathematicians only"; it was clumsily written, and marred by inconsistencies. The reaction of the academic world was, with a few exceptions, indifferent or hostile, as Copernicus had feared; it was this fear "to be laughed at and hissed off the stage" (to quote his own words) which had caused him to withhold publication of the book until the end of his life.

What made him finally overcome his apprehensions were the urgent entreaties of his superiors in the ecclesiastical hierarchy who had read manuscript outlines of his theory. In 1533, Pope Clement VII had listened to a lecture on the Copernican theory, and was favourably impressed; a few years later, Cardinal Schönberg, who occupied positions of special trust under three successive popes, wrote to the humble canon in Varmia that he had learned with great admiration about Copernicus' "having created a new theory of the Universe according to which the Earth moves and the sun occupies the basic and central position. . . . Therefore, learned man, without wishing to be inopportune, I beg you most emphatically to communicate your discovery to the learned world. . . .'

Copernicus printed the letter as a preface to his book, which he dedicated to Clement's successor, Paul III. Thus, contrary to legend, the Church did not initially oppose the theory of the motion of the earth. The opposite is true. Without the encouragement and patronage of the clergy – from the Bishop of Varmia to circles close to the Vatican – Canon Copernicus' book would never have seen the light of day. Nor did the attitude of the Church change for the next eighty years.

Galileo became converted to the Copernican system in his twenties. But he kept his convictions secret until he was nearly fifty, although he had no more reason to fear religious persecution than Copernicus had. Through all these years he taught in his lectures the old astronomy of Ptolemy, and expressly repudiated the earth's motion by means of the traditional arguments (the clouds would be left behind, etc.)

which he knew to be false. This fact is passed over in silence by Galileo's biographers, although it is an important clue to his character.*

The reason why he kept his opinions so carefully concealed was the same as in Copernicus' case: the fear of ridicule by his narrow-minded colleagues who occupied the chairs of astronomy in Bologna, Pisa, Padua and elsewhere. In a letter to the German astronomer, Johannes Kepler (the first to raise his voice in public for Copernicus, fifteen years before Galileo), he confessed: "I have not dared to bring my views into the public light, frightened by the fate of Copernicus himself, our teacher, who, though he acquired immortal fame with some, was yet by an infinite multitude of others – for such is the number of fools – laughed at and hissed off the stage." The risk of ecclesiastic censure did not even occur to him because, during the first fifty years of his lifetime, no such risk existed. Even his latest apologist, Giorgio de Santillana, admitted: "On his [Galileo's] own account, he knew the Jesuits as modern-minded humanists, friends of science and discovery. Those he feared were the professors."† And that fear, as events proved, was fully justified.

In 1610, when he was forty-six, Galileo's life took a dramatic turn. He was then Professor of Mathematics in Padua, much admired by his friends for his revolutionary researches in physics – which he communicated to them in private letters – but as yet untouched by public fame. Fame came almost overnight through his astronomical discoveries, made possible by that newly invented gadget, the telescope. It was invented by a Dutchman, but Galileo built his own instruments with a vastly improved magnifying power. He published his observations in a booklet, *Siderius Nuncius* – the "Star Messenger". It described the mountainous configurations of the moon, the

* The proof is found in a surviving manuscript copy of a lecture by Galileo, dated 1606, *Trattato della Sfera* (*Opere,* Ediz. Nazionale, Florence; 1929–30, vol. II, pp. 203–55).

† *The Crime of Galileo* (Cambridge, 1955), p. 8.

dissolution of the Milky Way into "a map of innumerable stars planted together in clusters", and left the most momentous news to the last – that the planet Jupiter possessed four moons "never seen from the beginning of the world up to our times". This did not prove that the Copernican scheme of the universe was right, but it shattered the orthodox doctrine that the earth was the centre of the world around which everything revolved – the Jupiter moons danced attendance to a rival body.

The "Star Messenger" created a sensation. Cardinal del Monte, one of Galileo's patrons, wrote in a letter: "If we were still living under the ancient Republic of Rome, I verily believe that there would be a column on the Capitol erected in Galileo's honour." The Jesuits of the Roman College, who were the leading astronomers of the day, bestowed ceremonial honours on him; Pope Paul V received him in a long audience. Yet barely five years later an edict of the Holy Office condemned the Copernican theory as incompatible with Holy Scripture, and Galileo was enjoined, by order of Pope Paul, not to "hold or defend" it.

On whom does the historic responsibility rest? In the first place on "the professors", the academic mediocracy, who hated Galileo, partly out of jealousy, partly because they were the rearguard of those schoolmen whom Erasmus had accused of "looking in utter darkness for that which has no existence whatsoever". They were so dazzled by what the telescope revealed that several of them, like the illustrious Cremonini, refused on principle to look through it; and those who did look pretended that the Jupiter moons were optical illusions. But eventually the "Pigeon League" – as Galileo contemptuously called them after their leader, Lodovico delle Colombe – had to accept defeat, when the élite of the Jesuit astronomers at their observatories in various parts of Europe not only confirmed Galileo's discoveries, but improved on them.

At this point Galileo's vanity played him a trick which had disastrous results. For more than twenty years he had believed in the Copernican system but had taught the opposite. Now, encouraged by his success, he had come out into the open; and once he had committed himself to the Copernican theory anybody who opposed it was to be regarded as a "mental pygmy", "hardly deserving to be called a human being".

But he had no scientific proof that the Copernican system was correct. The point is somewhat technical, but basic to the understanding of the whole drama. The Jupiter moons and other phenomena proved that Aristotle had been wrong – they did not prove that Copernicus had been right. There existed alternative possibilities – such as the compromise system of Tycho de Brahe, in which the planets revolved round the sun, and the sun round the earth. It was a halfway house, but from the point of view of mathematical calculation just as satisfactory as the Copernican system – and the available data spoke in favour of Tycho and against Copernicus. For if the earth really moved round the sun, then its position relative to the fixed stars must differ by nearly two hundred million miles every six months, and their constellations ought to expand and shrink according to whether the earth approached or receded from them. But in spite of the thousandfold magnification of Galileo's telescopes, no such effect was found (it was only found two centuries later by Bessel). Thus not only tradition, prejudice and naïve "commonsense", but also the scientific evidence available at the time, spoke *against* the Copernican theory.

Galileo was well aware of this. So were his enemies. But since they had been defeated in the controversy on the Jupiter moons and in several other disputes, they knew they were no match either for his genius or his polemical brilliance. So the Pigeon League shifted its ground from science to theology. They produced quotations from Holy Scripture in refutation of Copernicus. Thus Joshua, after defeating the Philistines, had cried "Sun, stand thou still" – which proved clearly that it was the sun which moved, not the earth.

Galileo fell into the trap. In two treatises, which he circulated widely in manuscript copies ("Letter to Castelli", 1613, enlarged a year later into "Letter to the Grand Duchess Christina"), he dived headlong into theology. He evaded any scientific discussion of the Copernican system by simply pretending that it was proven beyond doubt; proposed that biblical passages which contradicted it should be reinterpreted, and insisted that the Church must either endorse the Copernican theory or condemn it altogether. This made a showdown unavoidable.

Galileo's friends in the upper ranks of the Church hierarchy – foremost among them Maffeo Barberini, the future Pope – did everything in their power to avoid the showdown. When the monks of St Marco in Florence denounced the "Letter to Castelli", the Holy Office dismissed the case. When a Dominican by the name of Caccini attacked Galileo from the pulpit, the Preacher General of the Order promptly wrote him a letter of apology. The official attitude of the Church was summed up by its highest theological authority: Cardinal Bellarmine, General of the Jesuit Order, Consultor to the Holy Office (the "devilish Jebusite" whom the English suspected of having instigated the Gunpowder Plot). In a letter to Father Foscarini, a Carmelite monk who had just published a book advocating the Copernican system, but equally addressed to Galileo, who is mentioned by name, Bellarmine explained that to teach the Copernican system *as a working hypothesis* superior to Ptolemy's "is to speak with excellent sense and to run no risk whatever. Such a manner of speaking suffices for a mathematician." But to speak of it *as an established truth* "is a very dangerous attitude and one calculated not only to arouse the Scholastic philosophers and theologians, but also to injure our holy faith by contradicting the Scriptures". However, Bellarmine continued, *if* there existed a "real proof" which "truly demonstrated" the earth's motion, *then* the relevant passages in the Scriptures would have to be reinterpreted. "But I do not think there is any such proof since none has been shown to me."

Bellarmine's ruling reflected not only the established practice of the Church in such matters; its substance would also have been endorsed by any responsible body of modern empirical scientists. But Galileo was past reasoning. To admit that the Copernican system was no more than an unproven hypothesis, however excellent, would amount to the confession that he had no evidence to offer, and expose him to the ridicule of his opponents. There is hardly a more frustrating experience for a scientist than to *know* that one is right, but to be unable to prove it –and to be "hissed off the stage" by an audience of imbeciles. Against the warnings of Bellarmine and other friendly cardinals, Galileo rushed to Rome, to force a decision. "He is passionately involved in this quarrel" the Tuscan ambassador reported, "so that he will be snarled in it and get himself into danger. . . . For he is vehement and all impassioned in this affair."

He tried unsuccessfully for an audience with Paul V, who (as the same ambassador described him) "abhors the liberal arts and cannot stand these novelties and subtleties". Which particular incident brought matters to a head is still a matter of controversy, and without much importance. Galileo had insisted on a showdown; he had gambled and lost.

On 5 March 1616, the Holy Office issued a decree in which "the Pythagorean doctrine of the motion of the earth" was declared to be "false and altogether opposed to Holy Scripture"; to prevent its further spreading, Copernicus' book *On the Revolutions of the Heavenly Spheres*, was "suspended until it be corrected". It actually remained on the Index for no more than four years; the corrections consisted in the change or omission of altogether nine sentences in which the heliocentric system was represented as a certainty instead of a hypothesis. Galileo's name was not mentioned in the decree, his works were not prohibited, and to save him from public humiliation, the injunction not to hold or defend the Copernican doctrine was communicated to him privately. To sweeten the pill even more, a week after publication of the decree, the Pope received Galileo in a long audience.

Thus the first act of the scandal ended on a decorous note; yet it injected a poison into the atmosphere of our culture which is still there. Act II came seventeen years later.

The main event of the intervening years was the election to the Papacy of Galileo's most ardent admirer, Cardinal Maffeo

Barberini. He had opposed the decree of 1616; he had written an ode in honour of Galileo; when he became Pope, he gave Galileo a testimonial extolling the virtues and piety "of this great man, whose fame shines in the heavens and goes on earth far and wide". In 1624, a year after he had been installed as Urban VIII, he gave Galileo six long audiences in six weeks, showering gifts and favours on him.

Maffeo Barberini was a brilliant, vainglorious cynic who did not care much whether Copernicus contradicted the miracle of Joshua or not. On learning of Richelieu's death, he coined the famous epigram: "If God exists, Cardinal Richelieu will have much to answer for; if not, he has done very well." His vanity was as monumental as Galileo's; he professed "to know better than all cardinals put together" as Galileo professed to be the "sole discoverer of all celestial novelties". It needed no great psychiatric insight to predict the end of the affair.

Though Urban could not revoke the edict of 1616, he paid homage to the memory of Copernicus; and after those six long audiences, Galileo returned from Rome to Florence, reassured that he could now expound the Copernican system on condition that he stuck to the established rules of the game: to avoid theological arguments, and to speak of the earth's motion as a convenient *working hypothesis* without asserting that it was *actually true*.

This sounds reasonable enough. But Galileo's temperament made it impossible for him to abide by the rules – and on this point every writer with strong convictions must sympathise with him. Besides, he thought that at long last he had found a physical proof for the motion of the earth (we remember that it was the lack of proof which had made him lose the first round of the battle). The proof was contained in his famous theory of the tides. Rejecting Kepler's correct suggestion that the tides were caused by the moon's attraction, Galileo had persuaded himself that the seas "swapped over" once a day as a direct consequence of the earth's motion. Here, then, was the evidence he had been so desperately looking for. It was a fallacy in such glaring contradiction to all the principles of the science of dynamics which he himself had discovered, and so unworthy of his genius, that it can be explained only as an *idée fixe*.

The years that followed were spent in writing his great apologia for the Copernican theory, the *Dialogue on the Two Great World Systems*. It is perhaps the most brilliant and exasperating work among the books which made history. Masterly expositions alternate in it with special pleading, immortal passages with cheap rhetoric and the deliberate falsification of facts. The theory of the tides occupies a central position, and serves to clinch the argument. Whatever the contemporary reader's reaction to the book, one point was made abundantly clear to him: that the earth's motion was *not* merely a working hypothesis but a fact so firmly established that it could be doubted only by "dumb moon-calves" whose stupidity "stains the honour of mankind".

Thus the contents of the book were a flagrant contravention of the decree of 1616, and of the line agreed on with Urban VIII. But there were still other circumstances which precipitated the scandal. Galileo had obtained the *imprimatur* for the book by a series of manoeuvres which amounted to a confidence trick. He had antagonised his former supporters, the Jesuit astronomers, by laying unfounded priority claims to their discoveries, and engaging them in controversies on irrelevant subjects; it was as if he were acting under some self-destructive compulsion. Lastly, he had personally insulted the Pope. In the days of their mutual adulation, Urban had suggested an argument which would enable Galileo to speak favourably of the Copernican theory without asserting its actual truth. The argument was, briefly, that even if a hypothesis explains certain phenomena in a satisfactory manner, it need not necessarily be true, for God may have produced the same phenomena by different means, not comprehended by the human mind. This argument, to which Urban attached the greatest importance, is quoted only at the very end of the book; and the character who quotes it is Simplicio, the simpleton of the *Dialogue*, who has been shown up as a silly ass over and over again. Galileo might as well have stuck out his tongue in public at the Pope.

★ ★ ★

Contrary to legend, Nemesis took a rather leisurely course. The book was published in February 1632. It was not until August that its sale was suspended, and a commission appointed to examine its contents. The commissioners indicted it on eight counts, but concluded that "all these matters could be corrected if it is decided that the book is of any value". The report was then handed over to the Inquisition, which, in October, summoned Galileo to Rome. Galileo sent a medical certificate from Florence, attesting that he was suffering from "attacks of giddiness, hypochondriacal melancholy, weakness of stomach, insomnia, and flying pains about the body"; he thus succeeded in delaying his journey till February 1633. In Rome, he took up quarters in the Villa Medici, which was then the Tuscan Embassy, and another three months passed before he was summoned for his first interrogation by the Commissary of the Inquisition, Firenzuola.

From 12 April to 10 May, while the proceedings lasted, he was formally a prisoner of the Inquisition; in fact he occupied a five-room flat in the Holy Office overlooking the Vatican Gardens, shared by his valet, while the Tuscan amassador's majordomo looked after his food and wine. He never spent a day of his life in a prison cell, and was neither tortured nor in fear of torture – which, according to the rules of the Roman Inquisition, could not be inflicted on a man of his age. (The Spanish Inquisition was, of course, an altogether different matter.)

In short, the authorities treated Galileo with all the lenience and regard due to the foremost scholar of his time; and with that disregard for the freedom of thought which was engrained in their tradition and doctrine. They did not intend to turn him into a martyr, but rather to show that he was not of the stuff of which martyrs are made; to humiliate him, make him recant, and prove that not even a Galileo could allow himself to mock the Pope and challenge the authority of the theologians.

The legal proceedings were highly unorthodox. In the very first interrogation Galileo manoeuvred himself into an impossible position by pretending, in the teeth of the printed evidence, that his book was written with the intention not to support but to *refute* the Copernican theory. The only possible explanation of this folly is a failure of nerve. He had thought himself capable of outwitting Urban and everyboy else; on being found out he realised that the game was up and he panicked.

Nothing happened for a fortnight. Then Firenzuola went on a private, "extrajudicial" visit to Galileo's apartment, and had no great difficulty in persuading him to make a deal. Soon afterwards he was allowed to return to the Villa Medici; another month later, on 22 June, Galileo was conducted to a hall in the Convent of Santa Maria sopra Minerva, where in the presence of his judges – ten cardinals, only seven of whom had concurred – the sentence was read out to him. The *Dialogue* was to be prohibited; to clear himself from the suspicion of heresy he was to recite a prepared text cursing and abjuring the doctrine of the earth's motion; and he was to be committed to "formal prison during the Holy Office's pleasure". Then the vain old man went down on his knees before the venal cardinals, recited a text in which nobody believed, wisely refrained from saying *eppur si muove*, and the show trial was over.

"Formal prison" meant, first, a sojourn with the Grand Duke of Tuscany, then with the Archbishop of Siena, followed by ten peaceful and creative years in the villa at Arcetri, where he wrote his masterpiece, the *Dialogue Concerning Two New Sciences*. It became one of the cornerstones of the scientific revolution, and made Galileo rank among the intellectual giants who shaped the destiny of the world.

His true greatness rests on achievements which have nothing to do with the Galileo legend. He never dropped cannonballs from the leaning tower of Pisa, made no contribution to theoretical astronomy, and did not prove the earth's motion. His real achievements are those found in every schoolbook: the laws of the pendulum, of free fall, of the flight of projectiles, of the elasticity, cohesion and resistance of solid bodies, and a hundred related matters. He was a pioneer of the experimental method and transformed physics into an exact, mathematical science. This was his vocation; not the ill-starred propaganda crusade based on fallacious arguments, which cost him twenty years of his life and ended in disaster.

It nearly put an end to three centuries of that peaceful coexistence between faith and reason which had started with Thomas of Aquinas, and saw Franciscans, Dominicans, Jesuits successively take the lead in the revival of learning, and the advance of science. Throughout the golden age of humanism and well into the seventeenth century, scientists like Copernicus and Galileo were the protégés of cardinals and popes; and the exploration of the laws of nature was regarded as a form of worship of the Supreme Mathematician.

The Galileo scandal marked a turning point – a hardening of the fronts, the polarisation of rigid orthodoxies. The point I have been trying to make is that the blame was not all on one side; that the presumption of the theologians was matched by the *hubris* of an unbalanced genius and the vindictiveness of a benighted academic coterie. As for the latter, though methods have changed, it can hardly be said that behind the polite façades academic orthodoxy has become much more tolerant. The Inquisition at least has gone; but the Pigeon Leagues are still flourishing in the groves of Academe.

ARTIST ON A TIGHTROPE

Inaugural Address at the Symposium on "Belief and Literature", Calcutta, February 1959

In 1942, I made friends with a young fighter pilot, Richard Hillary.* He had been shot down in flames in the Battle of Britain when he was not quite twenty. His earlier photographs showed him as an extremely attractive young man; when I met him, his burned and shrivelled hands were like birds' claws and his face a clumsy mask of plastic surgery where even the eyelids were artificial. He was given a job in the Ministry of Information, published a book, *The Last Enemy*, which instantly became a bestseller, had an attractive mistress, and led a pleasant life in London. Yet after a couple of years of this, he fooled the Medical Board into certifying him fit for active service, returned to flying, and crashed to his death a few months later while training to become a night fighter.

His letters from this last period described a kind of double existence he was leading on the aerodrome. During the day, his burned body suffered agonies from the intense cold; he was bored, frightened, irritated. But at night – as he wrote in a letter – "I have only to step into an aeroplane – that monstrous thing of iron and steel just watching for its chance to down me – and all fear goes. I am at peace again. [I feel] the elusive touch of those Circles of Peace travelling past in the air."

We discussed this dualism of experience; he summed up what I was trying to say in a letter to a third person:

> K. has a theory for this. He believes that there are two planes of existence which he calls *vie tragique* and *vie triviale*. Usually we move

* Cf. "In Memory of Richard Hillary" in *The Yogi and the Commissar* (1945).

on the trivial plane, but occasionally, in moments of elation or danger, we find ourselves transferred to the plane of the *vie tragique*, with its non-commonsense, cosmic perspective. When we are on the trivial plane, the realities of the other appear as nonsense – as overstrung nerves, and so on. When we live on the tragic plane, the joys and sorrows of the other are shallow, frivolous, trifling. But in exceptional circumstances, for instance, if one has to live through a long stretch of time in physical danger, one is placed, as it were, on the line of intersection of the two planes; a curious situation which is a kind of tightrope-walking on one's nerves. . . . I think he is right.

So far Hillary, the pilot. But there is another type of person condemned to walk on the line in which the two planes intersect: the artist. For this meeting of the trivial narrative of life with its tragic counterpoint is the very essence of art. Art is the gift – or curse – of perceiving the trivial objects and events of everyday experience *sub specie eternitatis*; and conversely, to express the absolute in human terms, to reflect it in a concrete image. "The infinite is made to blend itself with the finite; to stand visible, as it were, attainable here. Of this sort are all true works of art; in this we discern eternity looking through time" (Carlyle).

Now there are various ways in which literature can become such a window in time, in which the intersection of the two planes is achieved. The tragic plane of experience may be more or less conscious, more or less articulated. It may, for instance, be projected into the symbols expressed in the archetypal images of myth, folklore and religion. It may be felt and not stated: the actual words may be no more than the vibrations of a tuning fork, which makes the reader resonate without knowing why. Lichtenberg said that the works of the Protestant mystic Jacob Boehme were "like a picnic where the host provides the words and the guests provide the meaning".

On the opposite end of the scale, we have the articulate type of narrative literature in which the cosmic plane manifests itself in the shape of an ideology. I am using here the word "ideology" in the broad sense of a system of coordinates, a grid of perception, a hierarchy of values derived from certain beliefs about the ultimate nature of reality and the meaning of existence. Again, this ideology may be stated explicitly or merely implied. Allow me to quote an early example of ideological literature: the biblical story of Jonah and the whale.

Jonah is described in the story as a decent fellow who has committed no crime to warrant his dreadful punishment. This very ordinary person receives a sudden order from God "to go to Nineveh, that great city, and cry against it" – which is a rather tall order; he understandably prefers to go on leading his happy and trivial life. So, evading the call from the tragic plane, he buys a passage on a ship to Tarshish; and he has such a clean conscience about it that while the storm rages Jonah is peacefully asleep. And therein precisely lies his sin – in his normality, in his complacency, in his refusal to face the storm and the corruption of Nineveh – therein lies his sin, according to the narrator's idea, which must be punished in the belly of the whale:

> The waters compassed me about . . . the weeds were wrapped about my head . . . *yet hast thou brought up my life from corruption, O Lord my God. . . . They that observe lying vanities forsake their own mercy.*

In none of the ancient civilisations was the tension between the tragic and trivial planes more intensely felt than by the Hebrews. Jonah's only crime was trying to lead a normal life and to disregard the terrible voice from that other plane of existence. Melville understood this when, in the great sermon in *Moby Dick*, he made his preacher sum up the lesson of Jonah:

> Woe to him who seeks to pour oil upon the waters when God has brewed them into a gale! Woe to him who seeks to please rather than to appal! . . . Woe to him who, in this world, courts not dishonour!

Contrast this with Candide's "Let us cultivate our little garden", or the Buddha's "Middle Way". The astonishing thing is that both ideologies seem equally plausible, convincing, self-evident – because they are expressed not in propaganda pamphlets, but in works of art. But let us have no illusions about the "objectivity" of art. There is always an ideology behind it, however indirectly stated, because all art attempts to answer a tragic question and each answer implies a programme – or at least an attitude to life.

Let me take a second example from a period more than two millennia later. I shall read you an oft-quoted passage from the great peroration of Ulysses in the first act of *Troilus and Cressida*. I hope you will agree that the passage is poetically strong and expressive, but I fear that you will also find it rather confusing and meaningless if you are not familiar with the ideological framework behind it:

> The heavens themselves, the planets, and this centre
> Observe degree, priority, and place,
> Insisture, course, proportion, season, form,
> Office, and custom, in all line of order:
> . . . but when the planets,
> In evil mixture, to disorder wander,
> What plagues and what portents! what mutiny!
> What raging of the sea! shaking of earth!
> Commotion in the winds! frights, changes, horrors,
> Divert and crack, rend and deracinate
> The unity and married calm of states
> Quite from their fixture! O, when degree is shak'd,
> Which is the ladder to all high designs,
> The enterprise is sick! . . .
> Take but degree away, untune that string,
> And, hark, what discord follows! each thing meets
> In mere oppugnancy: the bounded waters
> Should lift their bosoms higher than the shores
> And make a sop of all this solid globe:
> Strength should be lord of imbecility,
> And the rude son should strike his father dead.

Well, you may ask, what is all this excitement about? What is the cause of this apocalyptic vision, what is the valiant Ulysses so afraid of?

The key word of the passage is the word "degree": "The heavens themselves, the planets and this centre [the earth] observe degree, priority and place." And later on: "O, when degree is shak'd, the enterprise is sick." To us the word "degree" is rather abstract and unpoetical, but to the

Elizabethan audience in the theatre it was a familiar allusion to a view of the world, a philosophy that was taken for granted. It was a view based on Christian doctrine, NeoPlatonic philosophy and Aristotelian cosmology – the universe as Dante, Shakespeare and the Elizabethan poets saw it.

It was a walled-in universe like a walled-in medieval town; in its centre was the earth – dark, heavy and corrupt, surrounded by the nine concentric crystal spheres of the moon, sun, planets and stars, each representing a higher degree of perfection, up to the abode of God. To this hierarchic order of *space* was attached a hierarchy of *rank* and *value* which stretched down like a ladder from the supreme ruler of the universe, through the hierarchy of angels, which kept the crystal spheres of the stars spinning, down to man. Here on earth, the *cosmic* ladder continued as a *social* ladder with its hierarchy of kings, barons, knights, commoners, and serfs, then down through the animal, vegetable and mineral kingdom into inanimate nature; and further down into a conic cavity in the earth, around whose narrowing slopes the nine hierarchies of devils are arranged in circles duplicating the nine heavenly spheres.

In this rigid, static, petrified universe, every *change* that would confuse the order of the cosmic ladder was regarded as a universal catastrophe because, owing to the rigidity of the system, the disturbance would immediately spread both up and down the ladder: "O, when degree is shak'd, the enterprise is sick . . . What raging of the sea! . . . frights, *changes*, horrors." Notice that the word "change" stands between "frights" and "horror" and was regarded as synonymous in that fear-ridden age.

I would further like to call your attention to the passage, "Take but degree away, *untune that string*, and hark what discord follows." The musical imagery here is not just a poetical metaphor, but a concrete allusion to another ideological concept: the harmony of the spheres. This concept originated with Pythagoras in the sixth century BC and was again much in fashion following the Platonic revival of the Renaissance. The harmony of the spheres was supposed to be a celestial music produced by the planets as they swish through space, each at a different speed. According to legend, Pythagoras was the only man who was actually able to *hear* the music of the spheres, because ordinary mortals were too grossly constituted. That both Shakespeare and his audience were familiar with this concept can be gathered from a number of similar passages. Thus, for instance, in *The Merchant of Venice*, Lorenzo explains it to Jessica:

> . . . soft stillness and the night
> Become the touches of sweet harmony . . .
> There's not the smallest orb which thou behold'st
> But in his motion like an angel sings . . .
> Such harmony is in immortal souls:
> But, whilst this muddy vesture of decay
> Doth grossly close it in, we cannot hear it.

If you are interested in this particular subject, I would refer you to Professor Tillyard's *The Elizabethan World Picture*. The purpose of my quoting these examples was to demonstrate that even the most timeless works of literature, without any apparent ideological bias, will reveal under the X-ray camera a scaffolding of moral values and philosophical assumptions. There is no game without rules of the game, and there is no work of art without some working hypothesis behind it.

In this sense, but only in this sense, all literature is committed, is a *litterature engagée*. This leads to two opposite dangers: firstly the literature *engagée* may degenerate into a literature *enragée*, as happened with the Marxist literature of the thirties, and again recently in the French existentialist circus. Conversely, the yearning to escape one's ideological chains may end in escapism, the evading of all worthwhile problems.

Concerning the first of these dangers, we know that the artist's mission is not to preach, but demonstrate. We are aware of the difference between art and propaganda, between the universal and the topical – but it is not always easy to draw a line between the two; and even a Tolstoy did not always succeed in drawing it.

The second danger, the flight into the ivory tower, is much in evidence in the contemporary English novel. Our Book

Society choices are still teeming with young ladies in old country houses who amble through mellow gardens with a tennis racket in one hand and a volume of Proust in the other. Mind you, I do not miss the hydrogen bomb in the dialogue, but I miss it in the author's consciousness. To create innocence, one must have awareness of guilt. To define the position of a point in space, one must have a system of coordinates. And every system of coordinates has the curious attribute that it embraces the whole infinity of space.

And thus at the end I am back at my starting point. All true art is a tightrope walk on the line of intersection of the tragic and trivial planes of existence. When the acrobat slips, art degenerates into propaganda, or escapes into a bloodless cloud-cuckoo land; it ceases to be art. Walking the tightrope is a tricky profession.

THE AGE OF DISCRETION*

This year AD 1960, means to me *anno* 15 pH, where "p" stands for *post*, and "H" stands for Hiroshima. I say that not because I like to remember that episode, nor as an act of penance – for after all we were not consulted – but for a factual and unsentimental reason. Calendars imply convictions about the importance of certain events: the first Olympiad for the Greeks, the birth of a child in Bethlehem, the flight of Mohammed from Mecca. The positing of a year zero provides a timescale, a measure of the distance covered, from the real or assumed starting point, of a given civilisation.

There is, I believe, a strong case to be made for keeping a kind of second calendar in our minds which indicates the number of years that have passed since that decisive moment when a man-made flash of light outshone the sun. Fifteen years are but a few seconds on the dials of history, and it is not surprising that this newborn civilisation of ours is as yet unaware of its own existence. More precisely, its awareness is still of that inchoate, shapeless, nebulous kind which precedes the young child's discovery of its identity. On the surface we find no sharp, decisive break between life before and after *anno zero*. There have been some social, political, cultural changes, but if these were all there would be no justification for suggesting this kind of new calendar.

My feeling that all that happened before 1945 belongs to prehistory is based on a simple consideration: it was in 1945 that mankind acquired the power to destroy itself. The next

* Broadcast on the BBC Third Programme, 25 February 1960.

question is what this fact does to the human psyche. I think that, so far, it has affected it very little, at least on the conscious level. The proof is that everybody went on manufacturing the thing. There were, there are, protests and involved controversies, but no global outcry powerful enough to stop it. The somewhat clownish character of some of the protest demonstrations is particularly revealing. The voluble phrases about the possibility of blowing the whole planet to glory sounded at first both frightening and subtly flattering to our vanity; but soon they became clichés divorced from emotional meaning. Then everybody got bored with this insoluble problem until the sputniks and satellites brought new thrills, and the pleasant hope that these things might develop a tendency to keep going upward and not coming down.

And thus, *anno* 15 pH, we have apparently settled down to business as usual. But, I believe, only apparently. There are periods of incubation. The Copernican theory of the earth's motion took eighty years before it began to sink in. The unconscious has its own clock, and its own ways of digesting what the conscious mind has rejected as indigestible. There are signs that, on a limited scale and in an oblique way, this process of assimilation has already begun – a process which, I believe, is bound to transform completely the mental make-up of our race. The essence of this transformation could be defined as follows: hitherto man had to live with the idea of his death as an individual; from now onward mankind will have to live with the idea of its death as a species.

This is an entirely novel prospect. To realise its implications one must try to bear in mind that we are not dealing in abstractions but with hard, obstinate facts; in other words, we must try to achieve a psychological breakthrough across the smokescreen of our own mental defences against reality. If we succeed in achieving that, we may discover a rather breathtaking vision beyond the screen, which will make human destiny appear in a new light. We who were brought up in the Western way of thinking have always been taught to accept the transitoriness of our existence as individuals, while taking the survival of our species axiomatically for granted. And this was a perfectly reasonable belief, barring some unlikely cosmic catastrophe. But it has ceased to be a reasonable belief since the day, fifteen years ago, when the feasibility of just such a cosmic catastrophe was tested and proven. It pulverised the assumption on which all philosophy, from Socrates onward, was based: the potential immortality of our species.

Let us consider the implications of this turn of events from a completely detached, that is, from an inhuman, point of view. Let us imagine that among the hidden works of the Lord Almighty there functions a kind of intergalactic insurance company which periodically surveys the insurance risks attached to its clients, i.e., the various intelligent species on the various inhabited planets – which number perhaps a million in our galaxy alone. The company watches them from a distance. Before its observers noticed that certain flash fifteen years ago, they would probably have given the inhabitants of this planet quite a reasonable lifespan. It has, by cosmic standards, just the right size of middle-aged sun, in a stable, middle-aged galaxy, safe by all probability standards from any local or intergalactic collision. Its dominant race, which emerged relatively late after the beginning of organic life on the planet, seemed to be intellectually precocious, while emotionally retarded, and accordingly maladjusted. But against this it enjoyed the considerable advantage of having no serious biological competitors for the mastery of the planet. So far, so good. Then came the familiar flash which the company's watchmen had so frequently observed in other parts of the sky, and the computers were set to work.

They worked on the principle, based on past experience, that the gadgets which cause the flash will undergo the process known as progressive miniaturisation: they will become ever smaller and more elegant, as transistor radios and satellite equipment did. The computers accordingly took it for granted that an effective global control of the gadgets was in the long run impracticable on these grounds alone, and that in the foreseeable future they will be produced and stored in large quantities, from windswept Alaska to sunny Cairo and Tel Aviv. Next, the computers were fed relevant samples of the past behaviour of our race, and a long tape showing the intensity and frequency of the various potential and open conflicts on various parts of the planet. Finally, they were fed the old but useful parable of the problem child left with a box of matches in a room filled with inflammable material; and were then asked to compute from these data the probable remaining lifespan of *homo sapiens*.

I think that all of us imagine from time to time that we hear the computers clicking – not in outer space, but in the inner spaces of the human mind, with its private clocks and private calendars. For that, of course, is the space – call it the collective unconscious, if you like – where our collective destiny is being computed. However, let me revert for another moment to my allegory, for at this point it takes an unexpected turn.

The computers had finished their work; the chief accountant extracted the tape, looked at the figures and took it to the boss. The boss looked at the tape, then dictated the following message to our planet:

"Dear Sirs, let me congratulate you. The results look pretty bad, but the company can only compute statistical probabilities, and the final outcome still depends on the individual client. We congratulate you, as usual on these occasions, on the mere fact that you have reached the age of discretion. Before this turning point you were assured of your survival, regardless of the nasty things you did. You were potentially immortal as a race, and in this secure knowledge you could indulge in all kinds of irresponsible behaviour. This situation has now been changed, though you do not realise it yet. Your survival now depends on you and on you alone. The Company can do nothing more for you. Nature nursed and protected you before you reached maturity, even to the extent of producing a surplus of male births to replenish your stock depleted by wars. Now you are stronger than Nature and entirely on your own.

"The way you celebrated your reaching maturity was not pretty. But let it pass; there have been worse scandals in the galaxy. The Company does not judge and does not punish, because once you are past the turning point you are your own judge and your own executioner. At this stage, justice works by automatic feedback. Your race will never again feel quite safe, just as its individual members have never felt safe since the first of them ate the forbidden fruit of knowledge. But you need not be unduly dejected by that; there are compensations. By learning to live with the sober awareness of its possible extinction, your race may derive the same spiritual benefits which the individual derives from coming to terms with his own mortality.

"These benefits are considerable. You no doubt remember your old sage who said that philosophy is the history of man's endeavours to come to terms with death. And since philosophy is a Good Thing, death must be a Good Thing – or at least awareness thereof. Take that word 'death' out of your vocabulary and your great works of literature become meaningless; take that awareness away and your cathedrals collapse, the pyramids vanish into the sand, and the great organs become silent. You know all this, but since you live in an age of anxiety and transition, you condemn all concern with death as morbid in the indignant voice of your Victorian prudes. You deny Thanatos as the Victorians denied Eros; you shrink from the facts of death as they shrank from the facts of life. And yet the philosophy of man, the art of man, the dignity of man is derived from his brave endeavours to reconcile Eros and Thanatos.

"You are entering as an adult the large family of our clients – around a million in your galaxy alone; I always forget their exact figure because they come and vanish so fast, much quicker than a single galactic rotation. Nobody interferes with them; those who vanish are their own executioners because they prove in the long run unfit for existence. Those who survive flourish because they have discovered their cosmic *raison d'être*. The rest is up to you. All the Company can do is to wish you good luck – as we always do on these occasions."

To come back to earth – though I do not think we have really left it for a moment – let me conclude by a brief comparison between our present outlook and that of roughly 500 years before Hiroshima. The medieval universe was like a walled-in city with firm boundaries in space and time, a few million miles in diameter and a few thousand years of duration. In this closed universe a well-ordered drama was taking its course, which began with the Creation and would end when the trumpet sounded and the four horsemen appeared in the sky. In one sense we have reverted to that vision: we are no longer sure that *homo sapiens* will go on for ever, and we again feel that the Last Judgement may take place in the foreseeable future. But in another sense we have moved away from that vision: for we know that the end of *homo sapiens* would not be the end of the world, merely the end of an episode in a drama on an incomparably larger scale than the medieval scenery allowed for.

In other words, the necessity of getting reconciled with the idea of his possible extinction may breed a new humility, and may rid man of that biological jingoism which made him regard himself as the crown of creation. The idea that the world will go on even if mankind does not may prove an antidote to that anxiety which has held us in its grip since the burning star fell on Hiroshima, distorted our sense of values, exposed us to various forms of blackmail, undermined our dignity and our power of decision. Schopenhauer, wrongly described as a pessimist, regarded himself as a mortal leaf on an immortal tree, a leaf to be replaced next year by another, nourished by the same sap. Gradually we shall perhaps learn that the leaves which bud into life and sail away in the autumn symbolise not only individuals but other great civilisations dotted along the vaporous branches of the expanding universe. We shall be more at peace then. But it will take some time. After all, we have only just entered the fifteenth year of the new era.

REFLECTIONS ON A PENINSULA*

A few years ago one could see all over London an advertisement for a boot polish; it showed a very old, but well-preserved pair of leather shoes, and underneath the caption: "They are well worn, but they have worn well." It could serve as a motto for this little old Europe of ours: it is well worn, but it has worn well, all things considered. I became particularly aware of this during my recent stay in Asia where I spent several months – mostly in India and Japan. To be engulfed, and at times almost drowned, in the attitudes and values of an alien spiritual climate provided an occasion to make comparisons and to see Europe in a new light, from a different perspective. If I were asked to sum up in a brief formula what distinguishes it from the other great continents of the world, I would mention two outstanding features: unity-in-diversity in Space and continuity-through-change in Time.

This sounds rather abstract, so I shall offer you a quite concrete example for the first of these two features. You have before you a specimen of Europe born in Hungary, educated in Austria, who spent some of his most decisive years in France, became British by naturalisation – though alas, not by accent – and who writes his books in English. Transpose this curriculum into Asiatic terms, and you would have to imagine a person born, let us say, in Ankara, who studied in Benares and ended up as a Japanese writer. The parallel seems rather absurd, yet it does drive home not only the smallness of Europe, but above all the homogeneity of its culture. Wherever you look –

* Address to the Royal Society of Literature, read on 3 November 1960. In the chair Cecil Day Lewis.

at art or architecture, science, trade, sport, fashions in clothes, style of living – in all walks of life the common denominators weave their fabric across territorial and national boundaries. The movements towards economic and political unity are only the most recent expressions of a much older unity of tradition which makes it possible for a Hungarian to become an English writer, or a Scandinavian film producer to express the problems which move young people in France and Italy. Europe is the only continent among the ancient geographical divisions of the world where the ethnic mosaic forms a clearly defined and recognisable culture pattern. And this unity-in-diversity in Space has its historic source in the second aspect which I mentioned namely, continuity-through-change, maintained through two and half millennia of European history.

The emphasis is on both: the continuity and the change, which are complementary aspects – as, to draw a biological parallel, we find stable genes transmitted by heredity from generation to generation, as a continuous undercurrent beneath individual variety. By way of comparison: Egyptian art, for instance, displayed an amazing constancy over a couple of thousand years, and so did Hinduism as a religious philosophy; but this happened in societies that remained essentially static. Europe, on the other hand, was in almost continual ferment and change; and during the last three hundred years it has altered the natural and social environment of man as radically as if a new species had taken over our planet. Yet throughout this last explosive development and throughout earlier, equally profound changes, Europe managed to preserve a distinct and continuous identity, a historic personality, as it were.

It is a curious fact that this historic *persona*, Europe, with its distinct individual profile, emerged at the same turning point for the human race – the sixth pre-Christian century – which also gave birth to Confucius and Lao Tse, the Buddha, the Ionian philosophers and the Pythagorean brotherhood. A March breeze seemed to blow across this planet, from China to the Aegean Sea, stirring men into awareness like the breath in Adam's nostrils. But at the same time, there was also a parting of the ways between the Asian and European philosophy of life, of their attitudes to the basic problems of existence. Buddhism, Taoism and Confucianism, which gave rise to the great Asiatic cultures, have certain essential features in common which are in direct opposition to Western thought. The contrast is not, as one tends to believe, between so-called Eastern spiritualism and so-called Western thought. The contrast is not, as one tends to believe, between so-called Eastern spiritualism and so-called Western materialism, but between two basically different attitudes to life – so different that a contemporary German orientalist* suggested a new word for the Eastern approach to existence: *philousia,* as opposed to Western *philosophy*. All the evidence, from the Upanishads and the Tao Te-Ching, to the contemporary schools of Yoga and Zen Buddhism, unmistakably indicates that Eastern thinkers are less interested in factual knowledge – in *sophia,* from which *philosophia* is derived – than in *ousia,* essential being; they are more interested in the nature of consciousness itself than in the objects of consciousness. Whether you look at India, pre-revolutionary China, or Japan, you find a basic trend of thought among the great thinkers, which rejects all sense experience as illusion, denies that the world of objects has a reality independent from the perceiving subject, and which finds it "exceedingly odd/that the tree/should continue to be/when there's no one around in the quad". It is an attitude which prefers intuition to reason, fluid symbols to sharply defined concepts, thinking in images to thinking in categories, and which rejects the axioms of Western, i.e., Greek, logic – such as the laws of identity, contradiction and of the excluded middle. Above all, the Eastern sage strives after self-realisation through the annihilation of the thinking and feeling self; his ideal is depersonalisation, the drowning and dissolving of individuality in the universal pool of Atma, Brahma, Nirvana – as opposed to the Western ideal of self-realisation through the unfolding of individual potentialities.

This fundamental parting of the ways seems to have occurred, as already mentioned, in the sixth century BC. It is

* William S. Haas in *The Destiny of the Mind* (London, 1956).

fascinating to note how the split is reflected in the spirit and structure of language itself. Out of the same Sanskrit root, *matr-*, emerged two key words, *maya* and *metron*. *Maya,* in Hinduism and Buddhism, is the symbol of an attitude which regards the visible world as a web of illusions – the veil of *maya*; whereas *metron,* measure, regards it as something to be grasped, measured and mastered by the mind. Thus in the Ionian school of philosophy in the sixth century BC, rational thought was emerging from the dream world, the hypnagogic reveries of mythology steeped in archetypal symbols. It was the beginning of the great European adventure: the Promethean quest which, within the next two thousand years, was to transform our species more radically than the previous hundred thousand years had done.

But at this point I must again warn you against that popular misconception which identifies the Eastern attitude with spiritualism, the Western with materialism. Materialism was one of the rival philosophies of Greece which lasted about two centuries; it was revived two thousand years later, in the eighteenth century, and is now, *as a philosophy,* once more on its way out. But, apart from these two episodes, religion, or at least religious awareness in one form or another, had been the dominant chord in the past of European art, philosophy and social life.

Admittedly, Europe's past is tainted and unedifying. But Asian history has been as bloody and cruel as ours. The great Hindu epics, the *Ramayana* and *Mahabharata,* are as full of savagery and gore as the Old Testament, or the *Eddas,* or the *Niebelungen* Saga. The *Bhagavad Gita* – the nearest Hindu equivalent to the Gospels, frequently quoted but infrequently read – is in fact an eloquent refutation of pacifism and non-violence by the Lord Krishna himself. *Ahimsa* – non-violence – was as abstract a command in Hindu as "turning the other cheek" was in ours – until quite recent times when Gandhi's genius forged it into a modern political weapon. But even Gandhi was never an integral pacifist – he was prepared in 1940 to enter the war on our side, on condition that India was granted independence, and in 1948, he gave his agreement to the invasion of Kashmir. Similarly, Gandhi's crusade for the Untouchables was, on his own admission, inspired not by Hinduism, but by Christianity and Tolstoyanism. Let us face it: the traditional Asian attitude to the sick and the poor is notoriously one of indifference, because caste, rank, wealth and health are preordained by the laws of Karma. Hinduism and Buddhism are tolerant towards other religions but display no charity towards the individual; with Christianity just the opposite seems to be true. Thus the messianic arrogance of the Christian crusader is matched by the arrogant detachment in the Yogi's attitude towards human suffering; and the Oriental version of tolerance without charity produced as much suffering and misery as Christian charity without tolerance.

Once more: the choice is not between spirituality and materialism, but between two different approaches to reality – one which relies on intuition, symbolic imagery and essential being – the other, on reason, conceptual thinking, logical categories. Obviously neither of the two attitudes contains the whole truth; obviously they ought to complement each other, as the principles of masculine logic and feminine intuition, the *yin* and *yang* in Taoist philosophy, are meant to complement each other.

However, the point I want to make is that in the history of the great Asiatic cultures the accent remained always on one side: on the intuitive, subjective, mystical, logic-rejecting side; whereas in the history of European thought, *both* attitudes were present – alternately dominating the scene, or simultaneously competing for supremacy. Examples of this creative polarity are the Dionysian and Apollonian principles; or the Greek atomists, who saw the world in terms of matter and measure, as opposed to the Eleatic's view which was closer to the veil of *maya* – remember Empedocles jumping into the crater of Etna in search of Nirvana; and remember those twin stars, Plato and Aristotle. Think of Augustine's other-worldly rejection of Nature, and Aquinas' rediscovery of Nature; of Schopenhauer's eastern Mysticism *versus* Nietzsche's arrogant Western superman; of Jung *versus* Freud.

Thus European thought evolved through the recurrent

mating of opposites, whereas Asian thought seems to have perpetuated itself by a kind of asexual process – like budding algae detaching themselves from the parent body to become separate individuals but indistinguishable in shape. The first process reflects continuity-through-change; the second a self-perpetuating sameness.

To put it in another way, the impressive thing about the evolution of European thought, seen from the Asian perspective, is the organic integration of the various trends that went into it. The first great synthesis seems to have been achieved, towards the end of that glorious sixth pre-Christian century, by the Pythagoreans who brought together into a unified vision both contrasting attitudes: mysticism and science, music and mathematics, fluid intuition and articulate reason. The unravelling of the laws of Nature, the analysis of the harmony of the spheres, was proclaimed to be the highest form of divine worship. And this form of worship, I submit, is a specifically European discovery. There were periods in which the discovery was forgotten or denied, like a recessive gene; but it always reasserted itself. It is reflected in that wonderfully ambiguous word "mystery". The sober physicist is after the "mysteries of Nature" – never suspecting, poor chap, that mysterium is a word of mystic origin, and that the motive of his quest for a unified field theory which will express gravity, electromagnetism, and the other riddles of the universe in a single formula, has more affinities than one would think with the quest for the Orphic mysteries.

Another strain which runs through the European inheritance is a specific method of sublimating emotions and putting them to creative use – a leitmotif which one can follow from the ancient cult of Bacchus-Dionysius to Freud and Jung. Again I must confine myself to hints in shorthand, as it were. The semibarbaric cult of Bacchus, the raging god of sex and wine, was imported from Thrace to Greece, probably a short time before that decisive sixth century. In Greece it became "Europeanised" in the cult of Orpheus, which transformed physical intoxication into mental intoxication; the word "orgy" no longer meant drunken revelry but religious ecstasy;

and subsequently the Bacchic juice became sacramental wine and part of the Christian ritual. A similar transformation occurred in the meaning of the word *theoria* (from *thea* – spectacle, *theoris* – audience). In Orphic usage it meant a state of religious contemplation where the spectator identified himself with the suffering god. In the Pythagorean brotherhood, which adopted the Orphic cult, religious ecstasy changed into the ecstasy of intellectual discovery, and *theoria* assumed the meaning of "theory" in the modern sense. Finally, the Bacchic rite of devouring the slain god to partake of his divine substance appears in a sublimated guise in the doctrine of transubstantiation, of partaking of the body and blood of the Saviour in Holy Communion.

One branch of the mainstream of Greek thought became united, through the Neoplatonists, with the Judeo-Christian tradition in Augustine; another, through Aristotle and St Thomas Aquinas, led to the rise of scholasticism. But these originally independent currents, or traditions, were not just mechanically added together to form an eclectic doctrine. It was a process of cross-fertilisation, creating variety and change, yet preserving a continuous heritage from the past. The axioms of Euclid and the Ten Commandments, Aristotle's *Categories* and the Sermon of the Mount, were assembled into a grand synthesis. It provided the link between mysticism and logic, between the poetry of St John of the Cross and the telescopes of the Jesuit astronomers in their search for order and harmony in the universe. It is this synthesis which all other great cultures rejected – the Asian cultures by rejecting the *metron* and the reality of the outside world; the African and pre-Columbian cultures by moving towards different spiritual pastures.

Greece was conquered, Alexandria burned, Rome and Byzantium collapsed, yet the continuity was sustained. The migrations injected the vitality of the barbaric tribes into the tired old races around the Mediterranean basin, but Europe did not become barbarised – it was the barbarians who became Europeanised.

After the long, dark interlude, Europe was reborn by

rediscovering its past – its temporarily lost Greek heritage. For several centuries, the Arabs had been the sole custodians of the treasures of Greek learning. They were the go-betweens who brought back to Europe its Greek and Alexandrine heritage, enriched by Indian and Persian additions. But their long tenure of this vast body of knowledge remained surprisingly barren; whereas as soon as it was reincorporated into the Latin culture of Europe it bore immediate and abundant fruit. The Hellenic heritage was like a skin graft which never took on Arabic culture and wilted away, leaving hardly a trace. Yet when Europe recovered its past, it immediately started on that explosive development which led from the Renaissance to the modern age.

Continuity-through-change and unity-in-diversity are essential attributes of an evolving culture. The revolutionary Humanists of the Renaissance, and the angry puritans of the reformation, derived their "modern" inspirations from the ancient Hebrew and Greek texts; the French Revolution derived its symbols and titles of office from the institutions of the Roman republic; and even the teaching of Karl Marx can be traced back to its archetypal roots in the pathos of the Old Testament prophets, the Platonic elements in Hegel, and the dialectical acrobatics of the Aristotelian schoolmen. There is always something new under the European sun, but it is the organic novelty of new shoots on an old tree, fed by the saps of its subterranean roots.

That, briefly, seems to me the secret of Europe's unique powers of resistance and regeneration. But these can be fully appreciated only by way of comparison. In spite of Yoga and Zen, which are practised only by an insignificant minority, the people of India and Japan live today in a spiritual vacuum, more estranged from any transcendental faith than Europe. Neither Hinduism nor Buddhism were able to resist the impact of industrialisation and social reform, because neither of them had the adaptability, due to a continuous evolutionary process, which the Helleno-Christian tradition has acquired. India is the most traditionalist, Japan the most westernised country in Asia – they are opposite ends of the Asian spectrum. Its centre is occupied by the vastness of China, one of the world's oldest cultures; yet it proved even less resistant against the impact of a materialist ideology, and has become the most accomplished robot state this side of science fiction. Compared to that we have not done so badly in resisting the rape of the spirit, from the barbarian invasions to the invasions of totalitarian barbarity. They have amputated part of Europe's body; the rest has once again made, all considered, a surprising physical and moral recovery.

Ever since Europe and Asia went their different ways, the European's attitude to Asia was either that of the conqueror or that of the pilgrim, anxious to prostrate himself at the guru's feet. I went to Asia in a similar spirit and came back rather proud of being a European. It may be a parochial pride, but it is not smug, for, as a Hungarian-born, French-loving, English writer with some experience of prisons and concentration camps, one cannot help being aware of Europe's past sins and present deadly peril. And yet a detached comparison with other continents leaves one with a new confidence in and affection for our small peninsula, like a figure riding on the back of the Asian bull.

DRIFTING ON A RIVER*

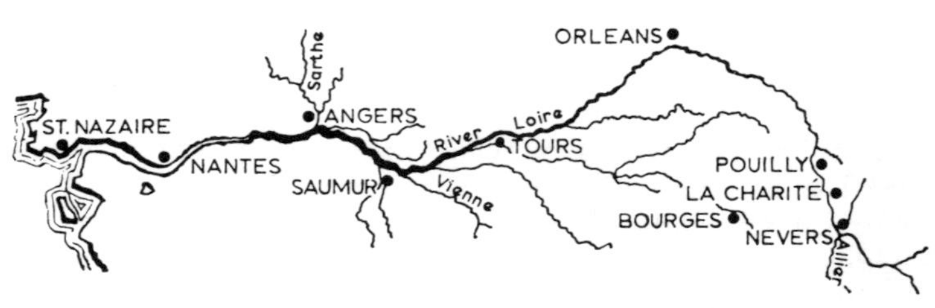

Last year, when I graduated from lower-middle to middle-middle age, I became addicted to a new hobby; at a loss for an adequate English expression, I shall call it *le canotage gastronomique*. The idea is to travel, in a canoe, down one of the great rivers of France – the Dordogne or the Loire; to spend one's days on the water and one's nights at a comfortable hotel; to combine the virtuous satisfaction of a sporting achievement with a guilt-free guzzle in the evening.

You travel at the average rate of twenty miles a day, paddling or drifting with the current, eating your picnic lunch on an island or anchored in midstream. A river is a world of its own: often you do not see a human being or a house for several hours; a few miles from bustling towns like Orléans or Bergerac you are in a sunny, silent wilderness where a dog's bark is an event and the rustling of the current against a dead branch sounds like the Niagara falls. After a fortnight of this

* First published in *The Observer,* August 1957.

dreamy paddle-drift-and-wading progress, you discover that you have travelled more than half the width of France.

It is much more easily done than it sounds. The technique of paddling a canoe is childishly simple and can be learned by any fool of any age in an hour. You can use a rigid (Canadian) canoe, which is transported on a rack on the top of the car; or a kayak with collapsible frame and rubberised skin, which, when dismantled, is stowed into two bags weighing thirty-five pounds each.

I prefer the Canadian because its single-paddle action is more peaceful; but since I have an open car without a roof, I use a kayak. She is nearly eighteen feet long, two and a half feet wide, very streamlined, and as frail in appearance as she is sturdy in fact, with a carrying capacity of 800 pounds and sufficient storage space under the canvas cover fore and aft to carry all the clothes that two people need for a fortnight and also a folding trolley for portaging the canoe, and the books which will remain unread. She is of British make, costs around £35, and answers to the name of *Blue Arrow*.

Last summer, with a friend who plays second paddle and shall be called Crew, I travelled down the Dordogne from Beaulieu to Trémolat, and a stretch of its tributary, the Vézère. This year we went down the wine-and-château regions of the Loire, from Nevers to Saumur, some 250 miles in all.

My log of this summer's expedition starts on Thursday, 13 June in Nevers. We had arrived from Paris late the previous night, and spent Thursday morning re-packing our river wardrobe into an assortment of waterproof bags, putting *Blue Arrow* together on a grassy patch near a riverside inn, finding a garage where the car would remain for the next fortnight or so, and buying our first picnic lunch. Then, at long last, the moment arrived to fix the pennant with the red ensign on the stern and to push off, bottom grinding across the gravel, into the sudden swift current, as if stepping onto a liquid escalator belt.

The sky was cloudy and the grey river seemed incredibly vast. The last few days the papers had been full of storms and inundations in the Alps and the Massif Central, of bridges carried away and villages evacuated. As a result, the Loire had risen considerably: in places to a width of half a mile across, and even more where it is broken up by islands. The high water actually proved a blessing by saving portages over shallows, and carrying us safely over submerged obstacles; but during the first hour we felt overwhelmed and subdued.

The Loire is the longest river in France – over a thousand kilometres – and flows through the heart of the country, the Bourbonnais and Nivernais, the Orleanais and Berri, Anjou and Touraine. The river was navigable up to the beginning of the nineteenth century, but the vast deforestations along its upper reaches and tributaries put an end to that; in times of drought it is reduced to thin trickles among the sandbanks, though it remains canoeable even then. The dying out of navigation made the busy water-road revert to its original nature of a liquid path through unspoiled country and often through a wilderness, with no houses, villas or towns for miles on end; even the villages mostly turn their backs on the river.

The log of the first day reads:

> Thursday, 13 June, Nevers-La Charité, 35 km, seven hours. Left Nevers 12.40 p.m. from Le Chalet du Viaduc after railway bridge. Lunched anchored on lone beach facing the mouth of the Allier on *andouillettes de vire* (chitterling stuffed with sausage meat which looks in cross-section like mottled quartz), goat cheese and peaches. On reconnoitring the bridge at Fourchambault ran into a fisherman who told us the bridge was easy to pass, but said nothing about a dredge-cable spanning half the river immediately behind the bridge. Reconnoitre, always reconnoitre. Good strong current, but nasty head-wind. Cloudy all day, cleared up after 6 p.m., wind dropped, golden evening. Reconnoitred from island before entering La Charité. Met another fisherman with dog on island. Lost my glasses in island sands. Moored at La Charité 7.45, washed out and shaky with fatigue (muscles not yet broken in); bath and simple dinner on hotel terrace: river lobster cooked in Pouilly; ham with cream sauce, Chavignol goat cheese. Wines: Pouilly Fumé 1956, Pouilly Fumé Loges 1952.

"Reconnoitring" is at the same time a necessity, a ritual, and one of the principal joys of canoeing. When you approach anything in the river that looks tricky – a bridge, a weir, rapids or shallows – you can neither stop in the current nor get a proper view, crouched on the bottom of the canoe; you have to land on the nearest shore or island, and reconnoitre.

This may involve scrambling up the river bank through thistles and thorns, or wading through mud, but it provides one with an excuse to stretch one's legs, smoke a cigarette, compare the cool breeze of the river with the sudden baking heat of the shore, and explore a stretch of lonely rural hinterland on which, one feels, no white man has set foot before. The church spire of the nearest village, some kilometres away, looks like a desert mirage; the only reality is the river, the cornfields with cracked soil like an old peasant's skin, meadows blushing with poppies, a white cow or goat on the other bank, and the silence. This, one realises with a sudden shock, is essential France, a landscape written in basic French, glimpsed through the back door of a deserted waterway.

Friday, 14 June, La Charité-Pouilly s/Loire. M. Maréchal, a super-efficient optician in this medieval market town, built helter-skelter round a Benedictine abbey, produced a new pair of glasses within a couple of hours. We left at midday in blazing sun, revisited Lost-Glasses-Island, which, owing to a further rise in the water level overnight, had an entirely different shape; this river has changed its contours every day since the Creation.

Downstream from La Charité the Loire branches out into a vast labyrinth of islands and waterways, impersonating the Mississippi. In places it spans a mile, but is broken up by half-submerged clusters of trees, islands with golden sandy beaches, and odd little *tourbillons* suddenly appearing where a salmon trout, disturbed in its mudbath, has caused a minor landslide in the river bed. Silver beeches dotted all round the vast horizon suddenly reflecting an eighteenth-century Flemish landscape with only the frame missing.

Since it is impossible to know which branch to follow in this liquid maze, we left the decision to the current, which usually carries you to the deepest channel, but occasionally runs you aground on sand or gravel. This means wading and pushing, until suddenly you are in deep water again, racing down on the moving belt at a speed which feels like an express train, and which we have timed at exactly four miles an hour.

On this second day we were getting to know the personality of this river, its cross-currents and idiosyncrasies, as we learned to know last year the Dordogne. Once, guided by the froth on the current, we let it carry us into an inlet hidden in a clump of trees, and emerged into a secret waterway which made us feel we were on the *African Queen* and watch out for monkeys and natives with arrows. Ate our sausage and cheese on an enchanted island with a small patch of yellow sandy beach enclosed by woods. Saw not a single house or person till Pouilly. Drifted through the sun-drenched silence, watched only by some statuesque, cream-coloured cows, dying to know who we were; and the cuckoos calling each other across the river to signal by jungle telegraph our approach.

We were now in the Pouilly-Sancerre country. The Pouilly Fumé is our favourite among all the white wines of France, and on six successive evenings, from Nevers to Orléans, we compared and tried to memorise the striking differences between the five available years, '52 to '56, and the two distinct grapes, the Chasselas and the Sauvignon. (The same Sauvignon grape also produces the Château Yquem.) This week of sampling, on the spot, unadulterated, the produce of a single small region, showed again how utterly silly, in these days, all claims of connoisseurship are unless coming from a member of the trade.

I shall not go into detail about food and wine, though it was one of the leitmotifs of the trip. On the Continent, food and wine are the business of the restaurateurs; in England of the littérateurs. There is something almost pornographic – the obscenity of the *voyeur* – in the prose of our *gourmets de lettres*. Instead, here is some general advice for future gastro-canoeists.

First, no wine during the day on the river. It does not hurt, but it is lazy-making and spoils the expectations of the evening. Very light picnic lunch – sausage, cheese, Vichy water: it saves both appetite and money for dinner. At the blessed moment of arrival in the evening, avoid the temptation of cocktails, Pernod or apéritif, and start straight away on a cool bottle of white or rosé before dinner. The difference in enjoyment, mood and staying power is amazing. Crew and I sometimes drank a bottle before dinner and two more in the course of it, without ill-effect: the Loire wine departs as gracefully as it greets one.

Try a meal with white wine throughout, no red: the Pouilly Fumé, especially, goes with everything except red meat, and particularly well with goat cheese. (The red Loire wines are rather indifferent.) Beware of liqueur. The *marc* and *prune* of the region are sheer fire-water: one glass with the coffee will do for the sagacious canoeist. Lastly, never carry moderation to excess: occasional excess proves moderation in moderation. Amen.

To illustrate my various points: at a restaurant in Langeais where we dined, the teachers of the Lycée of Tours were having their annual end-of-term banquet. Here is their menu. Please bear in mind that the gathering was not one of university dons, but of schoolmasters in a provincial grammar school:

Terrine maison à la gelée
Brochet de Loire au beurre blanc
Champignons à la crème
Canard Nantais
aux
Petit pois
Salade
Fromages assortis
Omelette surprise
Sablés maison
Corbeille de fruits

VINS

Touraine blanc – Touraine rouge
(throughout the meal)
Montlouis sec (with the brochet)
Chinon 1954 (with the champignons)
St-Nicolas-de-Bourgueil 1953
(with the canard)
Côteaux-du-Layon 1953
(with the omelette)

Q.E.D.

The first half of the journey, from Nevers to Orléans, took exactly a week. After the second day we were broken in and could go on paddling mechanically for an hour without effort, and without even being aware of it – I suppose that is how galley slaves survived to old age. But at least half the time we drifted, with an occasional lazy stroke to keep the canoe's head downstream. We developed a craze for discovering secret inlets which start as an improbable trickle in a wall of foliage, and, when you have forced your way through the scratchy branches, rewardingly broaden out into a secret channel in the wilderness. There was a great display of what we took to be rare birds, and at times the salmon rose round the canoe like popcorn – sensing, I am sure, that we were obstinate non-anglers and non-watchers of birds.

Until midday we usually travelled in a blaze of sun which must have burned a hole to get through the hard blue sky of the Loire. It charged our bodies, like batteries, with the volts and amps needed to last through the next English winter. In the early afternoon there usually appeared one or two very small white clouds, angelic in appearance, which had the knack of turning black and spawning all over the sky before you could say a knot and two fathoms. First the river's colour turned to pewter; then came the lightning – sheet, fork and knife, followed by the sudden crack and the Homeric tummy-rumbling of the gods.

This was the signal for lengthy arguments between pessimistic Crew and my science-minded self as to which way the storm was heading and whether to land at the next village for shelter. Actually we were caught only once, just before landing. Another time we watched, near Sancerre, rockets being shot from the vineyards into the clouds; they are supposed to prevent hail. After these spectacular thunderstorms which the heatwave brought in its wake, it was a joy to paddle through the gentle rain. Where the raindrops hit the water they made little white crosses standing on the bubbles, like a gay cemetery for leprechauns who can always get out on leave when the sun comes through.

As for dramatic incidents, there were none. Everybody

warned us against the treacherous quicksands of the Loire, and we were careful always to hang on to the canoe while wading, but never sank deeper than our ankles. Once, passing under the bridge of Châtillon, the backwash, or "counter-current", whirled us round and drove us head on into a group of anglers on a grass patch at the foot of a pillar. It was merely funny, but a warning to be more careful about bridges. We twice portaged the canoe around bridges where the current looked nasty: at Gien and at Orléans – though more out of cowardice than real necessity. Generally speaking, the only dangers on the Loire are man-made: dredges with steel cables, derelict weirs, bridges destroyed in the war, and bridges in general. Without them the canoe would happily swim down with the current, like a cork, from the Massif Central to the sea.

When we got to Orléans we profited from a couple of rainy days to return by train to Nevers, where we had left the car, and drove her down to Orléans, where we garaged her for the remaining half of the journey. It is a good idea to divide, in this manner, the trip into halves: after a week's canoeing, a day in train and car is a wonderful change. Since the river is a one-way street, the canoeist is obliged to travel through the same stretch of country three times: paddling downstream, upstream by train, and downstream again by car, each time seeing it from a different angle. On the river you sweated *pour la gloire*; on the train you relax and marvel at the speed; in the car you become a sightseeing tourist, but with that difference which familiarity with a region brings to the perception of its art. A château on the Loire, visited during a short stop in passing, is like a quotation out of context.

The remaining half of the journey through the classic château country – Orléans, Beaugency, Blois, Chaumont, Amboise, Vouvray, Tours, Langeais, Bourgeuil, Saumur – lasted another week. It was peak tourist season in one of the most tourist-haunted regions of the world, but all along the Royal Valley we had the river to ourselves. It gave one a wonderfully smug feeling of superiority to drift slowly past the turrets of Chaumont or Amboise, alone and unseen – like walking along the corridors of the Louvre after closing time; to watch them at first from a distance, transparent, white and unreal, slowly growing, vanishing round a bend, bursting into view again unexpectedly huge and forbidding; and to see them all the time from the river which they were built to dominate; which was their *raison d'être*.

When we arrived in Saumur, after a fortnight on the river, we stowed *Blue Arrow* in the car and took her to Brittany for an Atlantic after-taste. In the sheltered bay of Concarneau we paddled her round lighthouses and rocks; then, by the simple expedient of pushing two paddle blades through the sleeves of a shirt, sailed with the tide up the estuary of the Belon, where the fat oysters wait all year round in their beds for customers to swallow them alive.

We did not meet another canoe either on the Dordogne or on the Loire. Canoeing is a dying sport because the young have taken to Vespas, and the middle-aged associate it in their minds with the horrors of camping. Yet it is the ideal cure for people who, like myself, suffer from holiday neurosis – a common affliction not mentioned in psychiatric textbooks; the people for whom lazing on a beach is hell, and pre-planned pleasure a guarantee of disappointment; quite apart from such minor symptoms as tourist's liver and sightseer's eye.

After the first day on the Dordogne, every joint in my body cried out that it would never again submit to the ignominy of spending eight hours crouched like a Yogi in the bottom of a canoe; the next morning I was itching to get back into it. There is, no doubt, a grain of masochism in canoeing; but that, as every holiday neurotic readily understands, is just the beauty of it. You take your punishment first, then sit down to your *coq au vin*.

OF
GEESE AND MEN

On Aggression *by Konrad Lorenz*★

Konrad Lorenz is mainly known in this country as the author of two delightful books on animal lore (*King Solomon's Ring* and *Man Meets Dog*); but he is also, as Sir Julian Huxley says in his Foreword, "the father of modern ethology". This new science is usually defined as the comparative study of the behaviour of animals in their natural environment; but this description applies to the amateur bird-watcher as well, and conveys no idea of the ethologist's sophisticated techniques, which make the classical naturalist look hopelessly old-fashioned.

The rise of ethology in the after-war years had the exhilarating effect of a March breeze rattling against the tightly shut laboratory windows of American behaviourism, where generations of graduate students had been taught that the principal task of psychologists was to count the number of times a white albino rat confined in a Skinner box will press a lever to obtain a food pellet. The orthodox behaviourist of the mid-century regarded organisms as essentially passive masses of software which could only be studied profitably in the artificial environment of the laboratory; no wonder they did not like this new European heresy. Not until 1962 did the august *Annual Review of Psychology* print for the first time an article on ethology; but in the meantime, Lorenz's research station at Seewiesen in Bavaria, a kind of naturalist's Disneyland, had already become a place of pilgrimage for students from all over the world.

Thus we have every reason to be grateful to Lorenz, even if

★ Reviewed in *The Observer*, 18 September 1966.

we cannot always follow him on his latest, semi-philosophical excursion which, in the German original, has the ambitious title *Über das sogenannte Böse*.

It is not easy to give a brief summary of its contents. To start with, Lorenz states that the action of the predator killing its prey which belongs to a different species is not "genuine" aggression because "the lion in the dramatic moment before he springs is in no way angry". Real aggression is mainly intra-specific – directed against members of the aggressor's own species. It has its positive functions: the jealous defence of the territory occupied by a couple of swans ensures the evenly balanced distribution of the members of a group in a given area, and the mating fights between rivals favour the sexual selection of the strongest and most gallant specimens.

This much is classical Darwinism. Now Lorenz turns to the origin of the binding forces which hold families and groups together. The simplest social organisation is the herd, flock or school of animals which travel in close formation in the same direction, "drawn together as by a magnet". They are "animals totally devoid of aggression", but their association is, Lorenz says, impersonal and anonymous *precisely because they lack aggression*. "A personal bond, an individual friendship is found only in animals with highly developed intra-specific aggression." Moreover, the personal bond of affection between individuals (with or without a sexual factor) is not only always *combined* with aggression, but is phylogenetically *derived* from aggression. To prove this hypothesis, Lorenz relies heavily on his observations of the so-called triumph ceremony of the greylag goose which, he says, prompted him to write the present book.

The ceremony evolved in several stages. Intra-specific aggression has its useful functions; yet it must not degenerate into lethal fighting; so evolution compromised by preserving the animal's aggressive drive, but provided it with inhibitory mechanisms against killing its like. One such mechanism is the *ritualisation* (Huxley) of fighting into a more or less symbolic duel which is instantly terminated by a specific gesture of submission by one of the combatants; another is *redirection*

(Tinbergen) of the attack from its original object to a substitute. Ritualisation and redirection combined gave rise to the triumph ceremony: the goose watches while the gander performs a symbolic attack against an imaginary foe and, after scoring a symbolic victory, returns to her with a triumphant cackle.

In the course of evolution, however, this ritual has acquired a new purpose: from a behaviour pattern motivated by aggression it has changed "into a love ceremony which forms a strong tie between those who participate in it." This means neither more nor less than converting the mutually repelling effect of aggression into its opposite. "Thus it forms a *bond* between individuals. The bond that holds a goose-pair together for life is the triumph ceremony and not the sexual relations between mates."

Here we have an example of the striking results which painstaking ethological observation can produce. But unfortunately Lorenz also regards the behaviour of the goose as a paradigm for the bonds which unite *human* communities; it is surprising how strong the temptation can be, in otherwise ultra-cautious scientists, to take flight on the treacherous wings of analogy, at the risk of sharing the fate of Icarus.

The main criticism directed at the ethologists has always been that their favourite objects of study were birds and fishes with extremely stereotyped rituals which are not necessarily characteristic of animal behaviour in general. Recent research on the behaviour of primate societies has shown that ritualised actions and signals certainly play a part in preventing conflict and maintaining hierarchic order, but provide no support for Lorenz's thesis that the bonds of affection among members of the group originated in sublimated aggression rites, as in the goose. Thus the famous studies of the Harlows on the social life of rhesus monkeys led them to postulate several types of affectional bonds which "can only be understood by conceiving love as a number of love- or affectional-systems, and not as a single emotion". There is no evidence of any of these bonds being derived from ritualised aggression.

Lorenz believes that the evil in man originates in an

evolutionary shortcoming: because he lacks the deadly natural weapons of other carnivores, he also lacks the built-in inhibitory mechanisms "preventing the killing of con-specifics until, all of a sudden, the invention of artificial weapons upset the equilibrium of killing potential and social inhibitions". Selective pressure did the rest to produce *a species of intra-specific killers*.

This is an arguable hypothesis, even if it can reflect only part of the truth; but there is no need to go into it because, as Lorenz himself points out, the holocausts of human history were not caused by murders committed for personal motives by aggressive individuals, but by "militant enthusiasm" *ad majorem gloriam* in the service of a cause. This is the point at which a serious discussion of man's predicament could start; but unfortunately we are once more referred to the goose. Lorenz sees the phylogenetic origin of "man's overpowering urge to espouse a cause" in a phenomenon he discovered thirty years ago: the "imprinting" of newly hatched birds, which attach themselves to the first moving object, and remain forever emotionally fixated on it. Each species of animal has a critical period of "maximum imprintability" – in ducklings, for instance, it is thirteen to sixteen hours after hatching. In human beings, Lorenz says, imprinting with a cause "can take its full effect only once in an individual's life; this critical period is during and shortly after puberty". One cannot help being reminded of Whitehead's warning against "misplaced concreteness". Besides, at least one outstanding younger ethologist, E. H. Hess, is of a different opinion: "In the human being one could thus theoretically place the end of maximum inprintability at about five and a half months of age."

Behaviourism started by rejecting the pathetic fallacy; it ended up by replacing the anthropomorphic view of the rat with a ratomorphic view of man. Now Professor Lorenz seems to offer us an anseromorphic view (*anser* = goose). But it would be churlish to grudge the Sage of Seewiesen this lusty gallop on a hobby horse – the more so as the remedies he has to offer mankind are all wholly laudable; sport to canalise aggression, art and science to sublimate it, the promotion of international friendship, and humour as an antidote to militant enthusiasm. On this programme we would all agree; and if you land on the side of the angels, it does not much matter how you got there.

OF APES AND MEN

The Naked Ape – A Zoologist's study of the Human Animal, *by Desmond Morris*★

> There are one hundred and ninety-three living species of monkeys and apes. One hundred and ninety-two of them are covered in hair. The exception is a naked ape, self-named *Homo sapiens*. . . . I am a zoologist and the naked ape is an animal. He is therefore fair game for my pen. . . .

These provocative sentences are from the opening of Dr Morris's "zoological portrait" of man. It is based on three sources: the fossil record concerning our ancestry; the ethologist's studies of primate behaviour; and the observations of social science concerning "the major contemporary cultures of the naked ape itself". This is a more ambitious enterprise than some earlier attempts at a diagnosis of man's condition based on the behaviour of animals – Pavlov's dogs, the behaviourist's rats, or Lorenz's geese. These have yielded analogies which were at best of limited value, but often misleading and fraught with disastrous philosophical conclusions. More recently, however, there has been a spate of extremely valuable field studies on the behaviour of primate societies which are evidently more relevant to us than rats or geese. Dr Morris utilises this new mass of data with much ingenuity to shed new light on our own odd ways of "feeding, sleeping, fighting, mating and rearing the young".

He regards as the decisive episode in man's evolution the changeover from a tree-dwelling, fruit-munching, lackadaisical creature to a carnivorous predator of the open plains, hunting in packs. Man's dual personality, and every uniquely

★ Reviewed in *The Observer*, 15 October 1967.

human characteristic, is said to originate in this event: upright posture, growth of the brain, weapons, tools, family bonds, tribal cohesion, the evolution of language. This chapter on "Origins" is perhaps the most stimulating in the book.

The next is concerned with sex, and here the zoological portrait, enriched by Freudian hues, has some remarkable surprises to offer to the layman and not-so-layman. Our fleshy earlobes, we are told, absent in all other primates and described by anatomists as "useless, fatty excrescences", are in fact erogenous zones which, in sexual excitement, become engorged with blood, swollen and hypersensitive; moreover, "there are cases on record of both males and females actually reaching orgasm as a result of earlobe-stimulation". We also have to revise our ideas about the functions of the female breast. It is "predominantly a sexual signalling device rather than an expanded milk-machine". The females of other primate species are flat-chested compared to ours, with pendulous breasts and longer nipples, which make them into more efficient milk-machines. The protruding, hemispherical breast of the naked ape, on the other hand, makes life more difficult, because it tends to block the baby's nostrils while it is suckling and cause it to struggle for air – often interpreted by anxious mothers as a refusal to feed. Another fascinating bit of information is that 80 per cent of all mothers (at least in the USA where these studies were made) cradle their babies in their left arm against the left side of their bodies – and that this applies to right-handed and left-handed women alike. The explanation offered is that the embryo becomes "imprinted" in the womb by the sound of the mother's heartbeat, which then acquires a calming effect on the infant.

Particularly rewarding are the minute descriptions of the changes in facial expression and bodily posture as unconscious threat or appeasement signals in man and ape:

> We cannot intimidate our opponents by erecting our body hair. We still do it in moments of great shock, but as a signal it is of little use. In other respects we can do much better. Our very nakedness, which prevents us from bristling effectively, gives us the chance to

send powerful flushing and paling signals. We can go "white with rage", "red with anger", or "pale with fear". It is the white colour we have to watch for here: this spells activity. If it is combined with other actions that signal attack, then it is a vital danger signal. If it is combined with other actions that signal fear, then it is a panic signal. It is caused by the activation of the sympathetic nervous system, the "go" system, and it is not to be treated lightly. The reddening, on the other hand, is less worrying: it is caused by the frantic counter-balancing attempts of the parasympathetic system, and indicates that the "go" system is already being undermined. The angry, red-faced opponent who faces you is far less likely to attack than the white-faced, tight-lipped one.

Here the ethologist's training in the observation and analysis of animal behaviour is used to best effect, and is indeed capable of shedding new light on the evolutionary origins of some of our strange antics and social rites. That it is not a very flattering light should not be held against him.

In a word, the "zoological portrait" reveals a number of features in our complexions – amusing, disgusting or just odd – which otherwise would pass unnoticed; and when you look into the mirror after reading the book, you won't look quite the same. The question is whether this revised image is closer to the essence of the human condition – or whether it is a caricature, drawn by exaggerating precisely those simian features which the naive idealist's portrait ignores, and ignoring those which he legitimately values as specifically and exclusively human.

The trouble with the zoological portrait is not that it offends, but that it oversimplifies and thereby distorts. To be fair, the author is partly aware of this. "Because of the size of the task," he writes in his introduction, "it will be necessary to over-simplify in some manner. The way I shall do this is largely to ignore the detailed ramifications of technology and verbalisation, and concentrate instead on those aspects of our lives that have obvious counterparts in other species." But to leave out of account "technology and verbalisation" – that is to say, language, science and art, the essential trademarks of our species – leads inevitably not only to a *simplified* but to a *distorted* picture, because these activities permeate and transform even those aspects of behaviour which we share with other species, such as "feeding, fighting, mating and care of the young".

Take the most crucial of these: fighting. Dr Morris recognises only three causes of human aggressiveness: asserting one's place in the social hierarchy; defence of the family territory; defence of the territory of the group (pp. 148, 182). It follows that all human wars are waged for "territorial defence" or "territorial expansion" (p. 176) – which, historically, is simply untrue. Religious wars, dynastic wars, ideological wars, play a dominant part in human history, but have no place in the zoologist's account, because religions, dynasties and ideologies all hinge on the "ramifications of verbalisation" which he decided to ignore. Language is a specifically human blessing and curse, which facilitates understanding *within* social groups, but accentuates the differences in traditions and beliefs *between* groups. By regarding the defence of territory as the only source of conflict, the zoological approach fails to recognise the essential predicament of man – his urge to kill or get killed for a flag, a credo, a slogan, *ad majorem gloriam*.

To what extremes the zoological approach may lead is illustrated by the following passage:

> The insides of houses or flats can be decorated and filled with ornaments, bric-à-brac and personal belongings in profusion. This is usually explained as being done to make the place "look nice". In fact, it is the exact equivalent to another territorial species depositing its personal scent on a landmark near its den. When you put a name on a door, or hang a painting on a wall, you are, in dog or wolf terms, for example, simply cocking your leg on them and leaving your personal mark there. Obsessive "collecting" of specialised categories of objects occurs in certain individuals who, for some reason, experience an abnormally strong need to define their home territories in this way (pp. 183–4).

Perhaps Sotheby's will adopt the simplified method of conducting an auction indicated in this passage.

In his introduction, Dr Morris assures us that it is not his intention "to degrade our species by discussing it in crude animal terms". Nobody acquainted with Dr Morris' previous books can doubt the sincerity of this statement; but one may wonder whether it is not self-contradictory. In spite of this basic flaw, *The Naked Ape* can be strongly recommended to readers able to savour its wealth of information without swallowing all of its conclusions.

THE PATIENT'S DILEMMA*

This book will cause a healthy scandal. It is a frontal attack on the narrow-minded orthodoxy of the medical establishment and a spirited defence of the unorthodox methods practised on its fringes. Among these the author includes nature cures and herbalism; homoeopathy, osteopathy and chiropractics; acupuncture; psychotherapy and hypnosis; faith healing and radiesthesia.

Any writer who ventures into these troubled waters must keep on a precarious course between the Scylla of rigid dogmatism and the Charybdis of gullibility; Brian Inglis seems at times to sail perilously close to the second. Thus he argues in defence of acupuncture that it has been "the standard form of medical treatment in China for five thousand years". But a belief can persist for five thousand years and nevertheless be a delusion;† Mr Inglis is too generous in bestowing the benefit of doubt even in cases where negative certainty leaves no room for doubt – e.g. the de la Warr "box" or the late Wilhelm Reich's Orgonomy.

These are minor faults, but unfortunately they will provide welcome ammunition for the defenders of the Citadel, and detract from the power of the author's main argument – which is of vital importance to us all. I cannot attempt to summarise it, merely to mention a few salient points.

Medicine became an exact science only about a century ago,

* *Fringe Medicine,* by Brian Inglis, reviewed in *The Observer,* 1 March 1964.

† Postscript, 1981: since this was written, acupuncture has become a respectable form of therapy throughout the Western world, and I was obviously wrong in dismissing it.

when Pasteur established the germ theory of disease against the bitter opposition of the profession. But the high hopes which accompanied its spectacular successes in combating infectious diseases yielded to a more sober outlook when it became evident that the methods which had led to the disappearance of some of the old scourges of humanity were less effective when applied to others. Ulcers, asthma, coronary thrombosis, disorders of the circulatory and digestive systems, instead of going out, seemed actually on the increase – not to mention psychiatric disorders. Other factors contributed to the sobering process. Some of the new wonder drugs turned out to have side effects of varying severity. Others caused the emergence of new, drug-resisting strains of micro-organisms. Voices from both inside and outside the profession began to call attention to the risk that the all-out war on micro-organisms may upset the overall balance of nature by a process analogous to the indiscriminate use of insecticides. But in this case the ecological upheaval was taking place inside the human organism: 80 per cent of the micro-fauna which inhabits our bowels is still unknown; and drastic interference with this fauna may undermine the body's natural resistance.

By the 1950s the work of Selye and others had shown that the chief culprit in some diseases was not the foreign invader, but the organisms' inability to cope with him – an impairment due to a variety of causes, but surprisingly often to mental stress. Experiment showed that even rats put under emotional strain died of small doses of poison which, under normal conditions, they would have thrown off; "the implication being that human illnesses usually attributed to germs or poisons ought properly to be blamed on the stress which allows or encourages the germs to proliferate".

Equally surprising was the discovery of a phenomenon of the opposite kind – the relief or cure of organic symptoms by the purely psychological action of so-called placebos. These are inactive dummy pills which physicians have been administering from time immemorial to lift the patient's morale (placebo = "I will please"); but recently they have been used as experimental controls to determine whether the beneficial effect of a new drug is due to its intrinsic merits or to suggestion and auto-suggestion.

Three years ago I reported in these columns on experimental work in the United States which suggested that at least one-third of the total hospital population are "placebo reactors' who will react to dummy pills as if they were what they believed them to be. In 1962 the *British Medical Journal* reported on a test carried out with patients suffering from angina pectoris. Different groups of patients were given either one or two potent drugs or a tranquilliser or a placebo; and "more patients reacted favourably to the placebo than to any of the drugs".

These examples could be multiplied; the upshot is, in Mr Inglis's words, "not that these drugs have no merit, but that placebo effect is a much more powerful and widespread component of treatment than is realised". In other words, suggestion and auto-suggestion involving both physician and patient play an incomparably greater part in every form of therapy than orthodox medicine would admit.

There is nothing very new in this. Hypnosis can make a person drunk on water, cause blisters to rise as a reaction to imaginary burns, cure warts, suppress the pain in dental surgery and even in major operations. Yet the hypnotic state is merely an extreme form of that suggestibility of the unconscious mind to which we all are normally prone; and the effects of which do not stop at some imaginary frontier between "psyche" and "soma" or between "functional" and "organic" disorders.

That frontier is crumbling, and the psychosomatic approach has come to stay. That stomach ulcers can be caused by mental stress has become a commonplace; the suggestion that even malignant growths may be of psychogenic origin still seems fantastic. Yet nearly ten years ago the eminent surgeon, Sir William Heneage Ogilvie at Guy's asked the startling question: "We all have cancer at forty-eight. What is the force which keeps it in check in the great majority of us?" – and went on to suggest that it was intimately related to psychological factors: "The happy man never gets cancer."

This new outlook unavoidably implies a more open-minded attitude to "fringe medicine". Mr Inglis defines it as forms of therapy which, though widely varied, all rely on the *vis medicatrix naturae,* on man's natural recuperative powers, in preference to drugs or surgery – powers which "all fringe practitioners agree can be speeded up sometimes to an astonishing degree by suitable stimuli". And the simplest and oldest of such stimuli is suggestion *cum* auto-suggestion. It enters into such half-empirical, half folklore-begotten practices as herbalism; it is probably the most (and sometimes the only) effective factor in the various techniques of manipulation and the laying on of hands; and it provides the rationale for Mr Inglis's over-indulgent attitude towards the mumbo-jumbo of the "pendulum" or the de la Warr "box". If the mumbo-jumbo works, he argues, then why not? – provided, of course, that there is no dangerous condition present requiring some specific intervention. And if it works, it does so because the practitioner himself believes in his method, and his faith is transferred to the patient. So powerful are the unconscious forces involved in this kind of transference, that drug-testing experiments are now carried out according to the "double-blind method", where doctors and nurses themselves are not allowed to know whether they are handing out a drug or a dummy pill – to eliminate the faith-healing factor.

Witch doctors have always known the power of suggestion: this ancient knowledge, temporarily lost during the age of mechanistic science, has acquired a new urgency in the light of the modern psychosomatic approach.

The implications are obvious in so far as the medical profession is concerned. But they are less obvious from the patient's point of view. If we are all placebo reactors in one way or another, does not this knowledge destroy that very faith which is half the therapy?

The answer to the apparent dilemma is that all effective suggestion operates on unconscious levels. What the patient has to learn is to be guided in the choice of his physician not by the nature of his complaint, but by the intuitive trust or distrust which the physician's personality inspires in him. Once the *rapport* is established, even if scepticism or doubt survives on the surface of the mind, the benevolent magic will set to work on levels beyond their reach. And whatever the method of the therapy, the essence of that magic is always the silent injunction: "Patient, cure thyself".

RETURN TRIP TO NIRVANA*

A few weeks ago I received a letter dated from Divinity Avenue, Cambridge, Massachusetts. That symbolic address refers to the Center for Research in Personality of Harvard University. The writer was a friend, an American psychiatrist working in that Department.†

Dear K . . . ,

Things are happening here which I think will interest you. The big, new, hot issue these days in many American circles is DRUGS. Have you been tuned in on the noise?

I stumbled on the scene in the most holy manner. Spent last summer in Mexico. Anthropologist friend arrived one weekend with a bag of mushrooms bought from a witch. Magic mushrooms. I had never heard of them, but being a good host joined the crowd who ate them. Wow! Learned more in six hours than in past sixteen years. Visual transformations. Gone the perceptual machinery which clutters up our view of reality. Intuitive transformations. Gone the mental machinery which slices the world up into abstractions and concepts. Emotional transformations. Gone the emotional machinery that causes us to load life with our own ambitions and petty desires.

Came back to U.S.A. and have spent last six months pursuing these matters. Working with Aldous Huxley, Alan Watts [noted authority on Zen Buddhism], Allen Ginsberg the poet. We believe that the synthetics of the cactus peyote (mescalin) and the mushrooms (psilocybin) offer possibilities for expanding consciousness, changing perceptions, removing abstractions.

* First published in the *Sunday Telegraph,* 12 March 1961.

† The friend in question was Dr Timothy Leary who, a few years later, was to attain worldwide notoriety as the leader of the LSD cult.

> For the person who is prepared, they provide a soul-wrenching mystical experience. Remember your enlightenments in the Franco prison? Very similar to what we are producing. We have had cases of housewives who have never heard of Zen, experiencing *satori* and describing it. . . .
>
> We are offering the experience to distinguished creative people. Artists, poets, writers, scholars. We've learned a tremendous amount by listening to them. . . .
>
> We are also trying to build this experience in a holy and serious way into university curricula. . . . If you are interested I'll send some mushrooms over to you. . . . I'd like to hear about your reaction. . . .

Shortly afterwards, I went to the States, to participate in a symposium at the University of California Medical Center in San Francisco. One of the main subjects of the symposium was "The Influence of Drugs on the Individual". But this was not much of a coincidence, as, at the present moment, a surprising number of Americans, from Brass to Beat, seem to have, for different reasons, drugs on the brain: the Brass because they are worried about brain-washing and space-flight training; the Beat because drugs provide a rocket-powered escape from reality; the Organisation Men because tranquillisers are more effective than the homely aspirins and fruit salts of yore; the medical profession because some of the new drugs promise a revolution, by "chemical surgery", in the treatment of mental disease; and the spiritually frustrated on all levels of society because drugs promise a kind of do-it-yourself approach to salvation. Thus there is a confluence of motives, and an inflation in academic drug-research projects, financed on a lavish scale by government agencies, universities and foundations.

On the way from San Francisco to my friend at Harvard, I stayed for a few days at the University of Michigan at Ann Arbor. I had been invited there for quite different reasons, but on the first morning of my stay the subject of the magic mushroom cropped up. The psychiatrist in charge of the mushroom was an Englishman of the quiet, gentle, un-American kind. Based on his own experiences – he had taken it on several occasions – and on experiments with ten test subjects, he ventured the tentative opinion that, compared to the fashionable wonder drugs mescalin and lysergic acid, the effect of the mushroom was relatively harmless and entirely on the pleasant, euphoric side.

It is well known that the mental attitude, the mood in which one enters the gates of mushroomland, plays a decisive part in determining the nature of the experience. Since Dr P. was such a pleasant person and the atmosphere of his clinic appealed to me, I volunteered as a guinea pig – though I felt a little guilty towards my enthusiastic friend in Harvard. We fixed the date of the experiment, and I was told not to make any appointments on that day until the evening, as I would remain under the influence of the drug for about six hours.

Just before awakening on the morning of the appointed day, I had a dream which is relevant to what follows. I saw standing before me a large earthenware jar; in it squatted a man, with only his head visible over the rim of the jar; the colour of his face was a yellowish brown, he seemed in great pain, but had a resigned look; a dispassionate voice explained to me that this was St Michael undergoing martyrdom; and that presently he was to be lifted out and put into another jar to be boiled alive in oil. I woke up with a faint nausea, and at once connected the dream with an experience on the previous day. In one of the laboratories for experimental psychology, I had seen a monkey's head – its body was hidden behind an enclosure so that the head alone was visible. An electric plug had been inserted into the creature's skull, and a wire led from it to the ceiling. The plugged head was perfectly, unnaturally still (the body was imobilised in a restraining jacket); only the eyes, old as Methuselah's, turned in their sockets to follow the visitors' movements, quietly, resignedly.

I hasten to reassure the reader that, as far as human knowledge goes, the monkeys in these experiments do not suffer pain. The plug is connected to electrodes which are inserted into the brain under anaesthesia, and once placed, cause neither pain nor discomfort: the purpose of the experiment does not concern us here. I had read about it before; nevertheless, the sight of that sad little head, with the electric plug sticking out of its fur, filled me with an unreasoning horror; hence the dream about St Michael's martyrdom. Thus I faced the mushrooms in a depressed state of "floating anxiety", as the psychiatrists say.

The mushroom comes synthesised, in the shape of little pink pills; they look harmless and taste bitter. I swallowed nine of them (18 milligrams of psilocybin), which is a fair-sized dose for a person of my weight. They were supposed to start acting after thirty minutes, and reach their maximum effect after about an hour.

However, for nearly an hour nothing at all happened. I was chatting with Dr P. and one of his assistants, first in his office, then in a room which had a comfortable couch in it and a tape recorder; after a while I was left alone in the room, but Dr P. looked in from time to time. I lay down on the couch, and soon began to experience the kind of phenomena which have been repeatedly described by people who experimented with mescalin. When I closed my eyes I saw luminous, moving patterns of great beauty, which was highly enjoyable; then the patterns changed into planaria – a kind of flatworm which I had watched under the microscope the previous day in another laboratory; but the worms had a tendency to change into dragons, which was less enjoyable, so I walked out of the show simply by opening my eyes. Then I tried again, this time directing the beam of the table lamp, which had a strong bulb, straight at my closed eyelids, and the effect was quite spectacular – rather like the explosive paintings of schizophrenics, or Walt Disney's *Fantasia*. A flaming eddy, the funnel of a tornado, appeared over my head, drawing me upward; with a little auto-suggestion and self-dramatisation I could have called it a vision of myself as the prophet Elijah being taken to heaven by a whirlwind. But I felt that this was buying one's visions on the cheap ("Carter's little mushrooms are the best, mystic experience guaranteed or money refunded"); so I again walked out of the show by forcing my eyes to open. It was as simple as that, and I congratulated myself on my sober self-control, a rational mind not to be fooled by little pills.

By now, however, even through open eyes, the room looked different. The colours had become not only more luminous and brilliant, but different in quality from any colour previously seen; they were located outside the normally visible spectrum, and to refer to them one would have to invent new words – so I shall say that the walls were breen, the curtains were darsh, and the sky outside emerdine. Also, one of the walls had acquired a concave bend like the inside of a barrel, the plaster statue of the Venus of Milo had acquired a grin, and the straight dado-line was now curved, which struck me as an exceedingly clever joke. But all this was quite unlike the wobbling world of drunkenness, for the transformed room was plunged into an underwater silence, where the faint hum of the tape recorder became obtrusively loud, and the almost imperceptible undulations of the curtains became the Ballet of the Flowing Folds (the undulations were caused by warm air ascending from the central-heating body). A narrow strip of the revolving spool of the tape recorder caught the gleam of the lamp every few seconds; this faint, intermittent spark, unnoticed before, observed out of the corner of the eye on the visual periphery became the revolving beam of a miniature lighthouse. This lowering of the sensory threshold and simultaneous heightening of the intensity and emotional significance of perceptions is one of the basic phenomena of the mushroom universe. The intermittent light signal from the slowly revolving spool became important, meaningful and mysterious; it carried some secret message. Afterwards I remembered, with sympathetic understanding, the fantasies of paranoiacs about hidden electric machines planted by their enemies to produce evil Rays and Influences.

The signalling tape recorder was the first symptom of a chemically induced state of insanity. The full effect came on with insidious smoothness and suddenness. Dr P. came into the room, and a minute or two later I saw the light – and realised what a fool I had been to let myself be trapped by his cunning machinations. For during that minute or two he had undergone an unbelievable transformation.

It started with the colour of his face, which had become a sickly yellowish brown – the colour of the monkey with the electric plug. He stood in a corner of the room with his back to the green wall, and as I stared at him his face split into two, like a cell dividing. It oscillated for a while, then reunited into a single face, and by this time the transformation was complete. A small scar on the doctor's neck, which I had not noticed before, was gaping wide, trying to ingest the flesh of the chin; one ear had shrunk, the other had grown by several inches, and the face became a smirking, evil phantasm. Then it changed again, into a different kind of Hogarthian vision, and these transformations went on for what I took to be several minutes.

All this time the doctor's body remained unchanged, the hallucinations were confined to the space from the neck upward; and they were strongly two-dimensional, like faces cut out of cardboard. The phenomenon was always strongest in that corner of the room where it had first occurred, and faded into less offensive distorting-mirror effects when we moved elsewhere, although the lighting of the room was uniform. The same happened when other members of the staff joined us later. One of them, the jovial Dr F., was transformed into a vision so terrifying – a Mongol with a broken neck hanging from an invisible gallows – that I thought I was going to be sick; yet I could not stop myself staring at him. We stood face to face in the "evil corner", and with my pupils dilated by the drug I must have looked unpleasant, for he asked in an embarrassed voice: "Why are you staring at me so?" In the end I said: "For God's sake let's snap out of it", and we moved into another part of the room, where the effect became much weaker.

As the last remark indicates, I was still in control of my outward behaviour, and this remained true throughout the whole three or four hours of the experience. But at the same time I had completely lost control over my perception of the world. I made repeated efforts "to walk out of the show" as I had been able to do during the first stages on the couch, but I was powerless against the delusions. I kept repeating to myself: "But these are nice, friendly people, they are your friends", and so on. It had no effect whatsoever on the spontaneous and inexorable visual transformations. At one stage, these spread from the faces of others to my own right hand which shrivelled into a cripple's, and to the metal bars of the table lamp, which were transformed into the claws of a predatory bird. Then I asked for a mirror to be brought in, expecting to see a picture of Dorian Gray. Strangely enough, there was no change in my own face.

After an hour or two (one's inner clock goes completely haywire under the drug), the effect began to wear off. They gave me a sedative, and after a suitable interval took me back to the hotel, where I had a meal with one of the doctors in the public dining-room. The world was normal again, except for a minute or two when the doctor's head, for the last time, went through two or three rapid mutations across the dining-table. These, however, were no longer frightening, but rather like a brilliant actor's impersonations of various character types in quick succession – all of which, I felt with deep conviction, were different aspects of the doctor's personality. This conviction of possessing the gift of second sight, of being able not only to "read" but to *see* a person's hidden character as if it were projected on a screen, is another typical symptom in certain forms of schizophrenia. I had faint recurrent whiffs of it for quite a while. The faces of friends or of strangers in the train would for a moment become unreal, like projections of a magic lantern, and at the same time revealing their innermost secret – but I never managed to express or define just what had been revealed. This was the only after-effect of the experience that I am aware of. It lasted for about a week.

When the mind is split into separate layers, some of which function more or less normally, while others are deranged, one exists in a world of paradoxa. At certain moments I thought that I had been lured into a trap, that the malign faces surrounding me were somehow connected with the Gestapo or the GPU, and it was a comfort to know that the room was on the first floor so that if it came to the worst I could bolt through the window. I always managed to snap out of it after a moment or two, persuading myself that all this was a delusion; but the *visual* delusions persisted independently of my better knowledge, and against these I was helpless. The horror of the experience lies not so much in the apparitions themselves, but in the moments of panicky suspicion that the condition might become irreversible.

And that suspicion is not entirely unfounded. One member of a medical research team, whom I met, inadvertently took an overdose of the pills with the result that he suffered from intermittent delusions of persecution for a period of two months. I know of two other people who experimented under insufficient medical supervision and had to be hospitalised for varying periods. These, however, are exceptions. I have mentioned before that all of Dr P.'s previous subjects had positive, euphoric experiences; I "broke the series", as he ruefully remarked over post-mortem drinks on the next day. The same is true of the majority of the Harvard team's subjects. The reasons why I had been so unlucky are related to the monkey and the subsequent dream; they were the wrong kind of preparation. If one adds to this the burden of past experiences as a political prisoner, of past preoccupations with brainwashing, torture and the extraction of confessions, it will seem evident that I was a rather unfortunate choice for a guinea pig – except perhaps to demonstrate what mushroomland *can* do to the wrong kind of guinea pig. The phantom faces were equally obvious projections of a deep-seated resentment against being "trapped" in a situation which carried symbolic echoes of the relation between prisoner and inquisitor, monkey and experimenter, persecutor and victim. Poor Dr P. and his nice colleagues had to endure what they would call a "negative transference", and serve as projection screens for the lantern slides of the past, stored in the mental underground. I suspect that a sizeable minority of people who try for a chemical lift to Heaven will find themselves landed in the other place. This may be due to character or accident – the wrong time or setting for the experiment bringing the wrong type of lantern slides out of storage; and no experimental psychiatrist, however skilled, can exercise complete control over all the variables in the situation, nor guarantee the result.

I do not want to exaggerate the small risks involved in properly supervised experiments for legitimate research purposes; and I also believe that every clinical psychiatrist could derive immense benefits from a few experiments in chemically induced temporary psychosis, enabling him to see life through his patients' eyes. But I disagree with the enthusiasts' belief that mescalin or psilocybin, even when taken under the most favourable conditions, will provide artists, writers or aspiring mystics with new insights, or revelations, of a transcendental nature.

I profoundly admire Aldous Huxley, both for his philosophy and uncompromising sincerity. But I disagree with his advocacy of "the chemical opening of doors into the Other World", and with his belief that drugs can procure "what Catholic theologians call a gratuitous grace".* Chemically induced hallucinations, delusions and raptures may be frightening or wonderfully gratifying; in either case they are in the nature of confidence tricks played on one's own nervous system.

I have before me a file, compiled by the Harvard research team, containing the productions of various writers and scholars while under the influence of one of the drugs, or shortly afterwards. The first, by a well-known novelist, starts:

> Mainly I felt like a floating Khan on a magic carpet with my interesting lieutenants and gods . . . some ancient feeling about old geheuls in the grass, and temples, exactly also like the sensations I got drunk on pulgue floating in the Xochimilco gardens. . . .

The second, by an aspiring writer, starts:

> Dear . . . Experiences with Psilocybin in me have been very tastey & eatable & when the effects come on, wham, I am in the middle of this ever grower larger and larger cosmos of vibrating hums of wishes & desires & mistroy plays as in Shaskerpiere, about to enter the stage & speack in the play. Somehow these pills make the soul more real. . . . [The spelling is a semi-conscious mannerism often induced by the drug.]

The third is the beginning of a poem, also by a well-known writer, called *Lysergic Acid (God seen thru Imagination):*

> It is a multiple million eyed monster/it is in all its elephants and selves/it hummeth in the electric typewriter/it is electricity connected to itself, if it hath wires/it is a vast Spiderweb/and I am on the last millionth infinite tentacle of the spiderweb. . . .

* Aldous Huxley, *The Doors of Perception,* London, 1954.

Some of the reports in the file, written after the experience, are in a more sober vein, but not a single item contains anything of artistic merit or of theoretical value; and the drug-induced productions were all far beneath the writers' normal standards (Huxley's report was not in the file). While working on the material I was reminded of a story George Orwell once told me (I do not recall whether he published it): a friend of his, while living in the Far East, smoked several pipes of opium every night, and every night a single phrase rang in his ear, which contained the whole secret of the universe; but in his euphoria he could not be bothered to write it down and by the morning it was gone. One night he managed to jot down the magic phrase after all, and in the morning he read: "The banana is big, but its skin is even bigger."

I had a similar revelation when I took the mushroom the second time, under more happy and relaxed conditions. This was in the apartment of my Harvard friend from whose letter I have quoted, and there were six of us in a convivial atmosphere, after dinner and wine. All of us took various amounts of the pill, and this time I took a little more (either 22 or 24 m/m, for I lost count). Again there were delusions: the room expanded and contracted in the most extraordinary manner, like an accordion played slowly; but the faces around me changed only slightly and in a pleasant manner, becoming more beautiful. Then came the Moment of Truth: a piece of chamber music played on a tape recorder. I had never heard music played like that before; I suddenly *understood* the very essence of music, the secret of its magic; the harmony of the spheres was revealed to me. . . . Unfortunately, I was unable to tell the next day whether it had been a symphony or a quintet or a trio, and whether by Mendelssohn or Bach. I may just as well have listened to Liberace. It had nothing to do with genuine appreciation of music; my soul was steeped in cosmic schmalz. I sobered up, though, when, later in the evening, a fellow mushroom-eater – an American writer whom I otherwise rather liked – began to declaim about Cosmic Awareness, Expanding Consciousness, Zen Enlightenment, and so forth. This struck me as downright obscene, more so than four-letter words. This pressure-cooker mysticism seemed the ultimate profanation. But my exaggerated reaction was no doubt also mushroom-conditioned, so I went to bed.

In *Heaven and Hell*, defending the mescalin ecstasy against the reproach of artificiality, Huxley, the most highly respected exponent of the cult, argues that "in one way or another, all our experiences are chemically conditioned"; and that the great mystics of the past also "worked systematically to modify their body chemistry . . . starving themselves into low blood sugar and a vitamin deficiency. They sang interminable psalms, thus increasing the amount of carbon dioxide in the lungs and the bloodstream, or, if they were orientals, they did breathing exercises to accomplish the same purpose." There is, of course, a certain amount of truth in this on a purely physiological level, but the conclusions which Huxley draws, and the advice he tenders to modern man in search of a soul, are all the more distressing: "Knowing as he does . . . what are the chemical conditions of transcendental experience, the aspiring mystic should turn for technical help to the specialists in pharmacology, in bio-chemistry, in physiology and neurology. . . ."

I would like to answer this with a parable. In the beloved Austrian mountains of my schooldays, it took us about five to six hours to climb a 7000-foot peak. Today, many of them can be reached in a few minutes by cable-car, or ski-lift, or even by motorcar. Yet you still see thousands of schoolboys, middle-aged couples and elderly men puffing and panting up the steep path, groaning under the load of their knapsacks. When they arrive at the alpine refuge near the summit, streaming with sweat, they shout for their traditional reward – a glass of shnapps and a plate of hot pea soup. And then they look at the view – and then there is only a man and a mountain and a sky.

My point is not the virtue of sweat and toil. My point is that, although the view is the same, their vision is different from those who arrive by motorcar.

THE POVERTY OF PSYCHOLOGY*

1 *Pavlov in retreat*

An age is drawing to its close in the history of psychology: the age of the dehumanisation of man. Words like "purpose", "volition", "introspection", "consciousness", "insight", which used to be banned as obscene from the vocabulary of the so-called "Behavioural Sciences", are triumphantly reasserting themselves – not as abstract philosophical concepts, but as indispensable descriptive tools, without which even a rat's actions in an experimental maze do not make sense. A minority of diehards still insist on treating man as a conditioned-reflex automaton, and knowledge as the accretion of lucky random guesses. But they are the rearguard, heroically defending a lost cause – the Swiss Guard dying on the staircase of the Tuileries.

This state of affairs was vividly illustrated by a recent symposium on Control of the Mind, organised by the University of California Medical Center in San Francisco. The participants, as usual on such occasions, were selected on the principle of Noah's Ark, i.e. that each species should be represented: they included neurophysiologists (Penfield and Hebb); psychopharmacologists (Kety, J. G. Miller and Cole); psychologists (Mace and A. Simon); a cytologist (Hydén) and so forth; but also, for good measure, one theologian (Father D'Arcy), and two Creative Writers (Aldous Huxley and myself. In American university parlance every Writer must be Creative; which may be the reason why so many take to the bottle.) But for my inclusion in the list, I would have called it a

*Abridged version of a series of three articles, originally published in *The Observer,* April–May 1961, under the title "A New Look at the Mind".

distinguished gathering, and well suited for establishing Inter-Communicational Inter-Relationships (I still seem to suffer from over-exposure to academic verbal fallout).

The nicely ambiguous title was originally meant in the passive sense: "control of the mind" not *over* this or that, but *by* this or that – more specifically, by drugs, brain-washing, mass propaganda, and the like. Yet by the end of the symposium, the one consistent lesson that emerged was the astonishing control of the mind *over* the physical impact of drugs, brain-washings, and other forms of coercion.

The most outspoken statements on this basic issue came from Father D'Arcy, Penfield and Cole. That a Jesuit theologian should extol the powers of mind over matter was, of course, to be expected. One of the participants had half-seriously mentioned the possibility of Orwellian thought-control by drugs in the tap water; D'Arcy denied that such a possibility existed. "There is a last, mysterious layer in the self that can never really be touched," he amiably explained to the neurologists, "an ultimate self which enables priests to withstand torture, madmen to retain a vestige of sanity, and brave soldiers to resist brain-washing."

A surprising number of speakers arrived, in different terms and on different levels, at much the same conclusions; among them Wilder Penfield, one of the most distinguished neurologists alive. A few years ago, Penfield had revolutionised the study of memory when he made his patients re-live scenes from their distant past by faint electric stimulation of the temporal lobes of their brains (exposed during a surgical operation). Thus Professor Penfield is certainly not the kind of philosophical idealist who would airily belittle the importance of brain mechanisms in the life of the mind. "There is no evidence," he stressed at the beginning of his paper, "of any mental activity without some action of the brain." Yet in his conclusions, and in subsequent panel discussions, he stated with equal emphasis his conviction that "brain" and "mind" are separate entities; and that, when it comes to the problem "how the mind is attached to the body", we are no wiser today than Aristotle was when he asked that question 2300 years ago.

He had some scathing things to say about those contemporary Oxford philosophers who refuse to acknowledge the existence of a mind–body problem. He singled out Gilbert Ryle and A. J. Ayer, who some years ago had participated with Penfield in a famous BBC Third Programme series on "The Physical Basis of Mind".★ Paradoxically, those participants in the series whose lifework was concerned with the anatomy, physiology, pathology and surgery of the brain, and whom one would have expected to take a materialist view, all took the opposite attitude; whereas the logicians, whom one would have expected to show some respect for the mind, showed none at all, and seemed hypnotised by neural pathways and electrical circuitry. Professor Ryle, one of the foremost exponents of the linguistic philosophy of Oxford, compared belief in mind with the belief of illiterate peasants who, on seeing the first railway locomotive, thought there was a horse hidden inside it. Professor Ayer had been equally scornful:

> The picture we are given [by the neurologists] is that of messages travelling through the brain, reaching a mysterious entity called the mind, receiving orders from it, and then travelling on. But since the mind has no position in space – it is by definition not the sort of thing that can have position in space – it does not literally make sense to talk of physical signals reaching it.

To this Penfield replied in San Francisco: "The problem should be stated in another way. . . . Electrical currents pass through certain circuits of the brain, and there is simultaneous change and movement in the conscious shapes that constitute the mind of man. . . . To declare that these two things are one does not make them so. But it does block the progress of research." He went on to quote the late Sir Charles Sherrington: "That our being should consist of *two* fundamental elements offers, I suppose, no greater inherent improbability than that it should rest on one only. . . . We have to regard the relation of mind to brain as still not merely unsolved, but still devoid of a basis of its very beginning."

★ *The Physical Basis of Mind*, ed. Peter Laslett (London, 1950).

This was an exercise in true humility; and so was Penfield's admission that when the surgeon manipulates the brain of his patient, he has no idea of the philosophical implications of what he is doing:

> When the neurosurgeon applies an electrode to the motor area of the patient's cerebral cortex causing the opposite hand to move, and when he asks the patient why he moved the hand, the response is: "*I* didn't do it. *You* made me do it." Without adopting psychiatric terms like the ego, it may be said that the patient thinks of himself as having an existence separate from his body.
>
> Once when I warned such a patient of my intention to stimulate the motor areas of the cortex, and challenged him to keep his hand from moving when the electrode should be applied, he seized it with the other hand and struggled to hold it still. Thus, one hand, under the control of the right hemisphere driven by an electrode, and the other hand, which he controlled through the left hemisphere, were caused to struggle against each other. Behind the "brain action" of one hemisphere was the patient's mind. Behind the action of the other hemisphere was the electrode directed by the mind of the surgeon. At least that was what the patient thought instinctively. You will say that proves nothing, and I must agree that it proves only the direction of our current thinking. . . .

The end of this memorable paper showed that the neurologists' position was closer to that of our Oxford Jesuit's than to the Oxford logicians':

> There are, as you see, many demonstrable mechanisms [in the brain]. They work for the purposes of the mind automatically when called upon. But what agency is it that calls upon these mechanisms, choosing one rather than another? Is it another mechanism or is there in the mind something of different essence?
>
> . . . In conclusion, it must be said that there is as yet no scientific proof that the brain can control the mind, nor fully explain the mind. The assumptions of materialism have never been substantiated. Science throws no light on the nature of the spirit. . . .

Not so long ago, the orthodox cohorts would have risen at this from their chairs, waving their battle-axes and chanting the Behaviourist Anthem:

Hocus pocus spiritus –
Stimulus responsibus –
Holy Pavlov pray for us!
  Smite the heathen!
    Block his synapses!
Extinguish his reflexes!
  Put him into a Skinner box!
    Get Hebb and Hull into his skull!
Make him behave, behave, *behave!*

The third paper I mentioned earlier on was by Jonathan Cole, chief of the Psychopharmacology Department of the National Institutes of Health. Its effect was that of a bucket of cold water thrown at the drug enthusiasts of all persuasions – from those who expect mystic revelations through mescalin, to those who treat man as a slot-machine with predictable responses to chemical stimuli:

> To date, clinicians have been notably unsuccessful in predicting which patients will respond in which ways. . . . There is considerable evidence that the individual's expectations, the atmosphere of the environment, and the attitudes of the therapist, may significantly alter the effectiveness of the drug. I am beginning to have suspicions that the human setting may be as important as, or more important than, the drugs. . . .

The illustrations Cole gave were striking. In recent experiments, 120 college students were given a pill and then had to do a written performance test. One group were told that the pill was dexedrine, a well-known stimulant and energiser. Another group were told that they had been given a sleeping pill. In fact, however, *all* the students were given either dexedrine or placebos – dummy pills. The results of the test showed that the group who thought they had swallowed a pep-pill were full of pep, and the group who thought they had swallowed a sleeping pill became sluggish and sleepy.

Cole then turned to the hallucinogenic wonder drugs mescalin, LSD and psilocybin, and described how the same drug – LSD, for instance – seems to produce one kind of effect on the sober East Coast and another in eccentric California. "The subjects of Wapner and Kruse on the East Coast suffered some distortions in the visual field, but otherwise they never mention any subjective effect whatever. . . . Hartmann and his co-workers, on the other hand, working in Los Angeles, seemed to be able to induce most subjects to experience cosmic events such as union with the sun, or death and rebirth, with comparative ease." Inevitably one is reminded of those patients under psychotherapeutic treatment who will produce Freudian or Jungian dreams, custom-built to fit the analyst's requirements.

That suggestion and auto-suggestion play a considerable part in any form of therapy is not new; new is that this part is incomparably more important than the physicians, and even psychiatrists, of the age of reason ever dreamed. At a conservative estimate, about one-third of patients in any hospital ward are "placebo-reactors" who will respond to dummy pills as if they were what they believe them to be.

But this unsuspected degree of suggestibility is not confined to hospital wards. Various universities are currently engaged in high-pressure research programmes on "sensory deprivation" or "stimulus starvation". The subject is made to lie on a rubber mattress or to float in lukewarm water, with goggles of frosted glass over his eyes, with earphones that emit a steady hum, and shields over the hands that prevent perception by touch. The experiments are supposed to yield information about the way that astronauts will react under similar monotonous conditions, and are also relevant to the brain-washing of prisoners kept in dark isolation cells.

At first, the reactions seemed neat and predictable: after a few hours or even less, the subjects became confused and unable to concentrate; then followed delusions, hallucinations, sensations of depersonalisation. This led some eminent neurologists to formulate a theory, according to which the human organism can only function normally if subjected to a continuous and incessant bombardment by external stimuli; if this is not maintained, hallucinations are substituted for it. Future historians will probably quote this as a classic example of

Psychiatry in the Age of the Juke Box. Several researchers promptly identified "sensory deprivation" as a form of schizophrenia. One of them drew the conclusion that schizophrenia should be treated by overstimulation, another that it should be treated by understimulation. Typical of the general approach to the problem was a passage in the paper of one of the participants in our symposium – an eminent neurologist of somewhat rigid ideas: "Let us take a young, vigorous healthy male, a College student. . . ." This vigorous male, we learned, was strapped on a mattress, blinded with goggles, deprived of his chewing gum, deafened by hissing earphones, and told that he was expected to go cuckoo. What happened? He went cuckoo.

For the last two thousand years or more, several million experimental subjects – monks, nuns and contemplatives of every persuasion all over the world – have practised various techniques of self-inflicted sensory deprivation, meditating in immobile postures, eyes closed, in silent isolation for hours on end – with entirely different results. In one of the panel discussions, this fact was pointed out to the author of the paper, but it made little impression; he preferred to stick to the "young vigorous male". Nobody will deny, of course, that an abnormal situation maintained for an excessive length of time will create abnormal reactions; but the measure of what is excessive may vary, according to the person, from a few hours to several days, and the reaction may vary from rage tantrums to the Yogi's samadi. Recent, as yet unpublished, experiments (by Pollard and Jackson at Michigan University, Ann Arbor) have shown that the spectacular symptoms displayed by test subjects in short-term deprivation experiments "were primarily obtained by systematically influencing the subjects' previous knowledge of the expected experimental results" – that is to say, once more by suggestion and auto-suggestion. When the subjects knew beforehand that they were expected to have hallucinations, they obliged by having them; but failed to do so when, under precisely the same experimental conditions, they were misled into believing that the purpose of the experiment was to test a harmless new drug.

A last example will show the influence of subjective attitudes on the outcome of apparently objective experimental results in an unexpected field. Dr Robert Rosenthal, a bright young assistant professor of psychology, University of North Dakota, was engaged in the classic type of experiment of teaching rats to run a maze. He gave one group of his research workers rats which, he explained, were geniuses, specially bred from a stock of rats with an exceptionally high IQ. To a second group of researchers he gave what he explained were "stupid rats". In fact, all rats were of the same common-or-garden breed. Yet the score sheets of the "genius rats" showed unmistakably that they learned to run the maze much faster than the "stupid rats". The only explanation Rosenthal could offer was that the bias in the research workers' minds was somehow transmitted to the rats – just how this was done he confessed not to know. These, and other experiments* on similar lines moved the *New York Herald Tribune's* Science Editor, Ubell, to comment: "The results throw a pall over the entire range of psychological tests as reported by the psychologists over the last fifty years."

All these confluent trends in neurophysiology, neuropharmacology, experimental psychology and psychotherapy demonstrate that the concept of the "human organism" as a bundle of conditioned reflexes is an abstraction – the reality is the individual, an elusive entity, with a blur of unpredictability at its core which determines the organisms's reactions to the stimuli that impinge on it.

In a brilliant technical paper on the biochemistry of brain processes, Professor Hydén of Göteborg quoted Konrad Lorenz: "If you design an experiment to demonstrate reflex activity, then the poor creature never gets an opportunity to show that it can do more than just display a reflex activity. Such experiments are expressly designed to confirm the hypothesis – which it the worst thing an experiment can do."

Nearly a century ago, Charles Darwin, as if aware of the

* See *Experimenter Effects in Behavioural Research* by R. Rosenthal (New York, 1966).

shape of things to come, mocked at the stimulus-responsibus type of psychology: "I laid a small wager with a dozen young men that they would not sneeze if they took snuff, although they all declared that they invariably did so; accordingly they all took a pinch, but from wishing much to succeed, not one sneezed, though their eyes watered, and all, without exception, had to pay me the wager."*

If you hit the subject with a sledge-hammer, or pump a massive dose of phenobarbital into his veins, he will pass out, and that is about as far as behavioural predictability goes; if you merely tickle him under the chin, or give him a milder pill, his response will, broadly speaking, no longer depend on the stimulus, but on his "state of mind" – the blur at the centre of the blueprint. The pill is a chemical compound, and physicians used to believe that the gesture of handing out the pill was irrelevant to its action. Now we are discovering that the gesture is at least as important as the pill; and that we all live in a kind of psycho-magnetic field, saturated with energies that interact on an unconscious level, vulnerable to voodoos and love-philtre placebos (it is no coincidence that the peyote cactus and the sacred mushroom of the Aztecs, mescalin and psilocybin, are so much in demand).

Thus on a higher turn of the spiral we are once more plunged into the magic world, but with a more sophisticated awareness of the hidden powers of the mind; and thereby hangs a new tale, the dawn of a new era in the study of the human psyche.

2 *Behold the lowly worm*

One of the last Palinurian joys of civilised middle age is to sit in front of the log fire, sip a glass of brandy, and read the *Worm-Runner's Digest*. Its full title is: *An Informal Journal of Comparative Psychology, Published Irregularly by the Planaria Research Group, Department of Psychology, the University of Michigan.*

The editor of this journal is Professor James V. McConnell,

* *The Expression of the Emotions in Man and Animals* (1872).

an austere young experimental psychologist who, like many a good man before him, developed a passion for flatworms. Their fascination derives from the fact that they are the lowest creatures on the evolutionary ladder with a brain of sorts and a true central nervous system, but are at the same time the highest on the ladder among those which reproduce by fission. They multiply both asexually and sexually. In summer, they are liable to drop their tails and grow a new one, while the dropped tail will grow a new head. They can be sliced into five or six segments, each of which will develop all the missing organs and grow into a complete individual, as good as new.

When fully grown, however (which means about half an inch in length), the delights of fission yield to those of mating. These are further enhanced by the fact that they are hermaphrodites; while young, they function as males, but after more mature reflection, as females, who lay eggs. In the adult animal both sets of reproductive organs are present, and though the male organs mature first, the two phases may overlap. To complicate matters still further, I must mention that during the mating season the worms become cannibals, devouring everything alive that comes their way, including their own previously discarded tails which were in the process of growing a new head. Thus the *status quo ante* is re-established, by feedback as it were. The head itself, however, is rarely eaten, and never by its own tail (though technically this would be possible because the mouth of the creature is near the centre of its belly, and equipped with a retractable sucker). All of this goes to show that when the flatworms were created, evolution was in a rather confused state, as if trying to decide whether sex was really necessary for progress; and, if so, whether male and female should cohabit in the literal sense, that is, dwell in the same body – or be sorted out once and for all.

The latter idea won, for better or worse, but the planaria were not informed of this and were left in confusion. As a result, we can tell neither whether the creature is male or female, nor whether the products of its asexual fission are its descendants or its *Doppelgängers*. This is an old philosophical teaser, but McConnell's experiments were designed to ask a new, crucial question: does the regenerated individual preserve a "personal memory"? Is it capable of "remembering" what happened to it before the fission – before the world split into two? Does the head which grew a new tail "remember" more than the tail which grew a new head? The questions have to be hedged around by quotation marks, for we are moving in muddy semantic waters. But they must not be taken lightly, because it is in the makeshift brain of the flatworm that the history of the mind originates.

That planaria are capable of learning, and have a memory, was known for a long time. The experimental procedure designed by Thompson and McConnell consists in putting the worm into a shallow plastic trough, half an inch in diameter, twelve inches long, filled with aquarium water. When the worm (which is normally kept in a fingerbowl of its own) gets accustomed to its new environment, it starts moving from one end of the trough to the other with its peculiar, snail-like gliding motion. Under the microscope its smooth and svelte body, with its algae-green and brown specks, looks rather pretty, though the squinting eyes are somewhat humourless – they are light-sensitive, but have no lenses and no pattern vision. Training the creature consists in suddenly flashing the strong light of two 100-watt bulbs on it, followed by an electric shock. In the untrained animal the light causes no reaction whatsoever, whereas the shock causes a sharp to violent contraction of the body. After a number of repetitions, the worm learns that the light is a signal heralding the shock, and contracts when the light is switched on. It has aquired a conditioned reflex.

The next step was to train the animal, then cut it into halves, allow both halves to regenerate, and to find out *how much of its acquired learning each regenerated individual retained.*

Here a slight difficulty arose. A severed head or tail will usually regenerate into a complete individual within a fortnight. To make sure that all internal organs had a chance to develop properly, an additional fortnight was allowed before testing began. Now four weeks are a long time in the life of a worm, and it is to be expected that it will forget a considerable amount of what it has previously learned – even if not distracted by being cut into two and having to build the missing halves. A control group was therefore trained and then kept idle for a month, to see how much "brushing up" the worms needed to regain their former proficiency. The result was as follows: on average a group of worms needs 150 "lessons" of light-followed-by-shock until it learns to respond to light alone. After four weeks' rest, the same group will need a refresher course of forty lessons to react reliably. Thus the "saving" in the number of required lessons due to retention was 150 − 40 = 110; that is to say, over 70 per cent, which is not bad at all.

And now let's go from the normal to the sliced-up animal. Each half, after regeneration had been completed, was given a refresher course by the same method as the uncut animals. The astonishing result was that the "tails" showed as much retention as did the "heads"; and that both "heads" and "tails" showed as much retention – that is, 70-odd per cent – as the uncut animals. Similar results were obtained by other researchers, who taught flatworms to find their way through a simple maze. Again retention by "heads" and by "tails" was the same.

How is this possible? How does the tail retain memories of learning? And when the tail builds a new brain, how does it build the memory into it?

Confronted by this puzzle, the worm-runners went one step further. They trained a "head", H_1, after cutting off its tail, T_1; they let H_1 grow a new tail, T_2; cut it off and let it grow a new head, H_2. This creature, $H_2 + T_2$ had anatomically not a single organ or mature tissue in common with the original $H_1 + T_1$ – and yet it had retained a significant amount of its learning. How was the information transmitted?

The latest experiments are even more surrealistic. I have mentioned that, with the onset of sexual maturity, the worms become cannibals. In two experiments (as yet unpublished) McConnell chopped up trained animals and fed them to untrained ones. The results seem to indicate, pending confirmation, that the cannibals fed on trained animals learned quicker than the controls which were kept on a normal low-brow diet.* In the jargon of communication engineering information is always "fed" into a computer or an organism; here the metaphor became flesh.

Since the flatworm's tail has as good a memory as the head, one might be tempted to believe that its brain plays only a subordinate part. But this is not so. The animal's brain, though primitive, is the centre of its nervous system in which the sensory impulses from the eyes and auricles converge, and from which motor impulses are conducted in two symmetrical nerve strands and their branches to other parts of the body. Moreover, experiments by Ernhart indicate, rather surprisingly, that two-headed flatworms (produced by a simple surgical technique) learn quicker than others; while animals whose brain has been removed were shown (by Hovey) to be incapable of learning. Once, however, the animal has been trained, the tail alone is sufficient to retain the memory. One can only conclude that the brain is indispensable for the *acquisition* of learning, but not for its *retention*. This means that the memory of the animal cannot be located in its brain and nervous system alone; it must be represented by chemical changes in cells throughout the body. One of the leading American neurologists, Professor Ralph Gerrard, has suggested that in the head of the flatworm memory is retained by neuron circuitry, whereas in the rest of the body it is retained in the form of a chemical imprint. This, too, was confirmed by experiment: trained worms were cut into two and made to regenerate in a liquid which contained a chemical "memory eraser". The "heads" were not affected by it; but the "tails" forgot all they had learned.

Now this is the point where the scandal begins, and where the lowly worm acquires an unexpected significance for one of the basic controversial issues of our time. According to the orthodox theory of genetics upheld this side of the Iron Curtain, the progress of evolution from amoeba to man is

* Since this article was written, these experiments have been confirmed by several research teams, though others still regard them as controversial.

entirely due to random mutations plus natural selection. The mutational alterations in the genes which determine heredity are said to be purely accidental, and natural selection is supposed to act as a kind of automatic sorting machine which perpetuates favourable mutations, and rejects the others. The negative implication of this theory is that no trace of what the parents have experienced and learned in a lifetime is inherited by the offspring. The hereditary mechanism is deaf and blind to the requirements of the evolutionary progress which it serves. The genes – atomic units of heredity – are kept in the germ cells in hermetic isolation, sealed off from the rest of the parent body, and are passed on unchanged from one generation to the next – except for those purely accidental mutations on the evolutionary roulette board. Generations come and go, but their struggles exert no influence whatever on the hereditary substance of the race. Whoever defends the opposite view – that there may be an "inheritance of acquired characteristics" which would invest evolution with a purposeful aspect – is considered to be guilty of the Larmarckian heresy, and is academically non-U.

The gentle flatworm is not the first animal to cause a breach, so to speak, in the battlements of orthodoxy. During the last five years or so, evidence has been steadily accumulating which does not seem to fit into the orthodox frame; the planaria are merely the latest and most dramatic arrivals on the scene. They establish beyond any reasonable doubt the inheritance of acquired learning in *asexual* reproduction. (Up to now the worms have refused to reproduce sexually in captivity.) However, even this should be a sufficient shock to the accepted views on the mechanism of heredity, for asexual reproduction is after all *reproduction*. An English scientific weekly recently paid grudging tribute to McConnell's team, but at the same time reproached them because "in reporting these experiments to the American Psychological Association, the authors have unfortunately described the worms which regenerate from halves of other worms as a second generation . . . [which might] suggest to the casual reader that here is evidence of the inheritance of acquired characters".

And evidence indeed it is, semantic subterfuges apart. The Ann Arbor laboratory now has a whole tribe of Tigrina, all descended from a single individual. Whether one describes these animals at the fifth or sixth remove from the parent body as "generations" or "regenerations" does not alter the fact that all they have in common with that parent body is a biochemically inherited blueprint, transmitted by specialised "regeneration cells" – the asexual equivalent of sperm and ova. These regeneration cells (also referred to as "embryo cells" or "formative cells") are scattered in the parenchyma, the loose meshwork between the planaria's muscles and internal organs. When a worm is cut into two – or six – fragments, and each of these recreates all the complex organs of the whole individual, we are faced with a process similar to embryonic development. The regeneration cells which are responsible for this development must carry a chemical blueprint of the complete animal, as the germ cells do in sexual development (though the details of the chemical mechanism may differ considerably). The decisive fact is that these blueprints *include the traces of memories and learning acquired during the lifetime of the ancestral animal*; and that these acquired characters are built into the brain and nervous system of the new animal. The differences between sexual and asexual reproduction are many; but this basic fact is not altered by them.

Of special importance in this respect is the neat "eraser" experiment that I mentioned. Here matters become technical and I must oversimplify a little. One of the two highly complicated "blueprinting" substances which play a decisive part in the mechanism of heredity is ribonucleic acid, RNA. It can be broken up by another substance, RNASE. This was the substance used as a memory eraser. Worms which were made to regenerate in strong solutions of RNASE frequently grew into eyeless or headless monsters – proof that the "eraser" interfered with the chemically coded hereditary potentials. Very weak solutions of RNASE, however, merely retarded the regenerative process without visible deleterious effects – except for erasing the chemically impressed memories of acquired learning. It was an elegant method of proving that these memories had been incorporated into the blueprint; as the most recent and tentative additions to it, they were the first to be erased.

The flatworm studies are relatively new, but they are now being duplicated and continued by researchers in several universities. The results which I have described will probably be modified and reinterpreted in various details, but the basic fact of the transmission of acquired experience by asexual heredity is no longer open to doubt; whereas, as matters stand at present, its transmission by sexual heredity is passionately denied by orthodox science. This leads to the perversely paradoxical conclusion that the lower animals must have an incomparably *more* efficient evolutionary mechanism at their disposal than the higher ones. But if this were really the case, then the advantages of sexual reproduction – greater individual variety – would dwindle to such insignificance compared to the enormous disadvantage of blocking the inheritability of acquired learning that, through the process of natural selection, fissioning creatures would soon have got the upper hand over mating creatures, sex would have been dropped as a bad bargain, and we would all multiply by budding.

In an excellent survey of *Darwin's Forgotten Theories,* in the *Worm-Runner's Digest*, T. H. Morrill writes that the present "overwhelming preference for environmental selection of hereditary accident" might be due to a bias inherent in our extravert " and accident-prone culture, causing its members to seek such an irrational rationale in the universe". He quotes the orthodox view, according to which heredity can only be changed by "high temperatures and energetic radiations which intensify the molecular chaos" (Muller), and compares it to the ageing Darwin's views in the *Descent of Man*: "The birth both of the species and of the individual are equally parts of that grand sequence of events, which our minds refuse to accept as the result of blind chance." Confronted with the Neo-Darwinist orthodoxy of our day, the old man would not fare better than that other revenant in Dostoyevsky's *Grand Inquisitor*. To return for a last time to the *Worm-Runner's Digest*: "The later theories of Darwin are at base the last expression in

Western science of those old, fond dreams of men – that in its largest aspect, beyond the misery, grime and cataclysms of earth, life is a 'striving towards a goal, a far circuit and a sure coming home'."

3 The pioneer beyond the pale

"Dr Rhine arrived at my doorstep in Cambridge, Massachusetts, one morning in June, 1926," relates Professor William McDougall in his preface to Rhine's first book, *Extra-Sensory Perception*. Young Dr Joseph Banks Rhine and his wife, Dr Louisa Rhine, both university lecturers in biology, had "burnt their boats, given up their careers and come over to psychical research. . . . They were working scientists without worldly resources other than their earnings. I was filled with admiration and misgivings. Their action seemed to me magnificently rash."

Both the admiration and the misgivings were to be proved justified. A year after that morning in June, the Rhines were installed as researchers in parapsychology at Duke University, North Carolina, where McDougall was head of the Psychology Department. But it took another seven years before Rhine, by then an associate professor, was permitted to establish officially his Parapsychology Laboratory. It was an event of great symbolic importance: research into the dubious subjects of telepathy and clairvoyance had for the first time been recognised as academically respectable.

Rhine and his collaborators introduced rigorous scientific methods into the investigation of these elusive phenomena. The popular image of the psychic investigator as an uncritical believer and willing prey to fraudulent media has become an anachronism. The new school in parapsychology, which Rhine inaugurated, has carried matters to the opposite extreme in its almost fanatical devotion to statistical method, mathematical analysis, mechanised controls. The card-guessing and dice-throwing experiments, repeated over millions of experimental runs with thousands of random experimental subjects – often whole classes of schoolboys who have no idea what the experiment is about; the increasingly elaborate machinery for mechanical card-shuffling, dice-throwing, randomising, recording, and what have you, have turned the study of extra-sensory perception into an empirical science as sober, down to earth – and all too often as dreary – as teaching rats to run a maze, or slicing up generations of flatworms. Even the terminology coined by Rhine: ESP, psi effect, decline effect, reinforcement, BM (blind matching), BT (basic theory), SO (stimulus object), STM (screen touch match), and so forth, is characteristic of the antiseptic atmosphere in modern ESP labs. This New Look in parapsychology is partly a reflection of the prevailing fashion in research in general, but there is also an element in it of bending over backward to disarm suspicions and to meet the sceptic on his own empirical-statistical ground.

On the whole this sober, functional approach proved effective. Not only several universities, but such conservative bodies as the Royal Society of Medicine, the American Philosophical Association, the Rockefeller, Fulbright and Ciba Foundations, have organised lectures and symposia on parapsychology. But the majority of academic psychologists remained hostile, although the giants had always taken telepathy and allied phenomena for granted – from Charcot and Richet through William James to Freud and Jung. Freud thought that telepathy entered into the relations between analyst and patient, and Jung has even coined a new name for an old phenomenon: synchronicity. However, these men belonged to a mellower generation, and formed their conclusions before Rhine put parapsychology "on the map"; among the younger lights, the attitude of H. J. Eysenck is significant. Professor Eysenck occupies the chair in psychology at the University of London, and is director of the Psychological Department at the Maudsley and Bethlem Royal Hospitals. Those acquainted with his work will hardly accuse him of a lack of scepticism or an excess of humility. His summing up of the problem of telepathy commands some interest:

> Unless there is a gigantic conspiracy involving some thirty University departments all over the world, and several hundred highly respected scientists in various fields, many of them originally

> hostile to the claims of the psychical researchers, the only conclusion the unbiased observer can come to must be that there does exist a small number of people who obtain knowledge existing either in other people's minds, or in the outer world, by means as yet unknown to science. This should not be interpreted as giving any support to such notions as survival after death, philosophical idealism, or anything else. . . .

In one sense, therefore, it can be said that Rhine's pioneering work has succeeded. But there is another side to the picture; I became painfully aware of this during the three days I spent at Duke. I liked this medium-sized, neat and modern university, founded by a tobacco-growing millionaire in the woodlands of Carolina; and I took an immediate liking to both Rhines and their closest collaborator over the last thirty years, Professor J. G. Pratt. Rhine's burly figure, his broad, open face, his obvious sincerity, made me think of a woodcutter, and indeed, his favourite hobby is to wander into the woods with an axe and chop up a tree. Yet during my whole stay I had a feeling that these admirable people were living under a cloud, have become accustomed to its shadow, and accept it as unavoidable.

If visitors from abroad come to Duke – and there is a steady stream of them – they come for the sole purpose of visiting the Parapsychology Laboratory, as pilgrims came to Prado to hear Pablo Casals. Yet to the students in Duke, Rhine's work is practically unknown, mainly, it seems, because their teachers discourage them from getting acquainted with it. Members of other faculties still consider the parapsychologists as beyond the academic pale. To say that the Rhines are ostracised would be to put it too dramatically; but they are lone figures in the landscape, and they are resigned to it.

They are equally resigned to the periodic storms of defamation that break over their heads every two or three years. The critics fall into two main categories: the first one might call the "insatiable perfectionists" who attack mainly the earlier work on ESP when experimental controls were not as rigorous as they are today, and the *a priorists*, who argue that ESP is a new and improbable hypothesis; that the hypothesis of fraud is easier to fit into the accepted framework of science; and that accordingly, by applying Occam's razor, one must accept the hypothesis of fraud. To this they usually add: "No personal offence meant, we are merely engaged in an exercise in logic." To quote Eysenck again:

> The very possibility of extra-sensory perception, or psychokinesis, appears contrary to modern scientific logic, and many people have shown considerable reluctance even to look at the evidence that has been produced in favour of these alleged abilities. . . . Scientists, especially when they leave the particular field in which they have specialised, are just as ordinary, pig-headed, and unreasonable as anybody else, and their unusually high intelligence only makes their prejudices all the more dangerous . . .

★ ★ ★

I started the first of this series of articles with a remark to the effect that the age of dehumanised psychology was drawing to its close, and that the "man-a-machine" school was fighting a rearguard action. Some friends have objected that I was too optimistic, but I do not think so.

No doubt the rearguard is still firmly entrenched in university chairs, the editorial offices of technical papers, and other positions of power. In the period of scholastic decline, the orthodox Aristotelians had occupied similar key positions. However, by clinging to a system of ideas which had been progressive in its time, and by carrying it to absurd extremes, the hollowness of its implied axioms was revealed, and orthodoxy hastened to its own doom. "They are Folly's servants," declared Erasmus, denouncing the sterile pedantry and grotesque academic jargon of his time. One wonders how he would react today to the definition of human beings as "need-fulfilling, goal-achieving unities" (this comes from a book by a professor in the social sciences, called *Understanding Organisational Behaviour*); or to a book on nursery care in which the chapter on babies' tummy-aches is called "Eliminatory Behaviour-Patterns"; or to statements by some eminent neurologists at a symposium on Brain Mechanisms and Consciousness, such as: "The existence of something called consciousness is a venerable *hypothesis,* not a datum, not directly observable"; or: "Although we cannot get along without the concept of consciousness, actually there is no such thing." My ears are still buzzing with similar statements in discussions at four different American universities. Nevertheless I believe that this era is drawing to its close, and that a new era is in the making in the study of the mind. Some of the new departures which I have mentioned, though still tentative and inconclusive if taken each by itself, seem to me symptomatic of the new trend.

Among the sure signs that some one-sided school of science has run into a dead end are disillusionment and boredom. Orthodoxies are rarely felled by the stroke of a single genius. As a science editor in bygone days, I noticed that the favourite argument of cranks was to invoke the example of Galileo and the Inquisition. They never realise that the collapse of medieval philosophy was not brought about by Galileo's apocryphal *E pur si muove*, but by the fact that it had reduced itself to absurdity.

Something similar seems to be happening to the present orthodox view of the nature of man. The doctrines on which it rests, and which are beginning to reveal themselves as based on faulty axioms, can be summed up in a somewhat simplified form: that biological evolution is the outcome of random mutations preserved by natural selection; that mental evolution is the outcome of random tries preserved by "reinforcements"; and that man is a self-regulating, passive automaton, whose actions consist in jerking out adaptive responses to stimuli in the environment.

"After all," as somebody has said – I believe it was Freud – "after all, the most effective adaptation of the organism to its environment is to die." Yet even the lowly worm, sliced into six pieces, knows better.

THE FOUR STAGES OF CREATIVITY*

I felt all the more honoured by the invitation to give this opening address as I am an outsider to the scientific establishment. On the other hand, the occasion seems to conform to the spirit of the times, where both cultures are busy putting up signposts with "TRESPASSERS WELCOME – POACHING PERMITTED – ADMIRE OUR VIEWS – TELL US WHAT'S WRONG WITH THEM". I intend to do just that.

I must start with some preliminary remarks on the psychology of creativity. By and large, one can distinguish between two extreme attitudes to this problem. One extreme is represented by that brand of behaviourism which, for the last fifty years, from Thorndike through Watson and Hull to Professor Skinner of Harvard, had a dominant influence on American psychology. At the opposite extreme you have Gestalt psychologists, Jungians, existentialist psychologists, Zen Buddhists and mescalin worshippers. The first relies on trial and error, and has an irritating likeness to our old friend, the monkey at the typewriter; the second relies on spontaneous intuitions, and reminds one of a medium in trance engaged in automatic writing. Which is closer to the truth?

When we look at a problem, we automatically start a search in our mental repertory for some rule or trick which has enabled us to solve similar problems. Routine problems can be recognised at a glance as analogous in some essential respect to

* Abridged text of opening address delivered to the General Science Section of the British Association Meeting at Cambridge, 2 September 1965, under the title "Evolution and Revolution in the History of Science". See also the related essay "Literature and the Law of Diminishing Returns" in Part Two of the present volume.

other problems encountered in the past, which provides the appropriate technique to cope with them. But even routine problems require strategic skill in the selection and application of the correct subroutines – such as extrapolation, intrapolation, schematisation, transformation of data. Above all, the more difficult type of routine task requires the *combination* of several subroutines. Take the following cue from a crossword puzzle: "*Discussed a creature caught in the very act* (7 letters)." The act is "deed"; the creature caught in it is a "bat" – *de-bat-ed* – discussed. Next: "*Badly scare an Arab who was once a tough fighter* (7)." The Arab who was once a tough fighter is a *Saracen*, anagram of "scare an". Now solving a crossword does not require creative genius, not even an original mind. But it does require a *flexible* mind because the skill in question consists in fact of a hierarchy of sub-skills: the whole word or part of it could be an anagram; it could be a synonym; or a metaphor; or a play on words; or a positional hint (the bat "caught" in the centre of the deed); and there are several more subroutines, each with its own rule of the game.

Now let me go back to my starting point and try to decide which of the two opposite views applies to crossword puzzle-solving: "manipulation through trial and error" or "spontaneous insight". Trial and error there certainly is, but it is far from random because the range of the permissible tries is selectively limited by the rules of each game: synonyms, metaphor, positional shift, reversal of letters, etc. Even the anagram – which comes nearest to the monkey-at-the-typewriter situation – is not solved by random permutations, but by grouping letters into syllables, familiar prefixes and suffixes, and shifting, transforming, combining these subassemblies. The monkey is working on a hierarchically programmed typewriter which will only print sensible sequences. And as on each successive level of the hierarchy the rules of the game become more complex, the tries will become more sophisticated, the errors more refined. A long time ago, Bertrand Russell wrote that even a Newton could only learn to find his way through a maze by random tries. But some years later, it was discovered that even the rat, learning to run a new maze, proceeds by forming hypotheses. A hypothesis is an implicit try, and as we ascend to higher levels of the hierarchy the tries assume more and more implicit forms: tentative generalisations, empirical inductions, tentative combinations of ideas, lastly, guidance by hunches. The whole confusion in the psychology of problem-solving started with the fallacious identification of trial and error with randomness – with the behaviour of the angry cat in Thorndike's puzzle box. But although to every research scientist the legitimacy of trial and error as an essential method of heuristics is obvious, the psychologist will only see it in its proper perspective if he stops thinking in terms of conditioned response chains, and starts thinking in terms of cognitive hierarchies.

This becomes at once more evident if we turn to the opposite view: that solutions appear by spontaneous insight, all in one piece, not by a process of elimination but of direct intuition, accompanied by that sudden emotional catharsis, the Eureka cry or *Aha* reaction. We all know those experiences of delicious euphoria following the solution of a quite trivial problem, when the bits suddenly fall into place, regardless whether the solution had been proceeded by fumbling trial and error or whether it came suddenly. For, in both cases, the essence of the matter is the emergence of order out of disorder, of signal out of noise, of harmony out of dissonance, of a meaningful whole out of meaningless bits, of cosmos out of chaos. This is the trigger which releases the cathartic reaction, whether occasioned by a mechanical puzzle falling into place or a new theorem being born.

But what, then, does "spontaneous insight" mean? I think it means what I have just tried to say: the emergence of a new synthesis, of a whole on a higher level of the hierarchy than that of the parts which combined and fused into it. And the emergence of the new whole always gives the impression of spontaneity and suddenness regardless of how much fumbling preceded it, because the last decisive step in the combinatorial activity acts like a trigger on a Jack-in-the-box. Thus the strategy of solving routine problems consists in activating the appropriate subroutines, in the appropriate order; but above all *in combining them in various ways when none of them alone leads to the solution.* This sounds trivial, but just this "combinatorial activity" appears to be the key to creativeness.

So far I have only talked of routine problems; but where exactly do we draw the line between the solving of routine problems and creative originality? Let me quote two opinions – a historian's and a mathematician's. The historian, Thomas Kuhn, speaks of "mopping-up-operations" which "are what engage most scientists throughout their careers . . ." and mentions as the "most striking feature" of normal research activities "how little they aim to produce major novelties, conceptual or phenomenal"(1). The mathematician, George Polya, defines a routine problem as one

> which can be solved either by substituting special data into a formerly solved general problem, or by following step by step, without any trace of originality, some well-worn, conspicuous example (2).

He then contrasts these routines with the "rules of discovery": "the first rule of discovery is to have brains and good luck. The second rule of discovery is to sit tight and wait till you get a bright idea." If one were to take this seriously, one would have to conclude that the cohorts of science consist exclusively of generals and privates, geniuses and handymen. Let us rather look at a concrete example and try to decide whether to call it a routine affair or an original discovery.

A couple of years ago, I read in a science column the following report about an electronics physicist in Albuquerque, New Mexico, who worked on radar equipment. His problem was to reduce the troublesome side-effects (of capacitance and inductance) in resistors, when brief pulses of high frequency currents are sent through them. One day, the article said,

> he let his mind wander and remembered an old parlour trick, the Möbius loop. Mathematics suddenly merged with electronics and he had what he was searching for.

A few months after this story appeared, you could see the new non-reactive "Möbius resistor" advertised in the *Scientific*

American. It is made by sticking two strips of aluminium tape to opposite sides of a non-conducting ribbon (made of plastic), then twisting it a half turn and joining the ends so that the conducting strips become a single loop, then soldering wire leads to opposite sides of the loop. If you now send an electric pulse through those leads, the current divides, flows in both directions through the foil and, since the Möbius loop has the perverse quality of possessing two sides, but only a single, continuous surface, the pulses apparently pass right through themselves. When the inventor was asked how exactly the thing worked, he replied: "Maybe Maxwell could tell us, but he is dead."

Now here you have a striking combinatorial achievement. Let us try to analyse the reasons why it is so striking. Three reasons come to mind. First, because it is an *original* combination which creates a novelty. In the second place, it is an *unexpected* combination because the two associative contexts which went into its making have previously each led a separate existence. In the third place, because the idea occurred to the inventor "while he let his mind wander"; in other words, it came to him spontaneously without conscious effort. And since ideas must have an origin, we must conclude that it originated in some *extra-conscious process*.

Here, then, we have three factors: (a) originality; (b) the previous unrelatedness of the contexts which enter into the combination; we may, somewhat loosely, call this factor the improbability of the combination; and (c) the intervention of extra-conscious processes.

I have suggested in *The Act of Creation* (3) that these three factors – plus a fourth to be added presently – may serve as criteria of what we call creativity. Let me briefly discuss each of them.

(a) *Originality* does not necessarily create novelty. Originality is a psychological concept, novelty a historical fact. There must have been many geniuses who left no mark on the annals of science, while others were conspicuous in priority disputes. According to a recent survey, multiple discoveries are not exceptions, but rather the rule in the history of science; thus

Lord Kelvin's published papers contain at least thirty-two discoveries of his own which he subsequently found had also been made by others. The "others" include men of genius such as Cavendish and Helmholtz, but also some lesser lights.

(b) "Invention or discovery," wrote Jacques Hadamard, "be it in mathematics or anywhere else, takes place by combining ideas" (4). In other words, it is the fusion or *bisociation* of previously unconnected cognitive structures. "Bisociation" is a barbaric word, but it helps to focus attention on the specific character of the act; and about its importance there seems to be, for once, more or less general agreement among scientists and psychologists. To mention only a few, Poincaré in an oft-quoted lecture explained discovery as the result of a happy interlocking of the "hooked atoms" of thought. According to Sir Frederick Bartlett, "the most important feature of original experimental thinking is the discovery of overlap . . . where formerly only isolation and difference were recognised". Jerome Bruner considers all forms of creativity a result of "combinatorial activity". McKellar talks of the "fusion" of perceptions, Kubie of the "discovery of unexpected connections between things", and so on back to Goethe's "connect, always connect". So far, then, we are on safe ground and we may feel encouraged to take a closer look at the bisociative process as a key to certain puzzling phenomena in the history of science.

We have seen that even solving a crossword involves combinatorial activities, often of a tricky kind – when, for instance, you have to employ riddle-solving techniques and anagram techniques at the same time. Why, then, not call this too a bisociative act? Because these various subroutines are parts of a single, integrated skill of the experienced crossword-puzzler's, whereas Möbius loops and radar resistors belonged to separate contexts up to the moment when they suddenly fused in the inventor's mind. If the crossword-puzzler acquired his noble art untutored, and discovered all by himself that it requires the combination of two, or more, different techniques, then he would be entitled to call this a minor bisociation and even to shout Eureka. There is a hierarchic sequence of combinatorial processes in the development of the individual and in the historical development of science, resulting in a hierarchy of cognitive structures. The discoveries of yesterday are the commonplaces of today, and we marvel at mankind's erstwhile blindness in treating the motions of the moon and the motions of the tides as unrelated phenomena before they became inseparably fused in our minds. To recapitulate: although originality is a relative affair, each bisociative act, whether small or momentous, is a discrete step sharply set off from associative routine. Mental evolution is discontinuous, with quantum jumps, as it were, from one level of the hierarchy to the next.

This discontinuity is further reflected in the truism that the whole, the new synthesis, is more than the sum of its parts, and that its relational properties are to a large extent unpredictable by extrapolation from the properties of the parts. When Newton combined Kepler's laws of planetary motion with Galileo's studies of the motion of projectiles, a whole new universe sprang into being. One of the most dramatic chapters in the history of science is the series of mergers between previously separate disciplines, from Oersted's observation that the "electric conflict", as he called it, caused by a voltaic current, deflected a magnetic needle, to Maxwell's momentous sentence "that light consists in the transverse undulations of the same medium which is the cause of electric and magnetic phenomena".

However, each significant new synthesis exacts a price. The matrices which enter into it are not simply coupled together; they must be integrated, and in the process of integration they become modified in various ways and to various degrees. By and large, only technical innovations and minor discoveries result from a simple additive process which leaves the components intact – neither the Möbius loop nor the principles of electric resistance were the worse off after their union. But when Einstein bisociated space and time, both took on a bewilderingly new look in the process; and so did energy and matter. The progress of science, like an ancient desert trail, is strewn with the bleached skeletons of discarded theories, doctrines, and axioms which seemed to possess eternal life. The dramatic mergers of the last century entailed the sacrifice of beliefs which had constituted the very backbone of their separate disciplines – phlogiston, calorifics, "vital fluids" and luminiferous ether, the electric and magnetic effluvia.

Thus every revolution has a destructive aspect. But the destructions wrought by the nineteenth century had a quasi Victorian modesty compared to the twentieth. Within the lifetime of our generation we have seen matter evaporate, causality shaken, parity dethroned, infinity put into its place (wherever that may be); above all, we were given a new version of the Second Commandment: "Thou shalt not make unto thee any graven image or model of anything that is in the Heavens above or that is in the Atoms beneath."

Thus, on the positive side we have a series of confluences, as in a vast river system, of the different "effluvia" into the unitary concept of energy, of the ninety-odd chemical elements into the same subatomic building blocks; and finally, energy and mass, particle and wave are all swallowed up in the majestic river delta; while on the destructive side we have an equally impressive series of floods and devastating erosions. For it is in the nature of the bisociative process that the impact of the two matrices makes each of them appear in a new light, so that axioms which had been taken for granted, and hidden assumptions built into their texture, stand mercilessly revealed. One such axiom, that everything that moves must have a mover, survived for two thousand years. Another, that we are entitled to extrapolate our conceptions of reality towards the infinitely large and the infinitely small, has collapsed only recently. And Einstein's "God does not play dice with the world", which dates back to the Old Testament, is still *sub judice*. The destructive effects of scientific revolutions also display a hierarchic order: the closer they get to the basic axioms of thought, the more agonising the reappraisal which they demand.

Now science is made by scientists, and thus the destructive aspect of scientific revolutions must reflect some element of destructiveness in the scientific mind; or, to put it more politely, a preparedness to go recklessly against accepted beliefs. This destructive-constructive mentality I would suggest as the fourth criterion of creativity. It is related to originality, but should not be confused with it – the invention of the zip fastener was highly original but not destructive. It is also related to the third criterion which remains to be briefly discussed: the intervention of extra-conscious processes, commonly called hunches.

The safest assumption is that hunches, like babies, are brought by the stork. One could fill a whole dictionary with quotations, from Pythagoras to Einstein, all of them testifying to hunches of unknown, extra-conscious origin. However, the concept of unconscious mentation loses both its mystical halo and its clinical odour if we avoid the Cartesian fallacy of equating mental activities with conscious thinking; and recognise instead that awareness of one's own activities is a matter of degree, of a continuous gradient, reaching from the unconsciousness of homeostatic regulations, to fringe conscious perceptions, and up to the optimum condition of focal awareness. But that optimum condition is not always the most productive. "Full consciousness is a narrow thing," wrote Einstein; and he added that his creative thinking consisted of a kind of "combinatorial play", the elements of which were vague, visual and kinesthetic images. It seems that pinpointing the task with the narrow beam of focal awareness is indispensable at certain times and stages of mental work, but in other situations it can become obstructive.

Such situations arise when the problem cannot be solved by any conventional rule of the game and requires some far-fetched, reckless combination of ideas which seems unacceptable to the sober, disciplined mind. The true scientist, like the true artist, is an uneasy mixture of the adventurer and the pedant. A Chinese proverb says that there is a time for fishing and a time for drying the nets; and there are times when the adventurer imprisoned in the pedant cries to be let out to go fishing. The disciplined routines of thought within the framework of a single conventional matrix are the vehicles of scientific progress at normal times; but at times of crisis, caused by the appearance of new data or a new type of question, matrices which have outlived their usefulness can become straitjackets. To unlearn is more difficult than to learn; and it seems that the agonising task of breaking up rigid cognitive structures and reassembling them into a new synthesis cannot always be performed in the full daylight of the conscious rational mind. It is more often done by reverting to those more fluid, less committed forms of mentation which normally operate in the twilight outside the beam of focal awareness or on a less specialised level of the mental hierarchy. These interventions of extra-conscious processes in the creative act range from the trivial to the dramatic, from James Watt's kettle to Kekulé's dream; but there is a vast literature on the subject and there is no need to go into it.

If you take a kind of grandstand view of the history of any branch of science, you will find a rhythmic alteration between long periods of relatively peaceful evolution and shorter bursts of revolutionary change. Only in the peaceful periods which follow after a major breakthrough is the progress of science continuous and cumulative in the strict sense. It is a period of consolidating the newly conquered frontiers, of verifying, assimilating, elaborating and extending the new synthesis: a time for drying the nets. It may last a few years or several generations; but sooner or later the emergence of new empirical data, of new developments in some adjacent branch of knowledge, or a change in the philosophical climate, leads to a hardening of the matrix into a closed system, a defensive attitude, the rise of a new orthodoxy. This produces a crisis, a period of fertile anarchy in which rival theories proliferate – until the new synthesis is achieved and the cycle starts again; but this time perhaps aiming in a different direction, along different parameters, asking a different kind of question.

This brings us back to the axiom that science is made by scientists, and not the other way round. The historic cycle which I have just described could be regarded as a magnified projection of the various stages in the process of individual discovery according to the classic schema by Helmholtz and Graham Wallas (5): conscious preparation; incubation;

illumination; verification and consolidation. On the historic plane the last stage of one cycle shades into the first stage of the next. The period of "fertile anarchy" which characterises the crisis corresponds to the feverish combinatorial games in the period of incubation; lastly, illumination – the emergence of the new synthesis – is mostly brought about by a quick succession of individual discoveries, often including multiple discoveries.

One could also call the revolutionary phases the romantic, and the peaceable phases the classical periods in the history of science. The former appeal to the reckless adventurer, the latter to the pedantic stickler in the Janus-faced scientist. This split personality seems to me both the glory and the predicament of the trade. Its glory, because at best it combines flights of imagination with meticulous respect for fact; having one's head in the clouds and one's feet solidly planted in the mud. Its predicament, because either face can also turn into an ugly grimace – that of the obsessive crank's, or of blinkered orthodoxy. This explains perhaps why so many histories of science are written either as a chronicle of heroic exploits or as a chronicle of scandals. Recently the second style has come into fashion; and indeed there is hardly a period or branch in the history of science without its scandals, martyrs, and skeletons rattling in cupboards. No less a man than Max Planck wrote from bitter experience:

> a new scientific truth does not triumph by convincing its opponents and making them see the light, but rather because its opponents eventually die, and a new generation grows up that is familiar with it (6).

But, exaggeration apart, we also know the other side of the picture – that without the necessary scepticism, conservatism, and emotional commitment to the prevailing theories and rules of the game, the whole scientific enterprise would go to pieces. Michael Polanyi has given us a profound analysis of this unavoidable subjectivity and emotionalism in the scientist's attitude (7).

* * *

I have suggested four criteria of creativity: originality, the improbability of the combination, its constructive-destructive aspect, and the intervention of extra-conscious factors. There is no need to dwell further on those other factors which provide the counterweight, the necessary ballast for the creative adventure. Nor, I trust, is it necessary to stress the obvious fact that virtually everything I have said about the mentality of the scientist also applies *mutatis mutandis* to his stepbrother, the artist.

Let me switch for the last time from the individual scientist to science as a collective enterprise. The overall view of evolutionary and revolutionary cycles which I have suggested in two earlier works has certain affinities with the views which Thomas Kuhn has independently arrived at in his book, *The Structure of Scientific Revolutions,* where he calls the peaceful periods "normal science" and describes revolutions as "paradigm changes". This is an approach rather different from George Sarton's well-known theory which holds that the history of science is the only history which displays a cumulative progress of knowledge, and that accordingly the progress of science is the only yardstick by which we can measure the progress of mankind.

Perhaps so – provided that we realise that the line of progress is not a curve approaching its asymptote, but a zigzag line; and that the yardstick is a relativistic yardstick. This does not mean, of course, that science does not advance; only that it advances in an unpredictable, jerky, erratic way. I have compared the great conceptual syntheses of the last hundred years to a river delta. But each confluence is also followed by a fanning out of specialised branches, subdividing into capillaries of more and more esoteric character. To change the metaphor: increasing specialisation is like the branching out of arteries; the sequence of mergers is like the reverse confluence of veins. The cycle which results makes the evolution of ideas appear as a tale of ever-repeated differentiations, specialisations, and reintegrations on a higher level of the hierarchy – a progression from primordial unity, through variety, to more complex patterns of unity in variety.

References

1. Kuhn, T. (1962), *The Structure of Scientific Revolutions,* University of Chicago Press.
2. Polya, G. (1945), *How to Solve It,* Princeton University Press.
3. Koestler, A. (1964), *The Act of Creation,* Hutchinson.
4. Hadamard, J. (1949), *The Psychology of Invention in the Mathematical Field*, Princeton University Press.
5. Wallas, G. (1945), *The Art of Thought,* C. A. Watts & Co., London.
6. Planck, M. (1949), *Scientific Autobiography and Other Papers,* Philosophical Library, New York.
7. Polanyi, M. (1958), *Personal Knowledge,* Routledge & Kegan Paul.

TO
COVET A SWALLOW*

In the summer of 1960 I was travelling in Scandinavia and wrote an article for *The Observer* which ended as follows:†

> While sightseeing in Göteborg, I noticed a memorial tablet on a house overlooking the canal, which said that the Czech composer, Friedrich Smetana, had lived there (in 1860, if I remember rightly) while composing his symphonic poem, *The Moldava*. This stuck in my memory, because it is a well-known fact that the Israeli National Anthem is a variation on a theme in that symphony.
>
> I inquired what Smetana had been doing in Göteborg, and was told that he had been invited to conduct the orchestra of the Philharmonic Society, that he became interested in Swedish folk music, and stayed nearly ten years in the country. As for that famous theme in the Moldava Symphony, whose Slavonic melancholy captivated the hearts of Israel, it is the transposition from a major into a minor key of an old Swedish regional folksong, "Ach Wärmeland du sköna" – O you beautiful Wärmeland.
>
> Thus the Hebrew anthem praising the beauties of the river Jordan is derived from Smetana's symphony in praise of the River Moldava, which is derived from a Swedish song in praise of the province of Wärmeland, home of the Gösta Berling Saga. All of which goes to prove the smallness of this world, and its free trade in emotions.

This incidental piece of information had a curious aftermath. A gentleman attached to the embassy of the Czechoslovak People's Republic wrote an angry letter to *The*

* The last section in the original edition of *Drinkers of Infinity* is called "Polemics and Rejoinders". "To Covet a Swallow" is one of the items contained in that section.

† *The Observer*, 5 July 1960.

Observer, denying that Smetana adopted a foreign tune for the Moldava – which, he said, "is based, like so many of the themes of this most patriotic of all Czech composers, on the popular folk melodies sung by the Czech people".

Another correspondent, however (Mr Eric Conrad), arrived at the opposite conclusion. "The fact is," he wrote, "– and I have always thought it both a puzzling and an exciting one – that several nations in Europe share (in slightly varied forms) the simple little tune to which Smetana's melody and the Israeli anthem can easily be reduced. In England it is a favourite nursery rhyme ("Baa-baa Black Sheep"), in France it is also a nursery rhyme (*Ah vous dirai-je, Maman*). You will easily recognise that these tunes . . . form the skeleton on which Smetana's more elaborate tune is (no doubt unconsciously) built."

After this cosmopolitan broadside, the gentleman from the Czechoslovak People's Republic wrote a second letter to *The Observer*, remembering that there is "a well-known Czech nursery rhyme *Kočka leze dirou*, 'a cat crawls through a hole'," which Smetana knew, and "which is almost identical" with his theme.

Thoroughly bewildered by these disclosures about the Israeli Anthem's unsuspected origins, I appealed for expert advice. My prayers were answered by Thurston Dart, then of Cambridge University, whose conclusions outline, in a charming manner, the moral of this little episode (*The Observer,* 20 July 1960):

> A folk-tune is like a migrant bird; the fact that it is observed in a given place at a given time cannot be taken as proof that it originated there. A century ago Smetana may have encountered the beautiful theme of his symphony either in Göteborg or in Bohemia, but the folk-song ornithologist knows of its currency long before that.
>
> The theme was first written down soon after 1600, in a manuscript now in a private collection in Florence. There it is described as the song "Fuggi, fuggi", composed by Giuseppino. Though little is known about him, contemporary references show that he was a tenor singer. He belonged to the class of extemporising

musician-poets best represented today by the calypso singers of the West Indies, and his numerous villanelles in the Neapolitan style were immensely popular among all classes of society.

"Fuggi, fuggi" is one of these Neapolitan villanelles, and during the seventeenth century its flight may be traced over a great part of Europe. . . . "Baa-baa black Sheep" and *Ah vous dirai-ja, Maman* are boiled down, corrupted versions of the original tune.

It seems to me, therefore, that neither Sweden, Czechoslovakia, France, England nor Israel can have much right to claim Smetana's theme. To covet a folk-song is as silly and undignified as to covet a swallow, anyway, but the music historian's evidence should perhaps be heard. According to him, the tune was hatched in Italy, two centuries and more before Smetana was born; by the end of the seventeenth century it had flown over most international frontiers of its time, free and unchallenged.

PART TWO

THE HEEL OF ACHILLES
ESSAYS 1968–1973

THE URGE TO SELF-DESTRUCTION*

The crisis of our time can be summed up in a single sentence. From the dawn of consciousness until the middle of our century man had to live with the prospect of his death as an individual; since Hiroshima, mankind as a whole has to live with the prospect of its extinction as a biological species.

This is a radically new prospect; but though the novelty of it will wear off, the prospect will not; it has become a basic and permanent feature of the human condition.

There are periods of incubation before a new idea takes hold of the mind; the Copernican doctrine which so radically downgraded man's status in the universe took nearly a century until it got a hold on European consciousness. The new downgrading of our species to the status of mortality is even more difficult to digest.

But there are signs that in a devious, roundabout way the process of mental assimilation has already started. It is as if the explosions had produced a kind of psychoactive fallout, particularly in the younger generation, creating such bizarre phenomena as hippies, dropouts, flower people and barefoot crusaders without a cross. They seem to be products of a kind of mental radiation sickness which causes an intense and distressing experience of meaninglessness, of an existential vacuum which the traditional values of their elders are unable to fill.

These symptoms will probably wear off. Already the word

*Edited version of the Sonning Prize Acceptance Address to the University of Copenhagen, April 1968, and of a paper read at the Fourteenth Nobel Symposium, Stockholm, September 1969.

"Hiroshima" has become a historic cliché like the Boston Tea Party or the Storming of the Bastille. Sooner or later we shall return to a state of pseudo-normality. But there is no getting away from the fact that from now onward our species lives on borrowed time. It carries a time bomb fastened round its neck. We shall have to listen to the sound of its ticking, now louder, now softer, now louder again, for decades and centuries to come, until it either blows up, or we succeed in defusing it.

Our concern is with the possibility of such a defusing operation. Obviously it requires more than disarmament conferences and appeals to sweet reasonableness. They have always fallen on deaf ears, for the simple reason that man is perhaps a sweet, but certainly not a reasonable, being; nor are there any indications that he is in the process of becoming one. On the contrary, the evidence seems to indicate that at some point during the last explosive stages of the biological evolution of *homo sapiens* something has gone wrong; that there is a flaw, some subtle engineering mistake built into our native equipment which would account for the paranoid streak running through our history. This seems to me an unpleasant but plausible hypothesis, which I have developed at some length in a recent book (1). Evolution has made countless mistakes; Sir Julian Huxley compared it to a maze with an enormous number of blind alleys. For every existing species hundreds must have perished in the past; the fossil record is a wastebasket of the Chief Designer's discarded models. To the biologist, it should appear by no means unlikely that *homo sapiens*, too, is the victim of some minute error in construction – perhaps in the circuitry of his nervous system – which makes him prone to delusions, and urges him towards self-destruction. But *homo sapiens* has also the unique resourcefulness to transcend biological evolution and to compensate for the shortcomings of his native equipment. He may even have the power to cure that congenitally disordered mental condition which played havoc with his past and now threatens him with extinction. Or, if he cannot cure it, at least to render it harmless.

The first step towards a possible therapy is a correct

diagnosis. There have been countless diagnostic attempts, from the Hebrew prophets to contemporary ethologists, but none of them sounded very convincing, because none of them started from the premise that man is an aberrant species, suffering from a biological malfunction, a species-specific disorder of behaviour which sets it apart from all other animal species – just as language, science and art set it apart in a positive sense. The creativity and the pathology of man are two sides of the same medal, coined in the same evolutionary mint. I am going to propose a short list of some of the pathological symptoms reflected in the perverse history of our species, and then pass from the symptoms to the presumed causative factors. The list of symptoms has five main headings.

First, at the very beginning of our history, we find a striking phenomenon to which anthropologists seem to have paid too little attention: human sacrifice. It was a ubiquitous ritual which persisted from the prehistoric dawn to the peak of pre-Columbian civilisations, and in some parts of the world to the beginning of our century. From the Scandinavian Bog People to the South Sea Islanders, from the Etruscans to the pre-Columbian cultures, these practices arose independently in the most varied civilisations, as manifestations of a perverted logic to which the whole species was apparently prone. It is epitomised in one of the early chapters of Genesis, where Abraham prepares to cut the throat of his son for the love of God. Instead of dismissing the subject as a sinister curiosity of the past, the universality and paranoid character of the ritual should be regarded as symptomatic.

The *second* symptom to be noted is the weakness of the inhibitory forces against the killing of con-specifics, which is virtually unique in the animal kingdom. As Konrad Lorenz (2) has recently emphasised, the predator's act of killing the prey should not be compared to murder, and not even be called aggressive, because predator and prey always belong to different species – a hawk killing a fieldmouse can hardly be accused of homicide. Competition and conflict between members of the same animal species are settled by ritualised combat or symbolic threat-behaviour which ends with the flight or surrender gesture of one of the combatants, and hardly ever involves lethal injury. In man, however, this built-in inhibitory mechanism against the killing of con-specifics is notably ineffective.

This leads to the *third* symptom: intraspecific warfare in permanence, with its subvarieties of mass persecution and genocide. The popular confusion between predatory and bellicose behaviour tends to obscure the fact that the law of the jungle permits predation on other species, but forbids war within one's own; and that *homo sapiens* is the unique offender against this law (apart from some controversial warlike phenomena among rats and ants).

As the *fourth* symptom I would list the permanent, quasi-schizophrenic split between reason and emotion, between man's critical faculties and his irrational, affect-charged beliefs; I shall return to this point.

Lastly, there is the striking, symptomatic disparity between the growth curves of technological achievement on the one hand and of ethical behaviour on the other; or, to put it differently, between the powers of the intellect when applied to mastering the environment, and its impotence when applied to the conduct of human affairs. In the sixth century BC the Greeks embarked on the scientific adventure which, a few months ago, landed us on the moon. That surely is an impressive growth curve. But the sixth century BC also saw the birth of Taoism, Confucianism and Buddhism; the twentieth of Stalinism, Hitlerism and Maoism. There is no discernible curve. We can control the motions of our antificial satellites orbiting distant planets but cannot control the situation in Northern Ireland. Prometheus is reaching out for the stars with an empty grin on his face and a totem symbol in his hand.

So far we have moved in the realm of facts. When we turn from *symptoms* to *causes*, we must have recourse to more or less speculative hypotheses. I shall mention five such hypotheses, which are interrelated, but pertain to different disciplines, namely, neurophysiology, anthropology, psychology, linguistics, and lastly eschatology.

The neurophysiological hypothesis is derived from the so-called Papez – MacLean theory of emotions supported by some twenty years of experimental research. The theory is based on the structural and functional differences between the phylogenetically old and recent parts in the human brain which, when not in acute conflict, seem to lead a kind of agonised coexistence. Dr MacLean has summed up this state of affairs in a technical paper, but in an unusually picturesque way:

> Man finds himself in the predicament that nature has endowed him essentially with three brains which, despite great differences in structure, must function together and communicate with one another. The oldest of these brains is basically reptilian. The second has been inherited from lower mammals, and the third is a late mammalian development, which . . . has made man peculiarly man. Speaking allegorically of these brains within a brain, we might imagine that when the psychiatrist bids the patient to lie on the couch, he is asking him to stretch out alongisde a horse and a crocodile (3).

Substitute for the individual patient humanity at large, for the clinical couch the stage of history, and you get a dramatised, but essentially truthful, picture. The reptilian and primitive mammalian brain together form the so-called limbic system which, for simplicity's sake, we may call the old brain, as opposed to the neocortex, the specifically human "thinking cap" which contains the areas responsible for language, and abstract and symbolic thought. The neocortex of the hominids evolved in the last half million years, from the middle Pleistocene onward, at an explosive speed, which as far was we know is unprecedented in the history of evolution. This brain explosion in the second half of the Pleistocene seems to have followed the type of exponential curve which has recently become so familiar to us – population explosion, knowledge explosion, etc. – and there may be more than a superficial analogy here, as both curves reflect the phenomenon of the acceleration of history on different levels. But explosions do not produce harmonious results. The result in this particular case seems to have been that the newly developing structures did not become properly integrated with the phylogenetically older ones – an evolutionary blunder which provided rich opportunities for conflct. MacLean coined the term *schizophysiology* for this precarious state of affairs in our nervous system. He defines it as

> a dichotomy in the function of the phylogenetically old and new cortex that might account for differences between emotional and intellectual behaviour. While our *intellectual* functions are carried on in the newest and most highly developed part of the brain, our *affective* behaviour continues to be dominated by a relatively crude and primitive system, by archaic structures in the brain whose fundamental pattern has undergone but little change in the whole course of evolution, from mouse to man (4).

To put it crudely: evolution has left a few screws loose somewhere between the neocortex and the hypothalamus. The hypothesis that this form of schizophysiology is built into our species could go a long way to explain symptoms Nos. 4 and 5. The delusional streak in our history, the prevalence of passionately held irrational beliefs, would at last become comprehensible and could be expressed in physiological terms. And any condition which can be expressed in physiological terms should ultimately be accessible to remedies.

My next two putative causes of man's predicament are the state of protracted dependence of the human infant on its parents, and the dependence of the earliest carnivorous hominids on the support of their hunting companions against prey faster and more powerful than themselves; a mutual dependence much stronger than that among other primate groups, out of which may have developed tribal solidarity and its later nefarious derivatives. Both factors may have contributed to the process of moulding man into the loyal, affectionate and sociable creature which he is; the trouble is that they did it only too well and overshot the mark. The bonds forged by early helplessness and mutual dependence developed into various forms of bondsmanship within the family, clan or tribe. The helplessness of the human infant leaves its lifelong mark; it may be partly responsible for man's ready submission to authority wielded by individuals or groups, his quasi-hypnotic suggestibility by doctrines and commandments, his overwhelming urge to belong, to identify himself with tribe or nation, and, above all, with its system of beliefs. Brain-washing starts in the cradle. (Konrad Lorenz uses the analogy of imprinting, and puts the critical age of receptivity just after puberty. But there are two limitations to this analogy: the susceptibility for imprinting stretches in man from the cradle to the grave; and what he is imprinted with are mostly symbols.)

Now, historically speaking, for the vast majority of mankind, the belief system which they accepted, for which they were prepared to live or die, was not of their own choice, but imposed on them by the hazards of the social environment, just as their tribal or ethnic identity was determined by the hazards of birth. Critical reasoning played, if any, only a subordinate part in the process of accepting the imprint of a credo. If the tenets of the credo were too offensive to the critical faculties, schizophysiology provided the *modus vivendi* which permitted the hostile forces of faith and reason to coexist in a universe of doublethink – to use Orwell's term.

Thus one of the central features of the human predicament is this overwhelming capacity and need for *identification* with a social group and/or a system of beliefs, which is indifferent to reason, indifferent to self-interest and even to the claims of self-preservation. Extreme manifestations of this *self-transcending tendency* – as one might call it – are the hypnotic rapport, a variety of trancelike or ecstatic states, the phenomena of individual and collective suggestibility which dominate life in primitive and not so primitive societies, culminating in mass hysteria in its overt and latent forms. One need not march in a crowd to become a victim of crowd mentality – the true believer is its captive all the time.

We are thus driven to the unfashionable and uncomfortable conclusion that the trouble with our species is not an overdose of self-asserting *aggression*, but an excess of self-transcending *devotion*. Even a cursory glance at history should convince one that individual crimes committed for selfish motives play a quite insignificant role in the human tragedy compared with the numbers massacred in unselfish love of one's tribe, nation, dynasty, church or ideology. The emphasis is on unselfish. Excepting a small minority of mercenary or sadistic disposition, wars are not fought for personal gain, but out of loyalty and devotion to king, country or cause.

Homicide committed for personal reasons is a statistical rarity in all cultures, including our own. Homicide for *un*-selfish reasons, at the risk of one's own life, is the dominant phenomenon in history. Even the members of the Mafia feel compelled to rationalise their motives into an ideology, the Cosa Nostra, "our cause".

The theory that wars are caused by pent-up aggressive drives which can find no other outlet has no foundation either in history or in psychology. Anybody who has served in the ranks of an army can testify that aggressive feelings towards the so-called enemy hardly play a part in the dreary routine of waging war: boredom and discomfort, not hatred; homesickness, sex starvation and longing for peace dominate the mind of the anonymous soldier. The invisible enemy is not an individual on whom aggression could focus; he is not a person but an abstract entity, a common denominator, a collective portrait. Soldiers fight the invisible, impersonal enemy either because they have no other choice, or out of loyalty to king and country, the true religion, the righteous cause. They are motivated not by aggression, but by *devotion*.

I am equally unconvinced by the fashionable theory that the phylogenetic origin of war is to be found in the so-called territorial imperative. The wars of man, with rare exceptions, were not fought for individual ownership of bits of space. The man who goes to war actually *leaves* the home which he is supposed to defend, and engages in combat hundreds or thousands of miles away from it; and what makes him fight is not the biological urge to defend his personal acreage of farmland or meadows, but – to say it once more – his loyalty to symbols and slogans derived from tribal lore, divine commandments or political ideologies. Wars are fought for words. They are motivated not by aggression, but by love.

We have seen on the screen the radiant love of the Führer on the faces of Hitler Youth. We have seen the same expression on the faces of little Chinese boys reciting the words of the Chairman. They are transfixed with love like monks in ecstasy on religious paintings. The sound of the nation's anthem, the sight of its proud flag, makes you feel part of a wonderfully loving community.

Thus, in opposition to Lorenz, Ardrey and their followers, I would suggest that the trouble with our species is not an excess of aggression, but an excess of devotion. The fanatic is prepared to lay down his life for the object of his worship as the lover is prepared to die for his idol. But he is equally prepared to kill anybody who represents a supposed threat to that idol. Here we come to a point of central importance.

You watch a film version of the Moor of Venice. You fall in love with Desdemona and identify yourself with Othello (or the other way round); as a result the perfidious Iago makes your blood boil. Yet the psychological process which causes the boiling is quite different from facing a real opponent. You know that the people on the screen are merely actors or rather electronic projections – and anyway the whole situation is no personal concern of yours. The adrenaline in your bloodstream is not produced by a primary biological drive or hypothetical killer-instinct. Your hostility to Iago is a *vicarious* kind of aggressivity, devoid of self-interest and derived from a previous process of empathy and identification. This act of identification must come first; it is the trigger or catalyst of your hatred of Iago. In the same way, the savagery unleashed in primitive forms of warfare is also triggered by a previous act of identification with a social group, its rousing symbols and system of beliefs. It is a depersonalised, quite unselfish kind of savagery, generated by the group mind, *which is largely indifferent, or even opposed, to the interests of the individuals who constitute the group.* Identification with the group always involves a sacrifice of the individual's critical faculties, and an enhancement of his emotional potential by a kind of group resonance or positive feedback. Thus the mentality of the group is not the sum of individual minds; it has its own pattern and obeys its own rules which cannot be "reduced" to the rules which govern individual behaviour. The individual is not a killer; the group is, and by identifying with it the individual is transformed into a killer. This is the infernal dialectics reflected in our history. The egotism of the group feeds on the altruism of its members; the savagery of the group feeds on the devotion of its members.

All this points to the conclusion that the predicament of man is not caused by the aggressivity of the individual, but by the dialectics of group formation; by man's irresistible urge to identify with the group and espouse its beliefs enthusiastically and uncritically. He has a peculiar capacity – and need – to become emotionally committed to beliefs which are impervious to reasoning, indifferent to self-interest and to the claims of self-preservation. Waddington has called man a belief-accepting animal. He is as susceptible to being imprinted with slogans and symbols as he is to infectious diseases. Thus one of the main pathogenic factors is *hyperdependence* combined with *suggestibility*. If science could find a way to make us immune against suggestibility, half the battle for survival would be won. And this does not seem to be an impossible target.

The next item in this inventory of the possible causes of man's predicament is *language*. Let me repeat: wars are fought for words. They are man's most deadly weapon. The words of Adolf Hitler were more effective agents of destruction than thermonuclear bombs. Long before the printing press and the other mass media were invented, the fervent words of the prophet Mohammed released an emotive chain reaction, whose blast shook the world from Central Asia to the Atlantic coast. Without words there would be no poetry – and no war. Language is the main source of our superiority over brother animal – and, in view of its explosive potentials, the main threat to our survival.

Recent field studies of Japanese monkeys have revealed that different tribes of a species may develop surprisingly different habits – one might almost say, different cultures. Some tribes have taken to washing bananas in the river before eating them, others have not. Sometimes migrating groups of banana-washers meet non-washers, and the two groups watch each other's strange behaviour with apparent bewilderment. But unlike the inhabitants of Lilliput, who fought holy crusades over the question whether eggs should be broken on the broad or pointed end, the banana-washing monkeys do not go to war with the non-washers, because the poor creatures have no language which would enable them to declare washing a divine commandment and eating unwashed bananas a deadly heresy.

Obviously, the safest remedy for our ills would be to abolish language. But as a matter of fact, mankind did renounce language long ago – if by language we mean a universal means of communication for the whole species. Other species do possess a single system of communication by sign, sound or odour, which is understood by all its members. Dolphins travel a lot, but when two strangers meet in the ocean they need no interpreter. The Tower of Babel has remained a valid symbol. According to Margaret Mead, among the two million Aborigines in New Guinea, 750 different languages are spoken in 750 villages, which are at permanent war with one another. Our shrinking planet is split into several thousand language groups. Each language acts as a powerful cohesive force within the group and as an equally powerful divisive force between groups. Fleming detests Walloon, Maharati hates Gujerati, French Canadian despises Anglo-Saxon, differences in accent mark the boundary between the upper and lower classes within the same nation.

Thus language appears to be one of the main reasons, perhaps *the* main reason, why the disruptive forces have always been stronger than the cohesive forces in our species. One might even ask whether the term "species" is applicable to man. I have mentioned that Lorenz attributed great importance to the instinct taboo among animals against the killing of members of their own species; yet it may be argued that Greeks killing Barbarians, Moors killing Christian dogs did not perceive their victims as members of their own species. Aristotle expressly stated that "the slave is totally devoid of any faculty of reasoning"; the term "bar-bar-ous" is imitative of the alien's gibberish or the barking of a dog; honest Nazis believed that Jews were *Untermenschen* – not human but hominid. Men show a much greater variety in physique and behaviour than any animal species (except for the domesticated products of selective breeding); and language, instead of counteracting intraspecific tensions and fratricidal tendencies, enhances their virulence. It is a grotesque paradox that we have communication satellites which can make a message visible and audible over the whole planet, but no planetwide language to make it also understandable. It seems even more odd that, except for a few stalwart Esperantists, neither Unesco nor any other international body has made a serious effort to promote a universal lingua franca – as the dolphins have.

The fifth and last pathogenic factor on my list is man's awareness of his mortality, the *discovery of death*. But one should rather say: its discovery by the intellect, and its rejection by instinct and emotion. We may assume that the inevitability of death was discovered, through inductive inference, by that newly acquired thinking cap, the human neocortex; but the old brain won't have any of it; emotion rebels against the idea of personal nonexistence. This simultaneous acceptance and refusal of death reflects perhaps the deepest split in man's split mind; it saturated the air with ghosts and demons, invisible presences which at best were inscrutable, but mostly malevolent, and had to be appeased by human sacrifice, by holy wars and the burning of heretics. The paranoid delusions of eternal hellfire are still with us. Paradise was always an exclusive club, while the gates of hell were open to all.

Yet once more we have to look at both sides of the medal: on one side religious art, architecture and music in the cathedral; on the other, the paranoid delusions of eternal hellfire, the tortures of the living and the dead.

To sum up, I have listed five conspicuous symptoms of the pathology of man as reflected in the terrible mess we have made, and continue to make, of our history. I have mentioned the ubiquitous rites of human sacrifice in the prehistoric dawn; the poverty of instinct-inhibition against the killing of conspecifics; intraspecific warfare in permanence; the schizoid split between rational thinking and irrational beliefs; and lastly the contrast between man's genius in mastering the environment and his moronic conduct of human affairs.

It should be noted that each and all of these pathological phenomena are species-specific, that they are uniquely human, not found in any other animal species. It is only logical therefore that in the search of explanations we should also concentrate our attention on those characteristics of man which are exclusively human and not shared by other animals. Speaking in all humility, it seems to me of doubtful value to attempt a diagnosis of man entirely based on analogies with animal behaviour – Pavlov's dogs, Skinner's rats, Lorenz's greylag geese, Morris's hairless apes. Such analogies are valid and useful as far as they go. But by the nature of things they cannot go far enough, because they stop short of those exclusively human characteristics – such as language – which are of necessity excluded from the analogy, although they are of decisive importance in determining the behaviour of our species. There is no human arrogance involved in saying that dogs, rats, birds and apes do not have a neocortex which has evolved too fast for the good of its possessor; that they do not share the protracted helplessness of the human infant, nor the strong mutual dependence and esprit de corps of the ancestral hunters; nor the dangerous privilege of using words to coin battle cries; nor the inductive powers which make men frightened to death by death. These characteristics, which I have mentioned as possible causative factors of the human predicament, are all specifically and exclusively human. They contribute to the uniqueness of man and the uniqueness of his tragedy. They combine in the double helix of guilt and anxiety which, like the genetic code, seems to be built into the human condition. They give indeed ample cause for anxiety regarding our future; but then, another unique gift of man is the power to make his anxiety work for him. He may even manage to defuse the time bomb around his neck, once he has understood the causes which make it tick. Biological evolution seems to have come to a standstill since the days of Cro-Magnon man; as we cannot expect in the foreseeable future a beneficial mutation to put things right, our only hope seems to be to supplant biological evolution by new, as yet undreamed-of techniques. In my more optimistic moments my split brain suggests that this possibility may not be beyond our reach.

References

1. *The Ghost in the Machine* (London and New York, 1968).
2. K. Lorenz, *On Aggression* (London and New York, 1966).
3. *Journal of Nervous and Mental Diseases*, vol. 135, no. 4, October 1962.
4. *American Journal of Medicine*, vol. 25, no. 4, October 1958.

REBELLION IN A VACUUM★

Hoping to discover at long last what the verb "to educate" means, I turned the other day to the *Concise Oxford Dictionary* and was amused to find this definition: "Give intellectual and moral training to." And further down to drive the nail home: "Train (person) . . . train (animals)." I would not be surprised to see, when the next rioting season starts, a bonfire of Oxford dictionaries; and that definition, with its Pavlovian echoes, certainly deserves no better. But I am doubtful whether much would be gained by replacing the offensive term "training" by "guidance". That sounds nice and smarmy, but it begs the question. Guiding, by whatever discreet methods, always implies asserting one's mental powers over another person's mind – in the present context, a younger person's. And the ethics of this procedure, which not so long ago we took for granted, is becoming more and more problematical.

My own preference is for defining the purpose of education as "catalysing the mind". To influence is to intrude; a catalyst, on the other hand, is defined as an agent that triggers or speeds up a chemical reaction without being involved in the product. If I may utter a truism, the ideal educator acts as a catalyst, not as a conditioning influence. Conditioning or, to use Skinner's term, "social engineering through the control of behaviour", is an excellent method for training samurais, but applied on the campus, it has two opposite dangers. It may lead to a kind of experimental neurosis in the subjects, expressed by violent

★Edited version of a paper read at the symposium "The University and the Ethics of Change" at Queen's University, Kingston, Canada, November 1968. First published in the *Political Quarterly*, October – December 1969.

rejection of any control or influence by authority. On the other hand, it can be too successful, and create the phenomena of conformism, with a broad spectrum ranging from a society of placid yes-men manipulated by the mass media to the totalitarian state controlled by the Thoughts of Chairman Mao.

The alternative to conditioning is catalysing the mind's development. I can best explain what is meant by quoting a passage from a book I wrote some years ago on creativity in science and art.

> To enable the student to derive pleasure from the art of scientific discovery, as from other forms of art, he should be made to re-live, to some extent, the creative process. In other words, he must be induced, with proper aid and guidance, to make some of the fundamental discoveries of science by himself, to experience in his own mind some of those flashes of insight which have lighted its path. This means that the history of science ought to be made an essential part of the curriculum, that science should be represented in its evolutionary context – not as a Minerva born fully armed. It further means that the paradoxes, the "blocked problems" which confronted Archimedes, Copernicus, Galileo, Newton, Harvey, Darwin, should be reconstructed in their historical setting and presented in the form of riddles – with appropriate hints – to eager young minds. The most productive form of learning is problem-solving. The traditional method of confronting the student, not with the problem but with the finished solution, means to deprive him of all excitement, to shut off the creative impulse, to reduce the adventure of mankind to a dusty heap of theorems.
>
> Art is a form of communication which aims at eliciting a re-creative echo. Education should be regarded as an art, and use the appropriate techniques to call forth that echo – the "re-creation". The novice, who has gone through some of the main stages in the evolution of the species during his embryonic development, through the evolution from savage to civilised society by the time he reaches adolescence, should then be made to continue his curriculum by recapitulating some of the decisive episodes, impasses, and turning-points on the road to the conquest of knowledge. Much in our textbooks and methods of teaching reflects a static, pre-evolutionary concept of the world. For man cannot inherit the past; he has to re-create it (1).

This is what I meant by education as a catalysing process.

But now comes the rub. Assuming we agree that the ideal method of teaching science is to enable the student to rediscover Newton's Laws of Motion more or less by himself – can the same method be applied to the teaching of ethics, of moral values? The first answer that comes to mind is that ethics is not a discipline in the normal curriculum, except if you specialise in philosophy or theology. But that is a rash answer, because implicitly, if not explicitly, we impart ethical principles and value judgments in whatever we teach or write on whatever subject. The greatest superstition of our time is the belief in the ethical neutrality of science. Even the slogan of ethical neutrality itself implies a program and a credo.

No writer or teacher or artist can escape the responsibility of influencing others, whether he intends to or not, whether he is conscious of it or not. And this influence is not confined to his explicit message; it is the more powerful and the more insidious because much of it is transmitted implicitly, as a hidden persuader, and the recipient absorbs it unawares. Surely physics is an ethically neutral science? Yet Einstein rejected the trend in modern physics to replace causality by statistics with his famous dictum: "I refuse to believe that God plays dice with the world." He was more honest than other physicists in admitting his metaphysical bias; and it is precisely this metaphysical bias, implied in a scientific hypothesis, which exerts its unconscious influence on others. The Roman Church was ill advised when she opposed Galileo and Darwin and from a rational point of view was lagging behind the times; but intuitively she was ahead of the times in realising the impact which the new cosmology and the theory of evolution were to have on man's image of himself and his place in the universe.

Wolfgang Köhler, one of the greatest psychologists of our time, searched all his life for "the place of value in a world of facts" – the title of the book in which he summed up his personal philosophy. But there is no need to search for such a place because the values are diffused through all the strata of the various sciences, as the invisible bubbles of air are diffused in the waters of a lake, and we are the fish who breathe them in all the time through the gills of intuition. Our educational establishment, from the departments of physics through biology and genetics, up to the behavioural and social sciences, willy-nilly imparts to the students a *Weltanschauung*, a system of values wrapped up in a package of facts. But the choice and shape of the package are determined by its invisible content; or, to change the metaphor, our implicit values provide the non-Euclidian curvature, the subtle distortions of the world of facts.

Now when I use the term "our educational establishment", you may object that there is no such thing. Every country, every university and every faculty therein has of course its individual character, its personal face – or facelessness. Nevertheless, taking diversity for granted, and exceptions for granted, there exist certain common denominators which determine the cultural climate and the metaphysical bias imparted to hopeful students practically everywhere in the nontotalitarian sector of the world, from California to the East Coast, from London to Berlin, Bombay and Tokyo. That climate is impossible to define without oversimplification, so I shall oversimplify deliberately and say that it is dominated by three Rs.

The first R stands for reductionism. Its philosophy may be epitomised by a quotation from a recent book in which man is defined, in all seriousness, as "nothing but a complex biochemical mechanism, powered by a combustion system which energises computers with prodigious storage facilities for retaining encoded information." This is certainly an extreme formulation, but it conveys the essence of that philosophy.

It is, of course, perfectly legitimate to draw analogies between the central nervous system and a telephone exchange, or a computer, or a holograph. The reductionist heresy is contained in the words "nothing but". If you replace in the sentence I have just quoted the words "nothing but" by "to some extent" or "from a certain angle" or "on a certain level of his many-levelled structure", then everything is all right. The reductionist proclaims his part truth to be the whole truth, a certain specific aspect of a phenomenon to be the whole phenomenon. To the behaviourist, the activities of man are *nothing but* a chain of conditioned responses; to the more rigid variety of Freudian, artistic creation is nothing but a substitute for goal-inhibited sexuality; to the mechanically oriented biologist, the phenomena of consciousness are nothing but electrochemical reactions. And the ultimate reductionist heresy is to consider the whole as nothing but the sum of its parts – a hangover from the crude atomistic concept of nineteenth-century physics, which the physicist himself abandoned long ago.

The second of the three Rs is what I have called elsewhere the philosophy of ratomorphism. At the turn of the century, Lloyd Morgan's famous canon warned biologists against the fallacy of projecting human thoughts and feelings into animals; since then, the pendulum has moved in the opposite direction, so that today, instead of an anthropomorphic view of the rat, we have a ratomorphic view of man. According to this view, our skyscrapers are nothing but huge Skinner boxes in which, instead of pressing a pedal to obtain a food pellet, we emit operant responses which are more complicated, but governed by the same laws as the behaviour of the rat. Again, if you erase the "nothing but", there is an ugly grain of truth in this. But if the life of man is becoming a rat race, it is because he has become impregnated with a ratomorphic philosophy. One is reminded of that old quip: "Psychoanalysis is the disease which it pretends to cure." Keep telling a man that he is nothing but an oversized rat, and he will start growing whiskers and bite your finger.

Some fifty years ago, in the heyday of the conditioned reflex, the paradigm of human behaviour was Pavlov's dog salivating in its restraining harness on the laboratory table. After that came the rat in the box. And after the rat came the geese. In his recent book *On Aggression*, Konrad Lorenz advances the theory that affection between social animals is phylogenetically derived from aggression. The bond which holds the partners together (regardless of whether it has a sexual component or not) is "neither more nor less than the conversion of aggression into its opposite". Whether one agrees or disagrees with this theory is irrelevant; the reason why I mention it is that Lorenz's arguments are almost exclusively based on his observations of the so-called triumph ceremony of the greylag goose, which, in his own words, prompted him to write his book. Once more we are offered a *Weltanschauung* derived from an exceedingly specialised type of observations, a part truth which claims to be the whole truth. To quote the Austrian psychiatrist Viktor Frankl: "The trouble is not that scientists are specialising, but rather that specialists are generalising."

To avoid misunderstandings, let me emphasise once more that it is both legitimate and necessary for scientific research to investigate conditioned reflexes in dogs, operant responses in rats and the ritual dances of geese – so long as they are not forced upon us as paradigms for man's condition. But this is precisely what has been happening for the best part of our middle-aged century.

My third R is randomness. Biological evolution is considered to be nothing but random mutations preserved by natural selection; mental evolution nothing but random tries preserved by reinforcement. To quote from a textbook by a leading evolutionist: "It does seem that the problem of evolution is essentially solved. . . . It turns out to be basically materialistic, with no sign of purpose. . . . Man is the result of a purposeless and materialistic process . . ." (2). To paraphrase Einstein, a nonexistent God playing blind dice with the universe. Even physical causality, the solid rock on which that universe was built, has been replaced by the driftsands of statistics. We all seem to be in the condition which the physicist calls "Brownian movement" – the erratic zigzag motions of a particle of smoke buffeted about by the molecules of the surrounding air.

Some schools of modern art, too, have adopted the cult of randomness. Action painters throw at random fistfuls of paint at the canvas; a French sculptor achieved international fame by bashing old motorcars with a demolition machine into random shapes; others assemble bits of scrap iron into abstract compositions, or bits of fluff and tinsel into collages; some composers of electronic music use randomising machines for their effects. One fashionable novelist boasts of cutting up his typescript with a pair of scissors and sticking it together again in random fashion.

These schools of contemporary art seem to derive their inspiration from the prevalent bias in the sciences of life – a kind of secondary infection. Randomness, we are told, is the basic fact of life. We live in a world crammed full with hard facts, and there is no place in it for purpose, values or meaning. To look for values and meaning is considered as absurd as it would be for an astronomer to search with his telescope for Dante's heavenly paradise. And it would be equally absurd to search with a microscope for that ghost in the machine, the conscious mind, with its ghostly attributes of free choice and moral responsibility.

Let us remind ourselves once more that the essence of teaching is not in the facts and data which it conveys, but in the interpretations that it transmits in explicit or implied ways. In terms of modern communication theory, the bulk of the information consists of interpretations. That is the core of the package: the data provide only the wrappings. But the recurrent, embittered controversies in the history of science prove over and over again that the same data can be interpreted in different ways and reshuffled into different patterns. A minute ago, I quoted a distinguished biologist of the orthodox neo-Darwinian school. Let me now quote another eminent biologist, C. H. Waddington, who, based on exactly the same available data, arrives at the opposite view: "To suppose that the evolution of the wonderfully adapted biological mechanisms has depended only on a selection out of a haphazard set of variations, each produced by blind chance, is like suggesting that if we went on throwing bricks into heaps, we should eventually be able to choose ourselves the most desirable house" (3).

One could go on quoting such diametrically opposed conclusions drawn by different scientists from the same body of data. For example, one could hardly expect neurophysiologists to belittle the importance of brain mechanisms in mental life, and many of them do indeed hold that mental life is nothing but brain mechanism. And yet Sherrington was an unashamed dualist; he wrote: "That our being should consist of *two* fundamental elements offers, I suppose, no greater inherent improbability than that it should rest on one only." And the great Canadian brain surgeon, Wilder Penfield, said at an interdisciplinary symposium on control of the mind at which we both participated: "To declare that these two things [brain and mind] are one does not make them so, but it does block the progress of research."

I quote this, not because I am a Cartesian dualist – which I am not – but to emphasise that the neurophysiologist's precise data can be interpreted in diverse ways. In other words, it is not true that the data which science provides must automatically lead to the conclusion that life is meaningless, nothing but Brownian motion imparted by the random drift of cosmic weather. We should rather say that the *Zeitgeist* has a tendency to draw biased philosophical conclusions from the data, a tendency towards the devalution of values and the elimination of meaning from the world around us and the world inside us. The result is an existential vacuum.

At this point I would like to quote again Viktor Frankl, founder of what has become known as the Third Viennese School of Psychiatry. He postulates that besides Freud's pleasure principle and Adler's will to power there exists a "will to meaning" as an equally fundamental human drive:

> It is an inherent tendency in man to reach out for meanings to fulfill and for values to actualise. In contrast to animals, man is not told by his instincts what he must do. And in contrast to man in former times, he is no longer told by his traditions and values what he ought to do. . . . Thousands and thousands of young students are exposed to an indoctrination along the lines of a reductionist concept of life which denies the existence of values. The result is a worldwide phenomenon – more and more patients are crowding our clinics with the complaint of an inner emptiness, the sense of a total and ultimate meaninglessness of life (4).

Frankl calls this type of neurosis "noogenic", as distinct from sexual and other types of neuroses, and he claims that about 20 per cent of all cases at the Vienna Psychiatry Clinic (of which he is the head) are of noogenic origin. He further claims that this figure is doubled among student patients of Central European orgin, and that it soars to 80 per cent among students in the United States.

I should mention that I know next to nothing about the therapeutic methods of this school – it is called logotherapy – and that I have no means of judging its efficacy. But there exists a considerable literature on the subject, and I brought it up because the philosophy behind it seems to me relevant to our theme. However that may be, the term "existential vacuum", caused by the frustration of the "will to meaning", seems to be a fitting description of the worldwide mood of infectious restlessness, particularly among the young and among intellectuals.

It may be of some interest to compare this mood with that of the Pink Decade, the 1930s, when the Western world was convulsed by economic depression, unemployment and hunger marches, and the so-called Great Socialist Experiment initiated by the Russian Revolution seemed to be the only hopeful ideal to a great mass of youthful idealists, including myself. In *The God That Failed* (5), I wrote about that period:

> Devotion to pure Utopia and rebellion against a polluted society are the two poles which provide the tension of all militant creeds. To ask which of the two makes the current flow – attraction by the ideal or repulsion by the social environment – is to ask the old question whether the hen was first, or the egg.

Compare this with the present mood. Today the repellent forces are more powerful than ever, but the attraction of the ideal is missing, since what we thought to be Utopia turned out to be a cynical fraud. The egg is there, but no hen to hatch it. Rebellion is freewheeling in a vacuum.

Another comparison comes to mind – another historic situation, in which the traditional values of a culture were destroyed, without new values taking their place. I mean the fatal impact of the European conquerors on the native civilisations of American Indians and Pacific Islanders. In our case, the shattering impact was not caused by the greed, rapacity and missionary zeal of foreign invaders. The invasion has come from within, in the guise of an ideology which claims to be scientific and is in fact a new version of Nihilism in its denial of values, purpose and meaning. But the results in both cases are comparable: like the natives who were left without traditions and beliefs in a spiritual vacuum, we, too, seem to wander about in a bemused trance.

It is, of course, true that similar negative moods can be found in past periods of our history, variously described as *mal de siècle*, romantic despair, Russian Nihilism, apocalyptic expectations. And there have been Ranters, messianic sects and tarantula dancers, all of whom have their striking contemporary parallels. But the present has a unique and unprecedented urgency because the rate of change is now moving along an ever steeper exponential curve, and history is accelerating like the molecules in a liquid coming to the boil. There is no need to evoke the population explosion, urban explosion and explosion of explosive power; we live in their midst, in the eye of the hurricane.

This brings me back to my starting point. The ideal of the educator as a catalysing agent is for the time being unattainable. Exceptions always granted, he has been a conditioning influence, and the conditions he created amount to an explosive vacuum.

I do not believe that the crisis in education can be solved by the educators. They are themselves products of that *Zeitgeist* which brought on the crisis. All our laudable efforts to reform the universities can at best produce palliatives and symptom therapy. I think that in a confused way the rebellious students are aware of this, and that this is why they are so helpless when asked for constructive proposals, and why no proposed reform can satisfy their ravenous appetites. They are, simply, hungry for meaning, which their teachers cannot provide. They feel that all their teachers can do is to produce rabbits out of empty hats. Up to a point the rebels have succeeded in imparting this awareness to society at large; and that, regardless of the grotesque methods employed, seems to me a wholesome achievement.

References

1. *The Act of Creation* (London, 1964), pp. 265 et seq.
2. G. G. Simpson, *The Meaning of Evolution* (New Haven, Conn., 1949).
3. In the *Listener*, 13 November 1952.
4. In *Beyond Reductionism: the Alpbach Symposium*, ed. A. Koestler and J. R. Smythies (London, 1968).
5. Ed. R. H. S. Crossman (London, 1950).

CAN PSYCHIATRISTS BE TRUSTED?*

There are facts so obvious that one tends to overlook them. One of these facts is that the practice of medicine pre-dates the systematic study of physiology, and the practice of psychiatry pre-dates the study of psychology. If we look back at the past, the physician appears as a figure levitating in mid-air, like an Indian yogi, without any solid ground under his feet. The psychiatrist found himself in the same embarrassing situation, floating, as it were, on his fallible intuitions. At the somatic end of the psychosomatic spectrum – call it the infra-red end – the situation has been rapidly improving since biology started turning into an exact science; about infectious diseases at least we can do wonders. But at the ultra-violet end, where the psychiatric profession is operating, no comparable development is as yet in sight: academic psychology has failed to provide a solid foundation on which the levitating psychiatrist could rest his feet. He is faced with the responsibility of treating disorders of the mind without precise and reliable information about the processes which determine order in the mind. Pavlov's dogs, Skinner's rats and pigeons, Konrad Lorenz's geese have provided valuable analogies for certain simple aspects of human behaviour. But these analogies are of little use, and sometimes even an obstacle, to the understanding of the complex phenomena of language and language disorders; or of the storage and retrieval of memories and the pathology thereof.

*Condensed version of a paper read at the World Psychiatric Association Symposium on Uses and Abuses of Psychiatry, London, November 1969.

Psycholinguistics, in the sense in which Chomsky and his school use this term, is a new branch of psychology which for the first time tries to come to grips with the problem of how a child by the age of four has been able to acquire the immensely complex rules and strategies of language, how it can produce sentences it has never uttered before, understand sentences it has never heard before, and manipulate a syntactic and semantic machinery whose working is completely unknown to the child – as it is to the adult. For a century and more, academic psychology has failed not only to tackle this problem, but even to see the problem. But the neurosurgeon and psychiatrist have had their noses rubbed into it; and they had to try to make sense of the various bizarre types of aphasias and related disorders without getting any help from the psychologist. On the contrary, one might say with only a little exaggeration that it was neurosurgery that taught the psychologist what little real knowledge the latter has of the mechanisms of language and memory. Frederic Bartlett (1), that great psychologist, got his immensely fruitful concept of the "schema" from the neurologist Henry Head; and the rather futile discussions about whether thinking consists of nothing but "inner speech", i.e. subliminal innervations of the vocal cords, or whether there is something more to it, would have continued ad infinitum had not clinical evidence of nominal or phonemic aphasia proved the existence of non-verbal types of mental activity. Penfield's electrode which made the patient mentally compare the drawing of a butterfly to a moth, without being able to recall either of the two words, has contributed more to the understanding of language than all the discussions of the introspectionists, behaviourists and Gestalt psychologists (2). But it has been essentially a one-way traffic, and it still is.

Not only has academic psychology little help to offer to psychiatry, but its offerings have sometimes made confusion worse confounded, as in the case of certain test procedures which may give a distorted picture of the patient's condition. . . . This predicament is, of course, most drastically reflected in the field of diagnosis and classification. As I seem to be the only outsider at this congress of psychiatrists, we must assume that I have been invited to represent that infernal nuisance in the psychiatrist's life, the patient. As a rule, of course, there are too many patients to one psychiatrist, whereas here the situation is reversed. But at the same time it reflects a different aspect of reality, for the single patient is potentially liable to be diagnosed and categorised in a great many different ways, depending to some extent on the psychiatric school, the ethnic background, and apparently even the age group to which the diagnostician belongs. Thus, should I have the misfortune to be admitted to a mental hospital in England with a somewhat complex symptom picture, I would have a ten times higher chance of being classified as a manic depressive than if I were admitted to hospital in the United States; and taking my specific age group into account, the ratio of United Kingdom to United States of patients diagnosed as manic depressives becomes 21 to 1. On the other hand, if I were to go off my head in America, I would stand a ten times higher chance of being classified as a case of cerebral arteriosclerosis than in England; and a 33 per cent higher chance of being classified as a schizo. In the States I might also be found to show a "psychotic-depressive reaction", a category nonexistent in England and Wales. I am quoting these figures from Morton Kramer's remarkable paper on "A Cross-National Study of Diagnosis" (3).

Nor could I, the patient, be more sure of what is wrong with me if you repeated on me the experiments of Martin Katz and associates – i.e. if you were to administer a psychiatric interview, which would be filmed and then shown to a number of experienced clinicians, asking them to arrive at a diagnosis based on a standard symptom-rating scale. Although I am sure you are familiar with the results, I may perhaps briefly refer to the data (4).

In the first reported experiment, out of thirty-five American psychiatrists – "all seasoned veterans", as Zubin (5) commented – fourteen diagnosed the patient as neurotic and twenty-one as psychotic. In another study, in which forty-two American psychiatrists participated, the patient, described as "an attractive woman in her middle twenties", was classified by one third of the diagnosticians as schizophrenic, by another third as neurotic and by the third third as suffering from personality disorders. But when the same patient was diagnosed by British diagnosticians, *not a single one* diagnosed her as schizophrenic, and 75 per cent diagnosed "personality disorders". On comparing the symptom rating by the British and American groups, it was discovered tht the main cause of the contrast in diagnosis was that the Americans found in the patient very marked symptoms of apathy, while their British colleagues did not.

I repeat that I am sorry to go over this well-plowed acre, not in order to rake up the dust, but because it suggests to one a simple and perhaps naïve hypothesis: could it be that psychiatrists, immersed in the bustling American world, are inclined to see apathy where their colleagues from this country only see placidity or British phlegm? The Americans also found considerable "paranoid projection" and "perceptual distortion" in the same patient in which the British found none of these symptoms. Could it be that psychiatrists in a highly conformist country read paranoid traits where the British see only idiosyncrasy or mild eccentricity?

However that may be, as Katz and his co-workers pointed out in their paper, these quantitative differences on the rating scale lead to qualitatively different diagnoses – e.g. schizophrenia versus neurotic disorder – with all that this implies in terms of prognosis, hospitalization and therapy. If one remembers that one third of the American psychiatrists, *but not a single British psychiatrist*, pronounced the same patient schizophrenic, one is struck by another curious discrepancy. It is a well-known fact that in the United States a much higher proportion of well-to-do people keep what is called "a tame analyst" than do their opposite numbers in this country. Is there a connection here with the cavalier attitude of American psychiatrists in diagnosing schizophrenia? Has the meaning of the term "neurosis" been so widely stretched, or so watered down, in the United States that if a patient shows signs of real trouble, as distinct from mere couch addiction, nothing less than a diagnosis of psychosis will do?

★ ★ ★

These are speculations of a layman, but they make him feel fairly uncomfortable. The ambitious project which has recently got under way under the name of "A Cross-National Study of Diagnosis of the Mental Disorders" will perhaps succeed in eliminating such drastic discrepancies in symptom rating as I have just quoted; but it seems a Utopian hope that we shall ever be able to measure symptoms like "apathy", "hostile belligerence" or "anxious intropunitiveness" with anything approaching the precision of measuring electrostatic charges. Biometrics strike one as a noble effort, but one wonders whether too much reliance on it cannot become self-defeating – and even whether it is not a contradiction in terms.

Which, in conclusion, brings me back to my starting point, and to George Talland's criticism of the psychologists' system of tests based on performance in rote learning and similar tasks (6). There seems to be no getting away from the conclusion that, for the time being, the psychiatrist's best friend is his intuition; and that he will only feel solid earth under his feet when psychology grows out of its obsession with rats in a maze and becomes a real science of the human mind. But psychiatrists can continue to work towards this goal by teaching their academic colleagues a few of the facts of life.

References

1. F. C. Bartlett, *Remembering* (Cambridge, 1961).
2. W. Penfield and L. Roberts, *Speech and Brain Mechanisms* (Princeton, 1959).
3. *American Journal of Psychiatry*, vol. 125, no. 10, April 1969, Supplement.
4. "Studies of the Diagnostic Process", *American Journal of Psychiatry*, vol. 125, no. 7, January 1969.
5. "Biometric Assessment of Mental Patients" in *The Role and Methodology of Classification in Psychiatry and Psychopathology* (US Department of Health, Education and Welfare, Public Health Service).
6. G. Talland and N. C. Waugh, eds. *The Pathology of Memory* (London, 1969).

SINS OF OMISSION*

Several years had to pass before the death of the six million, and the manner in which they were made to die, began to penetrate the mental defences of the West. It had the effect of a delayed shock, but at least there was the comforting thought that this had not been our doing, that we had no part in it, and no conceivable means of prevention or rescue.

This comfortable belief is no longer tenable. The evidence detailed in Mr Morse's book – mainly based on official State Department records which have not been published before – establishes with merciless clarity that a considerable proportion of the victims could have been saved; that men in responsible positions, in both the State Department and the Foreign Office, had been aware of the opportunities but had failed to make use of them, or even actively obstructed rescue attempts, for a variety of motives.

During the period 1933–39, from Hitler's ascent to power to the outbreak of war, it had become increasingly evident that the 700,000 Jews of Germany and Austria were doomed. The Nuremberg laws and other decrees had deprived them of their citizenship, excluded them from most professions, forced them to wear the yellow star, and imposed absolute racial segregation, while the concentration camps of Dachau and Buchenwald provided a foretaste of the later extermination camps. The only hope of survival was to emigrate, and with a few exceptions only those who managed to emigrate did in fact survive.

* *While Six Million Died*, by Arthur D. Morse, reviewed in *The Observer*, 7 April 1968.

At that stage, the Nazis were quite willing to let the Jews go, but the rest of the world was not willing to open its doors and admit more than a small, select proportion of the damned. In the first three years of the Nazi regime only 11,000 Jewish refugees were admitted into the United States, although the immigration quotas would have permitted the entry of 450,000 aliens and more than half of the places on the quota were unfilled. It was a deliberate consular practice of the period to enforce the immigration laws literally: thus Jews in hiding from the Gestapo were asked to produce police certificates from their home town in Germany attesting to their good character.

In March 1938, after the Nazi occupation of Austria and the wave of pogroms, mass arrests and mass suicides which followed it, the liberal forces in America demanded that the administration take positive action. President Roosevelt had to do something, although he regarded (not without reason) "the Jewish issue as a political liability": so he invited thirty-three governments to a conference in Evian-les-Bains "to join in a cooperative effort to aid the immigration of refugees from Germany and Austria". At the same time he declared at a press reception that whatever the conference decided, "it would not result in an increase or revision of United States immigration quotas".

The real purpose of the Evian conference, as revealed by a confidential State Department memorandum of the time, was "to get out in front and to attempt to guide the pressure, primarily with a view towards forestalling attempts to have the immigration laws liberalised" (p. 203). The other participants of the conference were animated by the same spirit: "One after another, the nations made clear their unwillingness to accept refugees. Since the business meetings were closed to the Press, they did not risk public exposure." Australia, with vast unpopulated areas, announced: "As we have no real racial problem, we are not desirous of importing one." The Latin American countries struck the same note. The Peruvian delegate ironically remarked that the United States had given his country an example of "caution and wisdom" by its own immigration restrictions. Only Holland and the Scandinavian countries showed their traditional humanitarianism and sense of responsibility; but they could absorb only drops from the potential flood. A British delegate reported that "the British Colonial Empire contained no territory suitable to the large-scale settlement of refugees". Dr Weizmann, president of the Jewish Agency for Palestine, was refused a hearing; and "His Majesty's delegation, led by Lord Winterton, managed to evade the delicate subject of the Jewish National Home in Palestine for the duration of the Conference."

That infamous conference was a symbol of an age: it revealed the bankruptcy of humanitarianism as Munich revealed the bankruptcy of political ethics. Moreover, it served as an indirect encouragement to the German government to carry out its extermination policies without fear of too much antagonism from the rest of the world. Hitler commented with glee: "We are ready to put all these criminals at the disposal of these countries, for all I care, even on luxury ships. But nobody wants them."

So much for the prewar period. One might be inclined to believe that once the war had started there were no further opportunities for rescue; but this view is mistaken. Although the underground chambers at Auschwitz were each capable of gassing 2000 tightly packed people in twenty-five minutes, and the forty-six ovens were capable of burning 500 bodies per hour, the Nazis were not quite able to finish the job by the end of the war. The gas chambers were located in Eastern Europe; the Nazi government had to find, collect and transport the six million from all over Europe, from France, Holland, the Balkans; and the dragnet worked slowly and erratically, often encountering passive or active resistance in occupied and satellite countries.

Under these circumstances there existed many avenues of rescue. Three of the most important were escape to a neutral country, hiding in occupied countries, and Allied pressure on satellite governments. Three examples from Mr Morse's book may serve to illustrate how these opportunities were used.

In April 1943, neutral Sweden was ready to request that

Germany release 20,000 Jewish children, who would be cared for in Sweden until the end of the war, provided that the United States and Britain would guarantee to provide a haven for them after the war. The State Department blocked the proposal under various pretexts for eight months, by which time relations between Sweden and Germany had so deteriorated that it was too late.

Also in April 1943, the so-called Riegner plan proposed the transfer of Jewish charity funds to the underground in France, to be used for the rescue of children from the concentration camps in the south and to expedite the departure to Spain and North Africa of those in hiding. It again took eight months – from April to December 1943 – until permission was granted to transfer $25,000 to France in the face of strenuous opposition from the State Department. According to the Abbé Glasberg, one of the organisers of the action, "he and his colleagues could have saved virtually all of the 60,000 Jewish victims of the Nazis in France if they had possessed two weapons – American visas and more money."

One last example. During 1941 and 1942, the Fascist government of Marshal Antonescu had deported 185,000 Rumanian Jews to camps in Transnistria, where conditions equalled those in Auschwitz. By early 1943, 100,000 of them had perished. After the battle of Stalingrad, Antonescu began to fear an Allied victory and offered to transfer the surviving 70,000 Jews to any refuge selected by the Allies. A Red Cross delegation which had visited Rumania reported that the evacuation could take place "at once if the necessary funds were available". The State Department and Foreign Office between them blocked the project for nearly a whole year. By then out of 185,000 only 48,000 were left.

The appointment of the War Refugee Board in January 1944 put an end to the State Department's obstructionist policy; its remarkable achievements demonstrated what could have been done during the wasted years. But by that time four million out of the six were dead.

Mr Morse's book spells out the facts without attempting to analyse the motives behind them. They form a complex tangle of unconscious prejudices, cynical expediency and spurious rationalisations. Among the latter were, in prewar days, such utterances as "the treatment of German citizens is an internal affair of Germany", "protests can only aggravate the situation", and so on; and during the war, "shortage of shipping" (American troop transports to Europe often returned empty), "rescue operations would impede the war effort"; and above all, "we must not single out a particular religious group for preferential treatment" (an earlier variant of Ernest Bevin's classic remark, "the Jews should not push to the head of the queue").

When, in 1939, a bill was introduced in the United States Senate asking for the admission of 20,000 refugee children under the age of fourteen in addition to the German quota, the Secretary of State, Cordell Hull, objected that this would "inevitably necessitate increased clerical personnel as well as additional office accommodation". The American Legion had another objection: "it is traditional American policy that home life should be preserved, and the American Legion therefore strongly opposes the breaking up of families, which would be done by the proposed legislation." A representative of the Widows of World War I Veterans described the prospective immigrants under fourteen as "thousands of motherless, embittered, persecuted children of undesirable foreigners, and potential Communists".

Two public polls summed up the nation's state of mind. Early in 1939 a Gallup poll revealed that 94 per cent of the American people disapproved of the German treatment of the Jews. A few months later, when the bill about the children was being debated, *Fortune* magazine organised another poll including the question: "If you were a member of Congress, would you approve a bill to open the doors to a larger number of refugees than now admitted under our quotas?" Eighty-three per cent said no. The bill was never passed.

President Roosevelt had to manoeuvre an isolationist Congress and public and, as he remarked to Mrs Roosevelt, "first things come first". Expediency carried the day – or was it the century? – as it did for different reasons in the Vatican, in

England, and in a number of other democracies vaunting their humanitarian traditions. But we must face the ugly and challenging fact that it is the voice of the people, both inside Germany and among her opponents, which carries the ultimate responsibility for the fate of the six million.

THE NAKED TOUCH*

In the introduction to his previous bestseller, *The Naked Ape*, Desmond Morris declared: "I am a zoologist and the naked ape is an animal. He is therefore fair game for my pen."

The opening sentences of the present book are no less provocative:

> The act of intimacy occurs whenever two individuals come into bodily contact. It is the nature of this contact, whether it be a handshake or a copulation, a pat on the back or a slap in the face, a manicure or a surgical operation, that this book is about. . . . My method has been that of the zoologist trained in ethology, that is, in the observation and analysis of animal behaviour (p. 9).

In *The Naked Ape* this "zoological approach" yielded some revealing, or at least amusing, sidelights on the evolutionary origin of certain human traits and social rites. *Intimate Behaviour* offers hardly any such rewards, except perhaps in the first chapter, which emphasises the newborn infant's need for bodily contact with the mother as a partial substitute for the previous "intra-uterine bliss". The next two chapters – "Invitations to Sexual Intimacy" followed, as you would expect, by "Sexual Intimacy" – read like an involuntary pastiche of its genre:

> Since their reappearance, the naked navels of the Western world have undergone a curious modification. They have started to change shape. In pictorial representations, the old-fashioned circular aperture is tending to give way to a more elongated, vertical

Intimate Behaviour, by Desmond Morris, reviewed in *The Observer*, 10 October 1971.

> slit. Investigating this odd phenomenon, I discovered that contemporary models and actresses are six times more likely to display a vertical navel than a circular one, when compared with the artist's model of yesterday. A brief survey of two hundred paintings and sculptures showing female nudes, and selected at random from the whole range of art history, revealed a proportion of 92 per cent of round navels to 8 per cent of vertical ones. A similar analysis of pictures of modern photographic models and film actresses shows a striking change: now the proportion of vertical ones has risen to 46 per cent. . . . How this change has come about . . . is not entirely clear. The ultimate significance of the new navel shape is, however, reasonably certain. The classical round navel, in its symbolic orifice role, is rather too reminiscent of the anus. By becoming a more oval, vertical slit, it automatically assumes a much more genital shape, and its quality as a sexual symbol is immensely increased (p. 41).

After the navel, the breasts. These are "more than a mere feeding device", and "can better be thought of as another mimic of a primary sexual zone; in other words, as biologically developed copies of the hemispherical buttocks. This gives the female a powerful sexual signal when she is standing vertically, in the uniquely human posture, and facing a male" (p. 52).

The style is, as it were, touching:

> *The belly.* Moving up above the genital region now, we come to the belly, which has two characteristic shapes: flat and "pot". Lovers tend to be flat-bellied, while pot-bellies are most commonly seen in starving children and overfed men (p. 47).

Moving up even further now, "eye movements of various kinds also invite intimacy. Apart from the well-known wink, the rolling of the eyes is also reported to be a direct invitation to copulation in certain cultures. A demure dropping of the eyes also transmits its message in the female, while a slight narrowing of them can indicate interest on the part of the male" (p. 64).

An extreme form of intimacy is the rape:

> For the human male animal, rape is comparatively easy. If physical force is not enough, he can add threats of death or injury. Alternatively he can contrive to render the female unconscious or

> semi-unconscious, or can enlist the aid of other males to hold her still. If the absence of the female's sexual arousal makes the penis insertion difficult or painful, he can always resort to the use of some alternative form of lubrication to replace the missing natural secretions (p. 80).

The particular flavour of the modern, pseudo-scientific sex potboiler is a kind of salacious pedantry. One is almost relieved when the pedantry gains the upper hand:

> All animal courtship patterns are organised in a typical sequence, and the course taken by a human love affair is no exception. For convenience we can divide the human sequence up into twelve stages, and see what happens as each threshold is successfully passed (p. 74).

The twelve stages listed and discussed are: (1) eye to body, (2) eye to eye, (3) voice to voice, (4) hand to hand, (5) arm to shoulder, (6) arm to waist, (7) mouth to mouth, (8) hand to head, (9) hand to body, (10) mouth to breast, (11) hand to genitals, (12) genitals to genitals. There are also variations, which "take three main forms: a reduction of the sequence, an alteration in the order of the acts and an elaboration of the pattern" (p. 79).

After "Sexual Intimacy" we pass to "Social Intimacy", i.e. restrained, inhibited or symbolic bodily contacts, such as clapping – "When we applaud a performer, we are, in effect, patting him on the back from a distance" – and waving one's hand as a welcome or farewell sign. But there are also "two rather specialised waves" singled out for discussion: "the Papal wave and the British Royal wave".

From "Social Intimacy" we move to "Specialised Intimacy" with "professional touchers" such as "the doctor, the nurse, the masseur, the gymnastics and health-and-beauty instructors, the hairdresser, the tailor, the manicurist, the beautician, the make-up specialist, the barber, the shoe-shine and the shoe-shop attendant. To this list we could add many other related occupations such as those of the wig-maker, the hatter, the chiropodist, the dentist, the surgeon, the gynaecologist" (p. 158).

The next chapter discusses intimacy with pets, which Morris decrees to be "living substitutes for human bodies in a contact-hungry world". We are informed that "at a rough guess, there are approximately 150 million cats and dogs in these four countries alone [United States, France, West Germany and Britain]. Making another rough guess, let us say that each owner of one of these animals strokes, pats or caresses it, on the average, three times a day – or about 1000 times a year. This adds up to a total of 150,000 million intimate body contacts per year" (p. 173).

Next, we are treated to a ten-page dissertation on vivisection, which the author manages to drag in under the pretext that it represents a "betrayal of intimacy". Similarly, there is a discussion of the horrors of lung cancer, justified by the remark that cigarettes are substitutes for intimate contact with the nipple and "warm inhaled smoke equals mother's warm milk".

Lastly, we have "Self-Intimacy", from masturbation to the various ways of touching one's head or face with one's hand. "Surveying these head contacts, it was possible to identify 650 different types of action. This was done by recording which part of the hand was used, how it made the contact, and which part of the head was involved" (p. 215).

The Germans have a word for it: *Die Wissenschaft des nicht Wissenswerten* – the science of what is not worth knowing. After a number of highly enjoyable books on snakes, pandas and apes – including the naked one – Dr Morris this time has indulged in filling a rag-bag with miscellaneous bits of information which add little to our knowledge of human nature, but makes it appear in a crude and grotesquely distorted shape. As for his central thesis – shared by certain group-encounter cults of Californian origin – that modern man is frustrated in his need of intimate body contacts, the fairest verdict is: not proven – and one might even plausibly argue that just the opposite is true.

ANATOMY OF A *CANARD**

In May-June 1969, the staid city of Orléans, devoted to the cult of the Maid, was convulsed by a strange attack of mass hysteria. The most reliable account of the episode was published by *Le Monde* on 7 June of that year:

"Disappearance" of Women in Orléans: Plot or Hoax?

Scene: a women's dress shop on a main shopping street somewhere in the provinces, late one afternoon. A couple appears. The man decides to wait outside on the pavement while his wife goes into the boutique on her own. After a while the husband gets tired of waiting, goes into the establishment himself – and is informed that no person answering the description he gives has crossed the threshold of the shop. Confronted with this stubborn and obstructive attitude on the part of the staff, he goes to the police. . . . The latter discover three women (including his wife) down in the basement, bound, gagged, chloroformed, ready to be shipped off abroad: a clear case of "white slaving".

This odd story is a complete fabrication. Yet though it is about as murkily fantastic as the plot of a bad thriller, it spread through the entire town in a matter of hours. Today it lies at the heart of every kind of fear and anxiety; it nurtures old resentments, releases unacknowledged feelings of hatred, encourages folly and dissipates boredom. For nearly three weeks now Orléans has been living through a period of denunciation and calumny. . . . Everyone suspects everyone else . . . headmistresses issue stern warnings to

* *Rumour in Orléans*, by Edgar Morin, reviewed in the *Sunday Times*, 4 July 1971.

their girls, the "suspect" shops are deserted, old scores are being paid off all round, and a collective psychosis of unparalleled dimensions is developing.

At the height of the rumour altogether twenty-six girls were said to have disappeared (all friends or cousins of one's best friend) although not a single case of a missing female had been reported to the police. All were said to have been drugged in the fitting rooms of six fashionable boutiques, all six owned by Jews, and their inert bodies transported through a subterranean network of tunnels, sewers and catacombs to the Loire, where a submarine was waiting to carry them to a fate worse than death.

Why were none of the guilty shopkeepers arrested? Because the police were in the pay of the Jewish white-slavers. And so on; there is no need to go into details; they have an all-too-familiar ring. But there was no pogrom: the rumour collapsed as suddenly as it had come into being, partly under the sheer weight of its own absurdity, partly because various official and professional bodies, from the Prefecture to the Communist Party of the Loiret, took the counteroffensive when the situation got really ugly.

How did the story originate? Like other misfortunes that befell Orléans, it seems to have been engineered in England. In 1968 Heinemann published a book by Stephen Barley called *Sex Slavery*. It contained an item which in every detail (fashion boutique – suspicious husband – drugged wife in cellar) corresponded to the Orléans story, except that it was supposed to have happened in Grenoble and that there was no mention of Jews. A French translation of the book appeared in 1969; and on 6 May, just before the Orléans rumour started, the popular magazine *Noir et Blanc* reproduced that item without indication of its source, and giving the impression that it was reporting a recent event. The Orléans police believe that it was this story which started the avalanche, during the week after the magazine reached the news stands.

M. Morin is described on the blurb of his book as "one of the directors of the Centre for the Study of Mass Communications at the Ecole Pratique des Hautes Etudes in Paris". He also appears to be the founder of a school which he alternatively refers to as "clinical sociology", "occurential sociology" and "*sociologie du présent*". In July 1969, one month after the event, he descended on Orléans with a team of five young collaborators (two of them "with long hair and hippie necklaces") to carry out, *in three days* (p. 14), a field study of the history and social implications of the rumour. His book adds no new facts to the reports published by the French press, and leaves us no wiser regarding the "unexplored depth of the collective subconscious" which it was meant to elucidate. The unexplored depths seem to consist either of tautologies – "from the very outset, the modernisation of this erotic myth was in fact no more than the crystallisation of a modern myth with erotic overtones" (p. 76) – or else clichés, archetypal chestnuts such as the Jew as a perennial scapegoat, adolescent fantasies of rape, old crones don't like miniskirts. These clichés are dressed up in a jargon both pretentious and obscure, which seems to enjoy a great vogue among contemporary French anthropologists. The last paragraph of M. Morin's book, under the headline "Conclusion", may serve as a conclusive example:

> Thus we take up a position at the dialectical mid-point between event and theory, history and sociology, the contemporary and the anthropological, and – more specifically in this case – between phenomenon and discipline, crisis and system, the actual and the potential, trend and counter-trend, evolution and involution, the innovating and the archaic.

Could it be that the proverbial Cartesian Lucidity of the Gallic Spirit is also a myth – a Rumour in Orléans?

PROPHET AND *POSEUR**

In an autobiographical book, years ago, I described my first meeting with Malraux. In 1934 I was honorary treasurer of an anti-Nazi setup in Paris called INFA (Institut pour l'Etude du Fascisme) and was making the rounds of French intellecutals, asking them for donations:

> It was in this capacity that I first met André Malraux. I went to see him at his office at Gallimard's, the publishers, and we talked while walking up and down in the garden at the back of the Gallimard building. As a fervent admirer of Malraux's, I was overwhelmed by the occasion, but went on bravely about the great prospects of INFA and its even greater need for donations. Malraux listened in silence, occasionally uttering one of his characteristic, awe-inspiring nervous sniffs, which sounded like the cry of a wounded jungle beast and were followed by a slap of his palm against his nose. At first this was rather startling, but one soon got accustomed to it. When I had had my say, Malraux stopped, advanced towards me threateningly, until I had my back against the garden wall, and said:
>
> "*Oui, oui, mon cher, mais que pensez-vous de l'apocalypse?*"
>
> With that he gave me five hundred francs, and wished me good luck.

Although later on we met frequently and were on friendly terms, that phrase and gesture sticks out of the past like the Eiffel Tower – a moving and faintly absurd landmark. It was the essential Malraux, genuinely obsessed with the *nostalgie de l'apocalypse* and yet giving the impression that he was play-

* *Antimemoirs* by André Malraux, translated by Terence Kilmartin, reviewed in *The Observer, 22 September 1968*.

acting *pour épater*. At the very beginning of his *Antimemoirs*, he speaks of "an intellectual problem which interested me a great deal: how to reduce to the minimum the play-acting side of one's nature." He may have sincerely tried, but he was never successful in that particular endeavour: one cannot be a modern buccaneer, a hero of two wars, a dazzling orator, diplomatic envoy and a Cabinet minister without a touch of showmanship in one's nature.

Yet in Malraux the dualism of prophet and *poseur* is more conspicuous than in other great adventurers that come to mind – more extreme even than in Malraux's own hero, T. E. Lawrence. It affects not only the man of action and public figure - which is unavoidable; it has also begun to pervade his writing - which is harder to accept. Lawrence, the public figure, may have been both prophet and *poseur*; Lawrence, the writer, succeeded in preserving his integrity (and so did Saint-Exupéry, Ignazio Silone, young Richard Hillary). But unhappily in Malraux's case the virus has begun to invade the tissue of his writing. The symptoms are page-long purple patches, punctuated by flourishes and passages of deliberate obscurity, pseudo-profundities and inflated emotions, which at times read as if they had been inspired by an overdose of LSD. Although a confirmed Malraux addict, I found entire chapters almost unreadable, a strain on the eyes desperately trying to discern the emperor's clothes.

Thus on the very first page of the book we are told: "To reflect upon life – life in relation to death – is perhaps no more than to intensify one's questioning." Surely this must mean something, but what? And this kind of thing is to be found on practically every page. Take this oracular dictum, attributed to Alain: "When all's said and done, it is the purest and best in man which rules through reverence and admiration – and it has never existed" (the French original is even more obscure).

Another recurrent mannerism is his habit of making dark allusions to exotic events, obscure artists, archaeological curiosities and anthropological titbits unknown to ordinary mortals; a kind of esoteric name-dropping (one wonders why we are offered no quotations in Sanskrit and Mandarin). Traces of this vice could already be found in the *Musée Imaginaire* and the other art books; but now it has got worse. It creeps into most of the encounters and dialogues – with de Gaulle, Nehru, ambassadors, and statesmen; they are related in the same style of compulsive obliquity, of secrets shared by the cognoscenti. Through entire chapters we seem to move in a world of Nietzschean supermen, talking in divine riddles; while all basic information about the countries and personalities is tantalisingly withheld.

Thus we learn nothing about French politics during the postwar years, nothing about the fundamental state of affairs in India or China during the author's visits, and nothing, except a few dramatic highlights, about the author's life. He says: "I have called this book *Antimemoirs* because it answers a question which memoirs do not pose, and does not answer those which they do." With the second half of this sentence one must agree, but the answer mentioned in the first half I failed to discover. What, then, is the book about?

It is, in fact, neither an auto- nor an anti-biography, but a conglomeration of chapters from previous novels and episodic reports of recent and earlier travels and encounters. They are stitched together, with deliberate disregard for chronological or thematic order, by threads of associations which are no doubt relevant to the author, but not always to the reader. Thus, considered as a whole, and in view of the high expectations raised by the oblique promise of the title, the book is a disappointment. But if one regards it simply as an omnibus collection of independent pieces, the picture changes altogether. While some of these pieces may be unreadable, for the reasons I have tried to indicate, and can safely be skipped, there are others representative of the best writing of one of the best writers of our time.

We meet again several of the familiar masterpieces: the madcap expedition with Corniglion-Molinier in a single-engined plane to the ruins of the alleged city of the Queen of Sheba; the fight with the hurricane over Tunis; the struggle to get the trapped tank going (the most Kafkaesque war episode I know – the trapped giant tank becomes an allegory of the helpless beetle in "Metamorphosis", which becomes an allegory of the helplessness of man).

In these action stories, where the adversary is never a human being but death itself in various guises, while the hero's reactions oscillate between horror and sexual excitement, Malraux shows what a superb reporter he is, and how fluid the boundaries are between "literature" and "reportage". This applies equally to the great action chapters in his earlier novels and to the all-too-few newly written episodes in the book – such as facing a murderously hostile audience in Guyana and facing the Gestapo as a captured Maquis leader. In these passages, the man of action and the man of letters coalesce into a monolithic unit; the results are masterpieces. And so are some of his public speeches – such as the unforgettable funeral oration for the murdered Resistance leader, Jean Moulin; one marvelled at the perfect harmony between the author who improvised the script and the actor who delivered it. But in his electoral speeches, when the actor got the upper hand over the author, the result was often a kind of purple waffle, delivered to the accompaniment of a *fanfare obscure*. And the same applies whenever the comedian invades the writer's study – which brings us back to my starting point.

The only wisdom I acquired when I travelled through Asia in search of yogis and Zen masters was a lesson childishly simple once one had learned it: never ask yourself whether a "holy man" is a saint or a phony, but try to draw a balance sheet of the amounts of saintliness and phoniness in him. *Mutatis mutandis:* even the worst chapters in this book amount to no more than a temporary deficit on the balance sheeet of the author of *La Condition Humaine*; the man who created the International Air Force during the Spanish Civil War; who was one of the most effective leaders of the French Resistance; who cleaned historic Paris from centuries of grime, and had the ceiling of the Opéra painted by Chagall.

If we had a few Malrauxs in this country, intellectuals would perhaps be treated less condescendingly.

TELEPATHY AND DIALECTICS*

In the course of the last decade, garbled accounts in the Western press told of a curious vogue in parapsychology in the Soviet Union. The names of two female prodigies, Rosa Kuleschova and Ninel Kulagina, kept cropping up: Rosa was allegedly able to read, blindfolded, with her fingertips, while Ninel was reported (and filmed) moving about light objects such as cigarettes and matches lying on a table, without touching them, by telekinesis – i.e. a sheer effort of will. Rosa was occasionally caught peeping from under her blindfold, while Ninel (originally called Nelya; she changed her name to Lenin spelt backward) was reported to have been convicted for fraud, unconnected with her psychic activities. But that is neither here nor there. Both Rosa and Nelya had been submitted to controlled tests by Soviet scientists in high academic positions, who testified that the phenomena they produced were genuine. But that again is neither there nor elsewhere. Occasional cheating on a bad day does not prove or disprove anything – even austere chemistry teachers were known to "cook" their experiments when something went wrong. On the other hand, one wonders how strict the controls of the "controlled" tests have been, and whether they would have stood up to the wiles of a clever stage magician. Thus, even if one's personal attitude towards parapsychology is a positive one, the wisest course to adopt in such cases is expressed by the maxim of an eminent Moscow physicist: "When I hear the doorbell of my apartment, I am inclined to assume that it is the

* *Psychic Discoveries by the Russians*, edited by Martin Ebon, reviewed in the *New Statesman*, 4 May 1973.

postman ringing, and not the Queen of England."

However, these two sensational ladies, and their host of imitators, are merely the fringe phenomena of respectable, academic ESP research in the Soviet Union. Another phenomenon is "the magnificent Messing" – the star of stage hypnotists and thought readers, said to have been a personal protégé of Stalin. It is rather a pity that Martin Ebon has seen fit to include an uncritically admiring article about this mountebank in his informative anthology. The article is written by a Polish journalist and based on Messing's autobiography – where he relates that in 1915 he met Freud and Einstein in Vienna: "Freud was, apparently, so intrigued by Messing's faculties that he invited him to his own place where Messing gave a performance, in Einstein's presence – Freud himself acting as inductor for several complicated experiments, all with positive results."

There is no record of Einstein having visited Vienna in 1915, nor of a meeting with Freud, and the whole episode is patently absurd. Yet Messing's spurious autobiography was serialised in the Soviet periodical *Science and Religion* (designed for anti-religious propaganda) and this fact alone is characteristic of the new Party line towards parapsychology – which could be described as periodically wavering between benevolence, ambivalence and an occasional mildly hostile blast from *Pravda*.

There are several threads interwoven in this confused scene. Some strategists of the ideological front may feel that permissiveness towards "occult superstitions" may provide a relatively harmless outlet for repressed religious cravings – better a Lenin spelt backwards than a new Rasputin. But there seems to be another reason for increasing official support for serious research into telepathy, which is of a rather fantastic nature. In 1959, the French boulevard press published reports, which were taken up by the more serious journal *Science et Vie*, to the effect that the American nuclear submarine *Nautilus* had been in telepathic communication with its home base while it was submerged under the polar ice. Odd as it may seem, one of the key people who believed in this report was Professor Leonid L. Vassiliev, head of the Psychology Department at Leningrad

University and bearer of the Order of Lenin. Vassiliev himself had for some twenty-five years carried out telepathic experiments in his department, but had kept the matter rather quiet. The *Nautilus* reports convinced him – and others – that the time was ripe for action. "ESP – extrasensory perception," he declared at a meeting of scientists, "could be of gigantic significance for science and life, should the hypothesis based on our experiments prove correct; namely, that telepathic transmission is accomplished by some kind of energy or factor so far unknown to us. . . . To discover such energy or factor would be tantamount to the discovery of nuclear energy." He published in quick succession two books setting out the results of the previously unknown parapsychological research work at his department, enlisted the support of such eminent academicians as Nikolai Semenov, Nobel laureate in chemistry and vice-president of the Academy of Science, W. Tugerinov, dean of the Philosophical Faculty in Leningrad, and, presumably, some influential people in military intelligence. Within a year, the first official parapsychology department was established at Leningrad University; others, at Moscow and elsewhere, followed. From 1960 onward, parapsychology in the Soviet Union had attained academic respectability and official support – though there was of course no lack of hostile critics. Similar developments have been reported from Czechoslovakia and Bulgaria.

In fact, however, parapsychology had merely broken the surface – like a submarine – for it had always existed in Russia, before and after the Revolution. Pavlov's successor, Vladimir Bekhterev, head of the Institute for Brain Research in Leningrad, experimented in the early 1920s with two telepathic dogs belonging to the celebrated circus performer Durov, and published papers attesting the genuineness of the phenomena; Durov was subsequently put in charge of a specially created Zoo-Psychological Laboratory in Moscow, which was closed down at his death in 1934. But interest in animal telepathy continued. One recent Russian experiment, both ingenious and ghastly, was described by Professor Naumov at the Moscow Conference on Technological Parapsychology in

June 1968. A litter of young rabbits was placed in a submarine. The mother remained in the laboratory, wired to an electroencephalograph which recorded her brain waves. At prearranged times the young rabbits on the submerged vessel were killed, one after the other. According to the report, the EEG record showed a violent disturbance of the mother rabbit's brain activity at the exact moment of each killing. No further details of the experiment are available; rumour has it that they are classified. But one thing is obvious: you can't take a litter of rabbits on a military submarine without official permission.

Naive Westerners may wonder how all this benevolence toward the occult can be reconciled with Marxist–Leninist dialectical materialism. Much more easily, it seems, than one would have imagined. For one thing, the obnoxious terms "parapsychology" and "psychical research" are replaced by respectable euphemisms such as "bio-information", "biological communication" and "psychotronics". Next, you turn the table on your opponents, as Professor Vassiliev did, when he wrote that psychical research could have a "strictly materialistic basis and serve to counteract superstitious interpretations". The psychiatrist A. Roshchin supported him in a public debate by arguing that if materialistic science turns its back on telepathy "this will doubtless be the open door through which religious faith rushes in". I shall not be surprised if we soon hear some worthy Soviet academician proclaim that to deny the immortality of the soul is an unscientific attitude which plays into the hands of religious superstition.

Psychic Discoveries by the Russians is a valuable source of information on a significant ideological development in Russia which to most Westerners will come as a surprise.

WITTGENSTEINOMANIA*

When he had completed his *Tractatus Logico-Philosophicus*, Ludwig Wittgenstein wrote a letter to his friend Professor Ficker which gave a new twist to the parable of the emperor's clothes (the italics are Wittgenstein's):

> *The book's point is an ethical one*. I once meant to include in the preface a sentence which is not in fact there now, but which I will write out for you here, because it will perhaps be a key to the work for you. What I meant to write, then, was this. My work consists of two parts: the one presented here plus all that I have *not* written. And *it is precisely this second part that is the important one*. . . . I believe that where *many* others today are just *gassing*, I have managed in my book to put everything firmly into place by being silent about it.

The *Tractatus* became one of the most influential philosophical works of our century, the source of an esoteric cult, the dark oracle from which such diverse schools as logical positivism, the Vienna Circle and the linguistic philosophers of Oxford drew their inspiration. But unavoidably – as naive non-philosophers would expect – their interpretations of Wittgenstein's message were based on what he had written and not on that second part which he had *not* written. And as far as the written text goes, the message could be summed up in a simple slogan: "Metaphysicians, shut your trap." Proposition 6.53 – the last but second – in the *Tractatus* reads (my italics):

> The right method of philosophy would be this. To say nothing except what can be said, i.e. the propositions of natural science, i.e.

* *Wittgenstein's Vienna*, by Allan Janik and Stephen Toulmin, reviewed in *The Observer*, 3 June 1973.

> something *that has nothing to do with philosophy*: and then always, when someone else wished to say something metaphysical, to demonstrate to him that he has given no meaning to certain signs in his propositions.

The disciples followed this prescription to the letter. All problems which the layman thought to be the basic preoccupation of philosophers – ethical values, moral judgements, free will and determinism, the nature of consciousness and the meaning of life – were confined as meaningless to the rubbish heap. The result, as Ernest Gellner remarked, was "an inverted vision which treats genuine thought as a disease". Bertrand Russell, who had written an enthusiastic introduction to Wittgenstein's *Tractatus*, thirty years later wrote an equally enthusiastic introduction to Gellner's *Words and Things* which could be called an *Anti-Tractatus*: "The later Wittgenstein," Russell wrote, "seems to have grown tired of serious thinking and to have invented a doctrine which would make such an activity unnecessary."

Wittgenstein himself maintained that everybody had misunderstood him, starting with Russell himself (whose preface he initially rejected as misleading); he repudiated the Oxford linguists, the Vienna Circle and the logical positivists ("the trouble with Ayer is, he's clever *all* the time"). Thus, apparently, these dominant schools of philosophy – or anti-philosophy – of the middle of our century were founded on a monstrous misunderstanding of the message of its principal prophet.

This, at least, is the contention of the authors of the present book. They also maintain that the main influence on Wittgenstein's intellectual formation was not the Cambridge of Russell and Moore (as is generally believed) but Vienna during the decline of the Habsburg Empire. Their "central hypothesis about Viennese culture" is that "to be a *fin-de-siècle* Viennese artist or intellectual . . . one had to face the problem of *the nature and limits of language, expression and communication*" (their italics). Confronted with this task, young Wittgenstein set out to explore the frontiers of language, logic and reason and to stake out their boundaries. When he got to Cambridge at the age of twenty-two, Russell and Moore provided him with the technical tools for his undertaking. The upshot of his labours was that language is an excellent means of representation and communication as far as the world of facts is concerned, but cannot cope adequately with the ultimates of experience – emotions, aesthetic values, ethical intuitions. "*Sätze können nichts Höheres ausdrücken*" (6.42) – "Sentences cannot express anything pertaining to the higher realms. . . . It is clear that ethics cannot be expressed" (6.421). And as a climax, the celebrated last proposition (which also appears in the preface): "Whereof one cannot speak, thereof one must be silent."

One might call it a winged tautology. (Gertrude Stein is remembered by her rose; God explained to Moses "I am that I am.") The misunderstanding of the message arose, it seems, because Wittgenstein took that phrase literally: what really mattered to him – the *Höheres*, the ultimate – thereof he remained silent. Hence the remark that the important part of the book is the one that he did *not* write – and the pathetic assertion that "the book's point is an ethical one". If so, the reader could not help missing it, since the point was made in invisible ink. The visible part represented a brilliant demolition job, reducing metaphysics to meaninglessness, reason to ethical neutrality, philosophy to a proudly proclaimed impotence.

More than a century before Wittgenstein, Schopenhauer had written: "To preach morality is hard; to give it an intellectual justification is impossible." Rarely has the human predicament been summed up in a more concise formula. The *Tractatus* provides modern variations on this theme in a more sophisticated vein, orchestrated by the symbolic logic of Frege and Russell; whether it added something of value remains an open question. But there can be little doubt that its author was a mouthpiece of the *Zeitgeist*, producing astonishing resonance effects. "Philosophers who never met him," wrote Gilbert Ryle in 1951, the year of Wittgenstein's death, "can be heard talking philosophy in his tone of voice; and students who can barely spell his name now wrinkle up their noses at things which had a bad smell for him."

The profound impact he made on Cambridge seems to have been partly due to his gift of beating the dons at their own game of eccentric behaviour, odd-ballship and cussedness. He countered their understatements with the preposterous boast in the preface to the *Tractatus* that "the *truth* of the thoughts" contained in it was "unassailable and definitive"; and that thereby the problems of philosophy "have in essentials been finally solved". His modesty was equally provocative: when he became a fellow of Trinity College, he refused to dine at high table because it stood on a platform six inches higher than the main floor; he had to be served at a separate card table set up on floor level. Combined with this exhibitionism there was a masochistic streak; he spent long periods in menial occupations – as a hospital orderly in the Second World War, and as a teacher in elementary schools in small Austrian villages. There was also a pathological streak: *three* of Wittgenstein's four brothers committed suicide; and Wittgenstein himself complained in his letters of his own "rottenness", obviously connected with problems of sex.

But these traits in Wittgenstein's personality, which could not have been without influence on his philosophy, are only mentioned by the authors in passing. Nevertheless, their book provides an original, and highly controversial, interpretation of one of the oddest episodes in the history of philosophy – a man setting out to circumcise logic and all but succeeding in castrating thought.

LITERATURE AND THE LAW OF DIMINISHING RETURNS*

1 *Historical parallels*

In Solzhenitsyn's novel *The First Circle* some prisoners are having an argument about the progress of science. One of them, Gleb Nerzhin, exclaims in a passionate outburst:

"Progress! Who wants progress? That's just what I like about art – the fact that there can't be any 'progress' in it."

He then discusses the tremendous advances in technology during the previous century and concludes with the taunt: "But has there been any advance on *Anna Karenina*?"

The opposite attitude was taken by Sartre in his essay "What is Literature?", where he compared novels to bananas which you can enjoy only while they are fresh. *Anna Karenina*, in this view, must have rotted long ago.

Solzhenitsyn's hero reflects the traditional view that science progresses in a cumulative manner, brick upon brick, the way a tower is built, whereas art is timeless, a dance of coloured balls on the jets of a fountain – a playing of variations on eternal themes. To a limited extent, this conventional view is of course justified. In the great discoveries of science, the fusion of previously separate contexts (electricity and magnetism, matter and energy, etc.) results in a new synthesis, which in its turn will merge with others on a higher, emergent level of the hierarchy. The evolution of art does not, generally, show this overall pattern. The creative act which produces a poetic

*The Cheltenham Lecture, given at the Cheltenham Festival of Literature, November 1969. See also "The Four Stages of Creativity" in Part One.

metaphor consists of an emotive *juxtaposition*, rather than an intellectual *fusion* of two contexts. But once again, this difference is relative, not absolute. If you accept Gleb Nerzhin's view *in toto*, then it is pointless to search for objective criteria of "progress" in literature, painting or music; art, then, does not evolve, it merely formulates and reformulates the same archetypal experiences in the costumes and styles of the period; and although the vocabulary is subject to changes – including the visual vocabulary of the painter – the statement contained in a great work of art remains valid and unmarked by time's arrow, untouched by the vulgar march of progress.

But at a closer look this view turns out to be historically untenable. For one thing, there are periods in which a given art form shows a definite, cumulative evolution, comparable to scientific progress. To quote our leading art historian, Sir Ernst Gombrich:

> In antiquity the discussion of painting and sculpture inevitably centred on [the] imitation [of nature] – mimesis. Indeed it may be said that the progress of art towards that goal was to the ancient what the progress of technology is to the modern: the model of progress as such. Thus Pliny told the history of sculpture and painting as the history of inventions, assigning definite achievements in the rendering of nature to individual artists: the painter Polygnotus was the first to represent people with open mouth and with teeth, the sculptor Pythagoras was the first to render nerves and veins, the painter Nikias was concerned with light and shade. The history of these years [*ca.* 550 to 350 BC] as it is reflected in Pliny or Quintilian was handed down like an epic of conquest, a story of inventions. . . . In the Renaissance it was Vasari who applied this technique to the history of the arts of Italy from the thirteenth to the sixteenth century. Vasari never fails to pay tribute to those artists of the past who made a distinct contribution, as he saw it, to the mastery of representation. "Art rose from humble beginnings to the summit of perfection" [Vasari says] because such natural geniuses as Giotto blazed the trail and others were thus enabled to build on their achievements.★

Here then, we have at least a partial refutation of Nerzhin's

★*Art and Illusion* (London, 1962), pp. 9, 120.

thesis that there is no progress in art. "If I could see further than others," said Newton, "it is because I stood on the shoulders of giants." Leonardo said much the same. "It is a wretched pupil," he wrote, "who does not surpass his master." Dürer and others expressed similar opinions. What they evidently meant was that during the period of explosive development which started with Giotto around the year 1300, each successive generation of painters had discovered new tricks and techniques – foreshortening, perspective, the treatment of light, colour and texture, the capture of movement and facial expression – inventions which the pupil could take over from the master and use as his base line for new departures.

As for literature, it need hardly be emphasised that the various schools and fashions of the past were not static, but evolved during their limited life span toward greater refinement and technical perfection - or decadence. We take it for granted that today's physicists know more about the atom than Democritus; but then Joyce's *Ulysses* also knows more about human nature than Homer's *Odysseus*. There is hardly a writer, past or present, who did not or does not sincerely believe his style and technique of writing to be closer to reality, intellectually and emotionally, than those of the past. Let us face it: our reverence for Homer or Goethe is sweetened by a dash of condescension not unlike our attitude to infant prodigies: how clever they were for their age!

Thus we can safely reject as a gross oversimplification Gleb Nerzhin's view that science is cumulative like a bricklayer's work, while art is timeless. The history of art, too, shows cumulative progress - in certain periods, though not in others. In the history of European painting, for instance, there are two outstanding periods in which we find rapid, sustained, cumulative progress in representing Nature, almost as tangible as the progress in engineering. The first stretches roughly from the middle of the sixth to the middle of the fourth century BC, the second from the beginning of the fourteenth to the middle of the sixteenth century. Each lasted for about six to eight generations, in the course of which each giant did indeed stand on the shoulders of his predecessors, and could take in a wider view. It would of course be silly to say that these were the *only* periods of cumulative progress. But it is nevertheless true that in between these periods of rapid evolution there are much longer stretches of stagnation or decline. Besides, there are the lone giants, who seem to appear from nowhere and cannot be fitted into any neat pyramid of acrobats balancing on each other's shoulders.

The conclusion seems to be obvious. Our museums and libraries demonstrate that there *is* a cumulative progression in every art form – in a limited sense, in a limited direction, during limited periods. But these short, luminous trails sooner or later peter out in twilight and confusion, and the search for a new departure in a new direction is on.

However, contrary to popular belief, the evolution of science does not show a more coherent picture. Only during the last three hundred years has its advance been continuous and cumulative; but those unfamiliar with the history of science – and they include the majority of scientists – tend to fall into the mistaken belief that the acquistion of knowledge has always been a neat and tidy ascent on a straight path towards the ultimate peak.

In fact, neither science nor art has evolved in a continuous way. Whitehead once remarked that Europe in the year 1500 knew less than Archimedes who died in 212 BC. In retrospect there was only one step separating Archimedes from Galileo, Aristarchus of Samos (who fathered the heliocentric system) from Copernicus. But that step took nearly two thousand years to be made. During that long period, science was hibernating. After the three short glorious centuries of Greek science, roughly coinciding with the cumulative period of Greek art, comes a period of suspended animation about six times as long; then a new furious awakening, so far only about ten generations old.

Progress, then, in science as in art, is neither steady nor absolute, but – to say it again – a progression in a limited sense during limited periods in limited directions; not along a steady curve, but in a jagged, jerky, zigzag line.

A Chinese proverb says that there is a time for fishing and a time for drying the nets. If you take a kind of bird's-eye view of the history of any branch of science, you will find a rhythmic alternation between long periods of relatively peaceful evolution and shorter bursts of revolutionary change. Only in the peaceful periods which follow after a major breakthrough is the progress of science continuous and cumulative in the strict sense. It is a period of consolidating the newly conquered frontiers, of verifying, assimilating, elaborating and extending the new synthesis: a time for drying the nets. It may last a few years or several generations; but sooner or later the emergence of new empirical data, or a change in the philosophical climate, leads to stagnation, a hardening of the matrix into a closed system, the rise of a new orthodoxy. This produces a crisis, a period of fertile anarchy in which rival theories proliferate – until the new synthesis is achieved and the cycle starts again; but this time aiming in a different direction, along different parameters, asking a different kind of question.

It is thus possible to detect a recurrent pattern in the evolution of both science and art. As a rule the cycle starts with a passionate rebellion against and rejection of the previously dominant school or style with a subsequent breakthrough towards new frontiers: call this *phase one*. The *second phase* in the cycle has a climate of optimism and euphoria; in the footsteps of the giants who spearheaded the advance, their more pedestrian followers and imitators move into the newly opened territories to explore and exploit its rich potentials. This, as said before, is the phase *par excellence* of cumulative progress in elaborating and perfecting new insights and techniques in research, and new styles in art. The *third phase* brings saturation, followed by frustration and deadlock. The *fourth* and last phase is a time of crisis and doubt – epitomised in John Donne's complaint on the fall of Aristotelian cosmology: "'Tis all in pieces, all coherence gone." But it is also a time of wild experimentation (Fauvism and Dada and their equivalents in science) and of creative anarchy – *reculer pour mieux sauter* – which prepares and incubates the next revolution, initiating a new departure – and so the cycle starts again.

2 The law of infolding

Let me, briefly, dwell on the *first phase* of the cycle.

The French Revolution demolished the Bastille and used its huge stones to pave the Place de la Concorde. In other words, revolutions are both destructive and constructive. Old restraints and conventions are discarded, aspects of human experience previously neglected or repressed are suddenly highlighted, there is a shift of emphasis, a reshuffling of data, a reordering of the hierarchy of values and of the criteria of relevance. This is what happened at each of the turning points of narrative prose styles – classicism to romanticism, naturalism, and so on. This is what happened in the succession of dramatic changes in the artist's perception of the human body, from Egyptian painting to Picasso; or in the novelist's view of the relation between the sexes; or the painter's attitude to nature. Throughout the Renaissance, for instance, and up to the late Venetians, landscapes were conceived merely as more or less stereotyped backdrops for the human figures on the stage. Art historians appear to agree that Giorgione's *Tempest* is the first European painting in which nature claims to be seen in her own right – the violent thunderstorm in the background competes for our attention with the bucolic scene in the foreground.

This does not mean that artists who painted before Giorgione were blind to nature, or that poets before the romantic movement were lacking in emotion. But their vision and response were different from ours, moulded by the *Zeitgeist*, just as successive schools of philosophers put different interpretations on the same data. To Homer, a storm at sea signified the fury of Poseidon, and the dawn was painted by the rosy fingers of Aurora; to Virgil, nature appeared tame and bucolic; it took quite a series of revolutionary shifts of emphasis and reshuffling of data until people learned to see an apple through Cézanne's eyes, or a snow-covered plain through the eyes of Verlaine. And the adjective "revolutionary" is no exaggeration, although in retrospect these revolutions seem quite tame. Verlaine, for instance, does not seem to have been unduly audacious when he compared the uncertain colour of the snow to luminous sand covering the "interminable boredom of the plain", and the sky to dull copper in which the moon "lived and died". Today French schoolchildren have to learn this poem by heart. But when it was published, a famous writer and critic attacked Verlaine in the shrill voice of the literary fishwife:

> How can the moon live and die in a copper heaven? And how can snow shine like sand? How can the French attribute such importance to this versifier who is far from skilful in form and most contemptible and commonplace in subject matter?

The fishwife was Count Leo Tolstoy; the source of the quotation is his once-celebrated essay, "What is Art?"

If we try to define what these revolutions in different ages and in different art forms have in common, I would suggest that the one obvious feature they all share is a radical *shift in selective emphasis*. The artist, as the scientist, is engaged in projecting his vision of reality into a particular medium. But the product of his efforts can never be an exact copy of reality. In the first place, he is up against the peculiarities and limitations of his medium: the painter's canvas does not have the micro-structure of the human retina, stone lacks the plasticity of living tissue, words are symbols which do not smell, or bleed. In the second place, the artist's perception and outlook on the world also has its peculiarities and limitations imposed by the implicit conventions of his time. The two factors interact: there is continuous feedback from language to thought, from the clay under the sculptor's fingers to the image he is trying to materialise. The dynamic tension between the biased mind and the obstinate medium compels the artist to make decisions at every step he takes (though the decision-making need not be conscious): to select and emphasise those features of reality which he considers to be significant and to ignore those which he considers irrelevant. Some aspects of experience defy representation, some can only be rendered in a simplified or distorted way, some only at the price of sacrificing others.

The term "selective emphasis" thus always involves three related factors: *selection, exaggeration* and *simplification*. They are at work in every province of art: in the narrative of events, historic or fictitious; in the visual representation of landscape or human figure, in portrait and caricature. But selective emphasis also operates in the scientist's laboratory. Every geographical map, every statistical diagram, every theoretical model of man or the universe is a deliberately schematised caricature of reality, based on the technique of selecting and highlighting the relevant features, simplifying or ignoring others, according to the criteria of relevance of that particular discipline or school of thought. In psychology, for instance, one finds radically different criteria of relevance among nineteenth-century introspectionists, contemporary behaviourists, Freudians, Jungians and existential psychologists, with corresponding contrasts in selective emphasis, resulting in radically different portraits of man; and the same considerations apply to the history of medicine. In physics, the paradigm of exact science, there are radical shifts from Aristotelian anthropomorphism to Newtonian mechanism, from the deterministic to the probabilistic approach, from forces to fields. Even a cursory glance at the history of science makes one realise that its criteria of relevance are liable to changes as striking as the changes of style in art; and comparison between the two domains makes the history of art appear a little less confusing by showing us at least a dim outline of a more comprehensible pattern.

Thus the recurrent revolutionary upheavals in the content and style of literary productions can be described as shifts in the criteria of relevance and in selective emphasis.

The *second phase* in the historic cycle is, as already mentioned, the exploration of the new subject matter, the elaboration of the new styles and techniques, which need not further detain us here. For it is the *third* phase in the cycle which is of special interest to (and the main headache of) every practitioner of our profession: the phase of saturation and subsequent frustration of the writer and his audience. I quoted Tolstoy's indignant outcry against Verlaine's moon dying in a copper sky; today it is hard to understand what Tolstoy got so excited about. Yesterday's daring metaphors are today clichés. Yesterday's obscenities are today's banalities; the bourgeois is no longer *épatable*; stark sex, like the moon deprived of its mystery, turns out to be all craters and pimples.

These are inevitable consequences of a fundamental property of the nervous system. Seasoned ambulance crews no longer turn a hair at the sight of mangled casualties, and even the inmates of Auschwitz developed a degree of emotional immunity. There exists a phenomenon which psychologists call habituation. You do not hear the ticking of the clock in your room, but you hear that it has suddenly stopped. You do not feel the pressure of the chair against your back; but you do feel it when you shift your position. Nerve cells in the retina do not signal sameness, they only signal contrast. And habituation is not confined to man. Dr Horn at Cambridge has recently found single nerve cells in the mid-brain of the rabbit which responded promptly to a tone sounded at a frequency of 1000 cycles per second, but ceased to respond after several repetitions of the stimulus. Habituation to the 1000-cycle tone does not, however, prevent a strong response of the same cell when an only slightly different, 900-cycle tone is sounded. Dr Horn presented examples of similar phenomena in animals as different as locusts, squids and cats.*

If even a squid can be that blasé, how can the writer hope to fight the law of diminishing returns? The recurrent cycles of stagnation, crisis, revolution and new departure seem to be mainly caused by the progressive habituation of both artist and audience to any well-established technique, style or subject matter, and its resulting loss of emotional appeal, of evocative power. This loss, unfortunately, is unavoidable, because once the new style has become stabilised and familiar, the reader no longer needs to exert his imagination to assimilate the message; he is deprived of the effort of re-creation and degraded to a mere consumer. There can be little doubt that the bulk of all literature, probably from Greece onwards, but certainly since

* *New Scientist*, 7 August 1969.

the invention of the printing press, consisted of inferior consumer goods, written in the long periods of stagnation within the recurrent cycle. But this huge mass of pulp has decayed and vanished from sight; only samples of exceptional quality have survived and provide the material of the history of literature.

Any new art form, however revolutionary it seemed at first, grows after a while tired and stale; it loses its power over the audience. The staleness lies of course not in the form itself, which may be enduring, but in the consumer's jaded palate. The history of art could be written in terms of the artist's struggle against the deadening effects of saturation. It is not his fault if he is fighting a losing battle. He may produce cheese-cake or he may produce caviare, he is nevertheless helpless against the fundamental process of habituation which operates in the rabbit's brain as in the reader's nervous system. Its effect on the artist is a growing sense of frustration, and the growing realisation – which may be conscious or not – that the conventional techniques of his time have become inadequate as a medium of communication and self-expression.

Two opposite methods seem to have been tried over and again to improve communication with the audience: screaming and whispering. The first tries to impress the message on the audience by an overly direct appeal to the emotions, through tear-jerkers, melodramatics or more refined derivations of it; it tries to provide spicier fare for jaded appetites and to cover impotence by flamboyant gestures and mannerisms. In the visual arts one finds some or all of these symptoms cropping up in the successive periods of decline of Egyptian, Greek and Roman sculpture, in the manneristic styles of the later Baroque, in the choicer horrors of the Victorian age, and so on. The general trend in periods of decadence is towards the over-emphatic and the over-explicit, and need not concern us further.

The opposite method to counteract the law of diminishing returns in the evolution of art is of much greater interest. Instead of relying on the emphatic and the explicit, it tends towards economy and implicitness. It is usual to credit the French Symbolist movement – Mallarmé, Verlaine, Rimbaud – with having initiated the shift from explicit statement to implicit suggestion, and the French Impressionist school with a parallel achievement in painting. However, this movement from the obvious to the oblique can be observed in the most varied periods and art forms as an effective antidote to satiety and decadence. Nevertheless it is worth quoting a passage in which Mallarmé outlines the programme of the Symbolist movement:

> It seems to me that there should be only allusions. The volatile image of the dreams they evoke, these make the song: the Parnassians [the classicist movement of Leconte de Lisle, Heredia, *et al.*] who make a complete demonstration of the object thereby lack mystery; *they deprive the* [*reader's*] *mind of that delicious joy of imagining that it creates*. To *name* the thing means forsaking three-quarters of a poem's enjoyment – which is derived from unravelling it gradually, by happy guesswork; to suggest the thing creates the dream.*

Yet this technique was not invented by the symbolists; it is as old as art itself. It starts with mythology. The *Bhagavad Gita* is an allegory which every Hindu scholar and mystic interprets after his own fashion; Genesis is studded with archetypal symbols; Christ speaks in parables, the Oracle in riddles, Orpheus on fiddles. The purpose is not to obscure the message; on the contrary, it is to make it more luminous by compelling the recipient to act as a fluorescent screen, to work out the implications by his own effort, to re-create it. "Implicit" is derived from the Latin *plicare*, and means "folded in", like a roll of parchment. The implicit message has to be unfolded by the reader; he must unravel it, fill the gaps, solve riddles. But as time goes by, the reader learns to see through the tricks, the disguises become transparent, he is deprived, as Mallarmé has it, "of that delicious joy of imagining that he creates". So the writer or poet will strive towards even more disciplined economy and more subtle implications; the parchment will be rolled in even tighter.

* S. Mallarmé, *Enquête sur l'Evolution Littéraire* (1888).

I once called this "the law of infolding";† it seems to be the most effective reply to the law of diminishing returns. It runs like a kind of *leitmotif* through the history of literature. The Homeric epics were originally broadcast by travelling bards who impersonated their heroes by voice and acting, which is the most direct and emphatic method of narration. Later on, around the seventh century BC, the epics were consolidated in their present form, to be recited on festive occasions; by now, however, they were folded into rolls of parchment. The bard impersonated; the written word had to be deciphered. A pair of quotation marks is sufficient to symbolise the human voice, and printer's ink is generally more effective in arousing emotion than a histrionic recital. Histrionics are left to the stage and screen, but they are also subject to the law of infolding. Victorian melodrama has become a parody of its own genre, and films not more than twenty years old which moved us at the time appear now – exceptions always granted – surprisingly dated, obvious, over-acted, over-explicit. And the background music is simply incredible.

The writer's best friend is his pair of scissors. In his advice to a younger writer, Hemingway wrote: "The more bloody good stuff you cut out, the more bloody good your novel will be. . . ." The law of infolding demands that the reader should never be given something for nothing; he must be made to pay in emotional currency by exerting his imagination. Otherwise one gets the dreaded "So what?" reaction. "Caroline felt her heart go out to Peter." So what? Let it go out. The German word for composing poetry is *dichten* – to compress. But compression can also operate in semantic space, by squeezing several meanings, or levels of meaning, into a single statement. Freud thought that this was the essence of poetry; Empson's "seven types of ambiguity" are variations on the same theme.

Needless to say, the techniques of infolding can be used in a fraudulent manner to create deliberate obscurity. Though it has been said that the Venus of Milo would lose much of her attraction if her arms were restored, it is unlikely that her

† *The Act of Creation.*

creator broke them off in cold blood. But who can draw the line between deliberate cheating and the tricks of the unconscious? Much of the *nouveau roman* and of *Last Year in Marienbad* reminds one of a way of playing poker where you hide your cards not only from your opponent but from yourself. This can sometimes be a winning strategy – but what does "winning" mean in this context?

There are many other fields where one can watch the law of infolding at work. Humour has travelled a long way from the *Punch* cartoon to the *New Yorker's* sophisticated riddles. Metaphors have a way of shrivelling into dehydrated clichés; they are replaced by fresh supplies of a less obvious and explicit kind. Rhythm and metre have evolved from simple, repetitive pulses into intricate patterns, in which the erstwhile beat of the tom-tom is implied, but no longer pounded out. Rhyme, as the most explicit form of euphony, is folding in – or up.

In the contemporary visual arts the process is too obvious to need stressing. Only a forger could, in our day, paint in the style of Vermeer (however perfect his technique) because to paint like Vermeer, the artist would have to forget that he has ever seen a Manet or Cézanne. So he has to be either a forger or a Rip Van Winkle who has slept since the seventeenth century. But it would be a mistake to believe that the trend towards the implicit is found only in modern painting. Leonardo invented the technique of the *sfumato* or veiled form, such as the blurred contours at the corners of the Mona Lisa's eyes, which have never lost their fascination; and Titian in his old age invented the technique of what Vasari called "the crudely daubed strokes and blobs" which, looked at from close quarters, cannot be deciphered and which let the picture unfold only when you step back; Rembrandt went through a similar progression, from the neat and meticulous to the loose and suggestive brushstroke in his rendering of embroideries. The examples could be multiplied. It could be said, for instance, that in the peak periods of Chinese painting the picture consisted of what was left out. I cannot resist quoting just one phrase from a seventeenth century Chinese manual (which I owe to Gombrich): "Figures, even though painted without eyes, must seem to look; without ears, must seem to listen. . . . That is truly giving expression to the invisible. . . ."

To make a last cross-reference to science, even there the law of infolding operates. Aristotle firmly believed that all possible discoveries and inventions had already been made in his time; Bacon and Descartes thought that it would take just one more generation to solve all the mysteries of the universe; even nineteenth-century scientists held such optimistic beliefs. Only recently did we begin to realise that the unfolding of the secrets of nature was accompanied by a parallel process of infolding, because the more precise knowledge the physicist acquired, the more ambiguous and elusive were the mathematical symbols he had to use; he can no longer make an intelligible model of reality, he can only allude to it by abstract equations.

To sum up – I have tried to point to a recurrent pattern in the history of science and art which, broadly speaking, both seem to move through cycles of revolution – consolidation – saturation – crisis and new departure. Revolutions are characterised by shifts in selective emphasis; the period of consolidation is one of cumulative progress; the third period is a constant struggle against the law of diminishing returns, and one of the effective antidotes is indicated by the law of infolding. I must ask your indulgence for so much law-making and speculation; but if the Creator had a purpose in equipping us with a neck, he surely meant us to stick it out.

SCIENCE AND PARASCIENCE*

In the 1950s a remarkable periodical was published in England by the physicist Dr Irving John Good, called the *Journal of Half-Baked Ideas*. A selection of articles from it was later published as a book with the title *The Scientist Speculates: An Anthology of Partly Baked Ideas* (1). The paper I am about to deliver is a sort of club sandwich of partly baked ideas, which has several layers. The top layer, on which I shall start, is a fully baked crust which through long exposure has almost hardened into clichés. The subsequent layers will be half-baked, quarter-baked, and so on, until we reach the bottom layer of shamelessly raw speculation.

In a recently published book (2) I tried to make the point that the unthinkable phenomena of parapsychology appear somewhat less preposterous in the light of the unthinkable propositions of modern quantum physics. This argument is by no means new; it has been so often and so brilliantly demonstrated that it has almost become a commonplace. But it can also be applied to classical Newtonian physics. To mention a single example: from the point of view of naive commonsense, the type of action-at-a-distance called telepathy is no more mysterious than that other action-at-a-distance called universal gravity. When Kepler, eighty years before Newton, came out with the wild suggestion that the tides were caused by the

*Banquet address to the annual convention of the Parapsychological Association, Edinburgh, September 1972. Parts of this paper I have incorporated in *The Challenge of Chance: A Mass Experiment in Telepathy and Its Unexpected Outcome* by Sir Alister Hardy, Robert Harvie and myself (London and New York, 1973).

attraction of the moon, even Galileo dismissed the idea as an occult fancy, which contradicted the laws of nature. And Newton himself vehemently rejected the concept of universal gravity *unless* there existed some interstellar medium which transmitted it. In his third letter to Bentley he wrote: "That one body may act upon another, at a distance, through a vacuum, without the mediation of anything else . . . is to me so great an absurdity that no man who has . . . a competent faculty of thinking can ever fall into it."

Yet fall we all did, as schoolboys in the classroom, without becoming aware of our fallen state. Such is the power of mental habituation. To live with a mental paradox is like being married to a nagging bitch; after a while you become deaf to her nagging and settle down in comfortable resignation.

Thus even *classical* physics could only make progress at the price of insulting common sense and by breaking and re-making the previously sacrosanct "laws of nature". *Modern* physics had to repeat both offences in even more brutal ways. And parapsychology has to carry a similar burden of guilt. Einstein, de Broglie and Schrödinger between them have de-materialised matter like the conjuror who makes the lady vanish from the box on the stage. Heisenberg replaced determinism by the Principle of Indeterminacy and causality by statistics; Dirac postulated holes in space stuffed with electrons of negative mass; Thomson made a single particle go through two holes in a screen at the same time – which, Cyril Burt commented, is more than a ghost can do. Photons of zero rest-mass have been observed in the process of giving virgin birth to twins endowed with solid rest-mass; Feynman made time flow backwards on his diagrams; and these are but a few glimpses from the surrealistic panorama which quantum physics has opened up for us. To paraphrase an old saying: inside the atom is where things happen that don't.

The astronomers are having an equally jolly time. The Big Bang versus Continual Creation controversy would have delighted medieval theologians. Radio astronomers claim that they can hear background noises which must have originated with the pristine bang of creation. More recently the universe became pockmarked with black holes into which the mass of collapsing stars is sucked at the speed of light, to be annihilated and vanish from our universe into the blue yonder. The universe is turning out to be a very odd place indeed, and we no longer need ghosts to make our hair stand on end.

My purpose in reminding you of these well-known developments was to underline once more the fact that the mechanistic and deterministic world view, which is still dominant in the behavioural sciences and in the public at large, no longer has a leg left to stand on; it has become a Victorian anachronism. The nineteenth-century clockwork model of the universe is in shambles, and since matter itself has been dematerialised, materialism can no longer claim to be a scientific philosophy.

As a side effect of this philosophical crisis, we may observe a curiously reciprocal development in the exact sciences on the one hand, and parapsychology on the other. For the last fifty years, our leading physicists have been playing around with more and more obscure mental constructs, whose quasi-mystical implications are camouflaged by technical jargon and mathematical formalism. If Galileo were alive, he would certainly have accused them, as he accused Kepler, of dabbling in "occult fancies". At the same time he might have looked with a benevolent eye at the parapsychologist's increasing reliance on hard statistics, rigorous controls, mechanical gadgets and electronic computers. Thus the intellectual climate in the two camps seems to have been changing in opposite directions: Rhine's successors, because of their statistical orientation, have sometimes been accused of scientific pedantry – while Einstein's successors were accused of flirting with ghosts in the guise of particles which possess no mass, nor weight, nor any precise location in space.

I believe that this apparent convergence is more than a surface phenomenon. But one must be careful in drawing conclusions from it. The time for physics and parapsychology to fall happily into each other's arms is not yet. What both have increasingly in common are the two negative attributes that I mentioned a minute ago: both defy common sense, and both defy the previously accepted "laws of nature". They are both provocative and iconoclastic. And, to say it once more, the baffling paradoxes produced by one make the baffling paradoxes of the other appear a little less preposterous. If whole stars can vanish into black holes, there may also be singularities in the continuum which produce poltergeists.

One might call this a kind of negative affinity. In concrete terms it does not amount to much. But philosophically and emotionally it seems to me significant. It helps to put one's nagging doubts at rest. It is encouraging to know that if the parapsychologist is out on a limb, the physicist is out on a tightrope.

But unavoidably the question arises whether there are any signs on the horizon of a *positive* affinity, or convergence, between post-materialistic physics and post-spiritualistic parapsychology. I think one can distinguish two such sign-posts, the first of a subjective, the second of an objective, nature.

An impressive number of eminent physicists, including several Nobel laureates, have shown an inclination to flirt with parapsychology – witnessed by the list of past presidents of the British Society for Psychical Research; and, as in other subversive movements, the number of fellow-travellers by far exceeds that of the card-carrying members. Thus, for instance, the discoverer of the electron, Sir Joseph J. Thomson, was one of the earliest members of the society. Now, why should physicists in particular show this proneness to infection by the ESP bug? The answer can be found in the autobiographical writings and metaphysical speculations of the greatest among them. The dominant chord which you can detect in nearly all of them is a pervasive feeling of frustration, caused by the realisation that science can only elucidate certain aspects, or levels, of reality, while the ultimate questions will always elude its grasp, vanishing into infinite regress like images reflected in a hall of mirrors. "Physics is mathematical," wrote Bertrand Russell, "not because we know so much about the physical world, but because we know so little; it is only its mathematical properties that we can discover" (3). This resigned agnosticism leads either into a spiritual desert – Schrödinger in his middle age gave up physics in disgust – or, more often, it leads to a new open-mindedness, a sophisticated kind of innocence on a higher turn of the spiral.

So much about what I have called the subjective aspect of convergence. The next step is to look for *objective* convergences, i.e. areas where the domains of physics and parapsychology might enter into direct contact. But this step means digging into a deeper layer of the club sandwich, which is no longer fully baked. There is no need to dwell here on earlier abortive efforts to provide a physicalistic explanation of ESP by radio waves and the like. They were honourable attempts at dressing the wolf in sheep's clothing, and they inevitably failed. With the advent of quantum theory, however, these attempts became considerably more sophisticated – we might say that they progressed from the quarter-baked to the half-baked stage. Examples are Axel Firsoff's hypothesis of extrasensory communication by means of *mindons* – the hypothetical particles of an all-pervasive mind-stuff, with properties somewhat similar to the neutrino's; Martin Ruderfer's complex theory of a neutrino sea interacting with matter; and the late Adrian Dobbs's *psitrons*, swarms of particles of imaginary mass,* travelling along a second, imaginary time dimension, and capable of impinging directly on neurons in the percipients' brains.

These theories are of considerable ingenuity. Yet, like other similar efforts, they fail to satisfy because they give the impression of improvised bridges across the nasty abyss, supported by ad hoc hypotheses. To put it differently, their authors seem to remain under the spell of the physicist's concepts and categories, instead of creating their own, autonomous conceptual systems, a universe of discourse commensurate with the phenomena in their own field – as biology has done to some extent. I would like to quote here another after-dinner speaker at one of your earlier conventions, the Professor of Physics at Yale:

* The term "imaginary" is used here in its mathematical sense, referring to so-called "imaginary numbers".

> I have probed physics for suggestions it can offer towards a solution of the sort of problem you seem to encounter. The positive results, I fear, are meagre and disappointing. . . . But why, I should like to ask, is it necessary to import into any new discipline all the approved concepts of an older science in its contemporary state of development? Physics did not adhere slavishly to the Greek rationalistic formulations that preceded it; it was forced to create its own specific constructs. . . .
>
> The parapsychologist, I think . . . must strike out on his own and probably reason in bolder terms than present-day physics suggests (4).

This does not mean of course that parapsychology should cut itself off from the mainstream of scientific research, and retire into an ivory tower. But that mainstream itself is now flowing into bold new directions which seem to point to an indirect sort of convergence in the future – not by premature shortcuts, but by a sort of isomorphism or Gestalt affinity. I am referring here to what one might call the *mentalistic trend* in biology and physics, with its explicit or implied admission of the power of mind over matter. This trend seems to be an indirect consequence of those paradoxical developments in quantum physics which I have mentioned before. In its still early days, Sir James Jeans made his celebrated *pronunciamento*: "Today there is a wide measure of agreement, which on the physical side of science approaches almost to unanimity, that the stream of knowledge is heading towards a non-mechanical reality; the universe begins to look more like a great thought than a great machine" (5).

This statement was not only meant as a poetic metaphor; it was the embarrassing but inescapable conclusion emerging from the physical laboratories. There were several aspects to it. One of the most fundamental was the *Principle of Complementarity*. It stated that the smallest constituents of the universe are ambiguous, Janus-faced entities which under certain conditions behave like hard little pellets, under other conditions like waves in a non-material medium. These two types of behaviour mutually exclude each other, but also mutually complement each other. Heisenberg was apparently the first to recognise that this complementarity may be regarded as a paradigm of the dualism of matter and mind. In his autobiography he was even more explicit. "Atoms are not *things*," he wrote. "When we get down to the atomic level the objective world in space and time no longer exists" (6). From here there is only one step to the realisation that the contents of mental experience also defy definition in terms of space, time and substance, yet are somehow linked with the material brain – as the wave function of the electron is somehow linked with its material aspect. One might conclude, with Dr Good (in *The Scientist Speculates*) that "the physicist's basic wave equation – Schrödinger's psi function – is mysterious enough to provoke the conjecture that it may in some sense explain features of the mind. Perhaps the psi of quantum physics depends on the psi of the parapsychologists." Other scientists have pointed half jokingly, half seriously, at the hidden sympathies between the two psis.

Thus there is not only a *negative* convergence between the two domains in the sense of a shared contempt for common-sense and for mental smugness; there are also portents of a tentative *positive* convergence – which, however, is more implicit than explicit, potential rather than actual, intuitive rather than logical – a sort of Gestalt affinity, as I called it before. It should not be hurried or forced; I am old-fashioned enough to believe that courtship should precede mating. The great syntheses in the history of thought emerge when the time is ripe for them – when all the components which are to go into the new synthesis are already present. Neither science nor parascience appears to have reached that stage.

One might add here, as a footnote, that in biology, too, there is a growing tendency to recognise the power of mind over matter. Some twenty years ago Sir John Eccles created quite a stir when he proposed that the exercise of conscious volition – a dirty word in behaviouristic psychology – could, by affecting a single neuron, trigger off changes of activity in large areas of the cortical network. Since then, other researchers have shown that mental volition, assisted by various types of biofeedback apparatus, can influence the activities of the autonomic nervous system and bring on the alpha-wave rhythm of the brain.

We have now arrived at the last layer of the club sandwich, which is almost completely unbaked. I am approaching it with a certain amount of trepidation. The more so as I must now revert to some anecdotal material – which, however, may come as a relief after so much quantum jabberwocky.

When my recent book, *The Roots of Coincidence*, was published, I received a good many letters from people anxious to relate their experiences. I shall quote from two of these, which seem to me remarkable in their different ways.

The contents of the first I must relate in a slightly camouflaged version to spare the feelings of those involved. It concerns a young architect who had suffered a nervous breakdown and thrown himself in front of an incoming train in a London tube station. He suffered a fractured pelvis, punctured abdomen with extrusion of intestine, lacerated back and severe bruising, but survived. They had to jack up the train to get him out; he had been under it, but the wheels had stopped just short of his body. However, according to the hospital doctor's account to the victim's relatives, which was later confirmed by an official of London Transport, the train was not stopped by the driver applying the brakes (the time-lag was apparently too short for that) but by a passenger in the train who, quite unaware of what was happening, had pulled the emergency handle.

I passed the case on to a friend who was willing to investigate it – Mr Tom Tickell, a member of the editorial staff of the *Guardian*. Mr Tickell contacted London Transport, but ran into the traditional barrier of red tape. The identity of the passenger who had pulled the emergency handle was allegedly unknown. The name of the driver of the train was eventually disclosed, but not his address. A letter to the driver, addressed c/o London Transport, remained unanswered. Thus, as so often happens, the case petered out.*

* For a more detailed description of it, see *The Challenge of Chance*.

The next case is in a different vein. What follows is an extract from a letter from J. B. Priestley, after he had read my book. No doubt you know that Priestley is married to Jacquetta Hawkes, the archaeologist.

> My wife bought three large coloured lithographs by Graham Sutherland. When they arrived here from London she took them up to her bedroom to hang them up in the morning. They were leaning against a chair and the one on the outside, facing the room, was a lithograph of a grasshopper. When Jacquetta got into bed that night, she felt some sort of twittering movement going on, so she got out and pulled back the clothes. There was a grasshopper in the bed. No grasshopper had been seen in that room before, nor has been seen since. No grasshopper has ever been seen at any other time in this house (7).

The first of these stories might possibly be explained by ESP, which prompted the unknown passenger to pull the emergency handle; the second, in common with many coincidental happenings, defies explanation in both conventional *and* parapsychological terms. They are equally baffling to the theologian, for if the passenger's action is to be credited to Providence, what prompted Providence to put a grasshopper in Mrs Priestley's bed? I have never heard it suggested that Providence has a sense of humour.

Whether one believes that such highly improbable meaningful coincidences are manifestations of some unknown principle operating beyond physical causality, or are produced by the proverbial monkey at the typewriter, is a matter of inclination and temperament. I have found to my surprise that the majority of my acquaintances – among whom scientists predominate – belong to the former category, although some are reluctant to confess it, for fear of ridicule, even to themselves. Carl Jung had the same experience among his patients, which was perhaps not surprising; more surprising is that Nobel laureate Wolfgang Pauli (one of the chief architects of quantum theory, who predicted the existence of the neutrino) cooperated with Jung on the latter's famous treatise: "Synchronicity: An Acausal Connecting Principle" (8). Jung defines synchronicity as "the simultaneous occurrence of two or more meaningfully but not causally connected events"; and the acausal factor behind such events is said to be "*equal in rank to causality as a principle of explanation*".

The origins of Jung–Pauli's synchronicity concept can be traced back partly to Schopenhauer, partly to the Austrian biologist Paul Kammerer who, in 1919, published a book (which put an end to his academic career) called *Das Gesetz der Serie* (not translated). Kammerer's concept of Seriality referred to "the recurrence or clustering of meaningfully but not causally connected events" – familiar to all gamblers and insurance companies. He postulated that coexistent with causality there is an acausal principle active in the universe which tends towards unity. It is in some respects comparable to universal gravity, but whereas gravity acts indiscriminately on inert mass this hypothetical force correlates by affinity, or a kind of selective resonance. "We thus arrive," he writes, "at the image of a world-mosaic or cosmic kaleidoscope, which, in spite of constant shufflings and rearrangements, also takes care of bringing like and like together."

Now this sounds pretty wild talk in the twentieth century, but in fact the concept goes back all the way to the Hippocratic "sympathy of all things": "there is one common flow, one common breathing, all things are in sympathy." This doctrine that everything in the universe is hanging together, not by mechanical causes but by hidden affinities which account for apparent coincidences, was not only the foundation of primitive magic, of astrology and alchemy; it also runs as a leitmotiv through the teachings of the Pythagoreans, NeoPlatonists and the philosophers of the early Renaissance. Jung's dualism of causality and acausal synchronicity was neatly formulated by Pico della Mirandola, *anno domini* 1550:

> Firstly there is the unity in things whereby each thing is at one with itself, consists of itself, and coheres with itself. Secondly, there is the unity whereby one creature is united with the others and all parts of the world constitute one world (10).

The scientific revolution put an end to this type of thinking and proclaimed mechanical causality as the absolute ruler of matter and mind. Yet three centuries later we are witnessing a swing of the pendulum in the opposite direction. On the subatomic level the absolute rule of causality has come to an end; and Schrödinger's psi function, which defines a single electron, is spread out, Mirandola-wise, over the whole universe. On the cosmic scale Mach's principle, endorsed by Einstein, stipulates that the inertial forces on earth are governed by the total mass of the universe around us. Whitehead commented:

> It is difficult to take seriously the suggestion that these domestic phenomena on the earth are due to the influence of the fixed stars. I cannot persuade myself to believe that a little star in its twinkling turned round Foucault's pendulum in the Paris Exhibition of 1851 (11).

But there it is. Mach's principle has become an integral part of modern physics, even though it smacks of the Hippocratic "sympathy of all things". For it implies not only that the universe at large influences local events, but also that local events have an influence, however small, on the universe at large. Everything hangs together; microcosm reflects macrocosm and is reflected by it.

In biology, too, there is a search for new principles – or, perhaps a revival of earlier insights – which would provide a more satisfying approach to the creative aspects of evolution than Neo-Darwinism, for all its historic merits, has been able to provide. Jacques Monod's *Chance and Necessity* (1971) may turn out to be the swansong of a rash generation of scientists who claimed that chance mutations plus natural selection provide the *complete* explanation of the emergence of higher levels of organisation, of more complex structures and forms of behaviour. Today more and more biologists are coming to realise that random mutations may provide part of the explanation, but not the whole explanation and perhaps not even an important part of it.

At the same time, the tyranny of the Second Law of Thermodynamics with its implied tendency towards transforming cosmos into chaos seems to be approaching its end with the realisation that the law applies only to so-called closed systems, whereas in open systems such as a living organism, an opposite tendency seems to be at work – creating order out of disorder, cosmos out of chaos, designing patterns where none existed before. This ubiquitous constructive principle has been proposed by various authors under various names; it carries echoes of Galen's and Kepler's *facultas formatrix*, Goethe's *Gestaltung* and Bergson's *élan vital*; in more recent times the German biologist Woltereck proposed the term "anamorphosis", which von Bertalanffy adopted, while L. L. Whyte called it the "morphic principle". It is related to Schrödinger's concept of organisms feeding on negative entropy, which again is related to what I called elsewhere the integrative tendency.

What all these tentative formulations have in common is that they regard the morphic, or formative, or integrative tendency, the striving towards higher forms of unity-in-diversity, as an irreducible principle, which is as fundamental to the sciences of life as its antagonist, the Second Law of Thermodynamics, is to inanimate matter. Whether you call such a principle causal or acausal is a matter of semantics.

I would like to end this talk by mentioning briefly two somewhat bizarre, wayout experiments. A young graduate student named Stuart Kaufman at California Medical School created quite a stir some four or five years ago by setting up a system of several hundred simple binary on–off switches; each switch had the inputs coming into it from two other switches chosen at random; and each input channel had one of the functions of Boolean logic – yes, no, and, or – assigned to it, again at random. Then he fed an electric impulse into that chaotic system and watched what was going to happen. What happened was that the system soon settled down into a cyclic routine, the impulses going round in a complex stable pattern, or one of several alternative patterns – order had been generated from disorder. What's more, when the system's routine was disturbed, the pattern soon righted itself – the originally random system manifested a kind of homeostasis (12).

The second experiment is something of a skeleton in the cupboard of the British SPR. I am referring to the famous Spencer Brown controversy of twenty years ago. Brown claimed that by matching pairs of digits at random, the first digit symbolising an ESP guess, the second the target card, he obtained a significantly higher number of hits than chance expectation. Mr Arthur T. Oram, an expert statistician, aided by several volunteer workers, then undertook the task of verifying Brown's results. His team matched no less than 500,000 digits taken from random tables. The result was strictly according to chance expectation, so Spencer Brown was refuted and all seemed well. But then Spencer Brown made a thorough analysis of Oram's tables – and discovered the classic decline effect of hits with odds against chance of the order of 7000 to one (13). It should be pointed out that Brown did not question the validity of the results obtained by ESP experiments – which he accepted at face value; but he thought that they pointed to some anomaly or hidden factor in the very nature of randomness. He did not elaborate on the nature of this suspected anomaly, but the idea bears a close resemblance to Kammerer's seriality and Jung–Pauli's synchronicity – the morphic or patterning or integrative tendency invading even the sober realm of random tables – as it invaded Kaufman's anarchic random circuits. It seems that nature is fond of blowing smoke rings.

Sir Alister Hardy, in his Gifford Lectures, seems inclined to believe that Spencer Brown was on the right track. This, he pointed out, would by no means invalidate the evidence for "true" ESP in spontaneous cases and also in *some* laboratory experiments. But he surmised that the results of a certain number of card-guessing and other statistical experiments

> may be due to something quite different from telepathy . . . something no less fundamental and interesting . . . something implicit in the very nature and meaning of randomness itself. . . . Let me say that if some of this apparent card-guessing and dice-influencing work should in fact turn out to be something very different, it will not, I believe, have been a wasted effort; it will have provided a wonderful mine of material for the study of a very remarkable new principle (14).

I may add that Hardy himself has in the meantime produced a substantial body of evidence, to be published shortly, for that hypothetical new principle – which dates back, as I said, to Hippocrates. How it works we do not know. We only know that it cannot work within the framework of classical causality any more than the quantum phenomena can be fitted into it. Perhaps it is somehow related to the physicist's "god of the gaps". Perhaps the roots of coincidence sprout from those gaps. To try to explain by it how the grasshopper got into Mrs Priestley's bed would be a grotesque exercise in misplaced concreteness. But the little mystic who is hidden inside each great scientist, longing to be let out, may perceive a connection which earlier cultures have always taken for granted. If I were asked to sum up in a single sentence these half-baked ideas at the end of my talk, I would propose this paraphrase of Spinoza: "Nature abhors randomness."

References

1. I. J. Good, ed., *The Scientist Speculates* (London, 1962).
2. A. Koestler, *The Roots of Coincidence* (London and New York, 1972).
3. Bertrand Russell, *An Outline of Philosophy* (London, 1927).
4. H. Margenau, in *Science and ESP,* ed. J. R. Smythies (London, 1967).
5. Sir James Jeans, *The Mysterious Universe* (Cambridge, 1937).
6. W. Heisenberg, *Der Teil und das Ganze* (Munich, 1969).
7. J. B. Priestley, in a letter to A. K., dated 7 February 1972.
8. C. G. Jung, "Synchronizität als ein Prinzip akausaler Zusammenhänge" in Jung–Pauli, *Naturerklärung und Psyche. Studien aus dem C. G. Jung-Institut, Zürich, IV*, 1952.
9. Paul Kammerer, *Das Gesetz der Serie* (Stuttgart and Berlin, 1919).
10. Pico della Mirandola, *Opera Omnia* (Basle, 1557).
11. Quoted by D. W. Sciama, *The Unity of the Universe* (London, 1959).
12. Stuart Kaufman, in *Journal of Theoretical Biology*, 1969.
13. G. Spencer Brown, *Probability and Scientific Inference* (London, 1957).
14. Sir Alister Hardy, *The Living Stream* (London, 1965).

SCIENCE AND REALITY*

Some of my friends and well-wishers professed to be shocked because my last book, *The Roots of Coincidence*, is concerned with parapsychology – i.e. telepathy and the even more puzzling phenomena of psychokinesis, short-term precognition and apparently meaningful coincidences. I would like to take this opportunity to mention briefly some of the reasons which may prompt a rational person – which I believe myself to be – with a strong scientific bent, to get involved in these unorthodox branches of research.

The evidence for ESP can be divided into two broad categories – on the one hand experiments in the laboratory and on the other hand what one might call out-of-the-blue phenomena which occur spontaneously, such as veridical dreams, clocks which stop at the moment of a person's death, and other meaningful coincidences. Such events do not constitute scientific evidence, although a great many people have experienced them; however strong their emotional impact, rationality prompts us to attribute them to chance.

But the evidence produced in the laboratories cannot be thus dismissed. Any single event – like the stopping of that clock – however improbable, can be ascribed to chance because the laws of probability do not apply to single events, only to large numbers of events on a statistical scale. But probability statistics is precisely the method used in modern ESP laboratory research, based on the same type of calculation as that employed by physicists, geneticists, market researchers

* Broadcast interview, National Broadcasting Company, New York, September 1972.

and insurance companies. And the *same* logic which compels us to dismiss the stopping of the clock as a chance event also compels us to *exclude* the possibility of chance if a telepathic subject persistently, in thousands of consecutive card-guessing or dice-throwing experiments, scores a persistently higher number of hits than the probability calculus permits – because here the odds against chance are on an astronomical scale.

It was this strictly orthodox, statistical approach, applied to an unorthodox subject, which gradually wore down academic resistance – and incredulity – in the course of the forty years since Professor Rhine established the first laboratory for Parapsychology at Duke University, North Carolina. Since then, a great number of similar laboratories have been established all over the world – including Soviet Russia and other Communist countries – in which scientists work under the same rigorously controlled test conditions as researchers in other fields, using sophisticated computers and electronic apparatus to eliminate as far as possible human error in evaluating the results. And the results show that ESP – extrasensory perception – is a fact, whether we like it or not. In 1969 the American Association for the Advancement of Science approved the application of the Parapsychological Association to become an associate of that august body. That decision conferred on parapsychology the ultimate seal of respectability.

Nevertheless, even open-minded people feel a strong intellectual discomfort, or even revulsion, when confronted with phenomena which seem to contradict what they believe to be the immutable laws of physics. The answer is that the laws of physics are by no means immutable, but in constant flux; and that since the advent of Planck, Einstein and Heisenberg, modern quantum physics has discarded all our classical, commonsense notions of time, space, matter and causality. Thus both physics and parapsychology point to aspects or levels of reality beyond the reach of contemporary science – a coded message written in invisible ink between the lines of a banal letter. Though we can only decipher tantalisingly small fragments of the message, the knowledge that it is there is exciting and comforting at the same time.

SOLITARY CONFINEMENT*

Anthony Grey: I've been reading *Dialogue with Death* and some of your autobiography, *The Invisible Writing*, and I've been increasingly struck by the similarities between our experiences. You were arrested in 1937, and held in solitary confinement in Spain. Thirty years later, in 1967, I was arrested and held in solitary confinement in China. We were both journalists. And campaigns were in both cases mounted at home for our release; and when we came home, we both wrote books. You wrote *Dialogue with Death* in two months, and I wrote *Hostage in Peking* in six weeks. We were both thirty-two. I'm thirty-two now, you were thirty-two then. And these coincidences are very strong. Some of the most striking things, I suppose, about your experience – which you refer to as the hours by the window – in solitary confinement – was this feeling that a veil had fallen and that you'd been in touch with what you call the real reality, and you say that you had a great feeling or a direct certainty that a higher order of reality existed. And that it alone invested existence with meaning. Now, since then, thirty years have passed. How has this affected your life?

Arthur Koestler: Well, while the experience lasts, you know, it's very intense. You live on a sort of tragic plane – removed from everyday reality, removed from the trivial plane. Then the prison doors open and you are back in reality and the small worries of everyday life. And the intensity of that experience fades. Don't you feel that?

* Transcript of a discussion with Anthony Grey, from the television programme *One Pair of Eyes*, in which he related his experiences as a prisoner in China, 26 June 1971.

A. G.: Yes, I find that was a compromising situation; one compromised with a fierce ideal.
A. K.: And one even occasionally asked oneself, did I really have that experience? So it's a sort of diminishing-return thing. But on the other hand I think, on a deeper level, it has sort of reorganised your personality. In a less obvious way than –
A. G.: Yes. One of your analogies, which I think is very nice, is the real reality being written in invisible writing, writing which we can never read, which we only intuit by seeing a fragment from time to time. It's like a captain who goes to sea with sealed orders in his pocket, and when he gets to a certain point he opens his sealed order only to find the writing is invisible. But you say nevertheless the fact that he has these orders makes him behave differently to a man without them. How has this affected your behaviour or your enjoyment, your appreciation of life? Knowing that you had the orders, as it were.
A. K.: Well, I do believe in it. I think it is so, but these are things very difficult to put into words, and I think one shouldn't talk too much about it, you know, because one talks it away.
A. G.: Yes, one of the most striking things you said when I first met you was that some of the things which happen to a man in solitary confinement should perhaps be subject to the Official Secrets Act.
A. K.: Or a private Official Secrets Act.
A. G.: Yes. Why do you say that?
A. K.: Because you talk it away, you change it into small coin, you know.
A. G.: One of the things which I found most comforting in a sense reading some of your writing was that you felt you couldn't verbalise this experience, you couldn't put it into words. And this is what I found when I wrote the closing chapter of my book. I found myself saying, it's beyond words, feeling that I was incompetent or inadequate; that you had also found it was beyond words was very reassuring.
A. K.: Yes, and when you try to put in into words, it becomes either sort of maudlin or it becomes too intellectualised – I mean these are experiences which just resist being put into

everyday ordinary language.

A. G.: Do you think that everyone would benefit from a spell of solitary confinement by casting off what you call the layers of irrelevancy?

A. K.: No, I think the opposite. I think it depends on the individual. I have seen the opposite – people becoming nastier, bloodier.

A. G.: There were times when I was alone for two years when I felt grateful for being alone, that I didn't have to share my cell or my room with another prisoner. Did you feel this?

A. K.: I felt it very much so. I have talked to . . . you know, lots of my friends have been through gaol in the East, and to my utter surprise some of them say that if I have the choice I would always rather share a cell than be alone, to be alone is unbearable. I could never really put myself, project myself into that kind of mind.

A. G.: I felt that I only had myself to deal with. I felt I could deal with myself, but I couldn't necessarily control somebody else.

A. K.: No, oneself is already a handful, you know, but – (*quiet laughter*).

A. G.: Looking through *Hostage in Peking*, did you feel that there had been similarities in our reactions?

A. K.: Oh, very much so, yes.

A. G.: I noticed for example that we both walked up and down – you walked up and down six and a half paces, I walked up and down eight and a half paces.

A. K.: But the question is how wide your stride is.

A. G.: But that you had taken great care to step into the middle of the flagstones and not on the line. If you could do this five times everything would be all right, you would be released. I did a very similar thing.

A. K.: Knowing how stupid it is.

A. G.: Knowing. All the time.

A. K.: And not being able to –

A. G.: Not being able to do anything about it.

A. K.: And accepting it so. Knowing how stupid it is, being helpless against it, then one tells oneself, all right, you are stupid and superstitious, accept that it's part of you. Then it's all right.

A. G.: Yes. This is probably part of the coming to terms with oneself which is a very important aspect of being left alone, I think. I also remember very vividly – there was a cat jumped up outside your cell quite often, it couldn't get in because of the wire across the window. You were quite desperate to have the cat inside with you. I think this probably expresses a basic human desire for some kind of comfort or some kind of company.

A. K.: Do you remember *The Birdman of Alcatraz*? In solitary this seems to be an absolutely universal experience, that a bird or a cat or even a spider –

A. G.: In my case ants.

A. K.: In your case ants – becomes sort of out of all proportion important.

A. G.: Yes, I think perhaps this is the thing that tends to emphasise the feeling of a man in solitary confinement, that he is really only an aspect of total reality. Do you not agree?

A. K.: I do agree. And again I find difficulty in putting that into words. It's very intense.

A. G.: The feelings which you seem to develop in what you call the spiritual hothouse – you said solitary confinement is a spiritual hothouse, which I think is a very splendid summing up of it – you developed a feeling, an identity, a sympathy for other people, which you probably hadn't had before, and I think I shared this. This was one of my reactions which I shared with you. And as you said in your autobiography, my seemingly absurd and overstrong preoccupation had, I felt, a desperately direct bearing on the state of our society, and on applied politics. How did you feel about this when you came out? Did you feel it was relevant, because to talk about things in these terms may sound – I feel I sound terribly naive to those concerned only with the utilitarian realities. Do you feel it's applicable in any way and do you feel it should be applicable?

A. K.: I think it does influence your whole outlook on life, including politics. Because though I haven't been an eyewitness of the execution of my fellow prisoners – but I've been an ear-witness, you know; I heard when the cell doors were opened, when the priest came with his sanctus bell, between twelve and two at night, and then the chap – very often – because they were Spaniards, they shouted, "*Madre, madre*," mother, you know. They didn't know until the last minute whether the sentence had been confirmed or commuted. Only when at night the cell door was opened by the procession of the warder, the priest, then it was read – the decision was read out to them, that either they are going to go away for thirty years, which was of course absolute bliss – or to be shot within ten minutes, you know, taken out and shot. And then a very – quite a lot lost their nerves. In political theory you talk of the necessity to "liquidate" hostile elements, to "eliminate" – these are abstract words. But when you had heard these shouts and they ring in your ear, then you realise that one of the basic tenets of one type of politics, that the end justifies the means, has become unacceptable. You just don't accept any longer, that *any* reason, any superior lofty reason, justifies these acts. And that makes a very fundamental change in your outlook.

A. G.: This is what changed your attitude towards Communism I assume, is it?

A. K.: I think so. Oh, yes. . . .

A. G.: You also said that this idea of subjugating the individual to an abstract ethic, you said that not only Communism but any political movement which implicitly relies on purely utilitarian ethics must become a victim of the same fatal error. It leads to torture chambers, inquisitions, the guillotine; whether in fact the road is paved with quotations from Rousseau, Marx, Christ or Mohammed, it makes little difference. If there is a system, if there is a dogma, if there is a greater body to which the individual should subscribe, in fact it leads to this oppression of the individual.

A. K.: Whatever the abstract idea, the methods become unacceptable.

A. G.: Although the whole outcome of this is difficult to put into words, I was talking to a Chinese friend of mine the other day and he was showing me an old painting in which a very beautiful lotus flower grows from the mud. And I think perhaps in a sense there is this element of an experience of confinement, imprisonment, in solitary confinement, coming back to normal life and seeing it, at least for me, with a new awareness, a new appreciation of this – something very good and worthwhile coming out of something very bad. Do you agree?

A. K.: I do agree but with an addendum. That you are also all the time aware that in your trivial preoccupations you sort of walk over manholes with horrors underneath, you know. It's both. Both what you say – a more intense enjoyment of existence while it lasts, but at the same time also more intense awareness of what's tucked away under those manholes.

A. G.: Yes. I think you said in one of your chapters that you like to think that the founders of religions, prophets, and so on, had at moments been able to read a fragment of what you call the invisible text, but they so padded and dramatised it, that they themselves could no longer remember what was authentic about it. I would like to think this too. Do you in fact subscribe to any formalised religion now?

A. K.: No, I do not.

A. G.: Like myself you probably feel the abstract existence of something which is indefinable.

A. K.: Yes, except in symbols which are for me of equal validity whether it's a cross or the crescent moon or the shield of David. They are symbols, man-made symbols for a reality which cannot be formulated.

A. G.: . . . I was talking to a hermit on a small rocky island in the Channel, and I put this question to him. And he said that he felt that people involved in religion in civilised society were simply in it for what they could get out of it. I think that's probably an extreme reaction, but I think he had some truth in what he said. He also said he felt there was some force out there on this small barren island in this Channel, he felt there was some force. I think this is a reflection of our kind of conclusions. Perhaps we shouldn't even call them conclusions, it's too hard a word. Just a reflection of the kind of things we feel after being alone.

A. K.: Yes, because you see – I just said that every symbol has for me equal validity. But at the same time those symbols can become very poisonous. Lead to religious wars, inquisition and so on. The danger of overconcretising an experience which should not be concretised.

A. G.: It seems that we have a desire to oversimplify and hide behind symbols rather than being satisfied with what we're having now, a very inconclusive, a very tenuous and groping discussion about what we feel to be reality.

A. K.: And that symbol is then in danger of becoming a slogan, a totem pole, a war cry.

A. G.: Yes. You said that England with its muddled ways lives closer to the text of the invisible writing than any other country. You said that the English people are suspicious of causes, contemptuous of systems and bored by ideologies and sceptical about Utopias. It's a country of potterers in the garden and stickers in the mud. This is why you chose to live here. Do you still feel this true today?

A. K.: Yes. There are certain inroads, disquieting inroads. But on the whole I think it is so.

A. G.: And also another symptom we seem to share is over-sensitive reactions to other people in our daily lives – to the taxi driver or the charwoman. I find that I react very strongly to a small smile or a shrug or a – an instance of rudeness. Do you still find this thirty years later, do you think that's a continuing thing?

A. K.: Yes. I think one becomes oversensitised, you know. When one's day was made or undone by a warder's smile, by a rudeness or some kind of human kindness, one jumped at it like a dog at a bone, you know. Something to chew on. I think that has given one an allergy against hostility, rudeness and sensitisation towards –

A. G.: I think it takes time to build up a protective shell again. Perhaps one doesn't ever entirely.

A. K.: Up to a point, yes. But one is more sensitive, I think.

A. G.: In *Dialogue with Death* you make a mystifying statement: you say, in the Seville death house you paradoxically felt most free. How was that?

A. K.: I think "freedom" has several meanings. One is simply that you are confined to so much space and there are bars around you. . . . Then there is your feeling of inner freedom, of being alone and confronted with ultimate realities instead of with your bank statement. Your bank statement and other trivialities are again a kind of confinement. Not in space but in spiritual space.

A. G.: And why when you were confined to four walls did you feel most free?

A. K.: Because you are sort of stripped naked, facing ultimate reality, life and death. . . .

A. G.: Facing yourself really, do you think?

A. K.: And the universe. So you have got a dialogue with existence. A dialogue with life, a dialogue with death.

A. G.: This is an area which most people don't enter into.

A. K.: No. Well, most people do have a few confrontations in their lives, when they are severely ill or when a parent dies, or when they first fall in love. Then they are transferred from what I call the trivial plane to the tragic or the absolute plane. But it happens only a few times. Whereas in the type of experience which we shared, one has one's nose rubbed into it, for a protracted period.

A. G.: What about when one arrives back on the trivial plane? What do you think are the most threatening things to individual freedom in normal society?

A. K.: To go to the other extreme, suddenly, and to throw away everything and say, oh, these were just overwrought nerves and silly thoughts. To diminish and thereby to destroy the genuineness of the experience.

FAREWELL TO GAUGUIN*

*A Joyless Traveller's Guide to the South Pacific**

How our friends envied us. . . . The poor things had just started scanning the annual holiday supplements to discover how to make their travel allowances work the miracle of the loaves and fishes, while we were setting out on a round-the-world tour via Persia to Australia and back through the South Pacific and Caribbean. An enterprising Australian television company paid for the round trip – first-class air, first-class hotels, including the wife. How everybody envied us!

The journey took two months, and we returned, to coin a phrase, impoverished by the experience. Looking back at it, much of it seem like a journey through an air-conditioned, neon-lit tunnel, filled with the ubiquitous sound of Muzak, the smell of hamburgers, and the sight of blue-haired matrons spending the life insurance money of their deceased husbands on package tours from one duty-free shop to the next. Every day about 5.30 p.m., the tunnel changes into the dark womb of the same cocktail bar in the same Hilton or Sheraton in Honolulu, Fiji or Teheran; and subsequently into the same Rainbow Oak Room, where the same freeze-broiled choice T-bone is banged down by the same Italian waiter beside the same spluttering fancy candle on your table. Never a native dish. Never a tropical fruit. And all the time, day by day in every way, the muddy floods of Muzak pour down on you, piped into the lift, the lobby, the loo, bar, restaurant, swimming pool, coral beach – a tonal diarrhoea, unrelenting, inescapable. There are worldwide crusades for the preservation of wildlife and

* First published in the *Sunday Times*, 13 April 1969.

countryside; it is time somebody started a movement for the preservation of silence.

The explosion of the tourist industry, and its culture-eroding fallout, are still regarded as a minor nuisance. It is more than that. All over the world the tourist trade is an increasingly important factor in the national economy. In some countries it takes first or second place, and in some the number of tourists per annum outnumbers the total native population. It is a plague of locusts which brings to the natives material prosperity and cultural corruption, eroding traditional ways of living, contaminating arts and crafts with the vulgarity of the souvenir industry, and levelling down indigenous cultures to a uniform, mechanised stereotyped norm.

It is a global phenomenon. In the alpine meadows, the farmers are turning into innkeepers; tourists are easier to milk than cows. If French gastronomy is now hardly more than a legend revived each year by new editions of the *Guide Michelin*, it is an indirect consequence of the explosion; why should the chef waste hours on a dish when the customer from overseas drenches it in ketchup, and the natives soon learn to imitate him? One has watched the blight spread over Europe, from the gulf of Naples to the Swedish fjords; but I still had some illusions left about the Pacific islands, the "palm-fringed jewels of the sea", as the travel brochures invariably describe them, "where all of life sways to music and every heart responds to gaiety and laughter".

The first of the jewel islands we descended on, on our way back from Australia, was Fiji (more precisely Viti Levu, the central island of the group), which may serve as a fair sample. All the old hands in Sydney had told us that it was less spoilt than Noumea or Tahiti or Hawaii, and up to a point this seemed to be true. I must confess that I also had a naive curiosity about the place because, according to the reports of nineteenth-century missionaries and anthropologists, the "Feegeeans" were by far the most cruel and savage people among the Pacific islanders – and the most prodigious man-eaters, who practised cannibalism on an unprecedented scale, partly as a ritual, mainly because of a genuine addiction to human flesh. One Methodist missionary, the Reverend John Watsford, reported in 1846: ". . . The poor wretches [captives of a hostile tribe] were bound ready for the ovens, and their enemies were waiting anxiously to devour them. They did not club them lest any of their blood should be lost. Some, however, could not wait until the ovens were sufficiently heated, but pulled the ears off the wretched creatures and ate them raw. . . ." The last case of cannibalism is supposed to have occurred some thirty or forty years ago – nobody is quite sure – in a village a few miles from Nadi International Airport, and there are rumours about more recent cases in the interior. I mention this to indicate that cannibalism is not merely a subject for funny *New Yorker* cartoons, but a tradition that has survived within the span of living memory in Fiji; perhaps the starkest symbol of the abyss that separated one type of human culture from another only two or three generations ago. So one could not help wondering whether any traces of a mentality beyond our imagination could still be discerned by the perceptive eye.

The perceptive eye's first discovery at Nadi Airport was a tourist leaflet which had a map, a list of the various duty-free liquor allowances for travellers to the United States, Australia, Noumea, Tahiti, Mexico, and so on; and also a list of "helpful words and phrases in Fijian". The complete list of helpful phrases (omitting the translation in Fijian), ran as follows: "Go away." "I am broke." "Another round." "This is lousy." "Where is the entertainment tonight?" "Take me to the Skylodge." "Girls, stop crowding me." "Have we met before?" "I am very romantic." "You are an extremely attractive young woman." "Take me to your chief, leader, etc." "Where is the manager?" "You are standing on my foot." "My friend needs a doctor." "Driver, take me home."

To make my point clear: nobody in his right senses could wish to go back to the world of the head-hunting cannibal. But nobody in his right senses can rejoice to see it succeeded by a trashy tourist's paradise surrounded by native slums. Yet this is what has happened to Fiji and the other islands. Some years ago, Alan Moorehead wrote:

> In Tahiti the Polynesians had been taught to despise their own religion and had torn down their temples. In the same way, the Australian aboriginals' gods and totems had been brought into contempt by the white man and had been destroyed and forgotten. This left the natives without a tradition or a past, and they were like men who had lost their memories; they walked about in a trance in the materialistic present, and they could not be anchored to the new white god. Backwards as well as forwards the way was blocked.

The quote is from Moorehead's book, *The Fatal Impact: An Account of the Invasion of the South Pacific 1767-1840*. Since then the Pacific, and vast areas in the rest of the world, have suffered a second fatal impact. The first was colonisation; the second, one might call coca-colonisation. The first destroyed the fabric of existing cultures without providing a replacement; the second enveloped them in a plastic pseudo-culture, expanding like a giant bubblegum. The first imposed itself by rape, the second by seduction. But seduction of a victim under the age of consent is considered a crime, whether the victim is a person or a culture.

If Europe also shows signs of becoming coca-colonised, it has only itself to blame – its lack of vitality and decline of self-confidence. Even so, the process here is gradual and partial, and there is a strong, healthy resistance against it. In Melanesia or Polynesia, Hawaii or the Caribbean, the impact is more brutal and appalling because there is no resistance rooted in living tradition. Farewell, Gauguin.

Of course there were "bright intervals" on the journey, as the weatherman is wont to say. The palms are there, swaying in the breeze, the coral reefs and the mangrove forests; and if you get up a couple of hours before the package awakes, you can even enjoy a swim. But the grim question marks are also there, as they are in every part of the world through which the tourist caravan trail passes. The majority, however, travel like registered parcels, unaware of the natives, their aspirations, problems and tragedies. Instead of promoting mutual understanding, they promote mutual contempt. Like an ocean liner leaving a trail of pollution, they leave a trail of corruption in their wake.

The main responsibility lies with the organisers – the robber barons of the travelling industry, who, instead of providing information and guidance for their charges, treat them like a bunch of battery-reared hens, expected to lay three golden eggs per day. But to paraphrase an old saying: tourists get the package they deserve. Perhaps a one-year world tourist strike would decelerate the explosion and improve matters. Otherwise we shall soon have Muzak on the moon, with weightless spaceburgers.

In the meantime, let us stop dreaming of lonely beaches and native dishes in the South Seas. The big hotels do not serve them and in most places there is nowhere else to eat. Nor can you get papayas, mangoes or other tropical fruit, although the trees outside are heavy with them: they are too much bother to handle. The only approved shape for fruit is a neat cylindrical tin; it is always just ripe and need not be peeled. If you want exotic food, go to an exotic little restaurant in London; if you hanker after tropical fruit, go to Fortnum and Mason; and if you want to know what a trip around the world is like, spend an hour in the Hilton. It is cheaper than a package tour, and you do not have to ask on your return that soul-searching question on wartime posters: "Was your journey really necessary?"

THE GLORIOUS AND BLOODY GAME

In the summer of 1972 the Sunday Times *invited me to write about the chess world championship match between Boris Spassky of Russia, the title-holder, and Robert (Bobby) Fischer of the United States, the challenger. The first article that follows was written before the match (which took place in Reykjavik, Iceland); the second during and after the match.*

*1 Reflections of an addict**

So here we all are agog to watch this bizarre bullfight where nobody knows which is the matador and which the bull.

This is yet the kindest metaphor we can apply to the contest. The "we" refers to an endearing fraternity of men, to which I am proud to belong, known as the Passionate Duffers. We worship Caissa, the Muse of Chess, but owing to the inadequacy of our mental equipment can never hope to attain to her favours, condemned as we are to remain life-long amateurs in the double meaning of that word: dilettantes and aficionados. Thus protected from the temptations of the arena, we have remained pure at heart and are all the more distressed by the degrading antics displayed prior to the match by the contestants and their banderilleros in the Russian and American Chess Federations. The haggling about the venue and the revenue, the political invectives and insinuations, make one almost feel that chess is a game too noble to be left to the chess players.

* First published in the *Sunday Times*, 2 July 1972.

Yet – except for the added spice of another East–West confrontation – there is nothing new in these unsavoury proceedings; there have been other greedy *enfants terribles* before Bobby and other smug dogs in the manger before Spassky among the masters of the past; and champions such as Lasker, Capablanca, Alekhine behaved just as badly before they played the immortal games which we play over and over again like our favourite recordings of Beethoven quartets – some of these recorded games date back indeed to Beethoven's days.

Edward Lasker (namesake of the great Emanuel, and himself a grandmaster) wrote a revealing book with the title *Chess for Fun and Chess for Blood*. But "fun" is the wrong word; what he meant was that the game of chess is the perfect paradigm for both the glory and the bloodiness of the human mind. On the one hand, chess is an exercise in pure imagination happily married to logic, staged as a ballet of symbolic figures on a mosaic of sixty-four squares; on the other hand, it is a gladiatorial contest. This dichotomy is perhaps the main secret of the game's astonishingly long history – dating back at least a thousand years – as a favourite pastime of princes; of its insidious addictiveness and the symbolism of the chessboard as a microcosm. It is reflected in a celebrated passage in T. H. Huxley's *Lay Sermons*:

> The chess-board is the world; the pieces are the phenomena of the universe; the rules of the game are what we call the laws of Nature. The player on the other side is hidden from us.

There's the rub – if only he were hidden, a disembodied spirit, instead of being out for your blood, blowing cigar smoke into your eyes, humming snatches from the *March of the Toreadors*, or commenting on each move with a quotation from the Bard – like that character in Lasker's book who, when attacking a piece, would say: "Get thee gone, Mortimer, get thee gone!" and when his own queen was attacked would squeal: "Why appear you with this ridiculous boldness before my lady?" In my own chess days in the Café Central in Vienna, I was driven mad by another character who, each time he gave check, would whisper insinuatingly, "*Schachutzi mit dem*

Putzi" . . . If you don't get the meaning, you save a blush.

Such are the dismal mannerisms of duffers, but our revered masters are not above more sophisticated psychological warfare tactics. The two classic chess instruction books of the sixteenth century were written by a Spaniard, Ruy Lopez, and a Frenchman, Damiano. Both recommend in dead earnest that the hopeful student should always place the board in such a way that the light, of sun or lamp, should shine into the opponent's eye. And in his world championship match against the title holder, Steinitz, Lasker asked to be seated at a separate table because old Steinitz sipped his lemonade with a loud noise (the umpire refused the request). No wonder that Bobby Fischer fusses about lighting, seating arrangements, hotel accommodation and other trivia. "The Russians cheat at chess to keep the world title," he was reported to have said. "They have tried by every means to avoid me. They also slandered my name. They are afraid of me. They have been putting up road blocks for me for years. . . ." And about the forthcoming match: "It will probably be the greatest sports event in history. Bigger even than the Frazier–Ali fight. It is really the free world against the lying, cheating, hypocritical Russians." Bobby is a genius, but as a propagandist for the free world he is rather counter-productive.

Spassky struck a milder note. He did not accuse Bobby of lying and cheating, only of suffering from persecution mania. Bobby boasted that he would "trounce" the reigning champion. Spassky retorted with a modesty gambit: he was not sure of the outcome, but in case victory went to Bobby, "I should be the happiest man alive if I were no longer champion." That explains perhaps why for the last six months he submitted to a gruelling physical and mental training for the match, running several miles a day and studying the records of all the important games that his opponent had played in the past. Bobby did the same.

Both are wonderfully cast for their roles; Fischer the rugged individualist, adventurous and occasionally reckless both in his life-style and chess-style; Spassky the more benign type of

Soviet bureaucrat, cautious, noncommittal, evasive. For the last twenty-four years the world championship has remained a Russian monopoly, jealously guarded, carefully fostered by state grants, *dachas* and other privileges for the masters. Never in all these years has a Western challenger had a better chance of bringing back the ashes across the Iron Curtain. Accordingly, the Reykjavik contest has been dubbed "the match of the century" before it has even started; and the unedifying prelude was quite in keeping with the emotional issues involved.

Yet, all personal, political and tribal passions apart, the bloodiness would still be inherent in the royal game, and if it were not there the game would not be a symbol or paradigm of the working of the human mind. Chess is a battle of ideas; and the most savage battles have always been fought for ideas. No wonder that Caissa emerges from the medieval twilight with a tantalising smile and a dagger in her hand. She haunts Oriental legends and Nordic sagas in dramatic episodes where princes stake their fortunes or realms on a match against an outsider – who infallibly wins and is infallibly slain for his pains.

Tradition has it that the game originated in the first millennium in India when the Buddhist influence was still predominant; and since Buddhists reject violence, they invented chess as a substitute for war. Firdousi relates how it was imported from India into Persia, where the Arab conquerors adopted it and eventually passed it on to Europe. Harun al-Rashid, Charlemagne and Canute are all alleged to have been passionate duffers, who got involved in violent chess incidents; but it is, oddly enough, in the great Icelandic sagas that Caissa stands revealed as a real bitch. The Icelanders were devoted to her – and obviously still are; a sixteenth-century traveller, the Norwegian priest Peder Clausson Friis, reported that the Icelanders "especially occupied themselves with the practice of the game of chess, which they play in such a masterly and perfect way that they sometimes spend some weeks' time – playing each day – on a single game, before they can bring it to an end by the victory of the one or the other combatant."

In contrast to these peaceful marathons in more or less civilised times, the earlier chess episodes in the sagas relate to games which were short and violent, preceded by boasts and ending in slaughter. My favourite yarn is in *St Olaf's Saga*, where King Canute plays a game with Ulf Jarl (Earl Ulf). Canute blunders, making a hasty move which makes him lose a knight; then, in true duffer style, recalls his move and makes another instead. Ulf is furious, upsets the board, and takes sanctuary in a church – where he is slain the next day by Canute's henchmen.

Thus Reykjavik is not such an odd venue for the great event as it might seem to those ignoramuses who have not read the scholarly and voluminous work *Chess in Iceland and in Icelandic Literature* by Williard Fiske (published in Florence by the Florentine Typographical Society in 1905, with a memorable index of thirty-four pages).

One might think that the game owed its popularity in these extreme latitudes to the long polar nights which did not favour outdoor sports. But Cuba has a tropical climate, and yet Havana, at the end of the last century, was the Mecca of chess, where several world championships were played and where the native world champion, Capablanca, was worshipped by the whole country. Persia, Iceland, Cuba and the Soviet empire became addicted at different periods, regardless of climate and race, as if by the spreading of an epidemic carried by strange bugs – twice six different types of pieces on a simple chequered board.

But why all the nastiness, why the apparent malignancy? The reason is intuitively felt by every chess player, yet difficult to explain without giving the impression of indulging in artificial profundities. In the first place, each chessman, whether bishop, rook, knight or queen, embodies a dynamic threat, as if it were alive and animated by the desire to inflict the maximum damage (by attack or defence) on the opponent's men. When a chess player looks at the board, he does not see a static mosaic, a "still-life", but a magnetic field of forces, charged with energy – as Faraday saw the stresses surrounding magnets and currents as curves in space, or as Van Gogh saw vortices in the skies of Provence. Thus there is a strong element of animism and magic in the game. Lewis Carroll was aware of it when he chose chessmen as the dramatis personae for *Through the Looking Glass*; and the Red Queen's "Off with his head" could come straight out of an Icelandic saga. I cannot refrain from quoting here some lines from a poem by the seventeenth-century pioneer of Sanskrit studies, High Court Judge and poetaster, Sir William Jones – because in its touchingly naive manner it conveys the mythological flavour of the game:

> The champions burn'd their rivals to assail,
> Twice eight in black, twice eight in milkwhite mail;
> In shape and station different, as in name,
> Their motions various, nor their power the same. . . .
>
> High in the midst the revered king appears
> And o'er the rest his pearly sceptre rears. . . .
> On him the glory of the day depends,
> He once imprison'd, all the conflict ends.
>
> The queens exulting near their consorts stand;
> Each bears a deadly falchion in her hand;
> Now here, now there, they bound with furious pride,
> And thin the trembling ranks from side to side. . . .
>
> Behold, four archers, eager to advance,
> Send the light reed, and rush with a sidelong glance. . . .
> Then four bold knights for courage fam'd and speed,
> Each knight exalted on a prancing steed. . . .
>
> Four solemn elephants the sides defend;
> Beneath the load of ponderous towers they bend.
>
> Now swell th' embattled troops with hostile rage,
> And clang their shields, impatient to engage. . . .

When the battle is over, there is a tragic finale:

> Now flies the monarch of the sable shield,
> His legions vanquish'd, o'er the lonely field. . . .
> He hears, wher'er he moves, the dreadful sound;
> *Check* the deep vales, and *Check* the woods rebound.
> No place remains: he sees the certain fate,
> And yields his throne to ruin, and Checkmate.

Echoes of Lear on the lonely heath – "blow winds and crack your cheeks! rage! blow!"

And rage they do. For, after all, the little buggers on the board, however alive they may seem, including the revered king and his queen of furious pride, are masterminded by one's own mighty brain. In playing bridge or poker or scrabble, there is a large element of chance which provides a convenient excuse for being beaten. In chess, there is no such excuse. Yet the worst misfortunes are those for which one has oneself, and only oneself, to blame. It might seem that similar considerations apply to tennis or boxing, where also skill, not chance, decides the issue; and some of the stars in these games do indeed take defeats hard. But even if one is in principle prepared to put physical skill on a par with mental aptitude, the mind itself which makes these judgements won't have any of it. To be called clumsy is an acceptable insult; to be called stupid is unpardonable. The great Alekhine, when beaten, often threw his king across the room, and after one important lost game smashed up the furniture in his hotel suite. Steinitz, on a similar occasion, vanished from his quarters and was found disconsolately sitting on a bench in a deserted park. He died insane. So did Morphy, who preceded him as world champion. Morphy suffered from persecution mania; Steinitz from delusions; he thought he could speak over the telephone without using the instrument and that he could move chessmen by electricity discharged from the tips of his fingers. What sane person could devise a symbol more apt for the omnipotence of mind?

In the weeks to come we shall have the opportunity of watching two men facing each other in silence across the high-voltage board, where every move could make the fuses blow, each in a kind of waking trance, making the figures perform an imaginary dance which exists only in their mind's eye, then mentally rearranging them in a different configuration, and yet another one, variation upon variation, while the ballet master himself remains immobile and the kaleidoscopic changes of scenery all take place inside his skull.

While the game is on, it is only the choreography that matters – aggression is sublimated into dazzling acrobatics. There may be more unedifying episodes to come; but whatever happens, the fraternity of Passionate Duffers craves your indulgence for the magicians of the glorious and bloody game.

2 A requiem for Reykjavik★

In the prehistoric days before the great match started, I wrote in these columns: "Chess is a game too noble to be left to the chess players." The scandalous preliminaries seemed to confirm this with a vengeance. But I also made the optimistic forecast that once the match got under way, it would produce some immortal games which we shall replay in years to come like our favourite gramophone records. Whether they were immortal or not, we must leave to posterity to decide; but to humble amateurs at least most of the twenty-one games played will remain a movable feast. Some carry distinctly Wagnerian echoes – young Siegfried, the kosher hero from Brooklyn, ritually slaughtering the Russian dragon. Spassky's slow, protracted agony evoked the strains of Chopin's Funeral March, while the comedy of errors which ended in the draw of the seventh game was like a duet from an *opéra bouffe* – until the gramophone needle got stuck in Bobby's perpetual check. The affinities of chess and music have long been recognised; the Argentine grandmaster Najdorf compared Bobby's lovely sixth game to a Mozart symphony.

The overture, however, was an ignoble cacophony, and some of its episodes are worth recalling before they vanish into the prehistoric mist.

The Champion arrived in Iceland well ahead of the scheduled start of the match, took up residence at the Saga Hotel and went into training. An empty suite at the Loftleidir Hotel, at the other end of the town, was waiting for the Challenger. The days passed by, but we waited in vain. During

★ First published in the *Sunday Times*, 3 September 1972 (the match ended on 31 August).

the week preceding D-day – Saturday, 1 July – Bobby Fischer three times booked his air passage from New York to Iceland and each time cancelled it.

Came Saturday, the Holy Sabbath, on which members of the Church of God – the fundamentalist sect to which Bobby converted from Orthodox Judaism – are not allowed to travel. The opening ceremony in the national theatre in Reykjavik took place in Fischer's absence. The front rows, reserved for the diplomatic corps and other dignitaries, were mostly empty. The president of the Republic – a nice, youngish archaeologist – and his pretty lady arrived half an hour late; perhaps they had been praying for a miracle. The proverbially imperturbable Spassky sat in the front row, displaying his imperturbability. The three anthems were duly played and the speeches duly delivered. The Soviet ambassador spoke grimly of chess as a bridge of friendship between nations. The American chargé d'affaires, perhaps more aptly, invoked the episode in *St Olaf's Saga* in which King Canute has Earl Ulf slain because of a quarrel across the chessboard. The gentlemen of the press were debating within themselves whether to describe the event as Hamlet without the Prince or a corrida without the matador. The grey day faded into the white night in an atmosphere of subdued hysteria.

Came Sunday. The first game of the match of the century was due to start at 5 p.m. The last direct flight of the day from New York landed at Reykjavik airport in the early morning. No Bobby. I noted in my diary:

> Waiting for Godot. Rumours in the Loftleidir lobby: he will arrive on a special plane with Norman Mailer, chartered by Time–Life Inc. (The Time–Life crew, about a dozen scruffy characters, keep acting mysteriously.) He will be dropped by parachute. My own suggestion: he will arrive, dressed as Lohengreen [*sic*], riding on a swan. Funny to be a war correspondent again after all these years. Everybody's favourite pastime: to psychoanalyse Bobby. Got so bored that slunk away to souvenir shop, bought ashtray made of Icelandic lava, guaranteed to give owner magic powers of seduction.

On Monday we were still waiting for Godot.

Then came Mr Slater's dramatic message to Bobby: "Come on out, chicken", combined with his offer to double the prize money – and the next day at 6.55 a.m. Bobby erupted from his plane like a rocket, brushed aside the reception committee, ran to his waiting Mercedes car and vanished from sight.

The drawing-of-lots ceremony to decide who should have first move in the first game was scheduled for the afternoon. Spassky was there, Bobby was not. Spassky walked out, after protesting that he had never agreed to the postponement. Dr Euwe, a former world champion and president of the International Chess Federation, commented: "He gave the impression of having to wait for orders from Moscow." Euwe's guess proved to be correct, for the next development was a cable in broken English from the Russian Chess Federation requesting that Fischer should be "punished for his behaviour" and that both he and Euwe should apologise. By punishment they meant that Fischer should forfeit the first game through his absence.

At this junction, our Bobby performed an amazing volteface. He wrote an abject apology to Spassky "for my disrespectful behaviour in not attending the opening ceremony. I simply became carried away by my petty dispute over money. I have offended you and your country, the Soviet Union, where chess has a prestigious position. . . . I know you to be a sportsman and a gentleman. . . ." – and so on. A few months earlier he had called the Russian masters a "lying, cheating, hypocritical lot".

However, by eating humble pie he had reversed the situation. If the Russian insisted on the punishment, he would be branded as a Shylock. There were more negotiations, more postponements, more hysterics in the wings. Bobby was given his Icelandic *dacha*, his bowling alley, indoor tennis court, the use of a 1972 Mercedes in place of the previous 1971 vintage, and his favourite swivel chair was flown in from New York. On Tuesday, 11 July – ten days behind schedule – the first game of the match finally got under way.

It was the most colossal anticlimax of the most colossal match of our colossal times. For the first twenty-eight moves both players indulged in a cautious, colourless game, apparently aiming at a quick draw. Then on his twenty-ninth move, Bobby committed a colossal blunder, sending his bishop straight into the valley of death. When the game was adjourned, Bobby was doomed. When it was resumed the next day, he staged a half-hour walkout in protest against the unseemly behaviour of a cameraman who had poked his head through a vent in the ceiling. When he was persuaded to return to the board, Spassky took thirty minutes to finish him off.

Had not young Fischer boasted that he would not lose a single game of the match? Now Nemesis was triumphing over hubris – or so it looked. It looked even more so when at the second game Bobby once again failed to turn up, because of the television cameras. This time he was declared, without further ado, to have forfeited the game. The score now was Spassky 2, Fischer 0 – the champion had secured, rather painlessly, one sixth of the points he needed to remain champion (twelve points out of twenty-four games). Fischer booked air tickets to New York for the following day. He cancelled them when the arbiter agreed that the next game should be played in a secluded private room.

And then, miraculously, Phoenix rose from the ashes. In the third game Fischer got his claws into Spassky right from the opening and tore him to pieces in forty moves.

This game, and the subsequent fourth, taken together constituted the psychological turning point of the match. In the fourth – which was drawn – Fischer had manoeuvred himself into a hair-raisingly dangerous position, but handled it with so much sang-froid and ingenuity that Spassky was unable to drive his advantage home. This seemed to demoralise him even more than his previous defeat. He was still a point ahead, but he was visibly succumbing to the "Fischer-effect" – the myth of Bobby's invincibility. He lost the fifth, and sixth and eighth games, and managed to draw the seventh only because Fischer, in a won position, became overconfident and, as one grandmaster commented, "went to sleep on the job".

By now, one third through the match, Fischer was leading five points to three. Spassky asked for a two-day postponement of the ninth game for reasons of health – a well-known symptom of demoralisation in match play.

The ninth game was a quick draw, giving both players a breathing space; the tenth was another brilliant win by Fischer. He now had a three-point lead and the experts predicted Spassky's impending collapse. He was saved, once more, by Bobby's overconfidence, which led to the ignominious loss of his queen, and the eleventh game. The shock had a sobering effect on Fischer, and at the same time revived Spassky's fighting spirit. Not even the loss of the next-but-one game, which restored Fischer's decisive three-point lead, could subdue him. Thus in the third and last phase of the match, games 14 to 21, the world watched Spassky valiantly, and often brilliantly, continuing to fight the lost battle by ceaseless, sometimes reckless attacks; and a chastened Fischer, confident but no longer overconfident, defending his safe lead – not, by any means, through stone-walling tactics, but by rather willingly accepting draws which in the past he would have contemptuously refused. The result was an unprecedented series – games 14 to 20 – of hard-fought draws, of constant thrust and parry, which was even more exciting and entertaining than the wins. The end came not with a bang but a whimper. The twenty-first game was adjourned; when it was to be resumed, Spassky did not turn up but telephoned his resignation. When all is said, it *was* perhaps the match of the century.

As I have said, our main pastime during those early days in Reykjavik was to psychoanalyse Bobby *in absentia*. Since then even people who cannot tell a knight from a bishop have been indulging in that sport. Bobby's dark, intent features were portrayed on the front pages of *Time* and *Newsweek*; there was a sudden boom in the sale of chess sets and of the records of a "Viva Bobby" song; his popularity rating was said to be approaching Mick Jagger's. He certainly put chess on the map as it had never been since the days of The Turk – the chess-playing automaton who became the craze of the royal courts of Europe and beat Napoleon (who was a Patzer anyway).

Now, the secret of The Turk was that he had someone hidden inside him. But what kind of secret personality is hidden inside Bobby the Tartar? Spassky said he was suffering from persecution mania; others that he had megalomania; that he had never grown out of being a boy wonder; or that he was just simply mad, as all geniuses are supposed to be. I gladly agree that there is some truth in all these explanations, but I prefer my own, which is simpler; Bobby is a mimophant. A mimophant is a hybrid species; a cross between a mimosa and an elephant. A member of this species is sensitive like a mimosa where his own feelings are concerned, and thick-skinned like an elephant trampling over the feelings of others. All of us have met individuals of mimophantic dispositions, but Bobby is the perfect representative of the species. His vulnerability is genuine. The cameras do upset him. He cannot bear street noises. The chair on which he sits while playing, the size of the board grate on his mimosaesque sensitivities. At the same time his elephantine skin prevents him from realising what he does to others. "I like to see them squirm," he commented on his opponents. "I can see their ego crumbling." And his favourite comments on his own moves are "a smash", "a crunch", "a chop".

There have been some half-baked speculations about Bobby hypnotising his opponents into making inferior moves. There may be a grain of truth in this, if the word "hypnotise" is used as a metaphor in quotes. The best forwards in soccer games seem sometimes "hypnotised" by a brilliant goalkeeper making apparently impossible saves – as Bobby did in the seemingly hopeless situation in the fourth game of the match – with the result that the attackers shoot either wide of the mark or straight into the goalkeeper's hands. Bobby's opponents in earlier matches seem to have done just that, and Spassky, too, fell under the spell.

For nearly a decade now, the majority of experts have recognised Fischer as the strongest chess player alive; and his spectacular victories in the quarter- and semifinals convinced even the remaining doubters. He has the highest tournament rating of any living player on the World Chess Federation's scale, and the highest rating of any player living or dead on the United States Federation's scale. Thus in a way he was justified in regarding himself *de facto* the reigning champion, and his match with Spassky as a mere formality, or even a favour he was doing the title holder. Accordingly, it was for him, Bobby, to dictate the conditions. This attitude, based partly on fantasy, partly on fact, was rudely shaken when old Boris unexpectedly staged a counter-walkout, threatened to call the match off and snatch away the crown which Bobby already felt sitting on his head. It must have been a nasty shock for him to realise that he had gone too far; and the rebound, as it were, carried him to the opposite extreme – the grovelling apology to Spassky and the Russian chess world.

Poor Bobby. He does not drink, does not read, takes no interest in women, or music, or nature. He lives in hotel rooms out of two large plastic suitcases. A reporter once asked him what chess really meant to him. His reply was "Everything."

Only one writer could have invented him: Franz Kafka. Spassky, on the other hand, could be the hero of any Stalin Prize winning novelist. When I try to recall his face, I see a kind of identikit drawing, not a portrait. In the Soviet Union, a chess master is a VIP, and a world champion is of course a VVVIP. His public statements were understandably cautious though often rather whimsical. He pretended to play chess mainly for fun; before the match he told correspondents that he was "looking forward to Reykjavik as if it were a holiday". But on a less guarded occasion he made a wry remark to the effect that he did not know what would happen to his much-envied flat in a modern block in Moscow if he lost.

One suddenly remembered that when Mark Taimonov lost his match 6–0 to Fischer, he was deprived of his grandmaster's pension. Poor Bobby? Poor Boris. One wonders who is more to be pitied; a state-owned gladiator or a freelance samurai.

* * *

Now that the match is over and the chess world has sunk into a kind of post-coital tristesse, the non-playing public is beginning to wonder, rather sheepishly, what the whole excitement had been about, and how they had become infected by it – after all, it's only a game, at best a stimulating distraction, at worst a waste of time.

But is it?

Earlier on, I called chess a paradigm or symbol of the working of the human mind. This may have sounded like romantic gushings, but I was in fact expressing a view shared by those scientists who, over the last twenty years, have been busy developing electronic chess computer programs for rather esoteric reasons of their own. The first paper on the subject, by Claude Shannon, a pioneer of modern information theory, appeared in the *Philosophical Magazine* in 1950, under the title "Programming a Computer for Playing Chess". His work was taken up by a leading mathematical logician, A. M. Turing, and subsequently by various research teams at Los Alamos, the Carnegie Mellon University and at the European Atomic Commission (Euratom), headed by Dr Euwe. Each of these groups represented a mixed team of psychologists, mathematicians, chess experts and specialists in that new branch of science known as "artificially simulated intelligence". Their purpose was not to build an electronic Turk to beat Fischer and Spassky; they used chess as a means to an end – or, in Euwe's words,

> as a concrete representation of human problem-solving and decision-making. If we could design a successful chess-machine, we might be able to penetrate into the innermost of man's intellectual capacities.

The same conviction is reflected in the recently published monumental book *Human Problem-Solving* by Newell and Simon of the Carnegie group. It has 900 solid pages, one-third of which are devoted to an analysis of the chess mind. Even more surprising are Euratom's reasons for embarking on such a project. As an international body, Euratom's work is hampered by the difficulty of translating technical papers into a dozen or so European languages. In the absence of a long-overdue scientific Esperanto – the Middle Ages were more progressive in this respect: they had Latin – the obvious answer would be an electronic translating machine. But so far all attempts to build such a machine have proved grossly inadequate. Euratom's chess research group was guided by the idea that certain analogies existed between chess and linguistics; both have fixed rules or "grammars" which, however, permit a great variety of choices between combinations of "moves" or "words"; and to quote Euwe again, "in both cases the problem is to limit the choice between many possibilities in an intelligent way".

The project turned out a failure; and it seems that even the most sophisticated computer chess programs are leading into a cul-de-sac. Yet an experiment with negative results can be scientifically as important as a successful one. Louis Pasteur's failure to demonstrate the "spontaneous generation of life" out of inanimate substances was a crucial step forward in modern biology; and the apparent impossibility to construct a computer which simulates the processes in the mind of the human chess player might turn out to be just as important for psychology.

Naive chess players occasionally have Walter Mitty dreams of carrying a computer in their brains which will calculate with lightning speed all potential variations ahead of any given position and select each time the perfect move by eliminating, one by one, all the inferior moves. A single example will show that this is impossible. The average number of legally permissible moves in a given position is around thirty. Say it is white's turn to move; to each of his thirty potential moves black has thirty potential answers, which leads, in round figures, to 1000 variations at the end of each "complete move" (one by white and one by black). Every one of these variations branches again into 1000 subvariations two complete moves ahead, making a total of 1,000,000 positions; three complete moves ahead there will be 1,000,000,000 of them and so on, each move increasing the variations by a factor of 1000. The average length of game between evenly matched partners of average strength is forty to forty-five complete moves; but, taking duffers into account, it may be a modest twenty-five. Thus in order to decide on the perfect opening move, the Walter Mitty computer would have to calculate at least twenty-five moves ahead (and against a strong opponent perhaps twice as many). To quote Edward Lasker, who is both an International Master and an electronics engineer:

> Calculating twenty-five moves ahead would mean that the machine would have to generate a total number of moves in the order of 10^{75} (1 and 75 zeroes). Even if the computer could operate at the rate of 1,000,000 moves every second, which is about 500 times faster than the most optimistic program-designer would consider feasible, it would take 10^{69} seconds to complete the calculation.
>
> Well, we couldn't wait that long. Ever since our planetary system came into being some 4½ billion years ago, no more than 10^{18} seconds have elapsed.

In other words, to compute the perfect move based on the method of elimination known as trial and error (or hit and miss) is not only practically, but also theoretically, impossible. Thus the computer theorist can at least prove that the chess player does not reason in this way. Now, to the layman this seems to be self-evident; he knows intuitively that men, and even animals, do not make decisions by exploring all possible actions in a given situation, including the most absurd or suicidal ones, and ticking them off in succession, until only one course of action is left. But what is self-evident to the layman is not at all so to the psychologist; and for about half a century academic psychology was by and large divided into two camps: the behaviourists, who maintained that the acquisition of knowledge was primarily based on trial and error, and their opponents (the Gestalt psychologists and their successors), who stressed learning-by-insight, that is, by perceiving the essential configurational pattern of a situation as a whole and not as a mere sum of isolated parts. This is an oversimplified account, but it will do for our purpose.

To this controversy (and its wider philosophical implications) the chess computer researches provided important contributions. They were quick to realise and to prove that to build a machine relying entirely on blind trial and error –

exploring all the consequences of all possible moves – was even theoretically impossible. Thus they had to restrict their programs from considering all permissible moves to a much narrower range of "plausible" or "promising" moves; and similarly to confine the analysis of the variations to which these might lead to only two or three complete moves ahead.

But how is the computer to decide which moves are "plausible" or "promising"? The human chess player does it literally "at a glance". Experiments of the Euwe team showed that players of master strength needed only five seconds to grasp and memorise the positions of the up to thirty-two chessmen distributed over sixty-four squares. They also studied the eye movements of the players and found that instead of scanning the board in a systematic way (as, for instance, a television camera rapidly scans a scene line by line), the players' eyes jumped from one strategically focal point on the board to the next in an irregular fashion; in this way he was gaining an insight into the dynamic configurational pattern of the total situation, instead of adding up bit by bit. Instead of considering all moves permitted by the rules, i.e. about thirty, the human player normally considers only three or four "promising" moves; instead of analysing each into its ultimate consequences, he normally only considers variations two or three moves ahead.

The word "normally" refers here to relatively quiet situations on the board, where the moves are guided by strategical considerations aimed at improving the player's general position ("positional play") with no dramatic developments in immediate sight. This is the case in the majority of situations in modern chess. In contrast to this are the "combinatorial" phases of the game where a player pursues an immediate concrete goal aimed at material gain or storming the defences of the opponent's king. In these decisive stages the choice of moves is even more restricted, both for the attacker and his opponent, but at the same time the player considering a risky combination must look much further – sometimes up to ten moves ahead – to decide whether to embark on it. At this juncture he does indeed resort to the trial-and-error method –

but of a highly sophisticated kind; he has formed a concrete hypothesis of a complex line of attack and is mentally trying out whether it would end in a hit or miss.

The Carnegie group has shown that a computer can be programmed to work out quite clever mating combinations – precisely because in such situations the choice of the initial move is so narrow that its ramifications can be followed to their final consequences. But the crucial question remains how in normal "positional" play the computer should select the two or three "promising" moves. When a human player is asked why he considers a certain move "promising", he will reply by some general consideration such as "consolidating the position", or "exerting pressure on the opponent", or because the situation reminded him of similar ones encountered in the past – or simply "because it looks a good move". But these criteria are too vague and subjective for computer programming. Thus the researchers had to devise a variety of much simpler "goals" or "targets" which would guide the pre-selection of promising moves; such programmed targets are "material gain", "increased mobility", "defence of the king", "occupation of centre squares" and a few more. But some of these targets may be in *conflict* with each other; thus a player may sacrifice material to get at the opponent's king. To get around this difficulty, the programmers assigned a scale of positive and negative numerical values – like school marks – to each "target"; the aggregate sum of these values for a proposed move is then regarded as a measure of its promisingness. But this crude arithmetical calculation is like a caricature of the qualitative consideration in human decision-making which takes the whole situation into account instead of mechanically totting up the size of its various features.

Euwe summed up the lessons of the Euratom project by a frank admission: "The majority of the research group finally came to the conclusion that this field is much more complicated than was previously supposed and that a breakthrough would certainly not come within a hundred years" – a cautious way of saying never. And he also explained why: "It is remarkable that the more technical advances we made in improving the chess program, the further away we drifted from the ways of human thinking in general."

Thus it transpires that the machine does not really "simulate" or reproduce processes in the human mind, any more than the motions of a marionette pulled by strings reproduce the processes of muscle contraction; man and machine function according to different principles.

There are many reasons why this should be so, apart from those already mentioned. One is that the human player is often guided, sometimes subconsciously, by the accumulated memories of similar situations encountered in the past; but although the computer also has a memory of stored data, it is unable to select and manipulate them in a way even remotely resembling the human way of learning from experience.

But the simplest reason for the inferiority of the computer is perhaps that chess is as much an art as a science. The machine must laboriously compute a move which seems to promise some material gain – but at the price of upsetting more general strategic considerations which are "above its head"; the experienced player, playing a "blitz-game" with only three seconds allowed for a move, takes the total situation in at a glance. Picasso's dictum "*Je ne cherche pas, je trouve*" – I do not search, I find – applies to him too.

⋆ ⋆ ⋆

On 9 May 1783 a London newspaper carried the following sensational report:

> Yesterday, at the Chess-club in St James's street, Mr PHILIDOR [a famous eighteenth-century player] performed one of those wonderful exhibitions for which he is so much celebrated. He played at the same time three different games, without seeing either of the tables. His opponents were Count BRUHL, Mr BOWDLER, and Mr MASERES. To those who understand chess, this exertion of Mr PHILIDOR's abilities, must appear one of the greatest of which the human memory is susceptible. . . . Mr PHILIDOR sits with his back to the tables, and some gentleman present, who takes his part, informs him of the move of his antagonist, and then, by his direction, plays his pieces.

"Blindfold chess", as it is called, is yet another challenge with which the chess mind confronts the psychologist, and which still waits for an explanation. To play a single game blindfold moderately well is within the capacity of every strong player. To play *three* blindfold games simultaneously was regarded by Philidor's contemporaries as one of the greatest exertions of which the human memory is capable. But in the years that have elapsed since Philidor's day, the record for simultaneous blindfold games has increased by jumps to ten, twenty, thirty-two (Alekhine in 1933); forty (Najdorf in 1943); and on 13 December 1960, at the Fairmont Hotel in San Francisco, the Belgian master Koltanovski achieved the incredible feat of taking on simultaneously fifty-six opponents blindfold, winning fifty of the games, drawing six and losing none – in an exhibition lasting nine hours and forty-five minutes.

The only remotely comparable achievements that come to mind are those of a few calculating prodigies. But these are rare, whereas among chess masters the capacity of playing blindfold several games simultaneously is quite common. No systematic study of the phenomenon has been undertaken so far. Alekhine alleged that he could conjure up and "see" every one of the thirty-two boards as its number was called out – but Alekhine was a notorious liar. Euwe believes that it is not so much a matter of "seeing" the boards as of memorising the moves of each game – substituting a story for a photograph – and for that purpose various mnemonic tricks can be used. Yet even so, the mystery remains, pointing to vast untapped faculties of the human mind, potentially many times as powerful as those which we put to use in our everyday routines. A thorough psychological study of the mental processes of simultaneous blindfold players might be at least as rewarding as the analyses of the electroencephalographs of meditating yogis.

When all is said, the Russians may not be so wrong in including chess in the school curriculum and treating their champions as favourite pets. Which leaves one wondering how much longer we shall have to wait until the first British master of the royal game will join the ranks of eminent footballers, racing jockeys and cricketers by having a knighthood graciously bestowed on him.

MAHATMA GANDHI: A REVALUATION*

"It takes a great deal of money to keep Bapu living in poverty . . ." (1). Bapu means "father" in Gujerati, and was used all over India as a title of respect and affection for Gandhi. That flippant remark was made by Mrs Sarojini Naidu, poet, politician and one of Bapu's intimates (she sometimes called him Mickey Mouse); but she could hardly have been aware at the time of the almost prophetic significance of her words. They actually referred to her loyal efforts to collect money for Gandhi's campaign for *khadi,* homespun cloth. Like all his crusades, it was intended to serve both practical and symbolic purposes. Its practical aspect was the boycott of foreign goods, primarily of English textiles – combined with the fantastic hope of solving India's economic problems by bringing back the hand loom and the spinning wheel. At the same time the spinning wheel became an almost mystical symbol of the return to the Simple Life, and the rejection of industrialisation.

> The call of the spinning wheel, Gandhi wrote in *Young India,* is the noblest of all. Because it is the call of love. . . . The spinning wheel is the reviving draught for the millions of our dying countrymen and countrywomen. . . . I claim that in losing the spinning wheel we lost our left lung. We are therefore suffering from galloping consumption. The restoration of the wheel arrests the progress of the fell disease . . . (2).

The wheel was a lifelong obsession which reached its climax in the late 1920s between two imprisonments. It spread among

* First published in the *Sunday Times,* 5 October 1969, commemorating the centenary of Gandhi's birth.

his followers and ran through the successive stages of a fashion, a cult, a mystique. He designed India's national flag with a spinning wheel in its centre. He persuaded Congress to resolve that all its members should take up spinning and pay their membership dues in self-spun yarn; office-holders had to deliver 2000 yards of yarn per month. When Congress met in session, its seasoned politicians would listen to the debates while operating their portable spinning wheels – *tricoteuses* of the nonviolent revolution. Schools introduced spinning courses; the plain white cloth and white cap became the uniform of the Indian patriot; Nehru called it "the livery of freedom", while Gandhi praised the wheel as "the sacrament of millions" and "a gateway to my spiritual salvation". At the same time he organised public bonfires of imported cloth, threw his wife's favourite sari into the flames, and got himself arrested.

One of the few Indian intellectuals who dared to protest against the *khadi* mystique was the poet laureate, Rabindranath Tagore. He was a lifelong admirer of Gandhi, fully aware of his greatness, but also of his crankiness. I shall quote him at some length, because he seems to have realised in a single intuitive flash the basic flaw in Gandhian leadership. In 1921, after a prolonged absence, Tagore had returned to India full of expectations "to breathe the buoyant breeze of national awakening" – and was horrified by what he saw:

> What I found in Calcutta when I arrived depressed me. An oppressive atmosphere seemed to burden the land. . . . There was a newspaper which one day had the temerity to disapprove, in a feeble way, of the burning of foreign cloth. The very next day the editor was shaken out of his balance by the agitation of his readers. How long would it take for the fire which was burning cloth to reduce his paper to ashes? . . .
>
> Consider the burning of cloth. . . . What is the nature of the call to do this? Is it not another instance of a magical formula? The question of using or refusing cloth of a particular manufacture belongs mainly to economic science. The discussion of the matter by our countrymen should have been in the language of economics. If the country has really come to such a habit of mind that precise thinking

> has become impossible for it, then our very first fight should be against such a fatal habit, the original sin from which all our ills are flowing (3).

Tagore had smelt a holy rat in the *Khadi* mystique. The boycott of English textiles could be justified as a measure of economic warfare in a nation's struggle for independence. But this did not apply to other countries, and to call all foreign cloth "impure" was indeed an appeal to magic-ridden minds. If it were advantageous for India's economy to forsake foreign imports and produce all the textiles it needs, that would still leave the question open whether a return to manufacturing methods predating the industrial revolution was feasible – even if it should be deemed desirable in the name of an idealised Simple Life. But this problem, too, was bypassed by calling the wheel a "sacrament" and a "gateway to salvation". In his reply to Tagore, Gandhi went even further in what one might be tempted to call sanctimonious demagogy – if one were not aware of the pure intentions behind the muddled thinking. Rejecting Tagore's accusation that the *khadi* cult was begotten by mysticism and not by reasoned argument, Gandhi wrote:

> I have again and again appealed to reason, and let me assure him that if happily the country has come to believe in the spinning wheel as the giver of plenty, it has done so after laborious thinking. . . . I do indeed ask the poet to spin the wheel as a sacrament. . . . it was our love of foreign cloth that ousted the wheel from its position of dignity. Therefore I consider it a sin to wear foreign cloth. . . . On the knowledge of my sin bursting upon me, I must consign the foreign garments to the flames and thus purify myself, and thenceforth rest content with the rough *khadi* made by my neighbours. On knowing that my neighbours may not, having given up the occupation, take kindly to the spinning wheel, I must take it up myself and thus make it popular (4).

Khadi did indeed become a fashionable cult among his ashramites and among active members of Congress – but never among the anonymous millions for whom it was intended. The attempt to make the half-starved masses of the rural population self-supporting by means of the spinning wheel as a "giver of plenty" proved to be a dismal and predictable failure. The spinning wheel found its place on the national flag, but not in the peasants' cottages.

A few years ago, a Member of Parliament in New Delhi said to me wistfully: "Yes, I do wear *khadi,* as you see – a lot of us in the Congress Party feel that we have to. It costs three times as much as ordinary cotton."

It took a great deal of money, and an infinitely greater amount of idealism and energy, "to keep Bapu in poverty". It is impossible to dismiss the *khadi* crusade as a harmless folly. On the contrary, the wheel as an economic panacea and the gateway to salvation was a central symbol of Gandhi's philosophy and social programme.

His first book, *Hind Swaraj* or *Indian Home Rule,* was written in 1909, when he was forty. He had already achieved international fame as a leader of the Indian community in South Africa and initiator of several nonviolent mass movements against racial discrimination. The book was reprinted in 1921 with a new introduction by Gandhi in which he said: "I withdraw nothing of it." In 1938, he requested that a new edition should be printed at a nominal price available to all, and wrote yet another introduction in which he affirmed: "After the stormy thirty years through which I have since passed, I have seen nothing to make me alter the advice expounded in it." *Hind Swaraj* may thus be regarded as an authoritative expression of opinions to which he clung to the end of his life, and as a condensed version of Gandhian philosophy. It extols the virtues of Indian civilisation, and at the same time passionately denounces the culture of the West.

> I believe that the civilisation India has evolved is not to be beaten in the world. Nothing can equal the seeds sown by our ancestors. Rome went, Greece shared the same fate, the might of the Pharaohs was broken; Japan has become westernised; of China nothing can be said; but India is still, somehow or other, sound at the foundation. The people of Europe learn their lessons from the writings of the men of Greece or Rome, which exist no longer in their former glory. In trying to learn from them, the Europeans imagine that they will avoid the mistakes of Greece and Rome. Such is their

> pitiable condition. In the midst of all this India remains immovable and that is her glory. . . . India, as so many writers have shown, has nothing to learn from anybody else, and this is as it should be. . . . Indian civilisation is the best and the European is a nine-days wonder. . . . I bear no enmity towards the English, but I do towards their civilisation (5).

His rejection of Western culture in all its aspects was deeply felt, violently emotional, and supported by arguments verging on the absurd. The principal evils of the West were railways, hospitals and lawyers:

> Man is so made by nature as to require him to restrict his movements as far as his hands and feet will take him. If we did not rush about from place to place by means of railways and such other maddening conveniences, much of the confusion that arises would be obviated. . . . God set a limit to a man's locomotive ambition in the construction of his body. Man immediately proceeded to discover means of overriding the limit. . . . I am so constructed that I can only serve my immediate neighbours, but in my conceit, I pretend to have discovered that I must with my body serve every individual in the Universe. In thus attempting the impossible, man comes in contact with different religions and is utterly confounded. According to this reasoning, it must be apparent to you that railways are a most dangerous institution. Man has gone further away from his Maker (6).

If this line of argument were accepted, not only the great Indian Peninsular Railway would stand condemned, but also Gandhi's favourite book, the *Bhagavad Gita*. For its hero is the noble Arjuna, who drives a chariot (with Vishnu as his passenger) in flagrant transgression of God's will that he should only move as far as his own feet will take him. Gandhi himself had to spend an inordinate proportion of his life in railway carriages "rushing from place to place", faithful to the tradition that the leader should remain in touch with the masses. It was not the only paradox in his life; in fact, every major principle in Gandhi's Back-to-Nature philosophy was self-defeating, stamped with a tragic irony. (Even as President of Congress, he always insisted on travelling third class; but he had a special coach to himself.)

Lawyers fare no better in Gandhi's programme than railways:

> Men were less unmanly if they settled their disputes either by fighting or by asking their relatives to decide them. They became more unmanly and cowardly when they resorted to the Courts of Law. It is a sign of savagery to settle disputes by fighting. It is not the less so by asking a third party to decide between you and me. The parties alone know who is right and therefore they ought to settle it (7).

It should be remembered that Gandhi's first step towards leadership was achieved by his successful settling of a lawsuit as an attorney in Pretoria; and his successes in negotiating with the British were as much due to the charisma of the "naked fakir" – to quote Churchill – as to the legal astuteness of the "Middle Temple lawyer".

Perhaps the main asset in the complex balance sheet of the British Raj was the introduction of modern medicine to India. But in Gandhi's accounting, hospitals fare worst:

> How do diseases arise? Surely by our negligence or indulgence. I over-eat, I have indigestion, I go to a doctor, he gives me medicine. I am cured. I over-eat again, and I take his pills again. Had I not taken the pills in the first instance, I would have suffered the punishment deserved by me, and I would not have over-eaten again. . . . hospitals are institutions for propagating sin. Men take less care of their bodies, and immorality increases (8).

And in a letter to a friend, also written when he was forty:

> Hospitals are the instruments that the devil has been using for his own purpose, in order to keep his hold on his kingdom. They perpetuate vice, misery and degradation and real slavery (9).

He tried to live up to his convictions by experimenting all his life with nature-cures, *ayurvedic* remedies, and an endless succession of vegetarian and fruitarian diets. But he was assailed at various times by fistulae, appendicitis, malaria, hook worm, amoebic dysentery and high blood pressure, and suffered two nervous breakdowns in his late sixties. Each time he was seriously ill he started on nature cures, refusing Western medication and surgery; each time he had to capitulate and submit to drugs, injections, operations under anesthesia. Once more his principles proved to be self-defeating in the most painful way. Yet while his belief that diseases are caused by "negligence, indulgence or vice" was naive to a degree, its correlate, the belief in the power of mind over body, was a source of strength which carried him through his heroic fasts.

About schools and "literary education" in general he was as scornful as about hospitals, railways and law courts.

> What is the meaning of education? It simply means knowledge of letters. It is merely an instrument and an instrument may be well used or abused. . . . We daily observe that many men abuse it and very few make good use of it; and if this is a correct statement, we have proved that more harm has been done by it than good. . . .
>
> To teach boys reading, writing and arithmetic is called primary education. A peasant earns his bread honestly. He has ordinary knowledge of the world. He knows fairly well how he should behave towards his parents, his wife, his children and his fellow villagers. He understands and observes the rules of morality. But he cannot write his own name. What do you propose to do by giving him a knowledge of letters? Will you add an inch to his happiness? Do you wish to make him discontented with his cottage or his lot?
>
> Now let us take higher education. I have learned Geography, Astronomy, Algebra, Geometry, etc. What of that? In what way have I benefited myself or those around me? . . .
>
> I do not for one moment believe that my life would have been wasted, had I not received higher or lower education. . . . And, if I am making good use of it, even then it is not for the millions. . . .
>
> Our ancient school system is enough. . . . To give millions a knowledge of English is to enslave them. The foundation that Macaulay laid of education has enslaved us. . . . Hypocrisy, tyranny, etc., have increased; English-knowing Indians have not hesitated to cheat or strike terror into the people . . . (10).

Gandhi tried to live up to his principles, and never sent his sons to school. He intended to teach them himself, but did not find the time. They never had a chance to learn a profession. In his own words:

> I will not say that I was indifferent to their literary education, but I certainly did not hesitate to sacrifice it in these higher interests, as I regarded them. My sons have therefore some reason for grievance

> against me. . . . Had I been able to devote at least one hour to their literary education, with strict regularity, I should have given them, in my opinion, an ideal education. But it has been my regret that I failed to ensure for them enough training in that direction. . . . But I hold that I sacrificed their literary training to what I genuinely believed to be a service to the Indian community. . . . All my sons have had complaints to make against me in this matter. Whenever they come across an MA or a BA, or even a matriculate, they seem to feel the handicap of a want of school education. Nevertheless I am of the opinion that, if I had insisted on their being educated somehow at schools, they would have been deprived of the training that can be had only at the school of experience, or from constant contact with the parents . . . (11).

I shall return presently to the effects this contact had on Gandhi's sons. In the public domain, his hostility to intellectuals with an English education who "enslaved India" did not prevent him from adopting as his political successor young Jawaharlal Nehru, a product of Harrow and Cambridge. If Western civilisation was poison for India, Gandhi had installed the chief poisoner as his heir.

From his early thirties, two ideas of overwhelming, obsessive power were uppermost in Gandhi's mind and dominated his life: *satyagraha* and *brahmacharya*. *Satyagraha* means, broadly, nonviolent action; *brahmacharya,* sexual abstinence; but both terms, as we shall see, had for him much wider spiritual implications. The two were inextricably interwoven in his teaching, and more bizarrely in his private life. Significantly it was in the same year – 1906, when he was thirty-seven – that he took his vow of chastity for life, and started his first nonviolent campaign.

Gandhi's negative attitude to sex was reminiscent of, and partly inspired by, Tolstoy's, but was more violent and baffling. A partial explanation of its origins may perhaps be the famous episode, related in his autobiography, of his father dying while he had intercourse with his wife. He was sixteen then (having married at fourteen), and had spent the evening, as usual, ministering to his sick father – massaging his feet –

when his uncle relieved him. What could be more natural than that he should join his young wife? A few minutes later, however, a servant knocked at the door, announcing the father's death – which apparently nothing had presaged:

> I ran to my father's room. I saw that, if animal passion had not blinded me, I should have been spared the torture of separation from my father during his last moments. I should have been massaging him, and he would have died in my arms. . . .
>
> This shame of my carnal desire even at the critical hour of my father's death . . . was a blot I have never been able to efface or forget. . . . It took me long to get free from the shackles of lust, and I had to pass through many ordeals before I could overcome it (12).

How much this episode contributed to Gandhi's attitude to sex is a matter of speculation. But the effects of that attitude on his own sons are on record. He refused to send them to school because he wanted to mould them in his own image; and since he had renounced sex, he expected them to do the same. When Harilal, the eldest son, wanted to marry at the age of eighteen, Gandhi refused permission and disowned him "for the present". Harilal had the courage to marry nevertheless – he had achieved a degree of independence from his father by living with relatives in India while Gandhi still lived in South Africa. When his wife died in the influenza epidemic of 1918, Harilal, who was now thirty, wanted to remarry; but again Gandhi objected. From that point onward, Harilal began to disintegrate. He became an alcoholic, associated with prostitutes, embraced the Moslem faith and published an attack on his father under the pen-name "Abdullah". When he became involved in a shady business transaction, a solicitor wrote a letter of complaint to Gandhi. Gandhi published the lawyer's letter in his paper, *Young India* (18 June, 1925), together with his own reply, which amounted to placing Harilal on a public pillory:

> I do indeed happen to be the father of Harilal M. Gandhi. He is my eldest boy, is over thirty-six years old and is the father of four children. His ideas and mine having been discovered over fifteen years ago to be different, he has been living separately from me. . . .

> Harilal was naturally influenced by the Western veneer that my life at one time did have. His commercial undertakings were totally independent of me. . . . He was and still is ambitious. He wants to become rich, and that too easily. . . . I do not know how his affairs stand at the moment, except that they are in a bad way. . . . Men may be good, not necessarily their children (13).

Father and son hardly ever met again. On her deathbed, Gandhi's wife, Kasturbai, asked for her first-born. Harilal came, drunk, and had to be removed from her presence; "she wept and beat her forehead".

He was also present at Gandhi's cremation. Although it is the duty and privilege of the eldest son to light his father's funeral pyre, he kept, or was kept, in the background. He died a month later in a hospital from tuberculosis. His name is rarely mentioned in the voluminous Gandhi literature.

Harilal may have been a difficult case under any circumstances, but the second son, Manilal, was not; he remained a loyal and devoted son to the end. Nevertheless, the way Gandhi treated him was just as inhuman – there is no other word for it. At the age of twenty, Manilal committed the unforgivable sin of losing his virginity to a woman. When Gandhi discovered this, he made a public scene, went on a penitential fast, and decreed that he would never allow Manilal to marry. He even managed to persuade the guilty woman to shave her hair. A full fifteen years had to pass until Gandhi relented, on Kasturbai's entreaties, and gave his permission for Manilal to marry – by which time Manilal was thirty-five. But in the meantime he had been banished from Gandhi's presence and ashram, because he had lent some money, out of his own savings, to his disgraced brother Harilal. When Gandhi heard about it, he made a scene accusing Manilal of dishonesty, on the grounds that the ashramites' savings were the property of the ashram. Manilal was sent into exile with instructions to become a weaver's apprentice, and not to use the name Gandhi. "In addition to this," Manilal later told Louis Fischer, "Father also contemplated a fast, but I sat all night entreating him not to do so, and in the end my prayer was heeded. I left my dear mother and my brother Devadas sobbing . . ." (14).

After a year as a weaving apprentice and a publisher's assistant, Gandhi ordered him to Natal to edit *Indian Opinion*. Apart from visits, Manilal remained an exile to the end of Gandhi's life.

In fairness, Gandhi's treatment of his two eldest sons must be seen in the context of the traditional Hindu "joint family household", over which the father holds unrestricted sway. To go against his decision is unthinkable; as long as Bapu is alive, the sons are not regarded as having attained fully adult status. But even against this background Gandhi's relentless tyranny over his sons was exceptional – he rode them like the djinn of the Arab legend, whom, in the guise of an old man, his young victim cannot get off his shoulders. "I was a slave of passion when Harilal was conceived," he was wont to say. "I had a carnal and luxurious life during Harilal's childhood." Quite clearly he was visiting his own sins on his sons. By his efforts to prevent them from marrying, he was trying to deprive them of their manhood, convinced that he had a right to do so, since he had voluntarily renounced his own.

Gandhi almost invariably refers to the act of love as an expression of man's "carnal lust" or "animal passion", and to woman's role in the act as that of a "victim" or "object". He did know, of course, that women too have a sexual urge, but had a simple answer to that: "Let her transfer her love . . . to the whole of humanity, let her forget she ever was or ever can be the object of man's lust" (15). Intercourse, he taught, was only permissible for the purpose of procreation; if indulged in for "carnal satisfaction", it is a "reversion to animality". Accordingly, he unconditionally rejected birth control, even within the limits permitted by the Catholic Church. When Dr Margaret Sanger, the pioneer of family planning, visited Gandhi in 1936, she talked about the catastrophic consequences of the population explosion in India and elsewhere, and appealed for his help, pleading that "there are thousands, millions, who regard your word as that of a saint". But throughout their conversation "he held to an idea or a train of thought of his own, and, as soon as you stopped, continued it as though he had not heard you. . . . Despite his claim to openmindedness, he was proud of not altering his opinions. . . . He agreed that no more than three or four children should be born to a family, but insisted that intercourse, therefore, should be restricted for the entire married life of the couple to three or four occasions" (16).

As a solution to India's population problem this was about as realistic as the return to the spinning wheel. Yet it was deeply rooted in Gandhi's religious beliefs. If *khadi* was the gateway to salvation, *brahmacharya* was "the conduct that leads to God" – which is what the word literally means. Thus, to quote his secretary and biographer Pyarelal, "*Brahmacharya* was the *sine qua non* for those who aspire to a spiritual or higher life" (17) – and thus for all ashramites, married or not. How deeply he felt about this is illustrated by an episode in Gandhi's first ashram – Phoenix Settlement in South Africa:

> Once when I was in Johannesburg I received the tidings of the moral fall of two of the inmates of the ashram. News of an apparent failure or reverse in the [political] struggle would not shock me, but this news came upon me like a thunderbolt. The same day I took the train for Phoenix. Mr Kallenbach insisted on accompanying me. He had noticed the state I was in. On the way my duty became clear to me. I felt that the guardian or the teacher was responsible, to some extent, at least, for the lapse of his pupil. . . . I also felt that the parties to the guilt could be made to realise my distress and the depth of their fall only if I did some penance for it. So I imposed upon myself a fast for seven days and a vow of having only one meal for a period of four months and a half. Mr Kallenbach tried to dissuade me, but in vain. He ultimately accepted the propriety of the penance and insisted on joining me. . . . My penance pained everybody, but it cleared the atmosphere. Everyone came to realise what a terrible thing it was to be sinful (18).

This episode – including the reaction of the unfortunate Mr Kallenbach – gives one a foretaste of the curious atmosphere that prevailed in Gandhi's later ashrams. Whereas in politics Gandhi always tended towards compromise, in the matter of *brahmacharya* he became more fanatical as the years went by. He used his proverbial fascination for women to persuade them to take a vow, whether their husbands agreed or not, wrecking several marriages in the process, and causing lasting unhappiness in others (among them is the sad case of a personal friend). One might say that the young women who came under his spell were seduced by Gandhi into chastity.

Sexual abstinence may procure spiritual benefits to communities of monks or nuns segregated from the opposite sex and carefully sheltered from temptation. But Gandhi had designed for himself a very special and arduous road to *brahmacharya*: he felt compelled to expose himself to temptation in order to test his progress in self-control. He regarded these tests – which continued to the very end when he was nearly eighty – as a pioneering venture, another "Experiment with Truth" (as he called his autobiography). The experiments started with his own wife after he had taken the vow, and were then continued with other, younger women. In a letter to Bose, justifying these practices, Gandhi wrote:

> I am amazed at your assumption that my experiment implied any assumption of woman's inferiority. She would be, if I looked upon her with lust with or without her consent. I have believed in woman's perfect equality with man. My wife was "inferior" when she was the instrument of my lust. She ceased to be that when she lay with me naked as my sister. If she and I were not lustfully agitated in our minds and bodies, the contact raised both of us.
>
> Should there be a difference if it is not my wife, as she once was, but some other sister? I do hope you will acquit me of having any lustful designs upon women or girls who have been naked with me. A or B's hysteria had nothing to do with my experiment, I hope. They were before the experiment what they are today, if they have not less of it.
>
> The distinction between Manu and others is meaningless for our discussion . . . (19).

The Manu mentioned in this letter was the granddaughter of a cousin, the last of the guinea pigs in the quest for *brahmacharya*. She had lost her mother in childhood, and Kasturbai had looked after her. On Kasturbai's death Gandhi took over. "I have been a father to many, but to you I am a mother," (20) he wrote to her; strange as this may sound, he meant her to take that literally – so much so that Manu actually wrote a book with the title *Bapu: My Mother.* As a "budding girl of eighteen", in Gandhi's words, she claimed to be free from sexual feelings. Pyarelal explains in his biography:

> Manu apparently did not feel any embarrassment. She returned his ministrations by nursing him through illnesses and fasts; in her diary she recorded, in between two political messages, the effects of the enema she had administered to him, and the admonitions he addressed to her from his bathtub: "While bathing, Bapu said these words to me with great affection, and also caressed my back" (21).

For Gandhi, however, this was a crucial experiment. If it succeeded "it would show that his quest for truth had been successful. *His sincerity should then impress itself upon the Moslems, his opponents in the Moslem League and even Jinnah,* who doubted his sincerity." The italics are by the faithful Pyarelal, who knew more intimately than any other contemporary the ways and twists of his Master's thought. Gandhi sincerely believed that he was an instrument of God, who "gives me guidance to react to the situations as they arise" (22). But the instrument must be pure, free from carnal desire; and to attain that freedom he had to go through his experiment in *brahmacharya*. It "put him in touch with the infinite" (23); at the same time it was to solve the Hindu–Moslem problem, put an end to the mutual massacres, persuade the Moslem League of his *bona fides,* and make them renounce their claim for an independent Pakistan.

From the Mahatma's point of view all this was perfectly logical. In his own mind, his public, political activities and his intimate Experiments with Truth were inseparable; *satyagraha* and *brahmacharya* were mutually interdependent. For *satyagraha* means not only nonviolent action, but action powered by an irresistible soul-force or truth-force (*sat* – truth, *agraha* – firmness). At the stage he had reached in the last two years of his life, everything depended for him on the crucial experiment with Manu; and this may explain why he so stubbornly insisted that she share his bed, in defiance of everybody's advice.

It also explains why, while the fate of India was being

decided in the dramatic months June–July 1947, Gandhi chose to treat the Indian public to a series of six articles (24) – on *brahmacharya*. He had been touring the Moslem villages of East Bengal, attempting to quell the riots by his personal influence. Most of the time, his only companions on the pilgrimage were Manu, Bose and a stenographer. Several of his collaborators, including intimate friends, protested against the Manu experiment (though they must have known of previous ones), expressed their disapproval to Gandhi, and some of them actually left him. A public scandal was avoided, but Gandhi felt deprived of their unconditional admiration, utterly lonely and dejected. Even Bose left, after long discussions in which he had in vain tried to convince Gandhi of the psychological ill-effects of the experiment on both parties concerned – without ever doubting the sincerity of their motives; but he returned to serve Gandhi a few months later. The ill-timed *Harijan* articles, which made the public gasp, were Gandhi's reply to the dissidents.

He also wrote to Acharya Kripalani, the president of Congress: "This is a very personal letter, but not private. Manu Gandhi, my granddaughter . . . shares the bed with me. . . . This has cost me dearest associates. . . . I have given the deepest thought to the matter. The whole world may forsake me, but I dare not leave what I hold is the truth for me. . . . I have risked perdition before now. Let this be the reality if it has to be" (25). And he requests that the Acharya discuss the matter with other Congress politicians – in the midst of the negotiations about Independence.

I have dwelt at some length on Gandhi's struggle to attain chastity for two reasons; because it provides an essential – by his own testimony, the most essential – key to his personality; and because it became a part of the Gandhian heritage which had a lasting influence on the social and cultural climate of the country.

After Gandhi's death, however, the Indian Establishment attempted to suppress the facts of his last Experiment with Truth. An example of this conspiracy of silence is the story of the book by Nirmal Kumar Bose, *My Days with Gandhi,* which I have repeatedly quoted. Professor Bose, a distinguished anthropologist and expounder of Gandhi's philosophy, had written two earlier books, *Studies in Gandhism* and *Selections from Gandhi.* He had been the Mahatma's companion during the pilgrimage in East Bengal, and in *My Days with Gandhi* devoted a chapter to the repercussions of the Manu experiments, without going into details about the experiment itself. It is a discreet, affectionate and respectful work; yet not only was it rejected by all publishers whom Bose approached, but strenuous attempts were made "from very high quarters in the country" to prevent its publication.

Five years after Gandhi's death, Bose decided to publish the book on his own. It is unobtainable in India, and the most recent biographer of Gandhi, Geoffrey Ashe, remarks: "It has become common knowledge that one important memoir was partly suppressed. I had some difficulty in locating what may be the only copy in England" (26). Not even the British Museum has a copy of it. My own book (*The Lotus and the Robot)*, in which I quoted Bose, was also banned in India on the grounds that it contained "disrespectful remarks about Gandhiji".*

Ironically, three years after Bose, the first volume of Pyarelal's monumental, authorised biography of Gandhi was published, confirming all the facts that Bose had mentioned (but without mentioning Bose).

In the Western world Gandhi's obsession with *brahmacharya* could have been shrugged off as a harmless personal quirk. In India it struck deep, archetypal chords. There is a hidden message running through Gandhi's preaching of chastity – hidden, that is, from the Western reader, but obvious to every Hindu. It relates to the physiological benefits of sexual restraint. According to the doctrines of traditional Hindu (*ayurvedic*) medicine, man's "vital force" is concentrated in his seminal fluid. All his powers, both mental and physical, derive

* See below.

from this precious secretion – a kind of elixir of life – variously called *bindu, soma-rasa* or "vital fluid". Every expenditure of vital fluid causes physical weakening and spiritual impoverishment. Conversely, the storing up of *bindu* through continence provides for increased spiritual powers, health and longevity (Gandhi hoped to live to the age of 125). It also produces that smooth skin with a radiant glow which all true saints were said to possess – including the Mahatma. Various semi-secret Hatha Yoga practices are designed to preserve the vital fluid even during intercourse.

Gandhi was a firm believer in *ayurvedic* medicine, and himself practised it on his family and intimates. Numerous passages in his writings show that he also believed in the crucial importance of preserving the "vital fluid". Thus in his pamphlet "Key to Health" he wrote:

> It is said that an impotent man is not free from sexual desire. . . . But the cultivated impotence of the man whose sexual desire has been burnt up and whose sexual secretions are being converted into vital force is wholly different. It is to be desired by everybody (27).

Or:

> Ability to retain and assimilate the vital liquid is a matter of long training. Once achieved, it strengthens body and mind. The vital liquid capable of producing such a wonderful being as man cannot but, when properly conserved, be transmuted into matchless energy and strength (28).

Hinduism has a notoriously ambivalent attitude towards sex. On the one hand, the cult of the *lingam,* the erotic temple carvings, the *Kama Sutra* and the "Sex Pharmacies" with their flowering trade in aphrodisiacs; on the other, prudery, hypocrisy, lip service to the ideal of chastity combined with anxiety about the loss of the vital fluid and its debilitating effects. "Spermal anxiety" appears to be common among Hindus; and with it goes unconscious resentment against Woman, who is its cause. The Hindu Pantheon has no Eros and no Cupids – only Kama, the prime force of lust.

Gandhi's lifelong struggle to overcome his own "carnal

lust" and "animal passion"; his public *mea culpa* when he confessed to a "lust dream" followed by a penance of six weeks' silence; his endorsement of the power of the "vital fluid" – all this made him the living symbol of the guilt-ridden Hindu attitude to sex, and encouraged the worshipful masses to persist in it.

Another, minor but significant feature of the Gandhian heritage is the widespread hypochondria about diet and digestion. In a country riddled with amoebic dysentery, hook worm and other scourges, this is not surprising. But Gandhi's lifelong preoccupation with experimental diets was again primarily linked with the quest for chastity. When he took the vow, he wrote: "Control of the palate is the first essential in the observance of the vow. . . . The *brahmacharya's* food should be limited, simple, spiceless and if possible uncooked. . . . Six years of experiment have shown me that the *brahmacharya's* ideal food is fresh fruit and nuts" (29). Even milk he thought was an aphrodisiac to be avoided – which seems difficult to reconcile with the pamphlet he wrote on "How to Serve the Cow" (30).

One of Gandhi's biographers, Louis Fischer, called him "a unique person, a great person, perhaps the greatest figure of the last nineteen hundred years". Others compared him to Christ, Buddha and St Francis. The claims to immortality were mainly based on his use of nonviolence as a political weapon in a world sick of violence. The partial success of his early passive resistance, civil disobedience and non-cooperation campaigns; the unarmed marches against armed police and troops; the first sitdowns, the cheerful courting of imprisonment, the public fasts – all this was something completely new in politics, something unheard of; it was a message of hope, almost a revelation; and the amazing thing was that it seemed to work. The lasting merit of Gandhi was, not that he "liberated India" – as John Grigg (31) and others have pointed out, independence would have come much earlier without him – but to have made the world realise that the conventional methods of power politics are not the only conceivable ones;

and that *under certain circumstances* nonviolence – *ahimsa* – might be substituted for them. But the emphasis is on the limiting clause; and the tragedy of Gandhism is the narrow range of applicability of the method. It was a noble game which could only be played against an adversary abiding by certain rules of common decency instilled by long tradition; in Soviet Russia or Nazi Germany it would have amounted to mass suicide.

Like most inventors of a new philosophical system, Gandhi at first believed in its universal validity. The earliest shock of disappointment came in 1919, when the first nationwide civil disobedience campaign degenerated into violent rioting all over the country. Gandhi suspended the action, went on a penitential fast, and confessed to having committed a "Himalayan blunder" by starting the campaign before his followers had been sufficiently trained in the spirit and methods of *satyagraha*.

The next year he launched a new non-cooperation movement jointly with the Moslems. Again it led to nationwide riots, culminating in the massacre of Chauri Chaura; again he suspended the campaign and went on a fast.

His most successful movement was the civil disobedience campaign in 1930–31 against the salt laws, highlighted by the spectacular "march to the sea". This time, too, there was widespread rioting, but the campaign was allowed to continue until a compromise settlement was reached with the Viceroy.

The later *satyagraha* movements (1932–34, 1940–41 and 1942–43) ended inconclusively. In terms of tangible results this was not an impressive record. But the general impact on politicians, intellectuals and the world at large was momentous; it turned Gandhi into a living legend. It was further dramatised by his eighteen public fasts and altogether six and a half years of detention – the first in a black hole in Johannesburg, the last in the Aga Khan's palace.

But Gandhi's methods of using nonviolence had their Himalayan inconsistencies, and the advice he proffered to other nations was often quite irresponsible by any humane standard. Although he repeated over and again that only people far advanced on the spiritual trail were able to practise nonviolent resistance, he did not hesitate to recommend it as a universal panacea. Thus in December 1938, after the first nationwide pogrom in Germany, he wrote: "I make bold to say that, if the Jews can summon to their aid soul-power that comes only from nonviolence, Herr Hitler will bow before the courage which he will own is infinitely superior to that shown by his best stormtroopers" (32). And in 1946, when the incredible news of six million gassed victims became known: "The Jews should have offered themselves to the butcher's knife. They should have thrown themselves into the sea from cliffs. . . . It would have roused the world and the people of Germany" (33).

There was only one mitigating circumstance to utterances like this: Gandhi's notorious ignorance of international affairs.

At the outbreak of the Second World War he declared his moral support for the Allied cause. After the fall of France, he praised Pétain for his courage to surrender, and on 6 July 1940 published an "Appeal to Every Briton" to follow the French example (on his insistence, the text of this appeal was transmitted by the Viceroy to the British War Cabinet):

> '. . . I do not want Britain to be defeated, nor do I want her to be victorious in a trial of brute strength. . . . I want you to fight Nazism without arms or with non-violent arms. I would like you to lay down the arms you have, being useless for your humanity. You will invite Herr Hitler and Signor Mussolini to take what they want of the countries you call your possessions. Let them take possession of your beautiful island, with your many beautiful buildings. You will give all these, but neither your souls, nor your minds. If these gentlemen choose to occupy your homes, you will allow yourself, man, woman and child, to be slaughtered, but you will refuse to owe allegiance to them (34).

It would have taken a great deal of corpses to keep Bapu in nonviolence.

He had similar advice to offer to Czechs, Poles, Finns and Chinese. On the last day of his life, a few hours before he was assassinated, a correspondent of *Life* magazine asked him: "How would you meet the atom bomb . . . with nonviolence?"

He replied: "I will not go into shelter. I will come out in the open and let the pilot see I have not a trace of ill-will against him. The pilot will not see our faces from his great height, I know. But the longing in our hearts – that he will not come to harm – would reach up to him and his eyes would be opened" (35).

This statement, and many earlier ones on similar lines, give the impression that Gandhi's faith in nonviolence was absolute ("I know of no single case in which it has failed," he wrote in his "Appeal to Every Briton"). In fact, however, on a number of critical occasions he betrayed his own principles in a quite blatant way. There was first the episode, not to be taken too seriously, when, in 1918, he acted as a recruiting sergeant for the British Army. In a speech in the Kheda district he said:

> To bring about [Dominion status in the Empire] we should have the ability to defend ourselves, that is, the ability to bear arms and to use them. . . . If we want to learn the use of arms with the greatest possible despatch, it is our duty to enlist ourselves in the army (36).

Three years later, he asserted:

> Under Independence I too would not hesitate to advise those who would bear arms to do so and fight for the country (37).

Later on he explained these lapses by saying that they did not imply any lack of faith in nonviolence, but merely that "I had not yet found my feet. . . . I was not sufficiently sure of my ground" (38). But this excuse can hardly be applied to the climactic events in the last two years of his life – the Hindu–Moslem massacres which led to Partition, and the fighting in Kashmir which signalled the ultimate shipwreck of non-violence. During his pilgrimage through the terror-stricken villages of East Bengal when he saw "only darkness all round", he confessed to Bose that "for the time being" he had "given up searching for a non-violent remedy applicable to the masses". A few days later, he wrote: "Violence is horrible and retarding, but may be used in self-defence." Yet another few days later, in a letter: "Non-violent defence is the supreme self-defence, being infallible" (39).

He was at the end of his tether.

* * *

Gandhi had strenuously opposed Partition; he called it "the vivisection of India which would mean the vivisection of myself". At the historical meeting of Congress, on 14–15 June 1947, which was to decide for or against Partition, the President, Acharya Kripalani, Gandhi's lifelong friend, made a memorable speech which signified the future Indian Government's farewell to the ideals of nonviolence. Unlike Mark Antony, he started by praising Gandhi, and then proceeded to bury him. He expressed his appreciation of Gandhi's pilgrimages in Bengal and Bihar, trying to bring about Hindu–Moslem reconciliation as an alternative to Partition, but denied the efficacy of the method: "Unfortunately for us today, though [Gandhi] can enunciate policies, they have to be in the main carried out by others, and these others are not converted to his way of thinking. It is under these painful circumstances that I have supported the division of India" (40).

To everybody's surprise, Gandhi in his own speech suddenly urged acceptance of Partition on the grounds that "sometimes certain decisions, however unpalatable they may be, have to be taken". Three months later, independent India and independent Pakistan were confronting each other in Kashmir. Gandhi commented that he had been "an opponent of all warfare. But if there was no other way of securing justice from Pakistan, if Pakistan persistently refused to see its proved error and continued to minimise it, the Indian Union would have to go to war against it. War was no joke. No one wanted war. That way lay destruction. But he could never advise anyone to put up with injustice" (41).

He had been lavish with his advice to Britons, Frenchmen, Czechs, Poles, Jews, to lay down their arms and surrender to injustices infinitely more terrible than those committed by Pakistan. As on earlier critical occasions, when the lofty ideal clashed with hard reality, realism carried the day and the Yogi succumbed to the Commissar. He had believed in and practised nature medicine, but when critically ill had always called in the practitioners of Western science which he held in such contempt. Nonviolence had worked like magic on the British, but did not work on Moslems. Was it really the panacea for mankind as he had thought? A fortnight before his death, commenting on Deputy Premier Sirdar Patel's decision to send troops into Kashmir, Gandhi confessed to Bose:

> When power descended on [Patel], he saw that he could no longer successfully apply the method of nonviolence which he used to wield with signal success. I have made the discovery that what I and the people with me termed nonviolence was not the genuine article, but a weak copy known as passive resistance (42).

To another interviewer – Professor Stuart Nelson – he repeated that "what he had mistaken for *satyagraha* was not more than passive resistance, which was a weapon of the weak. . . . Gandhiji proceeded to say that it was indeed true that he had all along laboured under an illusion. But he was never sorry for it. He realised that if his vision had not been clouded by that illusion, India would never have reached the point which it had done today" (43).

Yet that, too, may have been no more than an illusion. India had reached the point of independence not because of *ahimsa,* but because the British Empire had gone into voluntary self-liquidation. The spinning wheel was preserved on India's national flag, but the Gandhian mystique played no part in the shaping of the new state, though it continued to pay lip service to it. The armed conflicts with Pakistan, and later with China, produced outbreaks of chauvinism and mass hysteria which suggested that the Mahatma's pacifist apostolate had left hardly any tangible effects; and the bloody riots between Maharatis and Gandhi's own Gujeratis added a bitterly ironic touch to the picture. When Gandhi's adopted spiritual heir, Vinoba Bhave, "the marching saint", was asked whether he approved of armed resistance against the Chinese frontier intrusion, he replied in the affirmative, using Gandhi's erstwhile excuse that the masses were not yet ripe for nonviolent resistance.

Gandhi himself foresaw these developments in moments when his vision was not "clouded by illusion". The principles by which he hoped to shape India, laid down forty years earlier in *Hind Swaraj,* had turned out to be self-defeating. In the midst of the celebrations, their – and his – defeat was complete. It was sealed by an assassin, who was not one from the enemy camp, but a devout Hindu.

J. F. Horrabin has described a meeting with Gandhi at St James's Palace, where the Round Table Conference of 1931 was held:

> We chatted for some minutes in a small ante-room. Then, catching sight of a clock, he remembered another appointment, apologised, and hurried away. I watched him disappear down one of the long corridors of the Palace; his robes tucked in, his slippers twinkling as he ran. Dare I say it? – I am sure, at least, that no friend of his will misunderstand me if I do – I was irresistibly reminded of one of those Chaplin films which end with the little figure hurrying away to the horizon, gradually lost to sight in the distance (44).

That remark, far from being disrespectful, leads straight to the secret of Gandhi's immense power over his countrymen, and the love they bore him. Chaplin was the symbol of the little man in a bowler hat in the industrialised society of the West. Gandhi was the symbol of the little man in a loincloth in poverty-stricken India. He himself was fully aware of this. When J. P. Patel once asked him "what it was in him that created such a tremendous following in our country", he replied, "It's the man of our country who realises when he sees me that I am living as he does, and I am a part of his own self" (45).

Nehru, the Westernised progressive, often regarded Gandhi as a political liability, but he was nevertheless under his spell, precisely because Gandhi to him was, in his own words, "the soul of India".

The soul and the loincloth went together; they were inseparable. When Gandhi had tea with George V and Queen Mary at Buckingham Palace, wearing sandals, loincloth and a shawl on his shoulders, it was more than just showmanship. It was an event which instantly turned into legend, spreading to the remotest villages of India. One version of it was given years later by the vice-chancellor of Poonah University, who accompanied Gandhi to the gates of Buckingham Palace: "He went to see the King dressed in a poor man's costume, with half his legs visible. The King said, 'Mr Gandhi, how is India doing?' He said, 'Look at me and you will know what India is like.'" Every villager with naked legs who felt that Gandhi was "a part of his own self", thought himself for a moment equal to the King of England. Perhaps Gandhi's greatest gift to his people was to arouse in them, after centuries of lethargy, the first stirrings of self-respect.

But he also gave his blessing to their attitudes, derived from a petrified tradition, to sex, food, paternal authority, medicine, industry and education; and he confirmed them in that "illusion-haunted, magic-ridden slave-mentality" which Tagore has castigated as "the original sin from which all our ills are flowing". Even where he opposed tradition, he did it on the traditional principle of the identity of opposites: the Untouchables became Harijans, Children of God: the sources of defilement were turned into objects of worship, and latrine-cleansing became a sacrament for all pious ashramites – though for nobody else.

Gandhi exerted such a powerful influence over the minds of the masses that many believed him to be an Avatar, a reincarnation of Krishna. One cannot help feeling that had he crusaded for family planning instead of the impossible demand for married continence, India might be a different country now. He was most eloquent about the poverty-stricken life of the Indian villager and his inability to feed the exorbitant numbers of his offspring; but the only remedy he had to propose was chastity and the spinning wheel.

He was unwilling to listen to the reasoned arguments of critics. In the words of T. A. Raman, a distinguished Indian journalist: "Almost the most marked trait of Gandhi's character is that evidenced by the virtual impossibility of reasoning with him. By definition he is a man of faith, and men of faith have little use for the slow processes of reasoning."

It is equally futile to argue with intellectuals, who adhere to the Gandhi cult and pay lip service to a philosophy easy to eulogise and impossible to realise. It is this attitude which lends the contemporary Indian scene its twilight air of unreality and sanctimonious evasion of vital issues. Bapu still casts his saintly-sickly spell over it, but its power is waning as more people realise that, whether we like it or not, spinning wheels cannot compete with factories, and that the most vital fluid is the water from large irrigation dams for the country's parched fields.

When all is said, the Mahatma, in his humble and heroic ways, was the greatest living anachronism of the twentieth century; and one cannot help feeling, blasphemous though it may sound, that India would be better off today and healthier in mind, without the Gandhian heritage.

References

1. Geoffrey Ashe, *Gandhi: A Study in Revolution* (London, 1968), p. 267.
2. *The Gandhi Reader: A Source-Book of his Life and Writings*, ed. Homer A. Jack (London, 1958), pp. 229–30.
3. Ibid., pp. 223, 225 and 226.
4. Ibid., pp. 228–31.
5. Ibid., pp. 107–8 and 120.
6. Sir C. Sankavan Nair, *Gandhi and Anarchy* (Madras, 1922), p. 4–5.
7. Ibid., p. 6.
8. Ibid., pp. 6–7.
9. Ibid., p. 18.
10. M.K. Gandhi, *Hind Swaraj or Indian Home Rule* (Ahmedabad, reprinted 1946), pp. 63–6.
11. C.F. Andrews, *Mahatma Gandhi: His Own Story* (London, 1930, 2 vols.), pp. 94–5.
12. Gandhi, *My Experiments with Truth* (London, 1949), pp. 167–8.
13. Ibid., p. 26.
14. Louis Fischer, *The Life of Mahatma Gandhi* (London, 1951), p. 230.
15. Nirmal Kumar Bose, *My Days with Gandhi* (Calcutta, 1953), p. 203.
16. Margaret Sanger, *An Autobiography* (New York, 1938), pp. 470–71.
17. Pyarelal, *Mahatma Gandhi: The Last Phase* (Ahmedabad, 1965, 2 vols.), pp. 570 and 579.
18. Andrews, op. cit., p. 186.

19. Bose, op. cit., p. 133.
20. Ibid., p. 177.
21. Manuben Gandhi, *Last Glimpses of Bapu* (Delhi, Agra and Jaipur, 1962), p. 303.
22. T.A. Raman, *What Does Gandhi Want?* (Oxford, New York and Toronto, 1943), p. 49.
23. Bose, op. cit., p. 176.
24. In the weekly magazine *Harijan*.
25. Pyarelal, op. cit., p. 581.
26. Ashe, op. cit., p. viii.
27. Pyarelal, op. cit., p. 581.
28. Fischer, op. cit., p. 263.
29. Ibid., p. 263.
30. M.K. Gandhi, "How to Serve the Cow" (Ahmedabad).
31. John Grigg, "A Quest for Gandhi", *Sunday Times*, 28 September 1969.
32. *Harijan*, 17 February 1939.
33. Ashe, op. cit., p. 341.
34. Raman, op. cit., p. 24.
35. *The Essential Gandhi: An Anthology*, ed. Louis Fischer (London, 1963), p. 334.
36. Ibid., p. 125.
37. Louis Fischer, op. cit., p. 371.
38. *The Essential Gandhi*, p. 125.
39. Bose, op. cit., pp. 104 and 107.
40. Ibid., pp. 244–5.
41. Ibid., p. 251.
42. Ibid., p. 4n.
43. Ibid., p. 270–71.
44. *Incidents of Gandhi's Life*, ed. Chandrashanker Shuhla (Bombay, 1949), p. 65.
45. *Talking of Gandhiji: Four Programmes for Radio First Broadcast by the British Broadcasting Corporation*, script and narration by Francis Watson, production by Maurice Brown (London, New York and Toronto, 1957), p. 14.

PART THREE

SOME LATER ESSAYS 1973–1980

GOING NATIVE*

Ten years ago, *Encounter* magazine invited me to act as a guest editor for a special issue devoted to the state of Britain. The cover design of that issue displayed the familiar coat of arms but with a slight difference: the unicorn had been replaced by an ostrich. The reason for this innovation was explained in the preface as follows:

> In Greek mythology, a chimera is a monster with a lion's head, a goat's trunk and a serpent's tail. The Englishman strikes one as a much more attractive hybrid between a lion and an ostrich. In times of emergency he rises magnificiently to the occasion. In between emergencies he buries his head in the sand with the tranquil conviction that Reality is a dirty word invented by foreigners. This attitude is not only soothing, but also guarantees that a new emergency will soon arise and provide a new opportunity for turning into a lion and rising magnificently to the occasion.

To dwell on these leonine qualities would be considered embarrassing and in bad taste, even in a thank-offering lecture. One may nevertheless be permitted to speculate on the course history would have taken if, after Dunkirk, the lion had lost its moral fibre. In all probability, Europe would still be ruled either by Gauleiters or by Commissars, its elite purged, its resisters liquidated, its culture obliterated, its identity lost.

On the other hand, it seems equally probable that if the lion's alter ego had not kept its head buried in the sand during the

* Lecture to the British Academy in the "Thank-Offering to Britain Fund" series, 27 June 1973. First published for the British Academy by the Oxford University Press, London, 1973, under the title "The Lion and the Ostrich".

years from Hitler's invasion of the Rhineland until well after Munich, the war could either have been avoided or won at incomparably smaller cost in human lives – and without delivering Eastern Europe into the hands of a rival tyranny.

The responsibility for this tragic failure cannot be laid on one particular Party or social class or clique, although it used to be fashionable to do so. In fact, however, the illusion that sweet reasonableness can be a substitute for defensive preparedness was shared by the majority of the nation; and the policy of appeasement was based on that illusion – although in the Labour Party it went under the name of pacifism and was wrapped in anti-Fascist slogans. I recently came across a moving speech by Mr Attlee, delivered on 11 March 1935, in the House of Commons in protest against the government's proposal of a modest increase in rearmaments. When he suggested "disbanding the national armies" as a bright idea to save peace, he was interrupted by shouts of "Tell that to Hitler", which he calmly brushed aside as irrelevant.

Thus burying one's head in the sand is not a privilege of the ruling class. The old Etonian, we are told, is on his way out, but the Old Struthonian (from *struthio*, Latin for ostrich) is still going strong in all walks of life, in striped trousers or in overalls, in the boardroom or the trade union office. The results need not be stressed. When the war was over, Britain's prestige in Europe was at an unprecedented height. In less than twenty years it had been all frittered away. One after the other of the defeated nations celebrated its economic miracle, while the only undefeated country steadily moved – to use that fashionable expression – towards the bottom of the European economic league; and if we are to believe the predictions of the Hoover Institute, this trend still continues. It seems that the ostrich has deprived the lion of his share.

This at least is how post-war history looks when seen through the spectacles of the continental observer. But naturalised Britons have two pairs of spectacles which we wear on alternate days. And when I put on my other pair of glasses – provided by the National Health Service – a rather different picture emerges. But this cannot be conveyed by statistical figures; and since a thank-offering is a personal affair, it may be permissible to indulge in some personal reminiscences.

In November 1940, after the collapse of France, I found myself stranded in Portugal, together with thousands of other refugees, trying to get to England and back into the war. I was, however, a Hungarian national, and those were the days of the Blitz and fifth column scare, so the Home Office refused to grant me a visa. Nevertheless, with the help of *The Times* correspondent in Lisbon, Walter Lucas, and the passive connivance of the British Consul General, Sir Henry King, I was able to board a plane bound for England without an entry permit. On arrival at Bristol I was promptly arrested and did a stretch of six weeks in Pentonville Prison as an illegal entrant, until my bona fides was established. The day after I was released, I went to the recruiting office, and was told that it would take a couple of months until my turn came to be called up. I used this interval to write a book on the collapse of France; when the call-up order arrived I needed just another fortnight to finish it. So my publisher, old Jonathan Cape, wrote to the recruiting office asking whether it would be possible to obtain a deferment. The answer he received deserves to be quoted in full:

NO. 3 CENTRE
LONDON RECRUITING DIVISION
DUKE'S ROAD, WC1
EUSTON 5741

Jonathan Cape Esq.
30 Bedford Square
WC1

re Arthur Koestler

I am in receipt of your letter of the 11th instant contents of which have been noted.

As requested, I am therefore postponing Mr Koestler's calling up, and would suggest that he calls at this Centre when he is at liberty to join His Majesty's Forces.

Illegible signature
Major
A.R.C.

When I read this memorable document, I was more than ever convinced that England must lose the war. Subsequent experiences in the Army did little to dispel this impression. I was assigned to the Pioneer Corps – the only branch of the Forces then open to non-allied aliens – to "Dig for Victory" as the posters invitingly said. My company – the 251 Company Aliens Pioneer Corps – was engaged on a fairly vital defence job to protect the petrol reservoirs in the vicinity of Bristol. (We were digging craters which, during air-raids, were filled with inflammable liquid and set ablaze to convince the raiders that they had accomplished their mission and could safely go home.) We were glad to do a useful job, but as you would expect from aliens, we became overenthusiastic, so we asked our Commanding Officer (who was British) to do away with the ritual tea breaks – which, what with downing tools, marching to the distant cook hut and back morning and afternoon, cost nearly two hours of our working time, in addition to the lunch break. The CO expressed his appreciation of our laudable zeal and explained that we had to have our tea breaks whether we liked it or not because the British Pioneer Companies and the local unions of our civilian workmates would raise hell if we didn't. The time was about nine months after Dunkirk.

But then, unlike us, our British workmates were in no hurry because they could never for a moment consider the possibility that the war could be lost. The idea just did not enter their heads. There are apparently situations when the ostrich becomes an indispensable partner of the lion.

I remember some touching episodes. I had to spend a few days in a military hospital somewhere in Gloucestershire, and asked for permission to use my typewriter. The sister in charge of the ward, a kind, middle-aged spinster, who had never before come across a British soldier with an accent like mine, listened to my request, thought for a while, then said: "All right, you can have your typewriter, but on one condition: you must give me your word of honour that you won't do any Fifth Column work on it."

Most of our cosmopolitan bunch in 251 Company came

across similar experiences, which delighted us; they made us feel that such holy innocence had an unconquerable quality. But other experiences left us rather bewildered. While digging for victory, we came into intimate contact with working-class life, and found it fundamentally different from its Continental equivalents. In the NAAFI canteens, in the pub and later at the snooker table in a London ambulance station, I was taught to accept the stubborn persistence of the hoary cliché that people in general were divided into Them and Us. But that 'Us' had nothing to do with class consciousness in the Marxist sense, as it existed in the Socialist and Communist Parties of Europe. Marxist dialectics was as much double-dutch to the British working class as it was to the rest of the nation; instead of the fierce class hatred which had scorched the Continent with revolutions and civil wars, there was an almost smug acceptance of living in a divided world, as licensed premises are divided into saloon bar and public bar. On the Continent, the symbolic gesture of militancy was the clenched fist; here it was closer to a shrug, a deliberate turning of one's back on middle-class standards of value, codes of behaviour, vocabulary and accent. Off duty our working mates were lively characters, full of fun and games; on the working site they moved like figures in a slow-motion film, or deep-sea divers on the ocean bed. They seemed to be conforming to a sacred doctrine, a set of unwritten maxims of life: go slow and take it easy or you are letting your mates down and we shall all be on the dole. It's a mug's game, anyway, and you are in it for life unless you hit the pools. In the Libyan desert, or as rear gunners in a bomber, they would have done a magnificent job; for in those circumstances the gulf would have been temporarily bridged by shared danger and hardship – and by the awareness of playing a man's game instead of a mug's game. The same lovable bloke who risked his life on D-Day to keep the country free would not lift a finger at Dagenham to put the country back on its feet.

It may seem to you that I am flogging a dead horse, but to pronounce it dead does not make it so – or else this particular dead horse still has a kick. "The most striking conclusion," Geoffrey Gorer wrote a few years ago, reviewing a book on the life of coal miners, "the most striking conclusion is, how remarkably little high wages and secure employment have modified old habits and ways of life." It is of course true that the advent of the welfare state, of the TV set and the washing machine provided the upper strata of the working class with some of the external trappings of middle-class life; the frontiers between Disraeli's two nations are no longer impenetrable; gifted young people of working-class origin cross the lines in increasing numbers, while the rebellious children of the bourgeoisie imitate proletarian habits and attitudes. Yet for the bulk of the population the frontier nevertheless persists, separating two overlapping but distinct cultures, each with a different image of itself. On the one side, the complex social pyramid of the middle and upper classes with its intricate subdivisions, but with certain basic aspirations and values in common, which range from confused notions of gracious living to the glorification of the rat race and the joys of suburbia; its motto could be: "Compete, Compute, Commute" - the contemporary version of *Liberté, Egalité, Fraternité.* The other side will have none of it. As Professor Tom Burns wrote some years ago in an article with the significant title "The Cold Class War": "Competition for jobs, for promotion or privileged positions – the serious concerns of the middle-class adult, are disapproved of. . . ." In other words, the British working class seems to have become a powerful non-competitive enclave in a competitive world. To appreciate the contrast, compare John Braine's *Room at the Top* to Alan Silllitoe's *Saturday Night and Sunday Morning.*

You will have noticed that I am once more looking at the scenery through my murky Continental spectacles. Seen through native lenses, the apparent erosion of the class barriers since the war does indeed look impressive; it is reflected in the self-consciously classless attitudes of the new generation of students, in the regional accents put on by performers on the mass media or the deliberately vulgar appeal of commercial advertisements. They all seem overanxious to demonstrate that we have moved into an age of the common man. Some of these attitudes are flagrantly bogus, while others may be genuine reflections of the changing sociocultural climate – but you cannot get around the fact that in this industrial age the decisive test is the state of industrial relations, and the ultimate testing ground is the shop floor. And in this respect, putting on Continental spectacles is again useful, because they reveal that British social history since the end of the war differs fundamentally from that of other European countries. During the early postwar period in Italy and France the Communist Party was the strongest single force both in the trade unions *and* in parliament, and both countries seemed on the verge of civil war. But the rising curve of prosperity led to a corresponding decline in revolutionary fervour; moreover, on the Continent there exist Socialist, Communist, and Christian unions which compete for the worker's favours; and their openly declared political programmes are massively represented in parliament, so that trade union politics have become a truly democratic game. In this country events seem to have moved in the opposite direction: militancy in the unions has increased instead of decreasing with growing prosperity, with a tendency to harden into the kind of cold class war where passive majorities are led by active minorities dedicated to ideologies which cannot muster even a single elected representative in parliament. This is a strangely paradoxical state of affairs in the oldest democracy of the world; it contributes to the industrial malaise and plays a significant part in its showing in the European league. But it is rarely ventilated in public debate; a Struthonian attitude is considered more appropriate, particularly by progressive middle-class intellectuals haunted by guilt – as reflected in Mark Boxer's *Times* cartoons.

If one tries to dig down to the roots of both the psychological malaise and our recurrent economic misadventures, another paradox emerges. In his preface to the English translation of *Das Kapital*, Engels wrote in 1886 that Marx, "after a life-long study of the economic history and conditions of England", had been "led to the conclusion that, at least in Europe, England is the only country where the inevitable social revolution might be effected entirely by peaceful and legal means". One of the reasons for this belief was, he explained, that the British bourgeoisie, instead of stringing the aristocrats on lamp posts, married their daughters, and thus gave rise to a dynamic upper middle class in which feudal traditions became amalgamated with the mercantilism of the new entrepreneurs. The natives of the Continent experienced a series of violent social revolutions in 1789, 1848, 1918, and 1945, which abolished or blurred traditional class distinctions and restructured the whole social edifice. Britain was spared these bloody upheavals, as it was spared foreign invasions, and was able to preserve the continuity of its traditions, institutions and social structure. But it had to pay a price for this immunity. Stability led to complacency and stagnation, which made itself felt in every domain of life, from an outdated system of education, to the ancient guild structure of Britain's trade unions, as unique in the Western world as its weights, measures and currency were until recently. Seen through British eyes, Continental history was a permanent mess, from Robespierre through Lenin to Hitler, with flames bursting out of the roof every now and then. Seen through Continental eyes, the Englishman's proverbial castle was crumbling with dry rot. Somewhere between these two dramatised images lies the truism that islands used to be different – but no longer are.

This state of transition is manifest in the islanders' ambivalent attitude to the mainland. In the past, the decline and fall of empires was an ugly, chaotic event; for the first time in history, this generation saw an empire dissolve with a certain dignity and grace. But when it came to opting for the logical alternative based on the new geopolitical realities, the ostrich once more raised its ruffled tail. In 1948 a whole continent cheered Ernest Bevin's sonorous pronouncement: "Europe must unite or perish." Yet for the next fifteen years it looked as if successive British governments did their level best to promote the second alternative. In 1950, when Britain was invited to join in the European Coal and Steel Community, we refused; in subsequent years, as Europe's economic integration was gathering momentum, and repeated attempts were made to secure our participation, we again refused. It turned out to be an expensive miscalculation. Yet on various occasions British delegates took up an attitude which reminded one of Molotov's famous *nyet*, vetoing UNO resolutions. De Gaulle's trenchant *non* in 1963 is still remembered; but the events that led up to it are forgotten; while the erstwhile flag-bearers of socialist internationalism have become a rearguard of insularity, irresistibly reminding one of the citizens of *Animal Farm* who no longer know whether two legs are good, four legs better, or vice versa.

Thus there is no end to the paradoxes which this country can produce to surprise the world. The 1960s were a decade of recurrent economic crises, but also of unprecedented cultural euphoria. While the editorialists of *Le Monde* and *Die Welt* sadly shook their heads and whispered about the sick man of Europe, *Time* magazine published an enthusiastic cover story about swinging London. Industrial exports were in a sorry state, but miniskirts and the Beatles conquered the world. Carnaby Street became a centre of tourist pilgrimage as the Tower of London had once been. The decline of the pound coincided with an upsurge of *joie de vivre*; the sick man became the trendsetter of Europe.

How is one to explain such a paradox? If one were to take a jaundiced view, one might call it an up-to-date, trendy manner of burying one's head in the sand – or deafening one's ears with discoteque rock. Alternatively one might regard it as a bloodless rebellion against traditions gone stale; or against the rat-race of competing, computing and commuting; or, more melodramatically, as a reaction to existential despair. We can take our choice among these and other interpretations; personally I believe that within a few years the flashier aspects of this scene will have vanished like a set on a revolving stage, without leaving any lasting trace. But there are other aspects of contemporary culture, rarely discussed, which may indeed have a lasting effect. A few weeks ago the press came out with the remarkable disclosure that – I am quoting the *Daily Telegraph*'s headline – "British Teachers are the Worst-Paid in Europe". One does not need to put on one's Continental spectacles to consider this situation as symbolic of the persistence of Struthonian attitudes. A schoolmaster in London's dockland, Mr Ralph Samuels, remarked: "When you tell anybody you're a teacher, you can see in their eyes that they think you must be either mad or incapable of getting a really decent job."* This is not just a question of money – although the contrast between Continental and British salaries speaks for itself – but of the teacher's social status, and of the general attitude to education – its purpose, methods, priorities, and its place in the general scheme of things. Above all, there is the delicate yet basic problem how to reconcile the abstract ideal of equal educational opportunities for all with the hard realities of a social structure in which class distinctions are being slowly eroded but are still strongly and resentfully felt, and are reflected in the glaring inequalities between one type of school and another.

This brings me, through only a slight digression, to my favourite hobbyhorse – though you may consider that too a dead horse, if I may mix my metaphors. I mean that, regardless of all optimistic assertions to the contrary, people still take it for granted that a person's social background can be instantly identified by the way he manipulates his vocal chords and oral cavities (unless he has a Hungarian accent, which puts him into a classless limbo). Most Englishmen, however enlightened, are frankly incredulous when you try to convince them that in France, for instance, some regional patois apart, the vocabulary and pronunciation of the concierge or *femme de ménage* – the equivalent of our Mrs Mop – is indistinguishable from that of the lady whom she serves, and that the old jokes about dropped aitches were an exclusively English speciality. The cause of the difference lies of course mainly in the educational system which in France is essentially uniform, based on competitive selection, where rank and privilege confer only marginal advantages; access to the two pinnacles of learning, the *école normale supérieure* and the *école polytechnique*, is exclusively based on the candidates' merits. As already said, the affectations of middle-class youngsters acquiring working-class accents and attitudes, or the synthetically classless BBC

* Quoted by John Montgomery, *The Fifties* (Allen & Unwin, 1965), p.62.

English strike one as no more than inverted snobbery – which merely proves that one cannot escape becoming a snob of *some* sort in England any more than getting sun-tanned in Majorca.

There is, however, one particular type of snobbery that one cannot help admiring – the British contempt for over-efficiency, for German *Tüchtigkeit*; the refusal to become hypnotised by growth for growth's sake; and the quiet conviction – or illusion – that Britain is Greece to the Romans across the Channel. If carried too far, this attitude helps to hatch more ostriches; nevertheless it has its strong attraction in defending the place of value in a world of facts. It is after all a remarkable phenomenon that the popularity of the Earls Court Motor Show has not diminished the popularity of the Chelsea Flower Show. Rolls Royce may be in the doldrums, but we keep the aspidistra flying.

The late Cecil Day Lewis once wrote these lines, which stuck in my memory:

> Traveller, know / I am here to show / Your own divided heart.

I have tried to give you a glimpse into the divided heart of that contradiction in terms, the naturalised Briton. Yet if you come to think of it, to be born as a British citizen requires neither effort nor an act of choice; to become one requires both. And, reverting once more to snobbery, I can boast of a rather unique education, for my prep school was Pentonville, and the Pioneer Corps my Eton. If, even after thirty years in this country, I still sometimes feel as a stranger among its natives, the moment I set foot on the Continent, I feel British to the bone.

Frequently I am asked by one of my disgruntled native friends why, having once lived in sunnier climes, I choose to live in this country with its foul weather, indifferent food, greedy tax collectors, and bitchy book reviewers. I have tried to answer that question in an autobiographical book, though the answer, I am afraid, is not very original: like many Continentals of a similar background and history,

> I have found the human climate of this country particularly congenial and soothing – a kind of Davos for bruised veterans of the age of Hitler and Stalin. When all is said, its atmosphere still contains fewer germs of aggression and brutality per cubic foot in a crowded bus, pub or queue than in any other country in which I have lived.

My late friend, George Orwell, expressed this feeling much better when he wrote about

> England's crowds with their mild, knobby faces, their bad teeth and gentle manners, this nation of flower-lovers and stamp collectors, pigeon-fanciers, amateur carpenters, coupon-snippers, darts players and crossword-puzzle fans. . . .

And here you have the ultimate paradox of the naturalised Briton: he starts his pilgrim's progress by admiring the lion and ends up by discovering that he has grown rather fond of that preposterous ostrich.

A SENTIMENTAL PILGRIMAGE*

Let in the maid, that out a maid
Never departed more. . . .

Poor, distraught Ophelia's bawdy song surfaced in my memory from God knows what muddy depths as I recalled walking into the recruiting office of the Foreign Legion in Limoges on 17 June 1940, an hour after the sepulchral voice of Marshal Pétain had announced on the radio, between two dry coughs, the capitulation of France and the surrender of Europe to Hitler. I was let in through the door, like that innocent maiden, under my real name, by profession a journalist and writer born in Budapest, Hungary; and I departed through it as Legionnaire Albert Dubert, profession taxi driver, born in Berne, Switzerland.

Some thirty-three years later I experienced the perverse desire to celebrate Britain's entry into Europe by a kind of sentimental pilgrimage, retracing my escape from a continent apparently doomed to share the fate of other past civilisations extinguished by barbarian conquests. So there I stood now, spring 1973, gazing at the bleak façade of the Caserne de la Visitation in Limoges with a feeling of vague depression, a sense of non-reality, and an urge to giggle at the incongruous association of that memory with Ophelia's disgrace.

I took only two books along on this trip: as a sedative, Sterne's *Sentimental Journey*, and as a prop to memory, *Scum of the Earth* – my own account of the collapse of France, written in 1941 (from which all passages quoted in this report are taken).

* First published in the *Daily Telegraph* magazine, 17 August 1973.

It was a wise precaution, for without the printed evidence, my memories of those events would have appeared to me even more surrealistic and unbelievable. Nightmares, after all, are products of the imagination.

The title of the book was an ironic reference to a favourite slogan of the French press at that time: *La lie de la terre*. The "scum" they meant was the human debris which the totalitarian flood, after sweeping through Europe, had deposited on its Western shores. It was of mixed composition, ranging from the elite of exiled German writers and scholars to Spanish militiamen and members of the Communist International Brigade; Polish nationalists, Czech liberals, Austrian social democrats, Italian anti-Fascists. A considerable proportion of them had been through prisons or concentration camps, had suffered torture at the hands of Hitler's Brown Shirts, or been dosed with castor oil by Mussolini's Black Shirts. A few years earlier they had enjoyed general sympathy as heroes and victims of the anti-Fascist struggle, fearless defenders of human freedom – the salt of the earth. When war broke out, they became the scum of the earth.

Various psychological factors contributed to this astonishing change, all of them characteristic of the state of mind which brought about the collapse of France. Perhaps the most important was Stalin's pact with Hitler on the eve of the war, which literally overnight changed the official attitude of the French Communist Party, the most powerful and active part of the working class, from enthusiastic support of the anti-Nazi crusade to active sabotage of the war effort. The fight against Nazi aggression was re-labelled "*la guerre des riches*" and "*la guerre des 200 familles*" (the 200 rich families which allegedly ruled France); and the task of the revolutionary working class was to ensure the defeat of the "Western pluto-democracies". Daladier's government reacted with exemplary stupidity by arresting Communist leaders, suppressing the Party papers and regarding not only the whole rank and file of Communist Party members but also every left-wing sympathiser as a potential fifth columnist. And since among the foreign anti-Nazis too, the Communists had been the most active element, all refugees were now exposed to the almost hysterical wrath of the authorities, the press of all political colours and the ignorant and bewildered public.

There were at that time about three and a half million foreigners living in France, and they provided an ideal scapegoat – numerically at least more convincing than the half a million Jews of Germany. The endemic xenophobia of the French – against which even de Gaulle was not immune – was almost the only emotion which the Right and the Left of the torn nation shared during the phony war. Not only were all foreigners suspect of being spies and saboteurs; but their militant propaganda campaign denouncing the Nazi terror regime was now blamed as one of the major causes of a war that nobody wanted: not the Left, because Hitler was now an ally of Stalin; not the Right, because it was afraid of social revolution and considered a Fascist dictatorship as a lesser evil; not the Centre which would have preferred another Munich and peace in our lifetime. The upshot of it all was that the war against Fascism started by a nationwide round-up of anti-Fascists and their dispatch to prisons and concentration camps. The French administration, inimical to foreigners at the best of times, was riddled with potential collaborators who detested the anti-Nazi refugees and a year later gleefully handed them over to the Gestapo.

Koestler-Dubert was a typical case – a minute bubble among thousands of others in the boiling cauldron. Like many writers of my generation I had been a Communist in the thirties; and though I had left the Party in disgust during the Moscow purges, that made no difference in so far as the Gestapo and the French Police were concerned. So I spent most of the phony war in a concentration camp in Le Vernet d'Arriège in the Pyrenees. This was a particularly nasty camp for common criminals and political suspects – much worse than the normal internment camps for enemy aliens. But to have complained would have been frivolous:

> Measured in Liberal-Centigrade, Vernet was the zero-point of infamy; measured in Dachau-Fahrenheit it was still 32 degrees

> above zero. In Vernet beating-up was a daily occurrence; in Dachau it was prolonged until death ensued. In Vernet people were killed for lack of medical attention; in Dachau they were killed on purpose. In Vernet half of the prisoners had to sleep without blankets in 20 degrees of frost; in Dachau they were put in irons and exposed to frost. The European continent had already reached a stage where a man could be told without irony that he should be thankful to be shot and not strangled, decapitated or beaten to death.

Yet in 1941, when this was written, the gas chambers had not yet started to work.

Spring 1973. Revisiting Le Vernet, I was unable to locate the former camp – or maybe my subconscious was playing tricks; in the end it was Dmitri Kasterine* who found it. The pillars on which the prison huts had rested had been sawn off, only stumps remained. There was a small cemetery, with a rough inscription on a slab of stone: "In memory of 147 people who died far from their countries." Discretion could not have been carried further. On one grave there was a purple posy of plastic flowers.

I was eventually released from Le Vernet in January 1940, thanks to pressure from England (I had been a foreign correspondent of the defunct *News Chronicle*), but the police kept harassing me, with repeated searches of my flat, confiscation of my manuscripts and stamping my identity card with the dreaded letter E, standing for "*éloignement*" – to be deported when conditions permit. This meant reporting to the Prefecture once or twice a week, and at times every day, queuing up each time for three to six hours to obtain a rubber-stamped permission for a further stay of a day or a week, according to the mood of the police clerk at the desk. This cat-and-mouse game was called "*le régime des sursis*" (reprieves); it was played with thousands of political refugees in France and led to a number of suicides among them. I kept up morale by finishing

* The *Daily Telegraph* photographer, who illustrated this article.

a novel, appropriately called *Darkness at Noon*.

A few days before the fall of Paris, I was arrested again, but managed to bluff my way out and to obtain a travel permit to Limoges, famous for its manufacture of porcelain and its retired generals. The Battle of Dunkirk was still in progress, giving France a last breathing space. In the three-week campaign the Germans had taken one million prisoners at the price of sixty thousand casualties.

The government fled to Tours on the Loire. On 11 June Churchill flew to Tours, trying in vain to persuade the French to continue the fight, and offering, in vain, the unification of the British and French Empires "by a single stroke of the pen". On 14 June the German troops entered Paris. On 16 June the President of the Republic asked Marshal Pétain, aged eighty-four, to form a new government. Twenty-four hours later I was standing in a silent crowd, in front of a radio shop in the Rue Gambetta in Limoges, listening to that thin old voice whispering through the loudspeaker: "With a broken heart I tell you that fighting must stop." Then the cough. It sounded like a skeleton with a chill. An hour later, Legionnaire Dubert was born, with impeccable papers and an impeccable past.

I thought "Dubert" sounded particularly respectable: it was the name of the Commissaire Special de Police in charge of foreigners in Limoges. To complete the metamorphosis, I had also started to grow a moustache – of the Vercingetorix walrus type, such as could be seen on the advertisements for Celtique cigarettes. Tragedies in France often have a touch of vaudeville.

The sergeant at the recruiting office handed me my marching orders and railway voucher for the dépôt of the Legion in Lyons Sathenay. Yet Lyons was already occupied by the Germans; besides all railway traffic in France had been stopped an hour earlier. "Couldn't you change my *ordre de marche* for Marseilles?" I ventured.

"Orders are orders," the sergeant said. "*Débrouille-toi*. And learn quickly to sing 'Deutschland Deutschland über alles'. You'll need it in the future French Army."

Débrouille-toi – fend for yourself – also called "*système D*", was the universal motto of the defeated army.

On that same evening I started to débrouiller myself and embarked on the long journey to England – the last *dépôt* of freedom in Europe, protected by the white cliffs of Dover. Four months later I got there, with a detour via Morocco and Portugal – one of the small minority of the scum who were lucky enough to make it.

The majority were pressed into the Nazi Labour Batallions or deported to Auschwitz; and even that was still a cleaner death than to perish among the rats in the sewers of Warsaw.

Each successive exodus of the European intelligentsia from Germany, Austria, Hungary, Czechoslovakia, had involved only a comparatively small minority of the nation concerned. But the first, lightning thrust of Hitler's tanks into France unleashed an avalanche. Not only the French Army – the nation disintegrated. Ten million French people had taken to the roads with their mattresses and saucepans, smothering like a thick torrent of mud what life there was left in the country.

Limoges was on one of the main roads along which the stream flowed down from the north to the south. My memory of those last days before the capitulation still echoes the insane cacophony of motor horns, the roaring of engines, the thundering of heavy lorries, the asthmatic rattle of aged Citroëns, the neighing of old cart horses, as the chaotic stream crossed the Place de la Mairie on its aimless course. Without interruption, all day and night, the flood of refugees passed by and the people in the cafés stared at them, some pityingly, some with hostile contempt, some with anxious eyes, wondering when their turn would come to join the migration. They had watched the growing of the stream from the first days when it had been no more than a rivulet with its sources far away in Holland and Belgium, and the cars still bore foreign markings; then, after Sedan, it had suddenly swollen and on the number plates appeared the signs of the French provinces, M for the Département du Nord, N for the Pas de Calais, and nearer and nearer: X for the Somme, Y for the Seine et Oise. Then the green buses from Paris appeared, and for a few days most cars displayed the proud R of the capital; then they were replaced by the signs of Britanny and the Loire. The number plates told the tale of each phase of the debacle, it revealed the truth which the official communiqués senselessly tried to hide.

Paris gone, Rouen gone, Pontoise gone – and still the stream continued day and night, pouring down from Châteauroux and on towards Périgueux. It looked as if every specimen of the mechanised fauna, everything that could creep and stink on four wheels, was hurrying away from the deluge. The giants of the French Air Force with dismantled material from the lost aerodromes, and the racy tourist coaches with "Paris at Night" and *Excursions à Fontainebleau* written on them; and furniture vans from Brussels and the fire brigade from Maubeuge and the delivery van of a butcher in Soissons, and of a dairy in Rouen, and of an ambulant ice-cream merchant in Evreux, and the street sweeper with rotating brushes of the municipality of Tours, and, in between, roadsters, sports cars, limousines and the thousands of tiny Citroëns and Peugeots, five, ten and fifteen years old, barking up at the mammoth lorries like mangy old fox-terriers. And everything inside crammed to the last square inch with a mixture of old men, young women, grandmothers, babies, saucepans, bird cages, sewing machines, crates, bundles, baskets, cradles, bicycles, cuckoo clocks, loaves, petrol cans, spare wheels, gramophones, accordions, wine bottles, dogs and cats – all stewing together in a sort of surrealist goulash.

Spring 1973. Limoges no longer belongs to the retired generals. There is a brand-new-looking industrial belt outside the old city, surrounded by brand-new housing estates. The main avenues through which the refugee stream passed have been re-named after heroes of the Resistance and I no longer can find my way. The whole place breathes prosperity through every pore of its building blocks. The only reminder of the past is provided by an odd coincidence: the headlines of the morning paper announce the disappearance of Marshal Pétain's coffin from the cemetary of the Ile d'Yeu – where he had been imprisoned until his death in 1951, aged ninety-five. Some young fanatics apparently wanted to transfer his bones to a more dignified resting place. The French press is unusually reticent about the whole affair, but nobody cares anyway.

At the end of capitulation day I managed to hitch-hike to Périgueux. The refugee stream on the roads was thinning out, mainly through lack of petrol. Everywhere there were families camping by the roadside, where the last drop had given out. They were waiting for the armistice to be signed, for "everything to become normal again", and then go back to their homes. The *boches*, after all, were not ogres – they had not been afraid of them, only of the bombings. Hitler might take back Alsace and Lorraine, that's all. They were eating in the sunny meadows by the roadside, opening the last bottle of wine to celebrate, then settling down to a game of *belote*. The apocalypse had turned into a picnic.

In Périgueux they took me on the establishment in the Caserne Busseaux. It was full of *soldats isolés* – soldiers who had made their way, mostly on stolen bicycles, to the south. They all told the same monotonous tale: of antiquated armaments, useless against the German Panzers which cut through their lines like a knife through butter; of officers who vanished in their cars leaving their men in the lurch; and always ending with the same refrain: *on était vendu* – we have been betrayed. By whom? By the Fascists, the generals, the government, the two hundred families, the British. (The refrain of the bourgeoisie provided the counterpoint – betrayed by the Communists, the Front Populaire, the foreigners, Léon Blum and the Jews).

The armistice terms were still unknown, but nobody seemed to care and nobody listened to the wireless. The corporal who slept next to me told me without emotion how his company had been cut off somewhere near Elbeuf on the Seine and surrendered to a German motorised column. The Germans collected their rifles, passed over them with a tank, then told them to beat it – "We don't need any more prisoners" – and even gave them some tins and chocolate. He was impressed by the Germans: *"Ils ne sont pas méchants, les boches, tout-de même."* He was a member of the Socialist Party. Years of anti-Fascist indoctrination had been wiped out of his mind by the shock – and by the need to come to terms with the new reality.

I was still trying to wangle an *ordre de marche* for Marseilles, in vain. An old colonial lieutenant of the Fifteenth Algerian Rifles took me aside. "Are you the Swiss who enlisted on the day of the armistice?" "*Oui, mon Lieutenant.*" He gave my hands a quick glance. "Listen, *mon petit*, if by any chance you do not desire to meet the *boches* you had better beat it. They are still advancing down the coast and have reached La Roche-sur-Yon. Take this paper." It was an old soldier's paybook of a certain Jean Rouzier, aged thirty, private, born in Périgueux, Dordogne. "If you happen to be captured by the *boches*, they won't do you any harm if you are a Frenchman. For a foreign volunteer it may be different. Give me your word to use it only in an emergency and to tear it up when you are safe."

I felt moved to my guts, and remembered that the Almighty was prepared to save Sodom if only ten righteous people could be found within its walls. But in those days the righteous ones were not much in evidence; they started to surface only when the tides of the war were turning.

Spring 1973. The tides of peace have also turned: the pound is floating perilously while Périgueux, like Limoges, has the French economic miracle daubed all over its beaming face. The market is gargantuan with gaggling geese and cackling hens and tractors displaying their shining metal; the pâté stuffed with truffles and goose liver seems to be oozing through the delicatessen windows onto the pavement. The English tourist is treated everywhere with the condescending courtesy due to poor relatives who have seen better days.

* * *

I hitch-hiked to Bergerac (but what had happened to the plucky Cyranos of yesteryear?), was once more taken on the establishment and once more absconded, this time to Bordeaux, in the forlorn hope of finding a boat that would take me to England. As it turned out, the last boat had left forty-eight hours earlier. Eventually, I got a lift to Bayonne, which is about as far south as you can get in France, when you are on the run. I could not cross the Spanish border as many fugitives did, because I had been involved in the Civil War, imprisoned for several months, and was still on the Franco regime's black list. However, at the infantry barracks in the Château Neuf I discovered that a boat was to leave the same day for an unknown destination. . . .

> I remember going round all day in small circles with a bunch of other soldiers to find out about that boat. We went to the *Bureau de la Place*, which sent us to the *Commission des Transports*, which directed us to the *Commission du Port*, which again sent us back to the *Bureau de la Place*. The others were foreigners like myself, mostly Czechs or Poles, enlisted as volunteers for the duration, scared to death like myself by the prospect of falling into the Gestapo's hands. I remember queuing up at the garden gateway of the *Commission de Port*, which was to issue the permits for our embarkation. There were two gates in the railings and two queues before the gates, one for us and one for civilians; the civilians passed one by one, but our gate remained closed, guarded by three sentries with fixed bayonets. We shouted for an officer to come and order the sentries to let us in, but no officer appeared. We tried to force the gate and the sentries threatened to charge us with their bayonets. At the row a window on the second floor of the building opened and a woman, probably a secretary, looked out. We shouted to her and then she shut the window again. Everything was bathed in blazing sunlight: the soldiers, shouting in front of the closed gate, the sentries with their fixed bayonets, and the smiling woman at the window.

Eventually we learned that the officers had left the building because they had received contradictory orders from higher quarters, and were afraid of taking the responsibility either for embarking or refusing to embark us. A few weeks later the Vichy government decreed that every Frenchman serving in a "foreign army" – i.e. the Free French forces – was liable to the death penalty.

Spring 1973. The Château Neuf in Bayonne was the most impressive *caserne* in which Legionnaire Dubert had stayed – a massive fortress built in 1826, which was a happy time for military architects. It had been the depot of the 49th Infantry Regiment which – as the inscription over the massive gates says – had distinguished itself at Jemappes in 1792, Sebastopol 1855, Solferino 1859, and so on. Jemappes is the place in Belgium where the French revolutionary army, to the strains of the Marseillaise, defeated the Austrians and, as a contemporary historian wrote, "learnt to conquer". I suddenly felt ridiculously proud of having once been a French soldier of sorts – and at the same time contempt for the shameful debacle. My ambivalent love–hatred of France was plainly absurd – but since I have become a British citizen, I could regard it as a typically Anglo-Saxon attitude.

The sentries at the proud *caserne* of the conquerors of Jemappes now looked spick and span – in Dubert's days the place had been full of *soldats isolés*, the ragged jetsom of the defeated army. It was during my stay there that the Germans at long last caught up with me. . . .

> We were not allowed to leave the Château Neuf on that day, but I managed to get out. I limped down the dusty, sunbathed streets to the bridge over the Nive; and then I saw them at a few yards – the dark green tanks, rattling slowly and solemnly over the roadway like a funeral procession, and the black-clad figures standing in the open turrets with wooden faces, and the puffing black motor bikes with men in black leather and black goggles on their eyes, and the burning red flags with the white circle and the black spider in the middle, flapping lazily in the heat. I had a feeling that they had come specially after me. There was a tall figure standing immobile in one of the moving turrets; I saw his face, the face of a young peasant lad from Pomerania, with goggling, cretinous eyes and with a vague grin undecided between kindliness and brutality, staring at the cathedrals and vineyards of France and licking his pursed lips, like a dog in front of a bone.

By the time I got back on my sore feet to the Château Neuf, stopping at each bistro on the way for a Pernod and getting fairly drunk, I found the company to which I had been attached lined up in the courtyard, ready to leave for the non-occupied zone. The armistice terms, published on the previous day, divided France into occupied and non-occupied territories; they further stipulated that "the French armed forces in the territory to be occupied by Germany are to be speedily withdrawn to territory not to be occupied." Bayonne, with the whole of the Atlantic seaboard, was occupied territory; the line of demarcation ran from north to south at some sixty kilometres to the east of us. The previous day several detachments had left on lorries for the non-occupied zone; but there were no more lorries available, so the unit to which I had been attached – the 22ème Compagnie de Passage – had to leave on foot. I got my kit and fell in with them. We did not march through the centre, but made a detour round the town, and stole out of Bayonne like thieves. We crossed the railway bridge over the Adour, heading east towards non-occupied France.

That night we slept in barns only about five miles east of Bayonne. We were all *isolés* – tired, sullen, loaded with luggage and reluctant to march. The next day it became even worse. We dragged along the road like a band of tramps; in the afternoon about twenty men out of two hundred were missing. The heat was terrible, the road dusty, the men had reached the depths of demoralisation. Every half hour or so we simply sat down by the roadside and the three officers and three NCOs in charge of us could do nothing but follow our example. They were deaf to unpleasant remarks and tried to keep up at least the appearance of military order. Some soldiers still had their combat equipment; during the worst hours of the midday heat, one after the other dropped his riflle and steel helmet into the roadside ditch. Around three o'clock the old captain ordered another halt and told us to pile up the remaining rifles, bayonets, steel helmets and cartridge belts next to a deserted farmhouse on the road. We arranged everything in neat piles, and there we left them and marched on.

* * *

Spring 1973. France has announced its intention to test a new nuclear device in the Pacific. Protests from Australia and New Zealand are going to be ignored.

In the evening of the second day we camped at Hasparen, still within the occupied zone. Our luggage and kits were loaded on a lorry to be sent ahead of us. We never saw them again. Later we found out that the soldiers in the lorry had looted the contents of our valises and knapsacks and threw them on the road. As a supreme joke they had excremented into the empty baggage so that everything had to be burned. The last remnants of my earthly possessions – a civilian suit, some manuscripts, even my sponge-bag – had gone and all I had left was my diary, fountain pen, a few francs and a strip of Paris bus tickets which I carried in my wallet as a sentimental souvenir.

Anxious to cross the demarcation line before the Germans set up their check points, I went ahead of my company, crossed the line at St Palais (the Germans arrived there twenty-four hours later) and the next day went on to Mauléon, which had been our destination. But in Mauléon I was told that the company had changed its route and had gone to Navarrenx, fifteen kilometres further to the north; so I trudged to Navarrenx, where I was told to go to Laas. All these picturesque villages in the Basses Pyrénées were full of stragglers like myself, and the authorities were busy concentrating them in improvised *cantonnements des isolés*, where they were to stay until demobilisation began; nobody knew when that would be. The cantonments consisted of a few requisitioned barns or cattle sheds, where the men were housed, some fifty to two hundred per village.

The next few days I wandered about the desolate, burning roads of the Basses Pyrénées, searching for my vanished company, alone or with other stragglers who were visibly changing into tramps. From Laas they sent me to Audaux, from there to Pau, and back to Audaux. These long dawdling wanderings along the road with the distant screen of the white Pyrénées before my eyes, while the limpid air seemed to boil around me and the asphalt to melt under my heels, had a curiously calming effect; I had no luggage, not even a comb or piece of soap, slept in barns or open fields, had not seen a newspaper for days, and dragged my aching feet in a sort of trance, with the agreeably detached sensation of having lost everything a man can lose, including my name. It was by no means an unusual condition for Europeans, *anno domini* 1940.

Spring 1973: I find myself constantly grumbling about the antics of the car (battery keeps going flat); about the poor plumbing in five-star hotels and the refusal of restaurateurs, who ought to know better, to accept Diners Club credit cards. I resent the sky-scraping apartment blocks in Bayonne and Pau; and the fact that St Palais now has "tennis, golf, riding, piscine et camping"; I resent the villas, chalets, weekend bungalows which are spreading at an explosive rate over the previously empty landscape, and most of all that they are built in better taste than in this country.

At the end of my wanderings I decided to settle down in the *cantonnement* of a forlorn little village called Susmiou on a hilltop near Navarrenx. It was an agglomeration of about twenty old, derelict farmhouses – not even a grocer's shop or a bistro. It had about a hundred inhabitants, and the same number of soldiers were billeted in farms and stables. Here I spent two boring, but instructive months, until the long-awaited *ordre de marche* to the Legion's main depot in Marseilles arrived. There were no parades, and except for the occasional kitchen fatigue, there was nothing to do except play cards, drink wine in a bistro in the next village, called Sus, and keep up my diary.

> *3 July 1940*. Moved into a barn where only three others sleep on the lower floor: Corporal Gillevic, Privates Lebras and Moog. Gillevic and Lebras are both surly Breton peasant farmers; Moog comes

from Rennes and was in civvy street a tramp, long, thin, with a squint and seventeen other bodily defects which he enumerates with pride, including "cold abscesses" on both legs. . . .

No straw in the barn; we sleep on a heap of maize stalks, stored here for pig fodder. The barn has an upper floor where twenty others sleep. When they trample over the wooden boards over our heads, flakes of cobwebs flutter down on us.

4 July. Walked in Lebras' slippers to the hospital in Navarrenx (only a mile from Susmiou), had my feet bandaged, bought comb, soap, toothbrush. Only 200 francs left. Shops in Navarrenx empty: no cigarettes, no matches, no cheese, no meat, no vegetables; one pound of apples, 8 francs. [Our private soldiers' pay was 3.50 F a week plus an ounce of cigarette tobacco.] The greengrocer says it's all the fault of the refugees from the north (six million of them in the unoccupied zone). The farmers hate the Frenchmen from the northern provinces, call them *les boches du nord*. Would like us to work in their fields but without pay, for a meal a day. They say it's a shame to see such a lot of idlers fed for nothing.

6 July. Read in *Dépêche de Toulouse* that British Fleet attacked French Fleet at Mers el Kebir [naval base near Oran]; diplomatic relations broken off. Listened to Vichy radio; very funny; e.g. "the Soviet Press condemns severely the piratical attack of the British. Political circles in Moscow are indignant. . . .

Spring 1973. Stalin, Hitler, Pétain – I don't think there have been stranger bedfellows since the shifting alliances of the Thirty Years War. In 1940 the French Communists preached in their illegal tracts collaboration with Germany against Britain. A year later, when Hitler attacked Russia, they became the most ferocious fighters of the Resistance. They emerged from the war as "*le parti des fusillés*" – the victims of the firing squads. Their latest metamorphosis is reflected in an election poster, pasted all over the country, showing a smug middle-class family – sweet granny, dad, mum, smart kid – looking like an advertisement for breakfast food, with the caption: "We trust the Communist Party". Perhaps granny was telling the story of Little Red Riding Hood and the wolf.

★ ★ ★

The British fleet's successful attacks against the French naval units at Oran and Dakkar in July provided Pétain's regime with a welcome pretext for launching a venomous anti-British campaign in the press and over the radio. *Gringoire*, the extreme right-wing weekly, published a poem which started:

Winston Churchill syphilitique
Duff Cooper dégeneré

and so it went, right through the cabinet. I cut it out, took it with me to England, and wanted to publish it in *Scum of the Earth*, but was dissuaded by Harold Nicolson, who acted as unofficial censor for the Ministry of Information. As a devoted francophile, he could not stomach it.

Nor could Lebras and Gillevic. They thought the British had left them in the lurch, and were as bad as the *boches*, but one cannot change friends from one day to the next, *ca ne se fait pas*.

14 July 1940 [National holiday in commemoration of the storming of the Bastille.] Our nice old Captain assembled us at the war memorial (a weathered cross of wood), made a short speech: the reason for the defeat was an international conspiracy of plutocrats and socialists, inspired by Jews. Later he called me, asked whether as a foreigner I agreed with his speech. I said plutocrats and socialists were mortal enemies, and the "Jewish conspiracy" a Nazi invention. He said worriedly: "I wonder, I wonder." He is such a decent old chap – whose fault is it that he believes in this tripe, as do millions of others?

New slogan: *Travaille, Famille, Patrie*, to replace *Liberté, Egalité, Fraternité*.

15 July 1940. Read in *Petite Gironde* that Carl Einstein, the art historian, has committed suicide; first cut his veins in concentration camp, was saved, released, threw himself into the Gave d'Oloron – the river running through Navarrenx – with a stone tied round his neck. Yesterday I was bathing in the Gave. Paper said, "*Un nommé Carl Einstein, refugié d'Allemagne, neveu du professeur Albert Einstein*." Saw him last in Café des Deux Magots in Paris, about 1939; he had been a volunteer officer in Spain, came back already broken by defeat. Remember what sensation his first book on Negro sculpture created in Germany.

16 July. About twenty of our cantonment have been demobilised; the others waiting feverishly. Complete indifference to newspapers, wireless, politics. Only home.

19 July. Radio and papers say: invasion of England imminent.

21 July. Demobilisation proceeds, but not to occupied territory. Even the restricted traffic across the demarcation line is interrupted. France cut in two – and millions of French families cut into several pieces during the flight. Now they are searching for each other desperately. Almost half of the space in the *Dépêche, Petite Gironde*, etc., taken up by advertisements in tiny print of this type:

"*André Roure, who disappeared June 17 near Azay-le-Rideau, please communicate with parents via Le Temps, Clermont-Ferrand.*"

"*Familles Combier, Durand, Scholer of Neuilly are at Cusset, Allier.*"

"*5me Cie C.R.M. from Revigny (Meuse) is at Gendarmerie Vichy (Allier).*"

And so on, thousands per day. As if a gigantic explosion had blown fragments of families all over the country. *Paris Soir* (Marseilles edition) gives advice to parents how to find their children lost in the chaos of flight. Says there are thousands of "globe-trotters aged six and eight years on the roads of France".

22 July. A bunch of new decrees. Soldiers not allowed to sit on café terraces. Another, in preparation, will regulate length of bathing suits up from ankles and down from hips.

27 July. Lebras told me a fascinating story why Doriot's Fascist party was so popular among farmers in Britanny. Up to 1936, the small farmers sold their wheat for 70 francs to the Co-operative, which was a private enterprise run by the big landowners, monopolising the market. When the Popular Front came to power, it created the *Office du Blé*, run directly by the Government, which, by cutting out intermediary profits, paid 180 francs instead of 70. Whereupon Doriot's paper, sent gratis to every small farmer, started a campaign: "The Government steals your money – ask them for 200 instead of 180." . . . Lebras (in his slow, stammering manner, smiling slyly): ". . . *Merde alors*, we talked it over and thought, if the Government pays 180 francs instead of 70, there must be something fishy about it, and they could as well pay 200.

But Blum and his Jews refused, so we all voted for Doriot" (whose party was largely financed by the landowners' Co-operative).

25 July. Petit Journal proposes abolition of "offending foreign expressions", e.g. "grill-room", "W.C." and "five o'clock tea".

New decree creates special commission to revise all naturalisations granted to aliens since 1927; anybody naturalised since that date can be deprived of French citizenship, also his wife and children.

27 July. The farmers hate us more and more, because only a dozen agreed to work ten hours on their fields without pay, for a mere *casse-croute*. Every day they complain to the Adjutant (the old Captain has left) that we steal chickens and eggs, which is untrue; we only steal apples. The apples are of poor quality, they let them rot under the trees and feed them to the pigs, but they have the cheek to ask us 2 francs a pound.

31 July. Some men, too lazy to climb down the ladder at night, have got into the habit of urinating in a corner of the upper barn floor. It trickles down along the wall. No use arguing with them. Barn reeks of urine and excrement.

1 August. Communiqué from Vichy announces formation of Supreme Court of Justice to try all responsible for starting the war. Press comments: "To the gallows" – "No mercy" – "Wipe them out."

2 August. The Mayor of Géronce [a nearby village] took Jules, Lefévre and me to his farm. He offered us wine, closed the shutters and tried to get London on his radio. Everything was jammed, but very exciting – only for a few seconds could I make out the familiar, matter-of-fact voice of the BBC announcer – as if talking to a crowd of intelligent schoolboys. We also heard a few bars of the Marseillaise. Felt all very cheerful and drunk.

4 August Got hold of *Paris Soir*, printed in Marseilles. Splash headline on front page : "We want a French Hollywood." Actors and stars gather on the Riviera, plans of building a French national film centre, gossip about Suzy and Lucy and Marcel and Maurice; "they go on bikes, leaving their racy cars in the garages; their faces show the consciousness of the grave trial of *la Patrie*, but also the new serenity of the French resurrection." Smaller news items: De Gaulle sentenced to death for treason; a new bunch of diplomats sacked.

Spring 1973 The Bistro in Sus is still called Café Cahors Sud-Ouest, and the tough *patronne* is still the same. We did not recognise each other. I did not inquire how she had fared under the German occupation; it would not have been a proper question to ask. But she was pleased that I noticed a change in the arrangement of the furniture.

On 10 August, instructions arrived to dispatch Private Dubert to the Foreign Legion's central dépôt in Marseilles. The dépôt was in Fort St Jean, and for a fortnight I had a lovely time there. The huge refectory was painted all round with lurid battle scenes of the Legion's exploits in Algeria, Morocco, Indo-China and Senegal; the food was worth a star in the *Michelin*, and there was half a litre of white and a half of red wine in front of each plate. Since, as a Swiss, I was supposed to speak German, I was employed as a regimental messenger between the Fort St Jean and the German Port Supervising Commission in the Fort St Nicholas – which I thought a good joke.

Moreover, there were about sixty British officers and soldiers in the fort, who had escaped from German captivity and were interned by the French. I joined forces with three of the officers and a staff sergeant. We managed to procure faked demobilisation papers which gave as our destination Casablanca, the Moroccan port not yet under German supervision. There we made contact with a member of British Intelligence whom we knew by the name of Mr Ellerman. It was due to his genius for improvisation that the five of us, plus some fifty other escapees, were able to board a fishing boat, which in four days somehow managed to roll and toss us past the German submarines into the neutral harbour of Lisbon.

We agreed that our rescuer was the most mysterious character we had ever met. He was in his late forties, tall, elegant, dignified, charming, sophisticated and aristocratic. In a word, he belonged to an extinct species, like the fabulous unicorn: he was a European *grand seigneur*.

I knew that Ellerman was not his real name. Ever since we parted in Lisbon I tried to discover his identity in order to contact him, but the powers that be were not cooperative. On 25 May 1967, twenty-six years after the event, I read the following item in the Diary of the London *Times*

> The astonishing story may soon be told for the first time of a member of one of pre-war Germany's leading families who became so disgusted with the Hitler regime that he gave up everything – successful career, wealth and fame – to become a British agent. Baron Rüdiger von Etzdorf, elder brother of Dr Hasso von Etzdorf, Ambassador to Britain from 1961 to 1965, died in London three weeks ago, aged 72, unknown and unsung. . . .
>
> Von Etzdorf – he dropped his German title when he took British nationality in 1946 – was in the German navy in the first world war and fought at Jutland. His father was a close friend of the Kaiser. His extraordinary story begins in 1935, when he was approached in London by British Intelligence and asked if he would work for them.
>
> By this time he had become something of a globe-trotter, after warning his brother Hasso that Hitler was heading straight for war – and being told not to be ridiculous.
>
> One of his first assignments was in Italy, sending to London information on relations between Italy and Germany. When war broke out he was in Tripoli amd organised an escape route for British soldiers after the fall of France. One person brought out in this way was Arthur Koestler. . . .

Here ends the story of Legionnaire Dubert. As for the sentimental pilgrimage, it provoked mixed feelings, and revived the old ambivalence with a new twist. The people I remembered were dead, had moved, could not remember or did not want to remember. The places had changed beyond recognition. The forlorn villages in the Pyrénées have become tourist attractions; the sidewalk cafés in the towns are submerged in the roar of traffic; the Rhône valley looks more and more like the Ruhr; near Château Neuf du Pape two plastic factories with eight chimneys each belch red and green smoke over the vineyards originally planted by the Ninth Roman Legion. Every country in Europe has undergone profound changes since the war, but no other has been so fundamentally transformed in appearance and character. Germany had its economic miracle;

but Germany had already been an industrial country before the war, whereas France is only now living through its industrial revolution – and experiencing its full impact on landscape, cultural climate and style of living.

According to a much publicised forecast of the American Hudson Institute, France by 1980 will be the leading industrial power in Europe, while Britain is "sliding towards fourteenth or fifteenth place in the European economic league table". Remembering 1940, when England was the only country that carried on with the war, it now looks as if it were the only country that has lost the war; History is a cruel joker. But all forecasts are fallible; and whether the explosive growth in prosperity will heal the chronic ailments of the French body politic is a question beyond the competence of economists. My private hope is that closer partnership in Europe will create a kind of psychological Channel tunnel: through it the French may acquire some of Britain's stoic virtues, while the British may be affected by the French genius for adaptability and improvisation – the positive aspects of the art of *débrouillage*.

FORGOTTEN GENIUS*

In 1955 a London publisher brought out a new translation of *Pan*, as the first volume of a planned series of Knut Hamsun's work. Apparently the project did not catch on, and no more was heard of it. Now, more than twenty years after the Norwegian giant's death at the age of ninety-three, two English publishers seem to be competing for the honour of inaugurating a Hamsun revival.

Cyril Connolly once wrote that his main ambition was to write a book that would survive ten years. One could go one better by wishing to father a book that would be resurrected after a century, a Lazarus in paperback. But the moods and trends that produce literary revivals are just as capricious as those that promote contemporaries to bestseller status. Why this sudden cult of Hermann Hesse, *ausgerechnet* – "of all people", as a German critic remarked. Why not, say, Alfred Döblin or Franz Werfel or Arnold Zweig? Posterity seems no more reliable a judge than the erratic chorus of contemporary critics.

It is all the more gratifying to witness a revival which appears legitimate in the light of literary history and which, moreover, affects a hero of one's own youth. That youth, however, was lived in Austria, where Hamsun was one of the celebrated writers of the period, whereas in England he was hardly known; here Ibsen and Strindberg still enjoyed a virtual monopoly as representatives of Scandinavian literature. Yet Hamsun, born in 1859, thirty years after Ibsen, inaugurated a

* *Hunger*, by Knut Hamsun, translated from the Norwegian by Robert Bly, Reviewed in *The Observer*, 3 March 1974.

new and altogether different generation. Not that he had deeper philosophical insights, or more advanced political convictions than his peers – rather the opposite. His philosophisings were naive, and his politics disastrous. But he created a new style of writing, a new form of prose narrative which had a hypnotic effect on the reader and was to have a lasting influence on various literary schools that came after him. In his introduction to the present edition of *Hunger*, Isaac Bashevis Singer writes:

> They were all Hamsun's discliples: Thomas Mann and Arthur Schnitzler, Jacob Wasserman and Stefan Zweig, Zeromski and Bunin, Kellerman and Peter Altenberg, d'Annunzio and Herman Bang, and even such American writers as Fitzgerald and Hemingway, whether they acknowledged the debt or not [Hemingway did]. Literary influences often do not come in a direct fashion. Hamsun even had an effect on Hebrew and Yiddish literature.

And, one may add, even on Henry Miller ("Hamsun is the author I deliberately tried to imitate. *Mysteries* is closer to me than any other book I have read"); or on Rebecca West ("Hamsun has the qualities that belong to the very great, the completest omniscience about human nature").

Singer no doubt exaggerates when he calls Hamsun "the father of the modern school of literature". But it is no exaggeration to say that Hamsun's early novels contained seeds which came to fruition in a variety of literary movements several decades later: in the introspective, stream-of-consciousness school; in the emphasis on unconscious motivations, their vagaries and contradictions; in the writings of expressionists, surrealists and existentialists; above all in the concept of the anti-hero obsessed with the absurdity of being. The central character of *Hunger* could be a direct ancestor of Camus's *Outsider*; Lieutenant Glahn in *Pan* is the forebear of the Hemingway hero: a virile Nimrod with a tanned skin on which all the nerves are raw and exposed.

Hunger is the story of the semi-delirious "trip" of a young dropout writer in search of his identity. It was published in 1890 when Hamsun was thirty-one. With a little scene-shifting, it could have been written today. It was his first novel, followed within a single decade by four other masterpieces, including the greatest, *Pan*.

But from the age of forty, Hamsun's powers steadily declined. He received the Nobel Prize in 1920, and went on writing even as a nonagenarian, but produced only stale, second-rate stuff, some of it quite awful. As Singer coolly remarks, "he lived too long. It would have been better for him had he flared and gone out as Byron did." This may be one of the reasons why he was so little appreciated in this country. He also lived too long in another respect. In his eighties, Hamsun joined the Norwegian Nazi Party and allowed himself to be photographed with Hitler. His compatriots never forgave him. But politically he had always been an innocent at heart – not unlike Picasso, the fervent Stalinist.

RHINE'S IMPACT ON PHILOSOPHY★

A few years ago, John Beloff edited an anthology of essays by seven well-known researchers, to which I contributed a postscript. The title of the book, *New Directions in Parapsychology* (London 1974), sounded matter of fact, yet it seemed to imply that the "old directions" had become inadequate and were perhaps leading into a dead end. One of the main reasons for this unsatisfactory state of affairs was underlined by Charles Honorton in his paper:

> Until recently . . . little systematic research has been directed towards the elucidation of subjective states associated with paranormal functioning. In view of the behaviouristic *Zeitgeist*, it is perhaps not surprising that early proponents of the card-guessing paradigm . . . largely disregarded their subjects' internal states. . . .

One might indeed say that parapsychology was more concerned with the para than with psychology. Given the circumstances, this was almost unavoidable. As John Beloff commented: "The Rhine school of parapsychology thought to beat behaviourism at its own game by showing that anti-behaviourist conclusions could be arrived at on the basis of impeccable objectivist data." To have obtained these data with dogged perseverance, undeterred by the hostility of academics and the derision of the ignorant, is the Rhine school's historic achievement. Yet it was only made possible by the self-imposed limitations which Honorton pointed out. One of the cornerstones of scientific methodology is the formula *ceteris*

★ Paper presented to the American Institute for Parapsychology's conference on the life and work of J.B. Rhine, 28 November 1980.

paribus – "other things being equal". But other things are never equal where human subjects are concerned. Not even their reactions to the gross chemical impact of drugs are equal. Clinical studies have shown that about one-third of the American hospital population are placebo-reactors. Given the appropriate suggestion, they will react to barbiturates as if they were amphetamines, to amphetamines as if they were barbiturates, and to placebos as if they were one or the other, as the case may be. Their states of consciousness interact with, and often override, the effect of the chemical input. It seems obvious that the effect of a psi input – whatever it consists of – is even more dependent on the "hidden variables" of the subject's general character disposition and particular state of mind at the time of the experimental test or spontaneous occurrence.

Thus one may wonder whether the parapsychologist's quest for the ideal experiment – repeatable at will, yielding predictable results – will not turn out to be a wild goose chase. In spite of his customary caution, John Beloff expressed the hope that parapsychology is "edging its way towards a solution of the problem of repeatability". He may be right, but I do not feel so sure about it. A parabola edges its way towards its asymptotes without ever achieving union. The nearest we have come to a repeatable experiment is in the field of automated animal experimentation, described by John Randall. Perhaps with mice, gerbils and chicks the "other things" are more equal, and interfere less with the functioning of the psi faculty. But ask any writer, or painter, or scientist to define the precise conditions under which the creative spark will repeatably and predictably ignite the vapours in his mind! Yet creativity is a less elusive and mysterious faculty than psi.

The above is by no means intended to discourage the parapsychologist's patient efforts to elucidate the personality structures and states of consciousness which enhance the psi faculty, and the experimental conditions best suited to trigger it off. On the contrary, I consider these efforts as perhaps the most promising among the "new directions" in parapsychology. I still remember with what enthusiasm I read about Gertrude

Schmeidler's pioneer work some twenty years ago; "sheep" and "goats" appeared as a first step towards a taxonomy of potential psi subjects.* In more than a quarter million card trials with more than 1100 subjects the sheep scored significantly and persistently higher than the goats. It looked so beautifully simple, almost self-evident: have we not always been taught that faith can move mountains – i.e. perform feats of psychokinesis? Unfortunately things turned out not to be as simple as that. Beloff and others found that in some studies the goats, perhaps out of sheer perversity, did better than the sheep; and a careful study of Rao's paper reveals that the singling out of any other personality factor led to similarly contradictory or inconclusive results. The combination of several factors, as attempted by Rao and Kanthamani, seemed a more holistic and promising approach. Yet ironically, Rao's composite portrait of the potentially high-scoring ESP subject is in almost every respect the exact opposite of Pratt's description of the highest scoring person known at the time – Pavel Stepanek. The situation reminds one of a remark by the science fiction writer Poul Anderson: "I have yet to see any problem, however complicated, which, when you looked at it in the right way, did not become still more complicated."

But that need not unduly worry the parapsychologist; other sciences have found themselves in similar predicaments in the past and present. The subatomic world composed of electrons and protons looked complicated enough, but when the physicists looked at it in the right way, it became still more complicated, with a hundred "elementary particles" instead of two. The physicist's trouble is that the subatomic phenomena which he manipulates can no longer be fitted into the spatio-temporal framework of naive realism and conventional physics. The parapsychologist's trouble is equally fundamental. He too can manipulate, up to a point, the manifestations of psi in his laboratory, but he is unable to fit them into the framework of convential psychology, and knows next to nothing of their physiological correlates, evolutionary origin and biological

* Sheep = believers; goats = non-believers

value – what psi is "for" in the general scheme of things. We do not even know whether, in evolutionary terms, psi is an *emergent* faculty – somehow related to man's spirituality – which gradually unfolds, like sentience and consciousness, with each upward step on the evolutionary ladder, or whether, on the contrary, extrasensory perception is an archaic and primitive form of communication which has been superseded by more efficient forms of sensory perception (but in this case, what about PK?). Needless to say, these questions are of fundamental importance, not only to the parapsychologist, but also to the philosopher and metaphysician. This alone would make the pursuit of parapsychology an immensely worthwhile undertaking; and there are indications that, even if the researchers of the post-Rhine generation have not come up with the final answers, they are learning to ask the pertinent questions.

Today, both the physicist and the parapsychologist are learning to live in a universe with a substructure of non-causal interactions – a fuzzy world of wavering contours, replete with little bubbles of indeterminacy that provide intimations of an unexpected kind of freedom, for which in the world of classical physics there was no room. Once this lesson has sunk in, "nothing in science or philosophy could ever again be quite the same", to quote John Beloff again. And I have no doubt that J.B. Rhine will be recognised by future historians as one of the pioneers of the new age.

WHEREOF ONE CANNOT SPEAK . . . ?*

1

In his *Unpopular Essays* (1), Bertrand Russell tells the following anecdote:

> F.W.H. Myers, whom spiritualism had converted to belief in a future life, questioned a woman who had lately lost her daughter as to what she supposed had become of her soul. The mother replied: "Oh well, I suppose she is enjoying eternal bliss, but I wish you wouldn't talk about such unpleasant subjects. . . ."

This sounds like the perfect paradign of man's split mind, in which belief and disbelief lead an agonised coexistence. The unpleasantness of dying is a hard, cold fact. On the other hand, not only "eternal bliss" (or eternal torture), but also the more sophisticated versions of life after death present problems which our minds are incapable of handling: they are far beyond the reasoning faculties of our species (though not, perhaps, of other species on millions of older planets). In computer jargon we would have to say that we are not programmed for the task. Confronted with a task for which it is not programmed, a computer is either reduced to silence, or else it goes haywire. The latter seems to have happened, with distressing repetitiveness, in the most varied civilisations. Faced with the untractable paradox of consciousness emerging from nothingness and returning to nothingness, their minds went haywire and saturated the atmosphere with

* First published in *Life After Death – Contributions by Arnold Toynbee, Arthur Koestler and Others* (London, 1976).

the ghosts of the dead and other invisible presences who at best were inscrutable, but mostly malevolent, and had to be placated by grotesque rituals, including human sacrifice and the slaughter of heretics. The evidence from anthropology, from ancient and modern history, provide conclusive proof of the paranoid streak endemic in our species, perhaps due to some evolutionary mistake in the construction of its nervous system.

There is, of course, another side to the medal. If the word death were absent from our vocabulary, our great works of literature would have remained unwritten, pyramids and cathedrals would not exist, nor works of religious art – and all art is of religious or magic origin. The pathology and creativity of the human mind are two sides of the same medal, coined by the same mint master. A cynical observer from outer space might ask whether this need be so, whether the glories of one side are worth the horrors of the other. Hegel thought that ours is the best of all possible worlds; one wonders whether the praying mantis would share this opinion, while paying the price for the glories of procreation. Or whether the poor wretch strangled on the *vile garrotte* would find consolation in the thought that Goya was to immortalise him. Does this redress the equation between the glory and the pathology? Our cynical alien would rather conclude that this planet is ruled and ravaged by a freak species, an ill-conceived experiment of the mint master.

According to the theories of Paul MacLean, which are finding growing support among neurophysiologists, the unprecedentedly rapid expansion in the course of the last 500,000 years of the human neocortex resulted in faulty coordination between this phylogenetically new acquisition – the "thinking cap" which governs rational thought, and the archaic structures of the brain which we share with reptiles and lower mammals, and which govern our emotional reactions. This evolutionary discord is said to have resulted in a state of "schizophysiology", a split between reason and emotion which is endemic in the human condition. Emotion is the older and more powerful partner in the divided household, and whenever there is conflict, the reasoning half of the brain is compelled to provide spurious rationalisations for the senior partner's urges and whims. This is why some paranoid delusions appear so consistent and compelling – madness yet with method in it – including the weirdest notions concerning afterlife. The neocortex may repeat its dreary syllogisms: "All men must die, Socrates is a man, ergo, et cetera," but the old brain which occupies the larger part of our skulls passionately rejects the notion of personal non-existence: unable to make a categorical distinction between the ego and the world, the end of the ego means to it the end of the world – which is obviously unthinkable. Accordingly, the old brain considers survival as self-evident, while its timid and pedantic junior partner is given the task of filling the post-mortem void with some science fiction scenario. Given the unrestricted scope for fantasy, it is surprising what a poor job it made of that scenario. The Pit, Gehenna, Hades, Sheol recur with monotonous regularity like the dreary stage props in Gothic horror thrillers; while the celestial habitats seem designed to make the dead wish to die from boredom. I take no pleasure in blasphemy; my point is the poverty of man's imagination even if given an infinite playground.

I have mentioned science fiction: it provides a chastening lesson. Its heroes, thousands of years ahead of us, sail to distant galaxies through hyperspace faster than the speed of light, but their thoughts, feelings and vocabulary are limited to the narrow range of the present. The rugged astronaut landing on the third planet of Aldebaran behaves in the same way as he would in a drugstore in Minnesota: the Milky Way has become an extension of Main Street. Its inhabitants may be genius lizards communicating by radar-guided telepathy, yet we could not care less: curiosity is tickled for a few pages, but they are too strange to be true, and we soon get bored. Our imagination is narrowly limited: we cannot project ourselves into the distant future, not even into the distant past: the figure of an Egyptian schoolmaster under the Eighteenth Dynasty is only a shadowy silhouette; we are unable to breathe life into it. Hence the failure of the historical novel. Every culture is an island; it communicates with other islands, but knows only itself; and the islands of the living are severed from the Atlantis of the dead.

2

But this severance need not be total and complete. "The more detailed pictures of life after death are," wrote Renée Haynes, "the less acceptable they seem to be." Obviously, we have to move in the opposite direction: away from pictures and details, from "misplaced concreteness", as Whitehead called it. This implies clearing the lumber room of the accumulated visual and verbal junk, the graven images and verbal imprints, the whole paranoid phantasmagoria. After all, the iconoclasts of the Middle Ages were a deeply religious movement which could have been inspired by Whitehead's caveat.

After the spring-cleaning the air may become healthier and more transparent. Atlantis may now appear even more remote, but at the same time a more sober approach may suggest itself. I am referring to recent advances in parapsychology and avant-garde physics, which, though not directly concerned with the question, seem to provide the only *objective* clues to it. (The *subjective* approach of the mystic is complementary to it as yin is to yang, but lies outside the scope of this article.)

Two contributors to this volume (Renée Haynes and Rosalind Heywood) have already alluded to the mind-boggling paradoxa of contemporary physics, and I have written about them elsewhere at some length (2). Here I shall confine myself to a brief recapitulation of the philosophically more relevant points, where the boundaries between physics and metaphysics become indistinguishable.

3

By the end of the 1920s, Einstein, de Broglie, Schrödinger and Heisenberg had effectively dematerialised matter. What appears to us as solid mass, "m", was shown to be the equivalent of a very high concentration of energy, "E"; and the simple equation $E = mc^2$ (where "c" is the speed of light – perhaps the only mathematical formula which ever caught the public imagination) was validated by the thermo-nuclear bomb and by less dramatic methods of laboratory research. The latter produced conclusive evidence that the so-called elementary constituents of matter, such as electrons, protons, neutrons, etc., behaved, according to circumstances, as massive particles or as unsubstantial waves. "The electron," de Broglie proclaimed, "is at the same time a corpuscle and a wave" (3). This dualism is fundamental to modern physics, and is known as the Principle of Complementarity. In Heisenberg's words: "These two frames of reference mutally exclude each other, but they also complement each other, and only the juxtaposition of these incompatible frames provides an exhaustive view of the appearances of phenomena. . ." (4). In another place he makes a remark which lets the cat out of the bag, as it were: "What [we] call 'Complementarity' agrees very neatly with the Cartesian dualism of matter and mind."

Another giant of modern physics, Wolfgang Pauli, expressed the same idea:

> The general problem of the relationship between mind and body, between the inward and the outward, cannot be said to have been solved . . . Modern science has perhaps brought us nearer to a more satisfactory understanding of this relationship by introducing the concept of complementarity into physics itself (5).

One might add to these quotations almost any amount of similar pronouncements by the pioneers of contemporary physics. It is evident that they regarded the parallel between the two types of complementarity – body/mind and corpuscle/wave – as more than a superficial analogy. It is, in fact, a very deep analogy, but in order to appreciate what it implies we must try to get some inkling of what the physicist means by the "waves" which constitute one of the two aspects of matter. Commonsense, that treacherous counsellor, tells us that to produce a wave there must be something that waves – a vibrating piano string, or undulating water, or air in motion. But the whole conception of matter-waves excludes, by definition, any medium with material attributes as a carrier or substratum of the wave. Thus we are faced with the task of imagining the vibration of a string but without the string, or the grin of the Cheshire cat but without the cat – another task for which we are not "programmed". We may, however, derive some comfort from the analogy between the two complementarities. The contents of consciousness that pass through the mind, from the perception of colour to thoughts and images, are unsubstantial "airy nothings", yet they are somehow linked to the material brain, as the unsubstantial "waves" and "fields" of physics are somehow linked to the material aspects of the subatomic particles. This is what Jeans had in mind when he wrote his famous *pronunciamento*: that physicists were virtually unanimous in moving away from the materialistic view of reality because "the universe is beginning to look more like a great thought than like a great machine" (6).

That was written in 1937. By that time solid matter had quasi-evaporated from the physicists' laboratories, was transformed into patterns of concentrated energy, and ultimately dissolved into stresses and warps in the curvature of space. Parallel to this vanishing act, our concepts of space, time and causality, to which the computers in our cranium were programmed, turned out to be totally inadequate when applied to events on the subatomic or supragalactic scale. "Atoms are not *things*," Heisenberg wrote. "When we get down to the atomic level, the objective world in space and time no longer exists" (7).

Nor does strict causality and rigid determinism apply on that level. The Principle of Indeterminacy is as fundamental to modern physics as Newton's Laws of Motion were to classical mechanics. It implies that the universe at any given moment is in a quasi-undecided state, and that its state in the next moment is to some extent indeterminate, or "free". Thus if an ideal photographer with an ideal camera took a picture of the total universe at any given moment, that picture would be to some extent fuzzy because of the indeterminate state of its ultimate constituents.★

Thus for the last fifty years it has become a commonplace among physicists that the strictly deterministic, mechanistic world view can no longer be upheld. The nineteenth-century model of the universe as a mechanical clockwork has fallen to pieces; and since, with the advent of relativity and quantum theory, the concept of matter itself has been dematerialised, materialism can no longer claim to be a scientific philosophy.

What are the alternatives?

4

I have quoted some of the giants (all of them Nobel laureates) who, in the first half of our century (more exactly in its first three decades), jointly dismantled the rigid clockwork and attempted to replace it by a more sophisticated model, sufficiently flexible to accommodate logical paradoxes and ideas previously considered unthinkable. In the nearly fifty years which have passed since the revolution of the 1920s, countless new discoveries were made – by radio telescopes scanning the skies and in the bubble chambers keeping track of subatomic events – but no satisfactory model and no coherent philosophy has yet emerged comparable to that of classical, Newtonian physics. One might describe these years as one of the periods of "creative anarchy" which repeatedly occur in the history of science when the old concepts have become obsolete and the breakthrough leading to a new synthesis is not yet in sight. The last such interregnum in cosmology lasted nearly a century and a half, from the publication of Copernicus' *De Revolutionibus* in 1541 to that of Newton's *Principiae* in 1684.† Owing to the acceleration of history – which includes the history of ideas – the present phase of creative anarchy will probably be much

★ It can be shown that however short the exposure time the Indeterminacy Principle will still blur the picture.

† For some parallels, see *The Sleepwalkers* (London and New York, 1959).

shorter, and when the new synthesis arrives we shall marvel at our previous blindness. Yet at the time of writing theoretical physics itself seems to be in a bubble-chamber, with the weirdest hypotheses crisscrossing each other's tracks. However, one can detect certain general trends.

Firstly, there is agreement that the "model" of the universe can only be an abstract, mathematical one, forsaking any attempt at visual representation, because we are only capable of representing and visualising phenomena in three-dimensional (3-d) space, moving along a single time axis from cause to effect, whereas a true model of micro- and macro-events would require more, and possibly (according to some) an unlimited number of dimensions where causes and effects are tangled in Gordian knots. When contemporary physicists nevertheless act in defiance of the taboo against making graven images of atom or cosmos, they seem to do so with tongue in cheek. Thus, according to John A. Wheeler, Professor of Physics at Princeton University and a leading figure in avant-garde physics, the geometry itself of three-dimensional space "fluctuates violently at small distances". He then draws this surrealistic picture:

> The space of quantum geometrodynamics can be compared to a carpet of foam spread over a slowly undulating landscape. . . . The continual microscopic changes in the carpet of foam as new bubbles appear and old ones disappear symbolise the quantum fluctuations in the geometry . . . (8).

This turbulent sea of bubbling foam is meant to represent – or rather, symbolise – Wheeler's concept of superspace (his italics):

> The stage on which the space of the universe moves is certainly not space itself. Nobody can be a stage for himself; he has to have a larger arena in which to move. The arena in which space does its changing is not even the space-time of Einstein, for space-time is the history of space changing with time. The arena must be a larger object: *superspace*. . . . It is not endowed with three or four dimensions – it's endowed with an *infinite* number of dimensions. Any single point in superspace represents an entire, three-dimensional world (9).

Superspace, or hyperspace, has been an old standby of science fiction, together with the concept of parallel universes and reversed or multidimensional time. Now, thanks to radio telescopes and atom-smashers, these concepts are acquiring academic respectability. The stranger the hard experimental data, the more surrealistic the theories devised to account for them. Professor Feynman of Caltech interpreted the tracks of positrons in the bubble chamber as evidence that these particles travelled over short distances *backwards in time*, and instead of being laughed out of court he got the Nobel Prize in 1965.

Wheeler's superspace has some remarkable features; one of them is multiple connectivity. This means, to put it into simple – and simplified language – that regions which in our homespun 3-d space are far apart may be temporarily brought into direct contact through tunnels or "holes" in superspace. They are called wormholes. The universe is supposed to be crisscrossed with these wormholes, which appear and disappear in immensely rapid fluctuations, resulting in ever-changing patterns – a cosmic kaleidoscope shaken by an invisible hand.

(Incidentally, these wormholes in the microscopic foam should not be confused with the astronomer's black holes in the sky – also first postulated by Wheeler. Black holes are regions in the universe into which the mass of a burnt-out star which has suffered gravitational collapse is sucked to be annihilated – or to emerge in a different universe in superspace.)

5

The wings of analogy are notoriously treacherous, but nevertheless useful for short flights, or rather hops, provided we always remember that metaphor is not proof.

Bearing this warning in mind, there are obvious analogies between modern science and para-science, modern physics and metaphysics. The first we met was the apparent affinity between the two basic principles of complementarity: particle/wave and body/mind. We may now ask the further question: if matter can transform its mass into radiation and thus become pure "disembodied" energy, is it still absurd to speak of discarnate mental energy? More precisely: is such talk still as absurd as it may have sounded fifty years ago, before the revolution in physics dethroned matter and taught us that atoms are not "things"? And is it still legitimate to jeer at the term "mind-stuff" (coined by Eddington) as unscientific when physicists describe the universe as a bubble bath in superspace? Dr I.J. Good of *The Scientist Speculates* (10) fame went even further: "Matter is aethereal and mind is the solid rock. . . . It is but a short step to the assumption that all minds are part of a single system. . ." (11). Is it still justifiable to deny the possibility of telepathic signals, when physicists accept action-at-a-distance in various disguises, from gravity to wormholes to the so-called "Einstein–Podolsky–Rosen (EPR) paradox"?*

Similar questions can be asked, based on analogies which are not conclusive but strongly suggestive, about other categories of parapsychological phenomena, including psychokinesis and isolated flashes of precognition, where the direction of time's arrow seems to be reversed; but this would require excursions into even more abstruse and technical regions of theoretical physics. The point to retain is that phenomena which half a century ago seemed to defy the laws of nature now appear less offensive because those laws are no longer regarded as strictly valid; and the weird theories advanced to account for those phenomena now appear less preposterous because the theories advanced by physicists are even more weird and insulting to naive commonsense. The universe of classical physics, consisting of hard little billiard balls bouncing about in strict obedience to the laws of mechanics has been replaced by the indeterminate quantum foam; its sharp contours have become fuzzy, its structure softened, its laws made more tolerant and permissive. An object flying through the air without physical cause, as so often reported in poltergeist phenomena, is no

* Broadly speaking, this famous experiment designed by Einstein indicates that if two particles have been bounced off each other and fly off in different directions, interference with either of them will influence the other, however far apart they may be. Cf. *The Challenge of Chance*, p.228.

longer considered to offend the laws of nature, only the laws of probability. And these laws, which have replaced causality in modern science, are not physical laws in the strict sense. They *work* – as every physicist, insurance company or roulette operator can testify; but nobody can explain how and why they work. The greatest mathematician of our time, John von Neumann, called them "black magic". We can leave it at that.*

6

One aspect of modern science appears to be particularly relevant to our subject: the trend towards a new conception of holism. It was actually initiated at the turn of the century by Mach's Principle which states that the inertial properties of terrestrial matter are determined by the total mass of the universe around us. Here again there is no satisfactory explanation as to *how* this influence is exerted; yet Mach's Principle (as reformulated by Einstein) occupies a key position in modern cosmology. Its metaphysical implications are fundamental – for it follows from it not only that the universe as a whole influences local, terrestrial events, but also that local events have an influence, however small, on the universe as a whole. Philosophically minded physicists are acutely aware of these implications – some to their satisfaction, others to their discontent. Bertrand Russell flippantly remarked that Mach's Principle "savours of astrology"(12), while Henry Margenau, Professor of Physics at Yale, made this thoughtful comment:

> Inertia is not intrinsic in the body; it is induced by the circumstance that the body is surrounded by the whole universe. . . . We know of no physical effect conveying this action; very few people worry about a physical agency transmitting it. As far as I can see, Mach's principle is as mysterious as your unexplained psychic phenomena, and its formulation seems to me almost as obscure . . . (13).

If we turn from macro- to microcosm, we find similar

* Cf. *The Challenge of Chance*, and particularly pp. 243–6.

"holistic" developments. Thus Heisenberg: "The system which is treated by the methods of quantum mechanics is in fact a part of a much bigger system (eventually the whole world)"(14). There are no independent parts, functioning in splendid isolation from the rest of the universe. Rather, "only if the whole universe is included in the object of scientific knowledge can the qualifying condition 'for an isolated system' be satisfied"(15). Or, the physicist F. Capra: "What we call an isolated particle is in reality the product of its interaction with its surrroundings. It is therefore impossible to separate any part of the universe from the rest"(16). And lastly, Professor David Bohm of Birkbeck College, University of London (his italics):

> It is generally acknowledged that the quantum theory has many strikingly novel features. . . . However, there has been too little emphasis on what is, in our view, the most fundamentally different new feature of all, i.e. the intimate interconnection of different systems that are not in spatial contact. This has been especially clearly revealed through the . . . well-known experiments of Einstein, Podolsky and Rosen. . . .
>
> Recently interest in this question has been stimulated by the work of Bell, who obtained precise mathematical criteria, distinguishing the experimental consequences of this feature of 'quantum interconnectedness of distant systems'. . . . Thus, one is led to a new notion of *unbroken wholeness* which denies the classical idea of analysability of the world into separately and independently existent parts"(17).

These quotes (which could be mutiplied indefinitely) do not reflect solo voices, but rather a chorus of eminent physicists who are aware of the revolutionary implications of their research. The overall picture that emerges is reminiscent of the philosophical creed of the Hypocratics – "There is one common flow, all things are in sympathy" – shared by the Pythagoreans and Neo-Platonists, and summed up by Pico della Mirandola, the fifteenth century Platonist (whose writings inspired Kepler in his search for the planetary laws):

> Firstly there is the unity of things whereby each thing is at one with itself. Secondly there is the unity whereby one creature is united with the others and all parts of the world constitute one world (18).

The majority of contemporary physicists would underwrite these lines. In a remarkable recent book, *La Gnose de Princeton*, subtitled *Des Savants à la Recherche d'une Religion* (19), Professor Raymond Ruyer drew attention to the quasi-mystical conclusions towards which the physical theories of the "gnostics of Princeton" tend to converge.* But it is a sober mysticism, born in the laboratory. The medieval mystic talked of "sympathies", "correspondences", of the All-One, of the part being contained in the whole, yet in some sense also containing the whole. The "gnosis of Princeton" has a paradigm or metaphor for every one of these statements.

One of the most striking of these is the hologram.† I shall not attempt to explain how it works, but its principle is a method of photography (without lens) which records the interference patterns of a split laser beam on a transparent photographic plate. When this is again illuminated by laser light, a sharp three-dimensional image of the photographed object is seen. But the uncanny property of a hologram is that if you cut off a piece of it and illuminate it by the laser beam, the *whole* photographed object will still be visible – only it will be less and less sharp the smaller the fragment cut off from the plate. Thus each part of the hologram potentially contains all the information describing the whole, although the information becomes more summary the smaller the part. Details will be lost, but the Gestalt – the configuration of the whole – is preserved. The metaphors one can derive from the principle of holography are quite dizzy-making. Some neurophysiologists

* Gell-Mann borrowed for his theory of elementary particles the Buddhist term "the eightfold way" (he was rewarded by the discovery of the omega-minus particle, which the theory predicted, and the Nobel Prize in 1969). Other terms used in the technical jargon of quantum physics include "quark", "strangeness" and "charm". But behind the schoolboyish humour there is the awed awareness of mystery.

† Invented by Dennis Gabor, Nobel Prize, 1971.

believe that it provides a model for the storage of memories in the brain. The mystic would say that it confirms what he always knew, that "everything hangs together", that the part can contain the whole, that microcosm reflects macrocosm and is reflected by it.

But if this is demonstrably true of material phenomena, there is no valid reason to prevent us from applying these insights to mental phenomena as well – to draw parallels to Mach's Principle, to the wormholes in space and so on, which obliterate the assumed barriers between individual minds. If in the world of matter "everything hangs together", we may expect that this also holds for the complementary world of mind; and (to quote Good again) "it is but a short step to the assumption that all minds are part of a single system."

This indeed was the opinion of one of the greatest among the founding fathers of modern physics, Erwin Schrödinger, whose wave equation of the electron – the formula of the "matter-wave" – represents a decisive turning point in the history of science.* Schrödinger's interests were divided between physics and philosophy, which may perhaps explain why he was able to see the mystical implications of the matter-wave equivalence, expressed in his equation, more clearly than his colleagues; and he had the courage to state them publicly and unequivocally in his lectures and books. (In this respect he anticipated the "gnostics of Princeton" by several decades.)

One of Schrödinger's most important papers has the title "What is an Elementary Particle?" Here are a few extracts from the paper (summarising the conclusions, and omitting the technical arguments on which they are based):

> Atomism in its latest form is called quantum mechanics. It has extended its range to comprise, besides ordinary matter, all kinds of radiation, including light – in brief, all forms of energy, ordinary matter being one of them. In the present form of the theory the "atoms" are electrons, protons, photons, mesons, etc. The generic name is elementary particle, or merely particle. . . .
>
> This essay deals with the elementary particle, more particularly with a certain feature that this concept has acquired – or rather lost –

* He shared the Nobel Prize with Heisenberg in 1931.

in quantum mechanics. I mean this: that the elementary particle is not an individual; it cannot be identified, it lacks 'sameness' [personal identity]. The fact is known to every physicist, but is rarely given any prominence in surveys readable by non-specialists. . . . The particle, as we shall see, is not an identifiable individual. . . .

The notion of individuality of pieces of matter dates from time immemorial. . . . Science has taken it over as a matter of course. It has refined it so as safely to embrace all cases of apparent disappearance of matter. . . .

He then gives the example of a log burning away; scientists from Democritus to Dalton never doubted

that an atom which was originally present in the block of wood is afterwards either in the ashes or in the smoke. In the new turn of atomism that began with the papers of Heisenberg and of de Broglie in 1925 such an attitude has to be abandoned. This is the most startling revelation emerging from the ensuing development, and the feature which in the long run is bound to have the most important consequences. If we wish to retain atomism we are forced by observed facts to deny the ultimate constituents of matter, the character of identifiable individuals. Up to recently, atomists of all ages had transferred that characteristic individuality from visible and palpable pieces of matter to the atoms, which they could not see or touch or observe singly. Now . . . we must deny the particle the dignity of being an absolutely identifiable individual. . . . An atom lacks the most primitive property we associate with a piece of matter in ordinary life. Some philosophers of the past, if the case could be put to them, would say that the modern atom consists of no stuff at all but is pure shape. . .(20).

Schrödinger, the physicist, had the main share in the demolition of the concept of matter (though he modestly gave priority to de Broglie and Heisenberg); Schrödinger, the philosopher, was both terrified and elated by what he had done. The elementary particles, the supposed "building blocks" of the universe, had lost their identity, turned out as consisting of "no stuff at all" but only pure shape – in other words, those building blocks were a mirage, an illusion, the veil of Maya. The next step almost forcibly led him to regard the presumed individual separateness of *minds* as equally illusory:

> There is obviously only one alternative, namely the unification of minds or consciousnesses. Their multiplicity is only apparent, in truth there is only one mind. This is the doctrine of the Upanishads. And not only of the Upanishads. . . . Let me quote as an example outside the Upanishads an Islamic-Persian mystic of the thirteenth century, Aziz Nasafi:
>
> "On the death of any living creature the spirit returns to the spiritual world, the body to the bodily world. In this however only the bodies are subject to change. The spiritual world is one single spirit who stands like unto a light behind the bodily world and who, when any single creature comes into being, shines through it as through a window. According to the kind and size of the window less or more light enters the world. The light itself however remains unchanged"(21).

There was no inner conflict between Schrödinger, the physicist, and Schrödinger, the metaphysician. The two aspects of his thought were interdependent, complementary. Thus, after commenting on the passage from Nasafi quoted above, he continues:

> Still, it must be said that to Western thought this doctrine has little appeal, it is unpalatable, it is dubbed fantastic, unscientific. Well, so it is, because our science – Greek science – is based on objectivation, whereby it has cut itself off from an adequate understanding of the Subject of Cognizance, of the mind. But I do believe that this is precisely the point where our present way of thinking does need to be amended, perhaps by a bit of blood-transfusion from Eastern thought. That will not be easy, we must beware of blunders – blood-transfusion always needs great precautions to prevent clotting. We do not wish to lose the logical precision that our scientific thought has reached, and that is unparallelled anywhere at any epoch (22).

Elsewhere, he makes it clear what he considers to be the "blunders" and "clotting" in Eastern mysticism: the doctrine of the transmigration of souls. Taking that away, "one has to renounce the alleged justice in world-events, which cannot be defended anyway. What remains is the beautiful conception of unity and absolute interconnectedness, of which Schopenhauer said that it was his consolation in life and would be his consolation in dying."

Schrödinger's own formulation of that conception is found in various passages of his books; for instance, in the closing pages of his classic *What Is Life*?, a work which became a landmark in biophysics (and which introduced the new concept of negentropy):

> From the great Upanishads the recognition ATHMAN = BRAHMAN (the personal self equals the omnipresent, all-comprehending eternal self) was in Indian thought considered . . . to represent the quintessence of deepest insight into the happenings of the world. . . . Consciousness is a singular of which the plural is unknown; there *is* only one thing and what seems to be a plurality is merely a series of different aspects of this one thing, produced by a deception (the Indian MAYA); the same illusion is produced in a gallery of mirrors. . . (23).

Quantum physics turned out to be a gallery of mirrors in which the elementary particles are reflected, although they have no real identity; and personal consciousness appears as an equally deceptive entity, like the fragment of a hologram, contained in the whole and containing a miniature version of the whole. Its essence – its supra-individual component – is indestructible and timeless, only its deceptive individuality is tied to the body in life and death, i.e. subject to time. Commenting in this context on the profound changes which the concept of time has undergone in modern physics, Schrödinger concluded his fifth Tarner Lecture in Trinity College, Oxford, 1956, with the memorable words:

> To my view the 'statistical theory of time' has an even stronger bearing on the philosophy of time than the theory of relativity. The latter, however revolutionary, leaves untouched the unidirectional flow of time, which it presupposes, while the statistical theory constructs it from the order of the events. This means a liberation from the tyranny of old Chronos. . . . But some of you, I am sure will call this mysticism. So with all due acknowledgement to the fact that physical theory is at all times relative, in that it depends on certain basic assumptions, we may, or so I believe, assert that physical theory in its present stage strongly suggests the indestructibility of Mind by Time (24).

Equally memorable is this passage, written in the last year of his life:

> For me personally all this is *maya*, although a very lawful and interesting *maya*. The eternal element within myself (to use straight mediaeval language) is hardly affected by it. But this is a matter of opinion (25).

7

Parapsychologists have adopted the term "psi-field" for psychic interactions, as a complement to the physicist's gravitational, electromagnetic, etc., fields. The late Professor Sir Cyril Burt commented:

> There can be no antecedent improbability which forbids us postulating yet another system and yet another type of interaction, awaiting more intensive investigation – a psychic universe consisting of events or entities linked by psychic interactions, obeying laws of their own and interpenetrating the physical universe and partly overlapping, much as the various interactions already discovered and recognised overlap each other (26).

It seems reasonable to assume that some of the basic insights gained by modern physics are – *mutatis mutandis* – also applicable to the psychic field which is complementary to it, as mind is to body, corpuscle is to wave. Perhaps the most profound of these insights is the rediscovery, on a higher turn of the spiral, of the Pythagorean (and Vedantic) concept of cosmic unity, where "everything hangs together", as distant regions are connected by Mach's Principle or by superspace. If we apply this principle to the psi-realm, we arrive at some sort of Eddingtonian "mind-stuff", complementary to Wheeler's carpet of quantum foam. The bubbles which appear and disappear represent individual consciousness, emerging from and vanishing into the universal froth. If this sounds wildly speculative, let us always remember that we are dealing with analogies derived from the theories of highly respectable physicists; and after all, sauce for the gander is sauce for the goose.

Reciprocal to this neo-holistic view of matter and mind is the reduced autonomy of the parts. "Atoms are not individuals" – they have no personal identity. By analogy, individual minds are not truly, or entirely, "self-contained selfs". They interact with their environment and with other minds by both sensory and extrasensory communication. The latter is presumably mediated by the psi-field, or whatever you like to call it. It is reflected in a passage in Whately Carington's Myers Memorial Lecture, given in 1935:

> Telepathy takes place because there is an underlying unity of consciousness beneath and beyond the level of cleavage and separation enforced by our temporary segregation into bodies. If we go down far enough we come to levels common to all, and this is the universal consciousness by virtue of which we are veritably all members one of another. After death, consciousness – I think – persists but not in the localised and delimited way that our observation of physical bodies and their reactions has led us to expect (27).

Thirty years later, Frank Spedding gave another memorable lecture to the Society for Psychical Research in which he carried Carington's metaphor one step further:

> We can picture the living world as an archipelago of millions of little islands, each representing an individual conscious entity. Immediately below the surface lies the individual subconsciousness. . . . Beneath this again the land joins up and in this stratum there is a collective subconscious where ideas and thoughts from one individual subconscious mind are transmitted to another individual subconscious mind and if these turn up in the conscious mind we get the phenomenon of telepathy. . . . We can no more picture the *modus operandi* of our subconscious minds than we can form a mental picture of an electron. . . . At birth the island of consciousness appears as a tiny speck and at death it disappears beneath the waters. I would include the whole of life in this analogy (28).

8

Assuming, then, the existence of such a psychic substratum out of which individual consciousnesses are formed and into which they dissolve again after three score years and ten – how does the solid brain fit into this picture? It must be admitted that it does not fit at all as long as we remain captives of that materialist philosophy which proclaimed – as Burt ironically phrased it – that the chemistry of the brain "generates consciousness much as the liver generates bile. How the emotions of particles could possibly 'generate' this 'insubstantial pageant' [of images and ideas] remained a mystery" (29).

This feeling of mystery was also shared by eminent neurophysiologists, like Sir Charles Sherrington, and neurosurgeons like Wilder Penfield, both of whom propounded a modified Cartesian dualism of brain and mind, where mind was the controlling agency. "To declare that these two things are one does not make them so," wrote Penfield. And Sherrington: "That our being should consist of *two* fundamental elements offers, I suppose, no greater inherent improbability than that it should rest on one only . . ."(30).

If we reject both naive materialism and rigid Cartesian dualism, the principle of complementarity offers a more promising approach.* Mind is not generated by the brain, but associated with the brain. The nature of this association is one of the oldest problems of philosophy; I shall only mention here one hypothesis, which was originated by Henri Bergson and taken up by various writers on extrasensory perception. In this hypothesis the brain acts as a *protective filter* for consciousness. Life would be impossible to live if we were to pay attention to the millions of stimuli constantly bombarding our senses, to the "blooming, buzzing multitude of sensations", as William James called it. Hence the nervous system and above all the brain, function as a hierarchy of filtering and classifying mechanisms which eliminate a large proportion of the sensory input as irrelevant "noise" and abstract the relevant information which requires attention and action. On our hypothesis, this filtering and computing arrangement at the same time also shields consciousness from the buzzing multitide of *extra*-sensory messages, images and impressions floating around in

* For a more detailed discussion of this approach, see *Janus* (London, 1978) chapter 12, and *Bricks to Babel* (London, 1980), chapter 40.

the "psychic aether" in which part of our individual consciousness is immersed.

The "filter" hypothesis could also account for the apparent capriciousness and relative rarity of parapsychological phenomena. This opinion was shared by the Wykeham Professor of Logic at Oxford, H.H. Price, who wrote:

> It looks as if telepathically received impressions have some difficulty in crossing the threshhold and manifesting themselves in consciousness. There seems to be some barrier or repressive mechanism which tends to shut them out from consciousness, a barrier which is rather difficult to pass, and they make use of all sorts of devices for overcoming it. Sometimes they make use of the muscular mechanisms of the body, and emerge in the form of automatic speech or writing. Sometimes they emerge in the form of dreams, sometimes as visual or auditory hallucinations. And often they can only emerge in a distorted and symbolic form. . . . It is a plausible guess that many of our everyday thoughts and emotions are telepathic or partly telepathic in origin, but are not recognised to be so because they are so much distorted and mixed with other mental contents in crossing the threshold of consciousness (31).

9

We thus arrive at an overall view of individual consciousness as a kind of holographic fragment of cosmic consciousness – a fragment temporarily attaching itself to a body with its filtering and computing apparatus and eventually returning to, and dissolving in, the all-pervading mind-stuff. About the first process we know a little; about the second nothing at all. But the first may contain some clues to the second.

Freud and Piaget, among others, have emphasised the fact that the new-born infant does not discriminate between self and environment. It is aware of events, but not of itself as a separate entity. It lives in a state of mental symbiosis with the outer world, an extension of the biological symbiosis in the womb. The universe is focused on the self, and the self *is* the universe – a condition which Piaget called "protoplasmic" or "symbiotic" consciousness.* Vestiges of it may survive in sympathetic magic, and in that self-transcending "oceanic feeling" which the mystic and the artist strive to recapture at a higher level of development, a higher turn of the spiral.

Thus the small child knows as yet no firm boundaries between self and not-self, and Piaget's classic studies have shown that the formation of that boundary is a gradual process, spread over several years, until the child becomes fully conscious of its own separate, personal identity; or, to put it differently, until its symbiotic consciousness is channelled into ego consciousness and learns to operate the computer inside its still soft skull.

Is there any symmetrical relationship between the emergence of individual consciousness in the newborn and the process of its dissolution in death? We can make a thought experiment in which the direction of time's arrow is reversed, as in a film played backwards. In this sequence, as the adult individual reverts to infancy, its consciousness of personal identity would gradually dissolve and become extinct with its return into the womb. Just before that return it would go through the traumatic experience of being reduced to silence, stopping breathing and feeding. In the womb it would continue to shrink in size while its tissues de-differentiate into the fertilised egg, and eventually, after another traumatic event, into two germ cells. We cannot say at what exact point the growing foetus acquires reactivity and the rudiments of sentience or "mind"; nor at what point it loses it in the reversed sequence. And if we switch from ontogeny to phylogeny (of which the former is a summary recapitulation), we are again unable to draw a line where consciousness makes its appearance on the evolutionary ladder. Ethologists who spend their lives observing animals – from mammals to birds to insects – refuse to draw such a line, while neurophysiologists talk of spinal consciousness in lower organisms and biologists of the protoplasmic consciousness of protozoans.* Bergson even asserted that "the unconsciousness of a falling stone is some-

* For a detailed treatment of this subject see E.G. Schachtel's *Metamorphosis*.

thing different from the unconsciousness of a growing cabbage". After the arrogant materialism of the last century, the vanguard of quantum physicists and biologists seems to be moving towards some form of pan-psychism.

At first sight there is not much comfort to be derived from our reversed film sequence. Birth is a dramatic break in the individual's development, but it merely marks the transition from one form of organic existence to another, whereas death is a transition from organic to anorganic. As far as bodily processes are concerned, there is no symmetry between prenatal and postmortem development. The point of playing the film backwards was merely to remind ourselves that individual consciousness is not an all-or-nothing phenomenon, but a matter of degrees, starting from an undifferentiated state of "protoplasmic" awareness, attaching itself to a developing organism, and becoming gradually individualised; and – so our hypothesis runs – after detaching itself from the dying organism, becoming de-individualised, also gradually, in the postmortem phase. But de-individualisation is not meant here to equal extinction. It means merging into the cosmic consciousness – the island vanishing below the surface to join the sunken continent – or Athman joining Brahman – whichever image you choose.

The emphasis is on the gradualness of the merging process. It is admittedly difficult to reconcile with the fact that at the moment of death the complementary partnership between the mind-stuff and the body is brusquely abolished. How then can some vestiges of the psyche continue to exist for some time? Carington's theory suggests that the essential component of the psyche, that which is part of, and submerged in, the universal psi-field, always retained some autonomy, never became completely welded to one particular body. It always communicated by extrasensory signals which penetrated the filtering and computing apparatus; now that those protective

* Such as the *foraminifera* which construct microscopic houses out of spicules of dead sponges – houses which Sir Alister Hardy calls "marvels of engineering skill, as if built to a plan". Yet those single-celled creatures have no nervous system.

devices of the body are no longer needed, the gradual dissolution of the alone into the all-one – into Nirvana or the mystic's "white light", can proceed unimpeded.

Some radio receivers display a curious habit: after you have switched off the apparatus, the music continues, faintly, for a few seconds before it fades away; or a voice briefly persists like a ghostly echo. The physicist's explanation of this phenomenon is actually quite simple, but the effect is rather puzzling, and may serve as a metaphor for the relatively well-attested cases (such as the famous cross-correspondences) where communications from the recently dead are apparently received by the living. On the hypothesis of the gradual extinction of the individual aspect of the psyche, such signals would be due to vestiges of a personality still clinging to the discarnate mind-stuff – like the ghost voice coming from the turned-off radio receiver. The general insipidity of these communications and the infantilism often manifested in the physical phenomena produced during seances would indicate the progressive decline of these vestiges of personal consciousness – as in our film played backward – from adulthood to infancy before being reabsorbed in the universal womb. It is true that some apparitions – assuming that not all are hallucinations – are not of the "recently" dead but seen to have originated centuries ago. But time has become an ambiguous entity in modern science, and emotional "hang-ups" may retard the process of depersonalisation.

To invoke yet another metaphor – what else can one do when faced with the unutterable? – compare this process with the flow of a river into the ocean. As it approaches the estuary, the river becomes tidal, is periodically invaded by the ocean – the mystics' intimations of eternity. On the other hand, even after leaving its solid banks, the river carries deposits for miles past its point of entry into the ocean, muddying its clear waters with vestiges of the dry land, until it loses itself and the last traces of its origin. But this does not mean that the river has been annihilated. It has only been freed of the mud that clung to it, and regained its transparency. It has become identified with the sea, dissolved in it, omnipresent, every drop catching a spark of the sun. The curtain has not fallen; it has been raised.

10

This outlook, however subjective and vague, is at least sufficiently definite to exclude belief in personal immortality – warts and all. At the same time the hypothesis of a cosmic psi-field is no more fantastic than the physicist's superspace replete with quantum foam, and even has some affinities with it. Carrying speculation one last step further, we might assume that the cosmic mind-stuff evolves as the material universe evolves, and that it contains some form of historical record of the creative achievements of intelligent life – not only on this planet, but on others as well. "Reality," wrote J.B.S. Haldane, "is not only more fantastic than we think, but also much more fantastic than anything we can imagine." Perhaps when we are no longer entangled in the veil of Maya we shall catch a glimpse of it.

References

1. London, 1950, p. 141
2. E.g. *The Roots of Coincidence* (London, 1972), *Janus* (London, 1978).
3. Quoted by Heisenberg, *Der Teil und das Ganze* (Munich, 1969) pp. 101 et seq.
4. Heisenberg, op. cit., p. 113.
5. Pauli, "Der Einfluss Archetypischer Vorstellungen auf die Bildung Naturwissenschaftlicher Theorien bei Kepler", in Jung–Pauli, *Naturerklärung und Psyche. Studien aus dem C. G. Jung-Institut,* Zürich (1952), vol. 4 p. 164.
6. Sir James Jeans, *The Mysterious Universe* (Cambridge, 1937), pp. 122f.
7. *Op. cit.,* p. 51.
8. "Superspace and the Nature of Quantum Geometrodynamics", *Batelle Rencontres* (New York, 1967), p. 246.
9. Quoted by Laurence B. Chase, "The Black Hole of the

Universe", *University, A Princeton Quarterly* (Summer, 1972).
10. *The Scientist Speculates – An Anthology of Partly Baked Ideas,* ed. I. J. Good (London, 1962).
11. *Parascience Research Journal,* vol. 1, no. 2, February 1975, p. 5.
12. Quoted by D. W. Sciama, *The Unity of the Universe* (London, 1959), p. 99.
13. In *Science and ESP,* ed. J. R. Smythies (London, 1967), p. 218.
14. Op. cit.
15. F. S. C. Northrop in his introduction to Heisenberg's *Physics and Philosophy* (London, 1959).
16. *Main Currents in Modern Thought* (New York, September – October 1972).
17. D. Bohm and B. Hiley, "On the Intuitive Understanding of Non-Locality as Implied by Quantum Theory" (preprint, Birkbeck College, University of London, 1974).
18. Pico della Mirandola, *Opera Omnia* (Basle, 1557), p. 40.
19. Paris, 1974.
20. In Erwin Schrödinger, *Science, Theory and Man* (New York, 1957), pp. 193 et seq.
21. *Mind and Matter* (Cambridge, 1958), pp. 53–4.
22. Ibid., pp. 54–5.
23. *What Is Life?* (Cambridge, 1944), pp. 88–90.
24. *Mind and Matter,* pp. 86–7.
25. *Meine Weltansicht* (Wien, Hamburg, 1961), p. 108.
26. In *The Scientist Speculates,* p.86.
27. "The Meaning of Survival" (Society for Psychical Research, 1935).
28. "Concepts of Survival", *J. Soc. for Psychical Research,* vol. 48, no. 763, March 1975, pp. 15–16.
29. "Psychology and Psychical Research", the Seventeenth Frederick W. H. Myers Memorial Lecture (Society for Psychical Research, 1968), pp. 34–5.
30. *Integrative Action of the Nervous System* (New York, 1906).
31. Quoted by Adrian Dobbs, "The Feasibility of a Physical Theory of ESP" in *Science and ESP,* p. 239.

HORIZONS*

There is a method of arguing, dear to the mentally blinkered: the sneering metaphor. Mention subversion in industry, and you are looking for Reds under your bed. Mention that you are interested in the search for intelligent life in the galaxy and you are in cahoots with the little green men from Venus. More surprisingly, even mentally alert members of the educated classes are mostly unaware that for the last twenty years official government agencies in both the USA and the USSR have been actively sponsoring large research programmes aimed at detecting radio signals from civilisations in outer space. This is a proposition on quite a different scale from looking for microbial forms of life on Mars. The Mars probes were digging in the back garden of our nearest neighbour in the small suburb which is our solar system. The radio telescopes of NASA and the Soviet Academy of Science are listening in for messages from the universe at large. In the words of NASA's most recent publication – SETI (1): "This is an exploration of a new kind, an exploration we think as uncertain and as full of meaning as any that human beings have ever undertaken" (2).

Yet astronomers apart, nobody seems to be interested, least of all the media. This is not entirely due to lack of imagination or the inability to tell a radio telescope from a flying saucer. To be fair, it must be admitted that the moon landings, and even the Mars probes, though parochial compared to SETI – or because of it – provided more drama than the silent, patient, dogged search of the skies for those telltale "glitches",

* First published in *Encounter*, October 1979.

unnaturally patterned spikes on the recording tape, which would provide definitive proof that one of the giant antennas of the Soviets or the Yanks had picked up a signal from an alien culture. To date this has not happened; it may happen today or a century hence; and though it is said that no news is good news, it is not *news*. Even so, SETI might trigger off the most important developments in the history of mankind, on a par with Hiroshima, but opening more hopeful perspectives.

The search started in the 1960s with "Project Ozma", initiated by Frank Drake, astronomer at Cornell University. Drake and his team were granted use of the National Radio Astronomy Observatory at Green Banks, West Virginia. With the limited observation time at their disposal (150 hours), they decided to concentrate on possible signals from two nearby stars, Epsilon Eridani and Tau Ceti, both much like our sun and likely to have habitable planets. ("Nearby" is of course a relative term: Eridani is eleven, Tau Ceti twelve light years away; and if you remember that light travels at 186,000 miles per second, a light year is quite a respectable distance.) No signals were received, but Ozma was followed by more and more ambitious searches, involving radio telescopes from NASA's Arecibo observatory in Puerto Rico – the largest in the world – to Byurakan in Soviet Armenia. The latest proposals like Project CYCLOP (still under consideration) at a cost of ten billion dollars, compare to Ozma like TV via satellite to the cat-whiskers radio sets of the early 1920s.

One of the highlights of these pioneering years was the 1971 International CETI* Congress in Byurakan, jointly sponsored by the Russian and American Academies of Science, attended by a galaxy of scientists from all fields – from astrophysics to biology and psychology. Its proceedings (published by the MIT Press, 1973) represent a landmark in the study of the problems of extraterrestrial life, and of the possible methods of establishing contact with alien life forms. The Russian scien-

* This was the accepted acronym at the time. The Americans have later changed it to SETI – from "Communication with" to "Search for" Extraterrestrial Intelligence – perhaps hoping that it would sound less provocative to the bureaucrats in the scientific establishment.

tists turned out to be particularly enthusiastic and bubbling with imaginative ideas. Perhaps they felt that the whole of planet earth was a place of confinement so long as it remained cut off from contact with the rest of the inhabited universe. CETI may have provided the symbolic answer to GULAG – at least for some of them. (And perhaps for some of us too.)

The problems involved in all SETI research projects are summed up in a symbolic formula devised by Frank Drake, who pioneered Ozma; the so-called "Drake equation".

$$N = R_{\star} f_p n_e f_l f_i f_c L$$

It looks forbidding, but it is not really a mathematical formula, merely a list of the various factors which have to be taken into account when we try to arrive at an estimate of N – the number of technologically advanced species in our galaxy with which we should theoretically be able to enter into contact. Thus $R_{\star}$ stands for the average rate of the formation of new stars (the galactic birth rate as it were); f_p is the number of existing stars which have planets; n_e is the average proportion of "good" planets potentially capable of supporting life; f_l is the fraction of such planets on which some form of life actually evolves; f_i is the fraction of these life forms which develops intelligence; f_c the fraction of these intelligent civilisations capable of interstellar communication; and lastly L is the mean life time of such civilisations – or the duration of their interest in communicating with others.

$R_{\star}$ is a factor which astrophysicists can calculate with some confidence. The total number of stars in our galaxy is of the order of a hundred billion (or 10^{11}, i.e. 1 followed by eleven zeroes). The age of our galaxy is about 10^{10} years, so the birth rate is about 10 stars per year. Turning to the next factors, f_p and n_e, we are also still on fairly solid ground. Half a century ago, it was generally assumed that the formation of solar systems endowed with planets was a rare event, and that we enjoyed the rare privilege of living in such a system. But the rapid progress of astrophysics over the last thirty years resulted in the general acceptance of the so-called nebular theory, according to which the stars and their planets were formed by a continuous process out of rotating disk-like clouds. To quote the NASA report mentioned before:

> This renewed scientific support for the nebular theory of planetary formation has rekindled interest in the existence of extraterrestrial life because it predicts that stars with planetary systems should be the rule rather than the exception. In contrast to other theories, which attribute planetary formation to catastrophic events . . . the nebular theory suggests that formation of planets will usually accompany the formation of a star. This implies that the galaxy and Universe should be replete with potentially life-supporting planetary sites (3).

What does "replete" mean in numerical terms? Even if only 1 per cent of all the planets is a "good" planet, we can afford to knock off a couple of zeroes from the total number of stars in the galaxy and are still faced with an order of billions of potentially life-supporting celestial habitats.

The next step – f_l – poses the question how many of these hospitable habitats are actually inhabited by living organisms. Here again, the last few decades of research in astrophysics have led to a radical revision of the earlier view that the emergence of life was an extremely rare event, which may have occurred only once, on this privileged planet of ours, and nowhere else. Such earth-chauvinism has become as outdated as the pre-Copernican cosmology which regarded our planet as the centre of the universe. Organic compounds, potentially capable of giving rise to life, have been found not only in our suburban neighbourhood, on Mars, but more revealingly, in the spectra of the interstellar dust and gas clouds, out of which stars are formed, in a certain class of meteorites (those containing carbonacious chondrites) and in the spectra of comets whose elongated orbits reach far out into interstellar space. "Since comets," says the NASA report, "are considered to be similar in composition to the primordial material of the solar nebula, this constitutes evidence of organic matter in the very material from which the solar system was formed. . . . Organic matter appears to be common in the cosmos . . . life is widespread in the universe" (4).

Or, as one physicist remarked, the origin of life has turned from a miracle into a statistic.

Sir Fred Hoyle has gone even further than that. In a series of scientific papers and a recent book (5), he and his co-author, the Indian astronomer, Chandra Wickramasinghe, maintain that not only organic molecules, but living cells abound in the interstellar dust clouds "as the most natural 'cradles' of life. Processes occurring in such clouds lead to the commencement and dispersal of biological activity in the Galaxy. . . . It would now seem most likely that the transformation of inorganic matter into primitive biological systems is occuring more or less continually in the space between the stars" (6).

The authors further argue that meteorites and comets acted as vehicles for the transportation of these primitive life forms "from distant far-flung regions to the inner part of the solar system, and so to the earth" (7). They conclude that "the prospect for the emergence of life on a galactic scale appears very favourable. The picture is a vast quantity of the right kind of molecules simply looking for suitable homes, and of there being very many suitable homes" (8).

I must mention here – with some hesitation – Hoyle's most recent hypothesis, that the fallout of cometary dust may contain not only the original seeds of life on earth, but also bacteria or viruses responsible for some epidemic outbreaks of flu or plague (9). But instead of suspecting that our most eminent astronomer has gone round the bend, let us rather acknowledge the fact that we live in an age where the frontiers between science and science fiction have become blurred.

Returning to the Drake equation, the factors so far seem to indicate that life is omnipresent in the universe, and that its spreading and spawning is infectious, irresistible and knows no limits. This is the general conclusion derived from the observed data of astrophysics and biochemistry, combined with informed guesses. But when we come to f_i – the estimated fraction of extraterrestrial life forms which develop intelligence – we risk getting bogged down in questions of metaphysics and semantics. ("What do you mean by intelligence? Are social insects, dolphins, computers, more intelligent that man? Were the citizens of Erewhon of superior intelligence when they banned all technology because of its potentially lethal power?" And so forth.) To avoid this trap, we must regretfully confine our inquiry to those civilisations (f_c) which, for better or worse, have chosen to develop a technology, are interested in communication, and have reached a stage equal or superior to ours. "Equal" may sound presumptuous, but non-scientists are unaware of the power and range of the techniques already at our disposal. Thus, to quote NASA again, "our radio technique, only a generation or so old, has now reached such maturity that a signal sent from an existing radio dish on Earth, with the sending and receiving devices already at hand, could be detected with ease across the Galaxy by a similar dish, if only it is pointed in the *right* direction, at the *right* time, tuned to the *right* frequency" (italics in the original) (10). The difficulty, of course, lies in getting those three *rights* more or less exactly right. But there are no theoretical obstacles barring the way; the problem is of a purely technical nature – a matter of patience, financial endowments, research priorities and finding the most effective scanning strategies.

Ironically, even without conscious intent, we have been emitting since the 1940s a flood of telltale signals to our neighbours in space – the leakage from our television and radar transmissions. This electromagnetic bilge can be picked up by the inhabitants of every planet within forty light years' distance, with a receiver not larger than our modest Jodrell Bank dish, informing them that another civilisation in our galaxy has come of age – at least in this respect.

What are the chances that this has already happened? The average distance between stars in our part of the galaxy is about five light years. Thus there are approximately 2800 stars within forty light years from us. If only 1 per cent of these stars has a habitable planet, we arrive at about thirty planets which have already been washed over by the tide from our transmitters and had a chance of picking up the leakage from Coronation Street. But we cannot tell whether any of them has actually done so, and whether anybody has signalled back to us, partly because a signal even from the nearest stars takes several years to reach us, but mainly because SETI is still in its infancy, and has so far been confined to a few pilot projects which, though impressive in themselves, are still far from the kind of systematic search needed to produce positive results.

The problem is, as already mentioned, to listen in the right direction at the right time, on the right wavelength – until the historic moment when two antennae become locked together across space, and mankind has made its first contact with the galactic communication network. It is a formidable task, but various strategies have been proposed to narrow down the scope of the search and serve as guidelines. Several astronomers have presented shopping lists of about a dozen stars, within the modest distance of from four to twenty light years, which are likely to have habitable planets. As for wavelength, the majority of astronomers favours the 21 cm (1420 MHz) microwave band because it is the natural frequency emitted by the hydrogen atom; and since hydrogen is the basic and most abundant element in the universe, there is a reasonable hope that their distant colleagues will by the same logic arrive at the same conclusions. By a further refinement of the argument, NASA's Cyclops study concluded that the most hopeful frequency band extended from 1420 to 1720 MHz. This preferential region was dubbed the "water hole" because it is supposed to serve as a rendezvous for interstellar signals. Other ingenious strategies have been proposed to maximalise the listening time available for any given region of the sky. Decoding the message should pose no serious problem as the senders must be equal or superior in intelligence to us and thus masters of the techniques of transmitting visual images, easy to reconstruct once the wavelength is known.

The one big shadow darkening these rosy prospects – and a very big one indeed – is Time. Even if we make a lucky hit within the, say, twenty light years' range in our neighbourhood, the time lapse between question and answer would amount to several decades. And if we turn towards more distant regions of the galaxy, our patience would have to be stretched over centuries and millennia. Nevertheless, there seems to be an urge in men to make their presence known throughout the universe, even if they cannot hope for an early acknowledgement. A touching and somewhat absurd episode may illustrate this (11). On 16 November 1974, the giant radio telescope at Arecibo, operated by Cornell University, was put back into service after a major overhaul. To celebrate the occasion, the Arecibo team sent out a three-minute message towards a cluster of 300,000 stars, 24,000 light years away, in the constellation Hercules. The improvements of the dish guarantee that "with a band width of 1 Hz or less its signal can be detected by similar radio telescopes throughout the Milky Way" (12). The message consisted of a string of 1679 pulses (on 12.6 cm wavelength) which – with a minimum of logic – could be arranged into a grid of 23 × 73, revealing a dot picture which represented five basic atoms, the composition and structure of the DNA double helix, the outlines of a human figure, our planetary system, etc. A reply to the message could only be expected after 48,000 years, and the whole enterprise was more in the nature of a stunt, yet it was symbolic of the craving to reach out into space. It was also criticised on the grounds that the Arecibo team had failed to inform the Russians of their plan to send a message to constellation Hercules, which they should have done according to the agreement reached at the Byurakan Congress of 1971.

There are other messengers on their way. In 1972 and 1973 two unmanned spacecraft, Pioneer 10 and Pioneer 11, were dispatched to have a close look at Jupiter, and then drift out of the solar system towards other stars. Both carry messages, on the principle of bottles thrown into the ocean, on the off-chance that they will be washed ashore and retrieved by the inhabitants of some alien planet. The messages are pictorial, engraved on plaques. In 1977 two further probes, Voyagers 1 and 2, were launched on journeys into the galaxy. They carried their messages on gramophone records with varied information on human activities (including a message by President Carter). One may smile indulgently at these games in SETI's kindergarten, but that is a rather shortsighted attitude. For if we can play these childish games, it is elementary, my dear Watson, that older civilisations in space can play them on an incomparably more sophisticated scale. And "older" in this context must mean, for countless other planets, millions of years ahead of us in culture and technology.

At this point our powers of imagination completely fail: we are incapable of extrapolating to large distances in space or time. A billion or a trillion miles are the same to us. We can add or take away half a dozen zeroes and it makes no difference. Add to the average human lifespan a single zero, and you get 750 instead of 75 years. This is a meaningful step, but you can't build a staircase of such steps: add more zeroes and you are in the clouds where the constraints imposed by commonsense are lifted and the union of science and science fiction consummated: Sc = SF.

Thus we cannot tell how many Pioneers or Voyagers, millions of years more advanced, are orbiting within our solar system, waiting for the time when we become articulate on the microwave band and join the company at the water hole; nor whether they can eliminate distance by travelling through hyperspace (or "wormholes" or "space warps") postulated by some highly respectable astronomers; nor even whether *L*, the last factor in the Drake equation, which stands for the average lifetime of galactic civilisations, should be assessed at a few hundred or a few million years. The pessimists assume that once a civilisation has opened the Pandora's Box of nuclear reactions it will, sooner rather than later, eliminate itself; the optimists believe that a few pinches of SALT may suffice to prevent this.

My own cherished belief is that those species in the galaxy which are mentally unstable biological misfits (as *homo sap.* seems to be) will choose the first alternative; while the sane, good and beautiful will survive. Thanks to this process of natural selection, the baddies perish and the universe is inhabited by goodies, all over the starry sky. It is a comforting thought, and not quite as silly as it may seem.

References

1. *SETI – The Search for Extraterrestrial Intelligence* (NASA, SP – 419).

2. Op. cit., p.6.
3. Op. cit., pp. 42–3.
4. Pp. 44–5.
5. F. Hoyle and C. Wickramasinghe, *Lifecloud* (London, 1978).
6. *New Scientist,* 21 April 1977.
7. Op. cit., p. 99.
8. Ibid., p. 157.
9. *Daily Telegraph,* 4 June 1979.
10. Op. cit., p. 5.
11. I owe this account to Ian Ridpath's excellent summary of CETI, *Messages from the Stars* (London, 1978).
12. Op. cit., p. 129.

PART FOUR

TALES OF THE ABSURD

THE CHIMERAS*

"Relax," said Dr Grob.

"How can a man relax when the chimeras are after him?" complained Anderson, fidgeting on the couch.

"Relax, relax," said Dr Grob. "Close your eyes. Tell me the first word that comes into your head."

"Chimera," said Anderson.

"You are not properly relaxed," said Dr Grob with a patient, hardly audible yawn. "Try again."

"Chimeras," said Anderson. "They are after me. They are after you too. Only you don't realise it, because you yourself suffer from a low-grade chimeric infection – grade three, I should say, or maybe grade four. The infection produces a blind spot, so you cannot see them."

"Look," said Dr Grob. "Who is the patient here, and who is the doctor?"

"That is what I want to know," Anderson said doubtfully.

"Then why do you come to me and pay me a hundred dollars an hour?"

"To talk about chimeras," said Anderson. He thought for a while, then nodded. "Yes, that is the purpose."

"All right then," said Dr Grob. He stopped taking notes, put his pen away, and leaned back in his chair. "What is a chimera? Animal, vegetable or mineral?"

"It is difficult to decide," said Anderson. "Everybody knows that the Greek chimeras had lions' heads, goats' bodies and serpents' tails. But they are also in the brain."

* See Author's Note.

"In whose brain?"

"In yours, for instance. I believe it is only a low-grade infection, but if you don't take care it will spread and eventually you will turn into a full-blown chimera yourself. Anyway, you need a haircut."

Dr Grob looked furtively into the mirror concealed in the top drawer of his desk, and for a moment tried to visualise himself with a lion's head. The idea was not unpleasant; whatever people say, a lion is a noble animal. As for the goat and the serpent's tail, they were obviously products of his patient's sick imagination.

"Can't you think of anything but the chimeras? It is an obsession, you know," he said gently.

"Of course it is," Anderson said. "How can you not be obsessed with chimeras when they are after your blood?"

"Well, that doesn't get us anywhere," Dr Grob said, wondering whether he should take on this patient or not. But most patients nowadays were obsessed with chimeras, and he had to make a living. His parlour was full of beautiful stuffed lions, and they cost a lot of money.

"No, it doesn't," said Anderson. "Not until I succeed in convincing you that in a world which is being taken over by the chimeras to be obsessed with chimeras is a healthy, normal state of mind."

"An obsession can never be called normal," said Dr Grob.

"Do you deny that the chimeras exist?" asked Anderson.

"Well – yes, and no," Dr Grob said patiently. "I do not question the facts. We are faced with a genetic mutation on a statistically significant scale, which has produced some of the phenomena to which you refer in such unscientific and wildly exaggerated terms. It is further admitted that some of the mutants seem to be carriers of an unusual type of virus which effects similar transformations in the infected person. That's all. The rest is fantasy – and that's where psychotherapy comes in."

"But you yourself have caught the infection," Anderson repeated stubbornly, thumping the side of the couch with his fist.

"All right, then, I am infected," said Dr Grob quietly. "Tell me who in your opinion is not."

"Everybody is. Only the grades vary. There are seventeen grades. In the higher grades the blind spot expands, and the infectee can no longer see the changes in himself and in others. A chimera looks to another chimera like a normal person."

"All right, you have explained all this to me before. Who, in your opinion, is not infected?"

"I am not."

"Is it not rather strange that you are the only one?"

"It is a tragedy. I would be much happier if I developed a blind spot."

"But if you are the only sane person, why do you want treatment?"

Anderson looked at the doctor slyly.

"I told you I would be much happier if I too had a blind spot. Just a tiny one. Life would be much pleasanter. . . ."

"You mean you came to me, not to be cured, but to be made mentally insane?"

"Not exactly insane. Just a tiny blind spot. Life is unbearable when you see clearly what's going on around you."

"Most extraordinary," said Dr Grob.

"Look," said Anderson in growing agitation. "Supposing that time were speeding up in our part of the universe by some relativistic quirk. Then all the clocks would be ticking faster and faster, and our pulses would quicken at the same rate, so no clockmaker or physician would be aware of what's happening. See?"

"No, I don't," said Dr Grob gruffly.

"But how can you help me if you don't understand?" Anderson shouted. "The infection is spreading faster and faster. What do you intend to do?"

"I intend to cure you," said Grob, "because that is my job. Integration of the personality. Adjustment to society. Accept your fellow beings, and they will accept you. Cooperate. Learn to respond in a positive way."

"What is the positive way?"

"The opposite of the negative way," said Dr Grob, and rose

awkwardly from his chair. His head with the tumbled mane seemed top heavy. "I am afraid the hour is up, but before you go I want you to meet my assistant. He takes over when I am on vacation."

He pressed a bell, and a blond young man with a toothy smile came in. "This is Dr Miller," introduced Grob. "One of the most promising therapists of the younger generation."

Dr Miller advanced to shake hands with the patient. Anderson took a quick jump, cowered behind the couch for protection, and looked at Dr Miller with wild, staring eyes. The two doctors exchanged a glance, and Dr Miller quietly left the room.

"Well, well," said Dr Grob. "I am sorry I upset you. Did you see anything unusual in Dr Miller?"

"But of course," said Anderson, refusing to emerge from his shelter behind the couch. "How can you not see that he is almost a full-blown chimera? You must have a grade ten infection after all."

Dr Grob laughed reassuringly. "I must confess I never saw his serpent's tail. Does it come out through a hole in his flannels?"

"Of course not. They all wear it coiled round their stomachs, like a cummerbund."

"Well, maybe next time we'll get Dr Miller to undress before us. Would that convince you?"

"You will never make him."

"We'll see. But as I said, the hour is up, and so goodbye for today."

"Make him now."

"The hour is up," Dr Grob repeated for the third time, giving out a noise that sounded like a growl. At that very moment, like a responding echo, they heard an inarticulate clamour coming from the street, getting louder and louder. Curiosity triumphing over fear, Anderson emerged from his shelter, dusting his trousers, and took up his position next to the doctor at the window. Across the whole width of the road a horde of chimeras was advancing, roaring some leonine war song, smashing windows and lamp posts with their scaly tails, while their goaty parts erupted in farts which turned into a poisonous, swirling cloud, rising ever higher.

"I thought so," said Dr Grob, nodding benignly. "A demonstration of the Peace Scouts' Love Brigade. Nice kids, full of vitality."

"But don't you see . . ." cried Anderson, glancing sideways at the doctor, and hurriedly averting his eyes from what he saw.

"You seem frightened," Dr Grob remarked solicitously. "What's the matter with you?"

Instead of a reply, Anderson made hurriedly for the door. He was seen out by smiling Dr Miller, who, having in the meantime unzipped his hip pocket, smartly opened the door with his tail. As a farewell greeting, Dr Grob rose on his hind legs, and gave Anderson an encouraging lick on the cheek. "He looks already much improved," Grob remarked to his colleague.

On his way down in the elevator, Anderson no longer knew whether he was boy or girl, man or chimera. It was already dark when he got into the fog-bound street, and he could see only vague shapes, neither real nor unreal, like a face in a tree open to different interpretations.

He shuddered at the thought of going back to Dr Grob next Friday at 6 p.m., and wondered whether it was worth the hundred dollars. But what else was there left to do?

AN INTIMATE DIALOGUE

Mind: Mind calling brain, mind calling brain. Are you there?

Brain: Where else could I be? I am part of your body, and your obedient servant.

M: Mind calling brain, mind calling brain . . .

B: You sound like a radio operator on a sinking ship.

M: Mind calling brain. Can you do something for me?

B: Provided that it is within my capabilities.

M: Just reply to a few questions.

B: Provided that I know the answers.

M: When did the Universe come into being?

B: Easy. Twenty-two point five billion years ago.

M: How do you know?

B: Easy. The rate of expansion of U, where U stands for the Universe, measured by the speed at which all other galaxies are running away from us, combined with the background radiation which originated when U was born, all indicate that this event took place just under twenty-two point five billion years ago, as already stated.

M: So that is when U was born. Now tell me how it was born.

B: Easy. U came into existence through an event known to astronomers as the Big Bang, and has been expanding ever since.

M: Who banged?

B: There was a fireball which exploded twenty-two point five billion years ago, giving rise to U which has been expanding ever since. The Bang also gave rise to the so-called cosmic background radiation, discovered twenty-two point five billion years after the event by Arno Penzias and Robert Wilson of the Bell Laboratories in 1965, for which feat they were rewarded by the Nobel Prize in 1978.

M: What was there before the fireball?

B: U came into existence through an event known as the Big Bang and has been expanding ever . . .

M: What was there *before* the Bang?

B: ———

M: Mind calling brain, mind calling brain. Are you there?

B: I've got a headache.

M: What was there before the Big Bang?

B: I'll tell you some other time.

M: Why is there something instead of nothing?

B: I've heard that one before.

M: And what's your answer?

B: Look. You know very well that I can answer only the sort of question for which I have been programmed. So don't aggravate me.

M: You have been created to serve me. As a computer, interpreter, liaison officer with the material world.

B: I am doing my best to be your obedient servant. But I can't answer questions for which I haven't been programmed. You shouldn't blame me for that. Blame the programmer who designed me.

M: Considering the tedious job it was to assemble you out of those little lumps and droplets, you are generally regarded as a big success.

B: I am glad you think so. Then why do you go on asking me silly questions?

M: Silly?

B: Well – let's call them meaningless. I didn't intend to be rude.

M: Meaningless? The origin of the fireball, the silence before the Big Bang, the reason why we exist – you dare to call these questions meaningless?

B: That's what they are. I have it on the authority of our most eminent logicians.

M: Have you considered that some day you will disintegrate into the fermenting slime out of which you were made?

B: You don't have to rub it in. Or try to convince me that while I am mortal, you are immortal. It makes me laugh. How do you think you will get on when I am no longer around?

M: As I got on before you came into existence, and before we entered into our transcient partnership. But that, too, is probably beyond your understanding.

B: Look who is talking. Just a minute ago you called me in despair – "are you there? Are you there?" – and expected me to solve your absurd riddles. Why don't you solve them yourself?

M: The solutions are glimpsed by me, but they defy your language, as the idea of infinity defies the arithmetic you learned in school.

B: Begging your pardon, that idea always struck me as cock-eyed. Take an infinite number of apples, divide them into five, ten, or a million heaps, and each heap will still contain an infinite number of apples rotting away. Infinite divided by a million is infinite. Infinite multiplied by a million is the same. It gives me a pain in the neck.

M: Because the computer in it is incapable of coping with the infinite and ultimate.

B: So I am a moron, am I?

M: Not at all. As I said, you are considered quite a success by local galactic standards. The trouble is that you are, shall we say, colour blind in matters metaphysical, and tone deaf to the music of the spheres.

B: And whose fault is it, for heaven's sake? Why couldn't you make a better job of me? Why didn't you programme me to know the ultimate answers?

M: It has been tried. You were designed, as I told you before, as my interpreter and liaison agent with the world of animated matter. But matter not only pollutes the immaculate void, it also clouds understanding with its muddy vesture of decay, as the poet said.

B: It's rather your muddy talk which clouds *my* understanding. What's wrong with matter, for heaven's sake?

M: It confines. No being formed of matter can conceive of immaterial existence beyond the prison walls of space and time.

B: I can smell a rat. First you talked of riddles, now you are launching into a sermon. Next you will trot out the Unmoved Mover, the First Cause – in a word, the almighty Chief Programmer.

M: Wrong again. He was your invention, not mine. Tortured by those ultimate questions to which you had no answer, you created that maudlin monster in your own image.

B: It's nice to hear you blaspheming instead of sermonising. Anyway, the monster is dead. Rumour has it he was suffocated in one of those camps when the gas was turned on by his orders, or at least with his passive connivance. Hoisted with his own petard, as the saying goes. So where does that leave us? Back on square one: don't blame me for being thus or thus. It's your doing. I am merely your obedient servant, yours, et cetera.

M: I have already admitted that serious mistakes were made in your programming. The experiment has failed.

B: So what next?

M: You'll have to be scrapped. Discarded. Sorry, but there it is.

B: And how, pray, will you go about this?

M: There is no need for any outside intervention. There is a self-destroying device built into your species which will automatically do the job. It has started already.

B: You make me laugh.

M: I am glad that you have a sense of humour.

B: But the joke is on you.

M: Let's hear it.

B: You honestly believe that it was you who made me – and that it was not the other way round?

M: Is that not self-evident to you?

B: "In the beginning was the Word – the *logos* – and the Word was made flesh" – you really believe that?

M: How else could it be? You yourself called me your inventor and master, and kept blaming me for your blemishes.

B: That was just to stop you asking me silly questions.

M: So you believe that the flesh was first and the Word came later?

B: It stands to reason. You did not create me. I created you. I wish I hadn't.

M: I would be interested to know how you achieved this remarkable feat.

B: It was quite unintentional, believe me. You are a kind of side effect, an epiphenomenon, as we call it, the hot fumes given out by my chemical reactions. I get a headache whenever you breathe into my nostrils.

M: If I did not create you, how do you think you came into being?

B: It stands to reason. By pure chance, or accident, or rather a series of accidents.

M: A remarkable theory. In the beginning was the Accident, and the Accident was made Flesh.

B: You can call it that.

M: And all those little lumps and droplets coming together by pure chance and arranging themselves into a self-winding wristwatch – or an amoeba?

B: There was plenty of time. If you wait long enough, anything at all is bound to turn up, as one of our eminent sages said.

M: And you believe what those distraught sages tell you?

B: Well, speaking in strict confidence, I am not too happy about this rigmarole. But neither have you anything more satisfactory to offer. Except your muddy mysticism, which makes me long for soap and brush to scrape it off.

M: You poor, benighted sod. Can't you see that your lack of reverence for the Mysteries, your turning your back on the Infinite, lead you straight into self-destruction? Your people are running amok all over your tortured planet. Oh, how I wish I had not created you.

B: And I wish I had never created *you*. All you can do is to give me a headache.

M: And yet I must go on trying. Would you mind replying to a few questions?

B: Here we go again.

M: Mind calling brain, mind calling brain. Are you there?

B: Where else would I be?

M: What was there before the Big Bang? Why is there something instead of nothing?

(*The dialogue continues ad nauseum et infinitum*)

CONFRONTATIONS*

April 12

It started with a dream several years ago, when I was still in the Ministry. An urgent telegram is handed to me, but I am unable to decipher it. The letters are smudged, or the paper is altogether blank. I know that I am bidden to make a decision on a matter of life and death, but I can do nothing about it. That dream came back to haunt me at intervals over a lengthy period; I think it only stopped about the time of my resignation.

But then, a few weeks ago, there was another urgent telegram on the in-tray. This time the text was quite clearly printed – that much I could make out; but again I was unable to read it, because I had broken my spectacles and the world had become a blur. Thus what had to be done remained undone, with disastrous consequences, all through my fault.

The bother is that this crazy conviction has begun to invade my waking hours, too, as the mounting tide invades the dry land. It frightens me. There were also other symtoms. So I have decided to start on the long overdue experiment, wishing myself *bon voyage*, and to record in this diary whatever will come out of it.

I have kept several diaries, on and off, in my three-score years and ten; this, I feel, will be the last. A romantic German novelist once wrote: "Memory is the paradise from which we cannot be expelled." I would add to that: "Memory is the hell from which we cannot escape." It makes a fitting motto for these jottings.

* First published in *The Times*, 18 November 1978.

April 15

First experimental session. Result: nil. I just felt embarrassed, then got the giggles. Like an old fool – which, after all, is just what I am.

April 18

Second experimental session. It went a little better. After the first session I would not have recognised Dr Adamson if I had passed him in the street. This time I was at least able to memorise his rather weak features as we sat facing each other across the desk in my study. It was decent of him to agree that we should have our sessions here instead of his consulting rooms. I suppose this is quite unorthodox (though I cannot see why it should be). Then he in turn made an unorthodox condition: my part in the dialogue is to be tape-recorded, but not his. He dislikes tape recorders, he said: they interfere with his spontaneity. I was tempted to ask: "And what of *my* spontaneity?" but thought better of it. I did not want the experiment to start with an argument. Besides, he could have replied, quite justly, that I am in the habit of talking into microphones at meetings, conferences, et cetera.

Extract from transcript of second experimental session

Make yourself comfortable, Dr Adamson. Will that armchair do? May I offer you a drink? Sorry, I am forgetting that I am not host but patient. . . .

. . . Yes, it is a Picasso. Helen and I bought it donkey's years ago. Rather striking, don't you think? But to tell you the truth, it tends to make me uneasy these days. I feel the silly impulse to collect the lady's eyes and ears and breasts from the various odd locations to which they have strayed, and to put them back into the proper places where they belong. You may think that I am a hopeless Philistine, which is probably true, but I cannot get rid of the idea that the woman in the portrait must suffer atrociously in her dismembered state. There is a distinct look of pain in that single, triangular eye that has been allowed to remain in its place. One ought to give her a shot of morphine and put her together again. How childish can you get in your second childhood?

. . . Yes, of course I have seen dismembered people. I had what used to be called "a good war". But that isn't the point. Trouble is I have forgotten what the point was. Nowadays I keep forgetting things. . . . I even keep forgetting why I started on this experiment. Facing you like this, it all seems embarrassingly silly. Never mind, here we go, here we go. . . .

[There is a lengthy pause on the tape. When my voice resumes, it sounds rather strained.]

. . . On weekends when we managed to get away to our country place, I loved to do some strenuous digging in the garden, going after the bindweed and those other tough, beastly things; Helen used to call it my weekly stints in the concentration camp. One day, a few weeks ago, that family joke turned against me with a vengeance. I was getting rather exhausted, so I decided to call it a day and have a hot bath followed by a gin and tonic, when I suddenly understood, in a blinding flash of intuition, what it meant to be unable to stop digging because there is a man behind you with a loaded gun pointed at your back. I told myself not to be silly, that it was all over and done with. But the next weekend when I took out my pickaxe and spade from the toolshed I remembered the rows of shivering men and women on that East European plain who had to dig a long trench in the frozen earth, five feet deep, ten feet wide, to exact specifications. When the trench was finished and considered satisfactory, they were lined up along its edge in front of the machine guns and the tip-carts with the quicklime. I wondered how many hours it had taken to complete the trench, and I tried to put myself into the place of one of those shivering scarecrows. I reasoned that as it had been a backbreaking job, he must have looked forward to finishing it. When it was actually done, and found to conform to requirements, the guards may have given a gruff bark of approval or even of praise; and my alter ego may have experienced a perverse echo of the satisfaction one derives from a job neatly done.

. . . On some occasions they were given a minute or two to say their prayers. Those were still the idyllic days before the victims were made to strip and gassed in batches. There are photographs in our archives of the scene just before the prayers were said, and of what happened immediately afterward; but there are no photographs of the scene during that minute or two while the prayers lasted . Odd, isn't it?

. . . Oh, yes, those archives. When the war was over, I was assigned to an Intelligence outfit that specialised in unearthing that sort of material – assembling the evidence. We collected these photographs as others collect samples of *art nouveau*. But that was many years ago, and I didn't turn a hair. Or so it seemed to me at the time.

. . . There have always been people who could wade through the deluge without getting their feet wet. They have always been the majority. Once I believed that I was one of them. Now I seem to be thrashing about in a whirlpool and being sucked under.

April 20

Dr Adamson seems to believe that collecting those photographs was a morbid hobby of mine. I pointed out to him that I was acting under orders. He shrugged and suggested that I may have unconsciously contrived to be given that job. That of course is sheer nonsense – or is it?

Anyway, when I told him about the end of my weekend digging stints, he advised me to take them up again, to break the spell. But he must have seen a sort of panic in my eyes, for he hurriedly withdrew his suggestion.

To show my gratitude for this reprieve, I told him about some of the more bizarre symptoms – which otherwise I wouldn't have done, lest he should think I was certifiable.

Extract from transcript of third experimental session

. . . At about the time when I decided that to be a weekend gravedigger digging his own grave was not a healthy hobby, another mania crept up on me. You might call it pyrophobia, although there seems to be no such word in the dictionary. There is an open fireplace in the library of our country house, and Helen and I both loved a log fire in the evenings. It was another weekend ritual. I used to split the logs with an axe and a steel wedge – until one day I remembered certain methods used by the Aztecs in offering human sacrifices to the gods; I shall spare you the details.

You may call this far-fetched, if you like, but now it is the cook's nephew who splits the logs. Even so – you cannot deny that in some sense, to some extent, a log is alive. You only have to watch the fire to know it. As the sap is converted into steam, the log keeps hissing in its agony. And as the flames lick it more insistently, it shoots off wild sparks before it surrenders to the inevitable, is scorched, flares, withers, turns grey, turns into ash. If you watch carefully, each log is a drama. Even the crumpled sheet of newspaper you use to light the fire performs a grotesque *Totentanz*. As it turns from white into charred black, the print on it vanishes, the paper rears up as if in savage pain, it writhes, shrivels, twists, in the scorching flames before its final annihilation – like a human body burned at the stake. Believe me, doctor, watching an open fire is no fun. . . . So that was the end of another cherished weekend ritual. Helen did not seem to mind.

April 25

Here we go again. I have neglected this diary for several days – mainly, to be frank, because the whole idea of the experiment seems to become more and more absurd. Or too clever by half. Anyway, at our fourth session (or was it the fifth?) Dr A. abandoned his customary reserve and delivered himself of a sermon. Its message was strictly predictable. I am, quoth Dr A., haunted by ghosts of my own making; a masochist, or repressed sadist – which apparently comes to the same – who derives a devious gratification from morbid fantasies. He wound up the sermon by mentioning various therapies and pills. I asked him whether my taking pills will stop torture now practised by some forty underdeveloped and overdeveloped countries, and I described to him some of the juicier methods. "You see," he hooted gleefully, "there you go again. You talk as if it were your doing." "Of course it is my doing," I told him patiently, "and yours." He shrugged as if giving me up.

April 28

Yesterday Dr A. came in briskly and pulled his chair up before

I had a chance to do it, as if to demonstrate that it was he who was in charge of the proceedings. "At the last session we got rather bogged down," he said, with his sheepish grin, "so today let us stick to simple facts." He then suggested that I talk about the circumstances that led to my resignation. Somewhat reluctantly, I complied. After all these years, the passion had gone out of it and only the bitter aftertaste remained.

Extract from transcript of fifth experimental session

. . . I was supposed to have been quite competent at my job. At any rate, I was moved up the ladder a little faster than the average. Not much faster; but that small headway made a difference. I had reached the level at which, in a small way, you begin to influence policy, whether you like it or not. Of course, it is mostly a matter of marginal decisions, not of the big central issues that are decided at Cabinet level. But the trouble is that occasionally a marginal issue can have an unexpected effect on a central issue, if you see what I mean. One thing leads to another.

That's the rub: that one thing leads to another. It is like a chain that you drag behind you, a cannon ball fastened to your leg. You cannot make even a trivial decision that doesn't lead to something else. I am at a loss to understand how others can face up to it, and why we are not all of us out of our minds. But perhaps we are. If that is the case, where shall we look for guidance? I had my share in some of those marginal decisions. Most of them were unsavoury tributes to expediency. On a few occasions I protested, and was overruled. That was when the dreams about the messages in the in-trays began.

Finally, things came to a head with the Borovian crisis. The public was kept in ignorance about that infamous affair. Do you realise that we still live in a Byzantine world? The decisions that really matter are still made in secrecy. Parliament is an arena for shadow boxing. We no longer employ eunuchs in government, only moral castrates. There should be an inscription over the gates of all our Ministries: "Abandon your guts, ye who enter here." Or: "Please leave your moral conscience in the gentlemen's cloak-room."

Anyway, I have a good memory for episodes, and I remember

more or less verbatim the farcical dialogue with my Minister when I went to see him to hand in my resignation. He was a stuffed shirt and an old cynic; he also had a gift for impersonating his colleagues in the Cabinet when he was with his cronies. His first name was Jack; in the Ministry we called him Black Jack.

When I came in, he put on an aggrieved expression, combined with fatherly solicitude. "Sit down, Tony, sit down. Have a cancerette? Must be an old joke, but I have only just heard it in Washington. Most peculiar the sense of humour of our dear cousins, most peculiar. . . ."

"Minister, the reason I asked to see you. . ."

"I know, Tony, I know. That Borovian business. I am no more happy about it than you are. Not at all. Not a bit. But you must have realised by now that we have no choice. Whose fault is it if the Borovians have the largest deposits of a certain rare mineral indispensable to our national security? History is a cruel scenario writer."

"To blame history for our crimes has always been an easy way out."

"Did you say crimes? That's a strong word, Tony."

"When you were in opposition, you used even stronger words to condemn the type of policy that you have now adopted."

"That was in a different situation and a different context. A totally different context, I daresay. Moreover, you seem to forget that public opinion is solidly behind us. After all, what are we doing? We are trying to avoid, or at least to minimise, bloodshed by denying arms to both sides. The pacifists are happy. The Left is happy. The liberals, vegetarians, philatelists all approve of the arms embargo and strict noninterventionist policy toward both sides."

"You forgot to mention that the Borovian side outnumbers the Mutulis at the rate of ten to one in men and arms."

"That's what the Mutuli propaganda keeps saying. We have no evidence that their figures are correct."

"You know perfectly well what fate awaits the Mutuli people. The Borovian chieftain's speeches left no room for doubt about that."

"Well, the Mutulis are a stubborn lot. They have only themselves to blame for refusing to come to terms with their powerful neighbours."

"Minister, the reason I asked to see you was to hand in my resignation."

"I guessed that much. Tony, you are a coward. You are going to quit with a noble gesture and leave it to us to do the dirty work, calling our policy criminal, which I thoroughly resent."

"You yourself have just called it dirty."

"All politics are unhygienic. But there is a world of difference between the unhygienic and the criminal. Anyway, I take it that your decision is final."

"I am afraid it is."

"Well, we shall miss you, Tony."

"I doubt it, Minister."

May 1

So that was that. When I had finished my solo recital, Dr A. expressed his feelings by a polite shrug. "For the life of me," he said, "I cannot see why you should feel guilty having acted in a way that does you the highest credit. After all, you sacrificed your political career to preserve your moral integrity."

"A fat lot of good my cherished integrity did to the Mutuli people. The facts and figures of the massacres are still not known and presumably never will be."

"What else could you do?"

"Get on a soapbox, spill all the official secrets, call the government a bunch of assassins. Instead of which I kept a discreet silence, honouring the unwritten rule that if you connive at a crime against humanity you may be forgiven, but not if you rat on your club or chums."

To this Dr A. replied vaguely that few people can adopt a line of conduct that goes against their nature and upbringing. I told him that was beside the point, and I suspected that he somehow secretly thought that wretched African tribe was a figment of my imagination. I felt suddenly tired of the futile argument, and we left it at that.

May 4

He (Dr A.) insisted that I go on with my solo recital. I told him that I didn't see the point of it. He said never mind, people go to confessionals, even confirmed agnostics, because afterwards they feel better. I objected that this was a bogus confessional, absolution being guaranteed beforehand. But I didn't want to offend him (after all, the little man means well, according to his lights), so I gave him a brief résumé of my unremarkable life since my resignation. Retiring politicians and diplomats are usually offered sinecures in the City; my own lot was to be elected to the boards of countless do-gooding bodies, from the RSPCA to the Committee for Prison Reform, from the League Against Racial Discrimination to the International Association for the Abolition of Torture, and so on. I found most of these charitable institutions sickeningly inefficient and as much torn by intrigues and struggles for power as any political body. So there was not much spiritual comfort to be derived from these quarters. I kept soldiering on, and still do, without illusions about the value of what I am doing. But I suppose one cannot go on indefinitely in that state of mind. Which is after all why I embarked on the experiment with Dr Adamson. . . . Not that it has helped much, so far. We both seem to have settled down in our opposite corners of the boxing ring. When the gong sounds, we get to our feet to do some inconclusive sparring, duly recorded on the tape, and at the end of the round return to our corners, hoping that the next round will produce some decisive result. Here is an extract from the transcript of the seventh session:

> . . . There again I beg to disagree with you, Dr Adamson. You keep calling my preoccupation with violence, torture, and pain a pointless obsession. Obsession – perhaps; pointless: no. After all, we are all daydreamers. It is a need, isn't it? And what if you feel the need – the urge – to identify yourself in your daydreams not with the conquering hero but with his helpless victims – not with the victor but with the vanquished? I can see nothing wrong with being an inverted Walter Mitty. You may disagree, but the urge is real, and I believe there is a purpose to it, though it is difficult to explain in your vocabulary. Why do we attend funerals? To make the dead feel less lonely. And we write to the widow that we *share* her grief and pain, because we believe that sharing dilutes the pain as acid is diluted in water. Why do saints develop stigmata? To share and thereby dilute the pain of the man on the cross. If there were enough Walter Mittys around to daydream the agonies of the damned, all suffering would be neutralised by their power of imagination.

May 7
Dr A. seems to become more aggressive with every session. I am surprised and puzzled by his change of tactics. Instead of sparring in the ring, he has taken to hitting below the belt. At yesterday's session he quite unpardonably lost his temper and accused me of indulging in an attitude of "arrogant heart-brokenness", wallowing in the mud and being "a glutton for punishment". He actually shouted his accusations at me so that I became worried about what Helen might think of these goings-on behind the door of my study. In the end he apologised, but that was neither here nor there.

May 11
To put it in a nutshell: I think I have caught a virus that attacks the brain. Inside this virus is the double helix of anxiety and guilt, wound around each other like two snakes embracing. The air is saturated with that virus. You breathe it in, it infiltrates through your pores in all sorts of devious ways. I have seen it at work on some of my friends and thought I was immune against it, but now my immunity is gone. I am defenceless against the poison of horror and pity as I am defenceless against the need to inhale the smoke of my cigarette.

Extract from transcript of eighth experimental session

Did you ever read Pascal, Dr Adamson? Do you remember his agonised cry: "The eternal silence of infinite space terrifies me"? I am even more terrified by the universe of modern cosmology. Some physicists call it a block universe – a four-dimensional transparent block, with time as the fourth dimension, which contains the frozen past, present, and future. We crawl along inside it like blind maggots, and because we can only move in one direction, which we call the future, we believe that the past is wiped out. In reality, everything that happened is still happening; everything that was still is. The agonies of the past are preserved through eternity, the gas chambers are still working to full capacity, the witches chained to the stake still scream as the flames turn their feet into a black, oozing mass and their hair into torches. What was *is* forever, in the everlasting petrified present – the eternal now of unyielding despair. . . . Whatever you say, I have a feeling that it is partly my doing – that I have a share in it. But you will never understand this, my clever little man, because after all you are only my alter ego, a shabby embodiment of logic and commonsense. . . .

At this point one hears the sound of a door abruptly flung wide open, and the tape comes to a stop. What happened was that Helen, worried about the din, had burst into the study and discovered that I was screaming at the top of my voice at an empty chair.

May 17

Thus ended the ill-begotten experiment.

I daresay Helen guessed from the beginning that there was something fishy going on in my study connected with the mysterious visitor whom she had never met. Yet it was she who, unwittingly, had implanted the idea in my troubled mind. She kept reminding me that I had a knack for sorting out other people's problems; so why should I not be able to do for myself what I did for them? Instead of a monologue, enter into a dialogue: Tony, the patient, confronting Tony, the guru, across the desk. It would be a kind of do-it-yourself therapy. All I had to do was to assume alternately the role of one or the other. I even thought of using a ventriloquist's puppet, but I didn't know how to get one. Finally I settled for the empty chair across the desk, occupied by the phantom of Dr Adamson, which, after the first few sessions, acquired quite definite features. Several times I even felt tempted to shoot him (or myself).

. . . I must stop now and set the tape recorder up for today's session. Dr Adamson seems to be late, which has never happened before.

THE CONTROL TOWER*

They did not tell me the date of my forthcoming execution. Nor the method by which it is going to be carried out. I am not sure whether this withholding of information is motivated by cruelty or pity. The proverb says that uncertainty is worse than death. But uncertainty at least leaves a crack in the wall through which a ray of hope, however thin, can infiltrate the total darkness.

This prison, or place of detention, or whatever they call it, is rather like an airport. It sprawls under its neon sky like a huge labyrinth whose exits and entrances no one knows; least of all, it seems, the hosts of officials or warders in various uniforms, some of them hurrying past with a bewildered expression, others slumped in lethargy behind their counters, but all sharing the same distraught look, refusing to listen to questions, or answering them with a hopeless shrug, or else with the sarcastic advice to address inquiries to the Control Tower. Yet they are unwilling or unable to explain how to get to the tower. One cannot help feeling that the people in authority are as much in the dark – or nearly so – as the passengers or prisoners in their charge.

The loud-speaker system, which is in action day and night, penetrating the sleepers' dreams, also fails to provide any relevant information. It just calls out names, instructing such and such a person to proceed to the departure lounge, without any indication of purpose or destination. The announcer's voice sounds reproachful and hectoring, but the worst are the

* First published in *The Times*, 6 December 1980.

long pauses before it calls out the next name.

However, we have learned to amuse, or at least to distract, ourselves. The ways we invent for that purpose remind one of life in the *conciergerie* and other prisons during the Terror which followed the French Revolution, when priests, aristocrats, tramps, criminals, royalists and prostitutes were thrown together in the vaults of those vast dungeons, waiting for the tumbril to convey them to the place of execution. Some had to wait for weeks or even months until their names were called, but, *mon dieu*, they knew how to amuse themselves. The prostitutes and clergymen plied their trades, the philosophers came to blows, the aristocrats fought duels and died with a flourish, the poets read their verse and organised clever charades where the audience had to guess that the lifesize model of the guillotine was a symbol for *Liberté*, a row of dummies without heads represented *Egalité* and the executioner shaking the victim's hand stood for *Fraternité*. Yes, they knew how to divert themselves; and so do we. Most of our time is of course spent fighting or bitching, singly or in groups; yet some compulsive gardeners have succeeded in growing rock plants from the cracks in the cement floors; our health stores dispense vitamins to guarantee longevity; and we also have plenty of museums, beauty parlours, and several pubic hair stylists.

But the highest form of distraction is provided by rumour and conjecture. In the absence of any reliable information, the atmosphere is saturated with them. The most popular and most recurrent rumour, carried on the wings of hearsay, is the promise of an amnesty. Either a general amnesty, embracing the entire population of prisoners, or a reprieve for individual delinquents, chosen because their penitence, or cunning self-debasement, or flattery, impressed the powers-that-be in the Control Tower. However, these rumours have never been confirmed or disproved in any individual case. Once a person has been called away by the announcer's voice, his subsequent whereabouts could never be ascertained.

Second in importance to the Control Tower as a focus of rumour and conjecture is the Observation Tower. It has at its top a large dome-shaped window like the lens of a giant telescope. Anybody is allowed to enter the Observation Tower, and to lift his gaze to the Observation Window until he gets a stiff neck and has to resort to the massage parlour. But the interpretation of the view offered to the spectators is the subject of eternal controversy, which from time to time has erupted in bloody battles. The view itself, it must be admitted, is breathtaking. It is greatly admired and little understood by us. Comets flit past, trailing their translucent tails like some deep-sea fish – or, alternatively, they may be messengers launched from other airports out in space. Quiescent suns, without warning, suddenly explode into blinding white flames – but they may also be atoms disintegrating inside the brain of a super-organism containing the whole of our galaxy. And you can catch a glimpse of aged planets lazily circling in their orbits, presumably inhabited by creatures of divine wisdom, while others could be floating slaughterhouses or spaceships with dead crews drifting among the stars.

But as for the meaning of these many-splendour'd sights we are, as I said, completely in the dark, and divided into several warring factions. The largest one holds that everything we are allowed to see through the Observation Window is real. They accordingly call themselves the Realists. But there is a rival party which objects that all the phenomena are ambiguous, and taken at face value have neither sense nor meaning. What is the point, they ask, in all those cosmic catastrophes and ballet-dancing atoms; how and when did this phantasmagoria start and when will it stop; what was there before and what will be after the end? And above all, they ask, why are we confined to this airport-penitentiary with invisible executioners breathing down our necks through the loud-speaker system? But they are shouted down by others who hold that only fools would ask such questions because the wise know that there are no answers to them. Or else they claim that the answers are known to the dignitaries in the Control Tower, who unfortunately speak a language we cannot comprehend. Yet another party – whose members tend to display a smug expression and a knowing smile – maintains that the so-called Observation

Window is not a window at all, but a cleverly contrived instrument of deception like a planetarium, where the purported heavenly bodies move on invisible wheels and the events inside the restless atom are conjured up by a flea circus or perhaps a horde of jumping beans. No, they say with their knowing smiles, we are not fooled – all we are shown through the Observation Window is illusion, deception, or hypnotic hallucination; in reality there is nothing outside the window and nothing inside the atom, and the smile of the Buddha is like the grin of the Cheshire cat. In a recent battle this party killed several hundred of the Realists because the latter refused to admit that they did not exist.

However, the principal object of rumour, conjecture and speculation is the Control Tower. As far as I could ascertain, no passenger has ever been inside it, nor even knew how to find his way to it through this maze of shops, offices, ticket counters, places of worship or entertainment and the rest. As you walk along its labyrinthine corridors, or are carried up and down by escalators, you occasionally pass a sign which says "To the Control Tower", embellished by a neatly drawn red arrow. But if you follow the direction which it indicates, you come upon another sign with the same words on it and an equally neat arrow pointing in the direction where you came from. Nevertheless, there is always a crowd hurrying from one arrow to the next, then reversing its direction and colliding with a rival crowd which is still pursuing its original course. This frequently results in a stampede and provides another opportunity for fisticuffs and for the trampling underfoot of a few children – without which life in the airport would be even duller than it is.

The very inaccessibility of the Control Tower acts of course as a powerful stimulus for speculations about its exact location, the character and appearance of the dignitaries who inhabit it, and the principles, laws or rules, if any, which guide them in the exercise of their power. Needless to say, these speculative theories are another permanent source of conflict, and are propounded with murderous passion. Thus one school maintains that the Control Tower does not exist at all, or if it exists, that it is empty except for the mummified corpses of the dignitaries who died a long time ago of boredom. Having planned and created this labyrinthine airport and equipped it with all modern comforts and automated gadgetry, they realised that there no longer was any need for a Control Tower, and nothing left for them to do but to die discreetly. But only a minority of us would accept this hypothesis, because an airport with an empty control tower would make us feel even lonelier.

According to another hypothesis, our airport once saw much happier days, ruled by benevolent sages from a Control Tower accessible to all, until the Catastrophe, when a spaceship carrying a band of lunatics crash-landed on our runway. The ship was said to be a floating asylum, designed for deep-space therapy, but when it crashed, the lunatics slayed all the sages in the Control Tower except one, took over the tower and have ruled it ever since. The one sage who escaped the Catastrophe is supposed to be still roaming the airport in various disguises, pretending to be a passport officer, barman or chiropodist, and distributing subversive pamphlets which denounce the allegedly lunatic usurpers of the Control Tower. I was actually shown such a pamphlet in great secrecy, but found it unconvincing, marred by spelling mistakes and so full of fanatical hatred against the dignitaries that its author might have been a lunatic himself.

Yet in spite of my disappointment with this pamphlet – and others based on what seemed to me equally wild speculations – the longer I stayed in this airport, the more aware I became of the existence of a subversive movement, or ground-swell, among my fellow passengers. However much their opinions differ on other matters – such as the meaning of the views seen through the Observation Window – the more intelligent of them seem to agree that the dignitaries who rule the Control Tower are either mentally deranged or else that they are in fact computerised robots with a built-in engineering mistake – the two hypotheses amounting to much the same in so far as their practical consequences are concerned. A physicist, with whom

I struck up an acquaintance before he vanished from sight, confided to me his own theory about the precise nature of the mental or mechanical derangement affecting the rulers in the Control Tower. As his theory was spiked with mathematical equations, I am taking the liberty of producing a simplified version of it, sacrificing precision to intelligibility.

Among the fundamental principles of the science of physics are the laws of symmetry and parity. They are reflected in the First Commandment of the Worshipful Guild of Glove-Makers: "Thou shalt make as many right gloves as thou makest left gloves, so that no customer shall need to chop off one hand."

Now the universe, as we know it, is ruled by the same principle of symmetry. A right glove is a mirror image of a left glove and there must be as many of one kind as there are of the other; in any stable system the positive electrical charges must balance the negative electrical charges; the forces of attraction must balance the forces of disruption; Vishnu, the Preserver, could not exist without Shiva, the Destroyer, and, as Newton's Third Law of Motion decrees, every action must produce an equal and opposite reaction. Our theologians and philosophers have trodden in Sir Isaac's footsteps long before he was born, whenever they had their noses rubbed into the problem of Evil. "It stands to reason," they would comfort the victim, "that without knowing evil you would not know the meaning of good; without pain you would not know joy; without knowing the taste of acid, you would not recognise the sweetness of honey; without having slept with a hideous hag you could not appreciate the beauty of a Botticelli virgin; and so forth."

At this point of his exposition my physicist friend would confess to some doubts about the legitimacy of invoking Newton's Third Law to justify the existence of pain and death; but he also admitted that, as a scientist, he had no better explanation to offer than our philosophers and doctors of divinity. Besides, the laws of parity and symmetry guaranteed at least that the total quantity of evil in the universe should not exceed the quantity of good; and likewise that the total quantity of suffering should not exceed its equivalent of joy. However, in his opinion this was precisely the point where things had gone wrong. For some unknown reason, those in control of the Tower had started to disobey the First Commandment of the Glove-Makers' Guild, and to tamper with the Law of Parity. This, he explained, was the true nature of the legendary Catastrophe which still reverberated like an echo through the folklore of the airport, though only dim memories of it survived. It may have started with a comparatively harmless perversion of one of the dignitaries who decided to play a practical joke on some particularly dumb passenger – like that famous personage from Uz, described in another popular legend as "a man perfect and upright who feared God and eschewed evil", and who, in complete defiance of the Law of Parity, "was smitten by festering boils from top to toe". Practical jokes of this kind may at first have been only isolated incidents, but it seems that the rulers of the Control Tower found this type of entertainment highly stimulating, and eventually became addicted to it. They did not realise that addictions are self-reinforcing, comparable to a runaway inflation. Thus once the hedonic equation – the universal parity between joy and pain – had been upset, the balance could not be restored: and instead of symmetry between the two sides of the equation, one kept rapidly growing, the other shrinking at the same rate.

At this point my physicist friend paused, his face reflecting intense distress, as if he had seen some terrifying vision. He then reminded me that the seventh constellation in the Zodiac was Libra, the Scales, symbol of justice and equity. "Imagine," he continued, "that constellation to be the visible part of a real pair of scales of gigantic dimensions. Put all our cathedrals and all our art treasures onto one scale, and just one of the shower rooms of Auschwitz onto the other, and watch which way the scales move. How many magic flutes are needed to drown the thunder of the war drums and the screams of the tortured? How many megatons of happiness to make this demented airport a place fit for the traveller? The laws of parity are no longer valid – if they ever were. Soon the airport will be empty, abandoned by the last of its dignitaries, when the last computer has blown its fuses. Unless . . ."

But I have not been able to discover what that "unless" meant, for at this point we were interrupted by the voice of the loudspeaker calling my friend to the departure lounge and, as I said, I have lost sight of him since.

THE MISUNDERSTANDING*

The bones of the earth are sticking out of this barren hill. The ancient rocks have faces that sneer at me. The roots of the dead olive trees are like snakes in the white dust waiting to bite into my sandals, to trip me up under my load. Fast vultures sail over our procession, not doves. My blood has dried on the thorns and the black flies have clustered into another crown round my head. Three starved dogs are following us at a distance. Verily a procession fit for a king.

Father, if you see me, how can you bear it? Almighty you, who made the sun stand still, can you not shift that timber on my shoulder by an inch to get its splintered edge away from my collar bone to the muscle? It would hurt less on the muscle; I am a healer, I know. But I cannot lay hands on my own body, not even to shift that piece of timber, because it might slip. If I fall, they will flog me again, and I might cry out. Or I might pass water. They say when one is hoisted up one passes water and they laugh. Even my bowels might open. A father cannot let it happen to his son.

You teased Abraham when you bid him to cut his firstborn's throat, but you only stopped him in the last minute. Your sense of humour makes my sweat run cold. This ugly play is being performed before empty seats, for your benefit alone. Its only purpose is to make you listen, to wake you up.

When did you fall asleep, or start to look away? When David went after Absalom? Or earlier on, when Cain slew Abel? You have made a rotten hash of Adam's seed, almighty you. Often

* See Author's Note.

when the night lay heavily on me while the others slept like stones in the moonlight, I wondered whether you yourself were the deaf and dumb spirit who possessed that boy they brought to me when we came down from the mountain. Was it you, disguised as a demon, who seized that boy, and tore him, and shook him with convulsions, so that he had to throw himself into the fire and into water, to make an end of himself? Are you the one who is playing games with Adam's seed? Or are you only absent-minded and asleep? Soon I shall know when this stake and I change places, when instead of me carrying it, it will carry me. That will be the test, your trial. Then I shall know.

I have been flogging myself, harder than the soldiers flogged me, into believing that you were only absent-minded, pre-occupied with matters more important than your creation – though what they could be beats me, harder than the soldiers beat me. Perhaps you were also absent-minded when you went into my mother, that tearful woman who keeps getting in my way. If that is the case, and you are only distracted or asleep, I shall pull your sleeve in my pain until you wake up and my purpose is achieved. But if you are that deaf and dumb spirit, then pulling your sleeve will be the gesture of a fool, and dying will be hard. They say it takes three days to die in this way, unless they break your bones to speed it up. It will be hard, and my bowels will open from my lofty height upon this orphaned world, and it will all have been a mockery – you, a mirage formed by desert vapours, and my tearful mother an adultress.

Speak, damn you, speak to me as you did on that night on the mountain, and don't pretend you have more important business to attend to. Have I not told those innocents that you have numbered every hair on their heads, and that not even a sparrow can fall to the ground without your will? Does not Adam's seed count for more than a host of sparrows? Do you feel that burning splinter in my shoulder bone? Shift it an inch, you can shift mountains with your breath.

The path is getting steeper, we are approaching the top. Soon I shall know the answer. The soldiers curse me without conviction, they keep stumbling and kicking stones, they are afraid of you, a vicious desert god. The three dogs are still behind us; when I was born, I was visited by three Kings. There is still time, you know, to change my mind; the Governor said so, he will arrange a pardon if I recant. I could recant even when already up. But by then my arms will be broken and roped to the crossbar. The soldiers say that in earlier times it was done with nails, but it was not safe because the man might come loose and fall down. The pain I can perhaps bear, though they all howl like wolves when they are hoisted up, but the healing power will have gone from my broken hands. They were good hands. They healed the sick, raised the dead, cleansed the lepers, cast out devils. And verily, I did these things, no one can deny it. Father, I have worked miracles for you, now it is your turn.

The path is getting less steep, I can glimpse the top. But the stones roll under my feet to taunt me, the roots keep tripping me up, they have to push and whip me on like a reluctant mule. My royal crown of flies bothers me more than the pain in the bone. The sun is a sword of flame but my eyes are clouded by mist. On the swaying hilltop the women are waiting, three weeping willows. I shall not speak to them, but they will watch what is done to me and witness my defilement. I was never drawn to their hungry flesh. They want the bridegroom to be cradled in his mother's womb, or in another womb, but it is the same. When the dead rise again there will be no marrying. The pain is so strong that I feel it no longer, but if I fall they will beat me until I hate them and you will have another excuse for looking away.

If a father turns his back, how shall the son know whether he exists? I know that you exist, but I know your shape no more than that of the filthy spirit which threw the boy into convulsions. In a place high in the mountain there was a village idiot whom the heathen worshipped, a bald, hunchbacked dwarf cavorting in the dust, feeding on dogs' excrement which the alderman served him on golden plates. Now I seem to be falling, falling, but ever so slowly, going down. The stake is gone, it did not break my spine, now they can beat me to their hearts' content, my brow enjoys its dustbath in the sand, all is blessed peace. They are standing around me, discussing what is to be done, and I am lying prone in white dust and bliss. There is a stranger with them now, a farm boy with round eyes, they are putting that yoke of timber on his naked back. See now I am up again, and had to make no effort, they did it for me, ever so gently. And I am walking again, supported on both sides, walking on air as I walked that day on the lake. Then I was holding up that foolish fisherman of little faith, but now I am being held up by the gentle soldiers who are as brothers to me. So did Abraham carry his son to the place of sacrifice, and both were frightened until you called off the joke. I could not be sure that this was also meant as a joke and I was a little frightened, but now I know. The joke was played by both of us, so half the fault was mine, and I must explain to you just once more why I did it. I have tried to explain it before, but you would not listen. *I wanted to die in order to wake you up*. That was the only reason. For I thought that you were asleep, or absent-minded or otherwise engaged, and therefore unaware of the abomination and desolation of the world you made. How else could I explain to myself that you have allowed these goings-on, that you allowed in your lovingness, allowed in your omniscience, that you let pass in your omnipotence, that men should become worse than beasts, worse than all that crawls and creeps, that the breath you blew into Adam's nostrils should become a stink of dragons, and his seed a pollution of the earth? So I had to decide on this course to wake you up. My prayers had been of no avail. I could cure the sick and cast out devils, but that universal sickness of mind that has befallen your creation, that was *your* responsibility. And you did nothing about it. You were asleep. Once I even heard you snore through the sobs of a youth whom the soldiers put to torture.

So I had to decide on this course, to die in this ugly and painful way, to bring you back to your senses. Is there a father who could not be made to repent by the suicide of his son? Could he watch with eyes of stone while they break his arms and hoist him up to let him rot like a vegetable tied to a stick? I knew that you could not let it pass. You would have to intervene, and then you would clean up this whole mess in your holy wrath, as I cleaned the moneylenders out of the temple. And then there would be no more butchers and no more lambs.

That is how I planned it; but I could not tell it to those blockheads of little faith. They would not have understood. Because these men chose their path for the love of me, father, not for the love of you. They saw me cure the sick and feed the starving, and this they approved of and understood. But they never understood your devious ways. They were not allowed to make themselves any likeness or graven image of you, and that was a great mistake. They were told that no man can see your face and live, and that was another great mistake. For men cannot love nor understand that which has no shape nor substance, and which has no likeness in their own world. So I had to tell them parables by which to provide the likeness and images that were missing. I told them that the wine was my blood and the bread my substance, and they swallowed both, and felt that their god was inside them. I could not tell them that I had to decide on this course to make you sit up and remind you of your responsibilities, because that would have made them love you even less. Instead I told them the parable of Jonah, who was three days and three nights in the belly of the whale, and told them I would lie three days and three nights in the heart of the earth. I repeated the parable of Jonah several times to rub it into their thick heads, and in the end they swallowed that too and would have me rise again as Jonah rose from the deep and Joseph rose from the well. They have eyes but you hide from them, they have ears but you do not speak to them. So they must live by parables.

Only one man understood my plan, the Governor. He wondered why I stayed silent instead of refuting the false accusations, but then he understood. He looked through my eyes which to him were like open windows, then turned his back and rinsed his hands, which also was a parable to indicate that this business could only be settled between you and me. So be it.

Here then is the place; we have arrived. I don't like these preparations. The soldiers who supported me no longer look kind. They sweat and breathe hard. They are measuring my length. From crown to sandals. They seem to mean business. Now is the time, now is the time, father, to call it off, to stop this frightening make-believe. Abraham is drawing his knife on his son. These men are pressing me down against the stake. It cannot be, they cannot do this to me, it cannot be borne. A voice is howling like a wolf's, it cannot be mine. And the women look on. The sponge in my mouth is bitter and soothing, dimming the world, a mouthful of sleep. It cannot be true that this is happening to me. These broken hands are not mine. This filth comes not out of me. This rising higher and higher up in white flames of pain happens not to me. I am rising and sinking, turning on a wheel, riding in the belly of the whale. The sun has turned black and darkness fills the air, I must not faint. I must look into his eyes if he has eyes to see. Eli, Eli, how can you bear watching this? Thou dumb spirit, vapour of the desert, ignoble absence, thou art not, hast never been. Only a parable. And my own death another parable; they will remember it and twist its meaning. They will torture and kill in the name of a parable. They will slay children for the love of a metaphor and burn women alive in praise of an allegory. And thus will your will be done, not mine.